❧ ABOUT THE AUTHOR ❧

E. C. Hibbs is an award-winning author and artist, often found lost in the woods or in her own imagination. Her writing has been featured in the British Fantasy Society Journal, and she has provided artworks in various mediums for clients across the world. She is also a calligrapher and live storyteller, with a penchant for fairytales and legends. She adores nature, fantasy, history, and anything to do with winter. She lives with her family in Cheshire, England.

Learn more and join the Batty Brigade at

www.echibbs.weebly.com

❧ ALSO BY E. C. HIBBS ❧

RUN LIKE CLOCKWORK
Vol I: The Ruby Rings
Vol II: The Eternal Heart

THE FOXFIRES TRILOGY
The Winter Spirits
The Mist Children
The Night River

THE TRAGIC SILENCE SERIES
Sepia and Silver
The Libelle Papers
Tragic Silence
Darkest Dreams

Blindsighted Wanderer
The Sailorman's Daughters
Night Journeys: Anthology
The Hollow Hills Tarot Deck

Blood and Scales (anthology co-author)
Dare to Shine (anthology co-author)
Fae Thee Well (anthology co-author)

AS CHARLOTTE E. BURGESS
Into the Woods and Far Away: A Collection of Faery
Meditations
Gentle Steps: Meditations for Anxiety and Depression

RUN LIKE CLOCKWORK

VOL I
THE RUBY RINGS

To Jackie,
Thank you for
coming to the
Citynapes panel!

E. C. HIBBS

First published April 2022

Cover design, cover artwork, book production and layout by E. C. Hibbs

Cover images from Pixabay

www.echibbs.weebly.com

‣ For my parents. •
De familia mihi vires.

‣ And for Katie. •
Amicitiae nostrae memoriam spero
sempiternam fore.

PART ONE
NIGREDO
'CHAOS'

THE BODY IS REGARDED AS A
MACHINE WHICH, HAVING BEEN
MADE BY THE HANDS OF GOD,
IS INCOMPARABLY BETTER
ARRANGED, AND POSSESSING IN
ITSELF MOVEMENTS WHICH ARE
MUCH MORE ADMIRABLE,
THAN ANY OF THOSE WHICH CAN
BE INVENTED BY MAN.

CHAPTER I

The snow fell without pause and without direction. It covered the entire City: Level upon Level of buildings and streets and sleeping forms. The Tower pierced through the centre; its spire reached so high, the tip was lost among the clouds.

Behind one of its glass clock faces stood a figure: small and still, and alone. He looked human, but he wasn't, not completely. He hadn't been human in a very long time.

Time… Such a strange yet logical concept. It was his cage and his comfort, without beginning or end.

He gazed down at the West Quarter. It was hundreds of feet below, but he still saw every cobblestone, every headline pasted on walls, every shivering unfortunate huddled in doorways. Mechanisms laced themselves among the wafts and wefts of ancient magic. Other wintry nights ran alongside this one, some long ago and others far ahead. Simultaneously, the living walked hand in hand with their own ancestors and descendants. They died and birthed; ate and spoke; were torn from their graves under cover of darkness.

So much detail, so many paths, filled with infinite possibilities and losses. All relative, overlapping, moving together on an ever-spinning wheel.

This was the way of things: unchanged and unshifting. But not now. There was an old saying, so old that nobody remembered it anymore, that one couldn't see the forest for the trees. So ironic, in so many ways.

The figure glanced at his hand. The shadows of snowflakes drifted over it, each one filled with the infinite possibilities of where it would settle. Then he turned his eyes on the Bellamy manor, far below in the Fourth Level. The curtains were drawn, but through the second window on the first floor, he knew she was there. The little girl.

He didn't smile or speak, just nodded to himself. The critical moment drew closer by the second. It was almost time. And all was as it should be.

It had been a day like any other. Maids dusted the ornaments and gossiped about the handsome new footman. Lord August Bellamy was out, finishing work at his sanctuary house after the Parliamentary Moot. His wife, Lady Lena, took tea in the drawing room and quietly encouraged her daughter to remember her posture. But Charlotte only half-listened. She was eight years old, and there were far more interesting things she could be doing.

She watched the snowflakes drifting past the window. If she waited until tomorrow, it would be thick enough to build a snowman as large as herself.

When evening came, her mother lifted her into bed.

"Is Papa home yet?" Charlotte asked.

"No. Don't wait for him. Go to sleep."

Charlotte grumbled. The governess was calling in the morning, and all she had lectured about for the past week was how to join the letters in handwriting. Her father said it looked pretty, but Charlotte didn't think so. It made her think of a spider which had fallen into an inkwell and then ran across the paper.

"Can't you give me a day off?" she asked half-heartedly.

"You can have your day off at the weekend, like everyone else," her mother said.

She placed a doll into Charlotte's arms, then lowered the brightness on the nightlamp; wound the crank fully, so it would last until dawn. The faint clicks of cogs filled the air.

Charlotte tried a different approach.

"Can we invite Malcolm for afternoon tea, at least?"

Her mother chuckled. "It's a bit short notice! He has to work as well. Clocks don't fix themselves."

"It's been *ages* since we saw him!" Charlotte protested.

"Three weeks. Hardly ages."

"It feels more like three months!"

Her mother rolled her eyes and kissed Charlotte on the forehead.

"Enough now. Go to sleep," she said, and swept out of the room like a dancer.

Charlotte scowled. But the delicious heat from the warming pan reached her toes, and her eyelids became heavy. She didn't like to move once she had been tucked in. The slightest twitch of her leg would break the spell woven during that magical final contact. As long as she could still feel her mother's hands pressing on the blankets, and smell her sweet perfume, nothing could happen. Nothing at all.

She scarcely felt as though she had fallen asleep before the quarter-chimes of the Tower cut through her dreams. She was so used to the bells ringing, sometimes she forgot they were there. But tonight, somehow, they sounded different. Harsher.

She opened her eyes. At night, in the dark, the room seemed completely unlike itself. The wall mouldings reminded her of the nonsensical ways she might drag her fingers through dust to create a swirling pattern. She supposed that must be how the carpenters made the designs, but whenever she tried it, it never looked as pretty. A marionette hung up by its strings over the heating mechanism in the alcove. Beside it lay a bundle of other toys. If she squinted, the pile almost looked like the City of Forest itself: a mountainous pyramid, wide at the bottom and narrow at the top. She imagined the twelve Levels extending down the sides like steps, Interlevels running between them, filled with tiny carriages and even tinier people.

This huge, sprawling, three-dimensional City of steel and stone. It was all she had ever known.

The chimes faded. Three quarters. Fifteen minutes until midnight.

The front door opened, then snapped shut. Her father was home.

Charlotte frowned when she heard him coming up the stairs. It sounded as though he was taking them two at a time. He never ran like that. It wasn't gentlemanly. Then she heard snatched breaths, feet pounding across the carpet and something being shoved into a bag. The noises moved to the landing.

"Are you sure?" her mother asked. "It's impossible!"

"I know it is! But I know what I saw… *Who* I saw! They won't allow me to just walk away from that!"

"They let you leave tonight."

"I don't think they meant to. I don't think they realised I'd gone until after—"

"August, wait, let's think about this."

"There's no time! We need to go!"

"To where?"

"I don't know. I'll figure something out. Phoebe's arranged a coach for us."

"What about the servants?"

"They're not the ones in danger. Get Charlotte ready. The Vixen will be here soon — you know what she'll do to me!"

The door opened. Charlotte's mother ran over, swept back the blankets, and broke the spell.

"Get up, sweetheart," she smiled, trying to project a semblance of calm, but it didn't fool Charlotte for a moment.

Both her parents laced boots on her feet without socks, wrapped her in a coat and hat. Her father was still in his suit and long cloak, but her mother wore simple loungewear — not the kind of clothes to be seen outside in. She hadn't pinned her hair up or put on a wig, either.

Her wristwatch glinted in the low light as she forced gloves onto Charlotte's hands.

"Scarf, too," she said. "It's still snowing."

Charlotte knew they weren't going to play in it.

"What's wrong?" she asked. "Papa?"

"Hush."

Nerves curled around Charlotte's belly. His voice was lower than normal. Sharper. He never spoke like that.

She snatched her doll, then held her mother's hand as the three of them left the room. Her father entered the passages of the servants' wing, and shoved open a trapdoor to reveal a stone shaft. It was the emergency exit — all the large houses had them — but Charlotte had never needed to go through it. The walls pressed around her like a coffin.

"I don't like it!" she protested.

"It's alright," her father said. "I've got you. Just keep going."

Charlotte closed her eyes. Somehow, that helped. It was better than keeping them open and still seeing only darkness.

A sharp rush of cold air filled her lungs as they stumbled into the manor grounds. Her father urged them through a side gate and down the abandoned street. He glanced over his shoulder at their footprints: a clear line in the virgin snow.

"We need to get where there's people. The more, the better."

Charlotte looked at the bag in his hand.

"Where are we going?" she cried.

"Ssh," her mother whispered. "We're taking a holiday, sweetheart. Now, stay quiet. Papa needs to concentrate."

That confused Charlotte even more. Nobody holidayed in the middle of winter. And why had they left in the middle of the night, with no luggage? Why hadn't they changed into travelling clothes?

Eventually, they reached the Interlevel: the main transport link between the Levels in Forest's ever-descending layout. They took the pedestrian walkway to bypass the road. The wide vertical tunnel dug through the rock and metal, circular walls painted with the pasty glows of small lighting mechanisms. Their components ticked loudly and echoed through Charlotte's head.

Where was she? They had run so quickly, she didn't even know anymore.

At the bottom of the Interlevel, her father paused. His ring glinted red as he wiped sweat from his forehead. Charlotte worried he was going to faint, the way some ladies did when their stays were laced too tight. But he wasn't wearing stays, and nothing ever scared him.

Suddenly, a tall woman stepped out of the shadows. She was dressed in the dark blue of the Constabulary, and a coal black braid swept over her shoulder, tied so firmly, it looked like an insect sting.

"A little cold for a stroll, isn't it, Lord Bellamy?" she said, then pressed something against his back.

Charlotte leapt behind her mother's skirt in fright.

"No!" her father whimpered. "Just leave my family alone! Let them go, please!"

The woman's eyes shone, harder than rock, sharper than razors.

"If that was what you'd planned to say, wouldn't it have been easier to leave them in bed, and go running by yourself?" she said. "Don't try anything foolish. I'm not alone tonight. There's no need to make this messier than it has to be."

A thunder of footsteps began to build. Charlotte tried to place it, but it seemed to be coming from everywhere. Whoever it was, there were a lot of people. Moving towards them like a monster.

Then there was a loud crash, as though something heavy had fallen over. The woman looked away.

Charlotte's father slammed the bag into her face. The object flew from her hand. It was long and shiny, with a hole at the end. Charlotte had never seen one with her own eyes before, but she knew what it was.

Her parents snatched her arms and ran.

"Who was that?" she cried.

"Please tell me the carriage is near!" her mother snapped. "Is Phoebe there?"

Her father didn't reply, didn't stop. His breath came in ragged gasps, short with panic.

Once-familiar routes bled together into a cloudlike haze. A stitch stabbed in Charlotte's side. Her boots slipped each time they came down. They were fancy things; the kind she had worn for tea that afternoon. Not for playing in. Not for *this*...

Her father rounded a corner, pointed down the street. It opened into a square, surrounded by grand buildings. A sparse crowd flocked about the central fountain — Charlotte could tell, from the way they staggered, they hadn't long left the taverns. A pair of street lighting mechanisms stood on either side, clicking with ice. The smallest of their gears was the size of a cartwheel, the largest was the height of Charlotte's ceiling.

There were only two ways in and out. The family stood at one, and directly opposite, on another street, she saw the black outline of a carriage.

The footsteps returned, louder this time, sharper. Her father's grip grew so tight on Charlotte's hand, she lost the feeling in her fingers. His entire body shrunk in on itself.

"It's too far away. Too open. They'll catch us."

"We can make it!" her mother insisted. "Come on, August! *Come on!*"

He shook his head, pressed a frantic kiss on her lips.

"I love you both. I'll hold them off. Go! I'll catch up if I can!"

"No! You can't leave us!"

"Just go! It's me she's after! Go! *Now!*"

He pushed them away, so hard, Charlotte almost tumbled over. Dread pierced her chest like teeth.

"Papa!" she squealed. "No! *Papa!*"

Her mother pulled her wrist; forced her to move. Snow and voices and breaths swept past as though in a dream. Her feet were a hundred miles away, separate from herself. Her father was running as well, but slowly. Too slowly. Deliberately so. There was a dull shine in his eyes: the kind which told Charlotte he knew exactly what was about to happen.

The footsteps became louder. Even the drunkards paused when they heard the noise. Nobody moved like that unless it was with purpose.

A horde of police officers churned into the square and fanned into two lines. All held the same long thin objects. Rifles.

The tall woman appeared.

"Lord Bellamy!" she shouted. "Come quietly!"

"Don't stop, Lena!" Charlotte's father yelled.

He tore the ring off his finger, threw it into the gutter. Then he looked at the Tower clock, looming above like a giant eye, and pointed at it.

"All of you, listen to me!" he cried. "The Timekeeper is up there! The Cor Aeternum put him there! He is—"

"Ad maius bonum!" the woman barked. She pulled the rifle off her shoulder, raised it, and shot Charlotte's father in the head.

Charlotte forgot to breathe. The edges of her vision blurred and blackened. Her mother howled in horror.

The woman turned to the officers.

"Seal the square! Leave none alive!"

Charlotte fell into the space between seconds. Her pulse filled her ears with the flat beat of a broken drum. And then came the screams: panicked, terrified. But even they didn't last long. The staccato notes of gunfire were louder.

The men shot mercilessly. A fleeing girl tripped on her own skirts; her head split open like an egg before she even hit the ground. The cabbie on top of the carriage tumbled out of sight in a spray of blood. Charlotte's mother gasped: a hollow, dull sound, more of shock than pain. The front of her dress bloomed red. A bullet had passed straight through from the back.

"Run!" she choked. More blood seeped between her lips. She collapsed and didn't move.

Charlotte wavered. Her lungs crushed under themselves like empty bellows. She couldn't leave. She had to get someone to help…

No. There were hardly any left standing, except the officers and the tall woman. All the adults were killing or being killed. And she would be next.

The carriage. Maybe if she got inside it, she could hide.

But no matter how hard she pushed, the distance didn't

close fast enough. The square whirled around her, reduced to flat lines and empty air. She stumbled over a chain in the lighting mechanism, and as she fell, something hit her shoulder.

It was so deep, so sharp, it took whole seconds before she realised what had happened. And as soon as she did, another bullet struck her in the arm.

Her cheek met the cobbles. She tried to drag herself away, but she knew already that it was pointless. The entire left side of her body felt as useless as a piece of meat.

She was going to die.

The lighting mechanism suddenly broke apart and clattered across the square. Charlotte curled into a ball as the gears tumbled and rolled like oversized wheels. One fell on top of her and pinned her down. Pain exploded through her in a sickly wave, but she couldn't scream. Her chest was too crushed...

How had that happened? She'd thought systems as large and important as those couldn't just *break*.

Bullets bounced off the metal gear. It was so loud, so incessant, even rational thought became impossible. She screwed her eyes shut; hoped against hope that if she opened them, she would be back in bed, surrounded by her mother's spell. She wouldn't try to sleep in, she would never complain about her lessons again...

How had she even kept hold of her doll? She couldn't remember. The world turned to water, swept her up and inside-out. She felt snowflakes on her lashes, as soft as feathers. Too soft.

The Tower chimed midnight. The sounds of the guns faded. Had the men shot everyone now? Or was it quieter because she was dying?

She tried to breathe, but couldn't. The massive gear pressed down too hard. The cold worked into her bones like needles. She wasn't here... she was in the manor grounds. Her father stood behind her and pushed the swing. To and fro, stop and go. Tick tock. She felt his hands on her shoulders.

Then, from the same place, blood. It was all over her back, hot and sticky. Her mother's perfume entwined with the acrid smell of gunpowder. She would be so annoyed to see Charlotte's nightgown ruined. It couldn't even be donated to the sanctuary house. All that blood would never wash out…

The pain drifted somewhere far away. All she wanted was to sleep. Maybe then, she wouldn't feel it anymore.

Fingers appeared on her face.

"This kid's alive!" a voice gasped. "Richie! Come help me lift this!"

It sounded distant, as though she were listening to it from behind a closed door. But she could tell it was a boy, older than her. He tapped her cheek again and she moaned in protest. That simple gentle touch felt like a hook snagging her insides. Why couldn't he let her sleep? Then she could wake up in bed and the spell would never have been broken…

The gear's weight disappeared.

"Are you still awake? Squeeze my hand if you can hear me."

Charlotte did.

"Good," he said. "Stay with me, alright? I'm taking you to the hospital."

The boy slipped his arms under her and ran.

CHAPTER II

Oscar and his fellow junior officers had been enjoying a night off, just a few streets away, when they heard the gunshots. They arrived at a scene straight out of a nightmare. Bodies lay everywhere, hemmed in by the high walls of the square. Many were sprawled haphazardly across the cobbles, brought down mid-stride. Not an inch of snow remained white. Even the fountain overflowed with blood.

Most of the teens froze in their tracks. Oscar almost vomited up the ale he'd been drinking. But he held himself together and began checking for survivors. That was the most important thing.

Gore covered his hands as he turned over casualty after casualty. He tried not to think about it. He had come from a dark place, but never imagined he would deal with something like *this*. In the lower Levels, in the North and South Quarters, perhaps; but not high up, in the prosperous higher Fourth West. *This* didn't happen *here*...

Then he heard a whimper of pain, so faint, he almost missed it. But it came again, like a tiny mouse. He listened hard, followed it to the fallen lighting mechanism. Barely visible under the components was a little girl. Two wounds gaped in her shoulder and arm. He could tell from the look of them that the bullets had lodged somewhere inside.

In one respect, she was lucky. If the gears hadn't collapsed the way they did, she would have certainly been dead.

"Hang on," Oscar muttered, more to himself than to her.

He sprinted faster than he ever had in his life. Her head rolled back, revealing a blood-streaked face.

Oscar's heart skipped a beat. He hadn't seen her before, but she had a look of someone he knew. Someone from not too long ago.

She was the spitting image of Lord August Bellamy.

Shock set his nerves afire, but he refused to slow down. He approached a hospital, burst through the door and bundled the girl into the arms of the nearest medic.

"She's been shot," he said. "There are more of them in Rene Square. I need to go!"

He ran back into the night. Every footstep pounded through his body. The ale threatened to come back up again. He shouldn't have had that stew, either. He stopped, clutched the wall with one hand and a stitch in his ribs with the other.

As he breathed through it, he caught the faint hint of something else on the air. Smoke. He ignored it — probably just a homeless urchin, burning scraps to keep warm.

By the time he returned to the square, everything looked worse. The blood filled the place with an awful meaty smell. Its warmth had melted the snow in places and exposed the rubbish beneath. Some of the trainees had seized a street vendor's cart and were loading bodies into the back. Others roamed about, checking for survivors, but their dismal expressions told all.

A nearby boy sniffed, trying to hold a sneeze. Oscar wasn't surprised. He was one of the lunafauna: a minority of the City, who could shift between animal and human forms. The canines, like him, always had the more sensitive noses, whether they stood on two legs or four. He was in his larger form now: spine straight, taller than Oscar, dressed in the same dark blue jacket as the others. But that was where most of the similarities ended. A faint sheen of red fur swept over his face and the long ears which fell past his chin. His nose was still a pointed snout, black and leathery at the end. Brown irises completely filled his eyes. His trousers had been specially cut to allow the backward bend of his legs, and he walked barefooted, paws in place of hands and feet. Oscar grimaced when he saw them. At least the humans wore boots. But there were no cordwainers who catered to lunafauna. When the boy returned to the barracks, he would need to scrub the blood out of his fur.

Oscar surveyed the faces lying atop the cart. Most were from the taverns — he could smell the alcohol on their clothes. Others were high-end whores, their necklines cut low in spite of the cold. Under one of them was a woman with an exit wound in her stomach.

Her feet caught his attention. All the victims were wearing simple boots, scuffed in places or watermarked from the snow. But hers were spotless: embroidered leather with hardly any grip on the soles. They were a rich woman's boots.

Oscar frowned. What was someone like *her* doing out at this time of the night?

His friend Richie stepped around the cart. Like all the trainees, they were both young, only fourteen.

"Did you get the kid to the hospital?" Richie asked.

"Yeah," Oscar said.

"How is she?"

"I don't know. I just left her at the door. No more luck?"

"No. And no sign of whoever did it, either. They're long gone."

Oscar went to rub his face, then stopped himself when he remembered the gore all over his hands. The girl had bled down the front of his jacket too. It was thick fabric, but he could still feel it had seeped through to his shirt.

He eyed the street at the side of the square. That was where the shots had been fired — he knew from the directions of the blood splatters — but any further signs were lost in the mess of footprints. Then his colleagues laid two more bodies on the cart. One's back was a mess of bullet holes, but the other had been shot at much closer range.

"Pistols," Oscar noted. "These two fell right next to each other and have different-sized wounds. So there was more than one shooter."

"How many, do you think?"

"I don't know. But pistols only hold four bullets at a time."

Richie jabbed his chin at another body. "Those aren't from pistols. They're rifles."

Oscar peered at the wounds. Richie was right. And that made him even more uneasy. Rifles were much harder to get hold of than pistols. Only thieves and police carried those.

Richie's mouth pressed into a grim line as he came to the same conclusion.

"I don't understand," he said quietly. "These people are all just... well, random. Look at 'em. You don't think it's King Rat, do you?"

Oscar shook his head. "Not his style. And too high up the Levels."

"Do you recognise anyone?"

"No."

"How would... Wait, can you smell smoke?"

Oscar sniffed again. The burning was stronger here. Closer.

A shrill whistle sliced the air and a figure ran down the street. Even before she came into view, Oscar knew it was Melissa Spectre: the Chief Officer. Her black hair, normally so perfect, was tangled with sweat, and her uniform was soaking wet. Had she fallen in the snow?

"All the trainees are to come with me right now!" she shouted.

At once, Richie and the other junior officers headed towards her, but Oscar hesitated. He motioned at the bodies.

"Madam Spectre—"

"I'm aware, Hargreaves," Melissa snapped. "I have backup coming to secure the place. Now, follow me!"

Her voice cut through him, sharper than a scalpel. There was no arguing with it.

As they ascended the Interlevel, the air grew hotter and heavy with the fumes of burning wood. The smell swept down Oscar's throat like fingers, and for the third time, he worried he might vomit.

In the distance, a black plume towered into the sky, and ashes fluttered among the snowflakes. His heart shuddered. That definitely wasn't a homeless person's fire.

They reached Leveson Street, and Oscar almost fell over in horror. The magnificent Bellamy manor was ablaze. Heat had splintered the windows and left only jagged shards, clinging to half-melted frames like broken teeth. Fire wardens were already there, pumping water through their hoses, and a small group of officers had formed a barricade to keep neighbours at bay. None of them looked injured, but Oscar felt their shock and fear as though it were his own. He had never seen anything like this.

It would be the wooden furniture which was burning. Nobody but the richest families, in the higher Levels, were able to afford so much of it. Wood was a rarity in Forest — a portion was from the faraway botanical farms, but most was antique, from before the trees disappeared centuries ago. The poorer areas knew only cheap stone and metal. No fires existed there save for what street urchins lit in bins.

"Help that line and get those people to safety!" Melissa barked at the trainees. She laid a hand on the pistol at her belt, darted through a gate to the manor's grounds, and disappeared.

Oscar joined the police in front of the crowd. He kept his eyes fixed straight ahead so he wouldn't be tempted to look at the fire. Even from here, the heat bristled the back of his neck. Gritty soot settled on his skin. When he touched it, it smeared into long black lines.

Another lunafauna stood beside him. There was a red circle embroidered on his left breast — Melissa had one of those too. But unlike her, the canine also wore a name badge. Yellen.

"Care to tell me what the hell's going on?" Oscar hissed.

"One of the servants knocked over a candle, or something," Yellen replied. "They're all still inside."

"The Bellamys?"

"No. They're on holiday, what I heard."

Oscar frowned. There hadn't been any gossip about them going away. And that girl he'd taken to the hospital… The Lord and his wife wouldn't have left their daughter home alone, surely.

He thought about the woman with the rich boots. He hadn't seen her face. Could she have been Lady Bellamy? If she was, did that mean her husband was dead as well? And even if Oscar was right, what would *they* have been doing in Rene Square at midnight in the dead of winter?

Apprehension grew in his mouth like a bad aftertaste. Something wasn't right.

Several loud, sharp cracks sounded inside the manor. Oscar spun around in alarm.

"What's the matter?" Yellen asked.

Oscar looked at him. "Didn't you hear that? Someone just fired!"

"Don't be silly."

"I heard it! We need to tell Madam Spectre!"

Another officer rolled his eyes. "Wood makes strange sounds when it burns, kid. Calm down."

The gate opened. Melissa emerged, streaked with ashes. She coughed so hard, her entire body convulsed. Richie went to help her, but she waved him off.

"I'm fine," she snapped. "Water."

Richie passed her his canteen. She nodded gratefully, drank almost the entire thing and smeared the rest across her face.

"I tried to get the servants out... I couldn't reach them," she wheezed. "Under no circumstances is anyone to go in there. It's too dangerous. Just wait out here until it's extinguished."

Oscar ran to her.

"Madam, I heard more shots!"

The reflection of the fire flashed in Melissa's eyes.

"I don't think so."

"But—"

"Hargreaves, if there were shots, I would have heard them. A cabinet fell inside the house when I was getting out — that's probably what it was. Go back to your post. I don't want anyone else near this place."

She coughed again, and did her best to smooth her jacket as she walked away. Oscar's eyes fleeted over her stained uniform, then locked onto her belt.

His breath caught, as though someone had driven a fist into his gut. Her pistol had changed position in its holster.

Charlotte opened her eyes and saw a flagged stone floor. She was lying on her stomach, in a bed with a hole through it to support her face. Everything hurt, even breathing. An intense knot of pain pressed against her back. She tried to move her arms and legs, but her whole body had turned to iron.

"She's coming round," said a woman. At first, Charlotte thought it was her mother, but then she realised the voice was too old. It wasn't her governess, either, or any of the servants.

"How are her vitals?"

"She's stable. I'll take her to the children's ward."

"Where am I?" Charlotte said. Her words fell over each other like dominoes.

The bed was wheeled away. She rounded several corners, then came to a halt. The woman covered her with a blanket, and as it settled around her, Charlotte smelled the soap it had been washed with. But it wasn't the same soap from home, and the woman tucked her in all wrong.

Panic sliced through her throat like a knife.

"Where am I?" she asked again.

"In Bentham Hospital, dearie," the woman said. "My name's Doctor Kelley. I'm a medic. Now, I know it's hard, but relax, alright? You're safe here."

Charlotte tried to look up, but it was impossible. She had never been so aware of her head's weight before. It felt as though a boulder was attached to her neck.

"Where's Mama?" she muttered.

"One moment, dearie. You can come in now, Mr Godwin."

"Is she alright?"

"Yes, but be gentle."

"Of course. Thank you."

Footsteps approached, but they were different from the doctor's. A man sat in a chair beside the bed. Charlotte saw his shoes through the hole: plain leather, dented buckles on the tops to hold them closed. His hand encased hers: large and rough, yet with the gentleness of a child. She recognised him before he even spoke.

"Malcolm?"

There was a small chuckle. "Yeah, kiddo. I'm here."

The stab of panic began to recede. At last, someone she knew.

Malcolm was a watch mechanic and a childhood friend of her father. They had always remained close, despite their class differences. Malcolm often joined the Bellamys for Sunday dinners and birthdays; had been a part of Charlotte's life for as long as she could remember.

He slipped something into the crook of her arm. She felt silk, hair, smooth porcelain. Her doll.

"There you go," he said. "You've still got Jessica."

Doctor Kelley's shoes appeared on the other side of the hole.

"Mr Godwin, make sure she doesn't roll over. Those stitches are fresh."

"Don't worry, I'll be staying for a while," replied Malcolm.

Charlotte opened her mouth to ask what he was doing there, but agony coiled in her left shoulder and fired into her arm. She remembered being told to wiggle her fingers if she thought a bone was broken, so she feebly tried it, but that only made it worse.

"It's alright," Malcolm said when she whimpered. "I've got you."

"It hurts!" Charlotte cried. "What happened?"

Malcolm swallowed so hard, she heard him gulp.

"You were… shot. You had to have an operation to get the bullets out. It will hurt more if you tense. Take deep breaths, alright?"

Charlotte sucked air in through clenched teeth. With his other hand, Malcolm fished a pocket watch from his jacket and flipped the lid open. She knew why. It was a habit he fell upon whenever he was thinking, or trying not to let nerves get the better of him.

Charlotte focused on the quiet ticking. The monotony of the simple sound wrapped around her like warm water, and the pain slowly began to recede.

"Are... Mama and Papa having op-things too?" she asked.

Malcolm's fingers tightened around hers.

"They're in another part of the hospital," he said in a gentle tone. "I went to see them before I came here."

"*I* want to see them," Charlotte insisted.

A memory of the square flashed in her mind. Her parents had been shot too. But they would be fine. Medics and alchemists were smart enough to fix anything.

"Are they asleep, like I was? Can you ask the lady to wake them up so they can come and see me? Don't *you* leave me, though. Stay here, please."

Malcolm hesitated. He closed the watch and put it back in his pocket.

"I'm not leaving," he promised quietly. "Charlotte, listen to me. They can't come. They're... not going to wake up. They're gone."

Time stopped. Charlotte's mind fell from her body; she made no move to stop it. A ball of horror and dread settled in her stomach like a stone. She wanted to cry, but she had no energy for it. She was too far away to do anything.

"Wake up," she whispered.

She didn't know whether she said it to herself or her parents. But either way, it didn't work.

CHAPTER III

Melissa Spectre pulled her cap down, trying to hide the ash still clinging to her skin. The rising sun pierced the sky, and everywhere she turned, the snow looked red. She strode through it and left a trail of deep, deliberate footprints.

Among the usual courses of opening shops and dragging market stalls into position, she heard the gossip. Word of the shooting hadn't stayed low-key for long, but she hadn't expected it to. There had been too much confusion, too many people involved. It was premeditated, the vendors were saying. To have killed so many, whoever was responsible knew what they were doing. It was already being referred to as the Rene Square Massacre.

Melissa touched her cheek, where August Bellamy had hit her with his bag. She cursed herself for giving him the opportunity to lash out. First, he had fled the manor with his entire family in tow, then he'd overpowered her, then the incident in Rene... She enjoyed toying with her marks on occasion, but that was a mistake a novice would have made. Not *her*. She was perfect, she had been from day one. And now, she'd been late, sloppy, and a square full of dead bodies was the cost. A crimson stain dripped onto her pristine record, and there was only herself to blame.

She approached a lighting mechanism. Hundreds like it filled the City: systems of six-foot-high gears connecting the streetlamps for each square mile. They were exposed to the air, so they could be maintained in the evenings by a lightsman. But as with every major machine in Forest, they never needed to be completely rewound. They were linked to the Tower, from which all power flowed. It was the Timekeeper's responsibility, high in the topmost chamber, to sustain everything.

Melissa opened a small hut behind the mechanism: the storage for the lightsman's tools. Inside was nothing remarkable, but she wasn't there for the cranks or cleaning cloths. Instead, she stamped five times on a large stone in the middle of the floor. A hidden hinge groaned and the whole thing swung wide like a trapdoor. She jumped through, landed in an underground antechamber, and a guard manoeuvred the stone back into position. Within seconds, there was no trace it had ever been moved.

"Good morning, Madam Spectre," he said.

Melissa went to reply, but turned away and coughed. She could still feel the smoke grating against her throat.

"My apologies."

"Is everything alright, Madam?"

"It will be."

Melissa entered an elevator and waited as it lowered through a mile of solid rock. The doors opened to reveal a colossal space of shadow and dancing light. The walls were so far away, she could barely see them. The only reminder that they were there at all was the faint shimmer of ancient magic, running over the mortar like water, keeping the entire structure sound from the inside-out. A complex network of staircases and bridges extended in every direction. Between them sat buildings, all fitted with fake windows to give the illusion of a view, and supported by pillars so high, their bases could be blotted out with a thumb.

It was called the Roots: a system of chambers and thoroughfares directly beneath the streets. And the Tower dominated even down here. It stood in the centre of the hive: a massive stone tree to which everything connected, far larger than even the largest structure above ground.

Melissa approached a building near its flank, the entrance guarded by one of her officers.

"Is he still here?" she asked.

"Waiting for you, Madam."

Melissa fought back a grimace. She wasn't sure if that was what she had wanted to hear or not.

She followed a lavishly-decorated hallway and stepped through the door at the end. An elaborate oak desk, dark with age, dominated the space. Behind it, his back to the window, sat a well-built man in his early thirties. He wore a filigree coat over a perfectly-tied cravat, but hadn't bothered to put on a wig — instead, his natural auburn hair was slicked back to give some semblance of effort. He sang of power. Even without the usual swathes of expensive clothes and perfumes, his presence filled the room, thicker than the humidity of a summer night. And it was all in his eyes, too. They settled on her, strikingly green, like a glass of absinthe. There were no other eyes like that.

"Hello, Daniel," said Melissa.

He didn't move.

"You took your time. I thought you weren't going to come."

Melissa gestured at the ashes still clinging to her jacket. The whole night had been an infuriating descent into a deeper and deeper hole, and she might as well have stood there with the shovel in her hands.

"There was a lot to clean up," she said.

"How many? I've heard conflicting figures."

"Twenty-three. Twenty-seven if you count the servants at the house. It's a good thing I thought to carry extra rounds."

Melissa tapped her pistol. She coughed again, then

plucked a cigarette from a silver case on the desk. If she was to have smoke in her lungs, it could at least be the kind she enjoyed.

Daniel glanced at the ring on his left index finger, and rubbed his thumb over the ruby in a half-hearted attempt to polish it.

"Are you hurt?" he asked.

"No."

"Good. But this was hardly the low-key operation I asked for."

"August tried to run. And then two lighting mechanisms collapsed. One in Rene and the other a few streets down. It blocked the route for the officers."

"Are you suggesting that all this is the fault of an incompetent lightsman?"

Melissa pursed her lips. "No, but it didn't help matters."

"What also didn't help is you setting the house on fire," Daniel pointed out sharply. "I heard about that. You say you had a lot to clean up? You're the one who made the mess in the first place."

Melissa took a long drag of the cigarette and blew out the smoke through her nose.

"August got ahead of me a few times. There, I admit it. Thirteen years an assassin, and now I've made one mistake. Are you really going to rake me across the coals for that?"

Daniel shook his head. "I don't have to. I know you've already raked yourself across them far worse than I could."

Annoyance rolled in Melissa's stomach. Daniel watched her carefully, but she looked straight past him. A part of her wished he *had* torn into her. It might have kept her from the tide of harshness she had set against herself.

"But," he continued, "thanks to the fire, now everyone will know that August and his family were involved in... whatever you're going to call last night. How do you intend to dismiss it?"

Melissa relaxed a little. She could punish herself for as long as she wanted, but if there was one thing she was good at, it was making unfortunate circumstances invisible. This was what she enjoyed. Logic, plans, all loose ends tied up so neatly, nobody needed to know they had ever been separate from the tapestry.

"Why do you think I went to the manor?" she said. "If August involved his family, I don't know if the servants overheard as well. I wasn't about to take that risk. The whole affair might have lacked subtlety, but who looks for bullets in burned bodies?"

"And what of Rene Square?"

"An escaped convict was the shooter, not us. I'll make it a lunafauna for good measure. I'll have one killed close to the scene, and a couple of guns will be left with him which match the bullet sizes. Just a horrible accident. And an unlucky coincidence that the fire happened on the same night."

Daniel got to his feet. "A clever, if not messy, solution."

The corner of Melissa's mouth curled into a smile. "We both know I can clear up messes. One way or another."

Daniel didn't blink.

"Except for the small matter of a survivor. I heard it through the grapevine, from your man Yellen. Is it true?"

The smirk slipped from Melissa's lips. She had hoped to approach that subject herself.

"I went to Bentham Hospital before I came here, to check," she said. "It's Charlotte Bellamy. The daughter."

Daniel snarled. "Of all the people! You managed to shoot every single drunkard and whore, but not *her?*"

"I *did* shoot her. Just not in the head," Melissa said tightly. "I told you, a mechanism went down. It fell around her; protected her from the worst of it. And a group of my trainees showed up before we could go in for point blank shots."

Daniel stayed still for a moment, then wandered to the window with a sigh. The movement was laboured, as though heavy weights were strapped around his legs.

"Why does it always have to involve children?" he muttered.

Melissa stubbed out her cigarette. Only yesterday, it had become obvious that Lord August Bellamy needed to be eliminated. But she knew Daniel had hoped to spare the family.

She approached him, laid a hand on his shoulder. His muscles were tense, harder than stone. At any other time, she might have liked it.

"Don't worry, I'll take care of her," she whispered.

"Not without my order."

"Then give it to me."

"After she's already cheated death once? A little girl?"

"I'll make it quick. I'll just go back to the hospital, slip a bit of laudanum into her arm, and nobody will suspect anything."

"No."

"You're being too soft."

"I'm being humane," Daniel argued. "She's only a child."

"That doesn't matter," Melissa said. "August was a child once, and you gave the order for him. She's a liability."

"Not necessarily," Daniel said. "Now I think about it, this might actually be an advantage."

Melissa stared at him. "*Advantage?* How?"

"Her survival will help to divert attention from the… incident. If *she* is still alive, then how could her family be the targets? What is anyone supposed to think except, like you said, it was just an accident?"

Melissa wove her fingers with his. Then she slipped her other hand around his waist.

"That's a profound risk. You do realise that?"

"We live our entire lives walking on the surface of risk," Daniel said. "And she's only seven, eight years old? She'll probably forget about it in time. At least to the point that distorts the event."

"Children remember more than one might think," Melissa insisted.

Daniel closed his eyes. "What harm can a little girl do?"

Melissa glanced at the ceiling. "Hopefully not as much as a little boy."

"He's not a boy," Daniel said, but a faint tremor came into his voice. "And we're not talking about him."

"Are you sure? Two lighting mechanisms collapsing within ten minutes? Either he did it on purpose or he's starting to slip."

"It's impossible for him to do something like that on purpose. Taking down a mechanism would be like cutting off a finger."

"Regardless, Charlotte Bellamy can't just be running amok, shouting *Aeternum* for anyone to hear. August spoke it in front of everyone in that square. Why else do you think I had to shoot them all? I would much rather have just killed one person instead of nearly thirty."

"I understand that," Daniel said firmly. "And I also understand you want to kill her so you'll feel better about the whole situation. But she's not going to remember how to say a word like *Aeternum*. And no matter how you went about it, your order was still only August. You should have dealt with him before he had a chance to go home and get his family involved. You shouldn't have... been in here."

Melissa tightened her grip on Daniel's waist.

"As you said, I can punish myself enough for that. But is it really going to be *your* official stance on the matter?" She brought her mouth close to his ear. "Because you had no stance at all when we were here ten hours ago. If I remember correctly, you couldn't even walk."

Daniel didn't move. He might give her orders — he might be the Potentate: the figurehead of the entire City — but he was her equal.

She moved her other hand up to his chest.

"What happened, happened," she said. "What matters is how we deal with it. Come on. I promise she won't feel a thing."

Daniel shook his head. "No, Melissa. She was never meant to die."

Melissa rolled her eyes. A cough tickled her throat and she swallowed before it could overwhelm her.

"Well, nobody will ever be so grateful for a lighting mechanism falling on top of them," she said acidly. "Fine. I'll have someone keep watch, and if the status quo changes, then we'll act accordingly."

"*Only* if it changes," Daniel repeated. "Now, I know the news vendors will be desperate to get hold of this, so let them have it. But only give them what they need to slake their thirst. I want this as smooth as you can get it. And do not disappoint me again."

"You won't be disappointed," Melissa replied. "Isn't that why you have me? So you can stop worrying that sweet head of yours?" She perched on the edge of the desk. "What are my other orders?"

"Am I correct in understanding Phoebe Feline had something to do with this?"

"Yes. She arranged the carriage."

"Very well," said Daniel. "Fetch Paley and go with him to Faunatown."

Melissa sighed with relief. At last, he'd made his first sensible decision of the entire meeting.

"My pleasure. That's one cat I wouldn't mind shooting. Or skinning."

She made no effort to mask her disdain. The only reason she allowed some of the lunafauna within her ranks was for their tracking abilities. The felines had superior sight and hearing, and the canines a sense of smell stronger than any human. They were useful, but no more so than any tool when put to proper use. And Phoebe Feline was a fool to think herself different.

"What am I to do in Faunatown?" Melissa asked. "Cut her tail off? An ear?"

Daniel tapped his fingers together in thought.

"No. Put a suppression device on her. There should be a few still available down here."

"There are," Melissa confirmed. "Standard procedure?"

"Block her from telling the truth, and from shifting," replied Daniel. "I don't want her causing any more trouble. And I alone will decide when it's time for it to come off. That should teach her a lesson."

He settled back into his chair with a groan. It wasn't physical tiredness, but the kind which came from dragging a great unseen weight for a lifetime. Melissa felt it herself, but she was much more active than him, moving all over the City like a ghost. It didn't make the load any lighter, but certainly served as a distraction.

"One more thing," Daniel said. "When you've dealt with Phoebe, bring Samuel Tiffin here to see me."

Melissa nodded, but her eyes took on a sharp shine.

"So you'll let the Bellamy girl go because she's an innocent child, but not the Tiffin baby?"

Daniel's expression turned darker than a thundercloud.

"You know I will," he said. "This has already been decided. It's for the greater good."

"And silencing the last witness isn't?"

"Do not try to guilt me now, Melissa."

She cocked an eyebrow. "I can't. You're too much like me in that respect. You do it well enough to yourself."

She held his gaze for a moment, unblinking. He stared straight back.

"I'll see you later," she said, honey at the edge of her voice. Then she left the building and climbed a flight of stairs away from the Tower. Overhead, through streets and rock, the great clock struck nine in the morning. Its chimes reverberated down and the walkways shook beneath her feet.

She coughed into her sleeve. The smoke felt as though it was leaving her lungs at last, but annoyance still simmered in her blood. Daniel was being careless, allowing Charlotte Bellamy to live, after everything she'd seen and heard. Melissa wished she hadn't pressed him so firmly. Then he wouldn't have forbidden her from acting, and she could have dealt with the matter herself.

There was nothing to do now but make the best of a bad situation. She would not fail. As always, no matter how she did it or how long it took, she would deliver.

She took the elevator to another antechamber. It was concealed from the surface not by a lightsman's hut, but a simple manhole, hidden in a dingy alley. The officer standing guard was one of her juniors, and she recognised him at once.

"Hargreaves? What are you doing here? I thought you'd be getting some sleep after last night."

The boy shook his head. "No, Madam. I thought it would be better to keep myself busy."

"Not tired?"

"No."

Melissa surveyed his face. He was tall for his age, with the faint shadow of black stubble on his chin. And he was stronger than he looked. He would have to be, to carry the girl to the hospital as quickly as he did. The feature which struck her most, however, was his eyes. They were almost as piercing as Daniel's, and just as unique: one brown and one blue.

"I heard you were the one who rescued that child," said Melissa. "Well done. Did you make sure she was seen to?"

"As fast as I could, Madam. I didn't stay long to find out."

"Did you stay long enough to find out her name? I'd like to send my condolences."

Melissa watched him closely. She knew he had met August Bellamy less than a year ago.

"I didn't," said Hargreaves. "But I think I know who she is. Charlotte Bellamy. She looks a lot like Lord Bellamy."

Concealed behind her lips, Melissa bit the tip of her tongue. Could the hole she'd dug get any deeper?

She kept calm, took stock of her options. Hadn't it been settled that she would deploy an officer to watch the girl? Daniel intended to use the Bellamy girl by keeping her alive. There was no reason why Melissa couldn't milk the same advantages with Hargreaves. She could plant him as the main lookout. And in order to do that, she would have to feed his potential and bring him into the fold.

"What's your first name?" she asked, although she already knew.

"Oscar, Madam."

"Well, Oscar Hargreaves, I'm impressed by how you acted last night. So I'd like you to be put through advanced tuition for my personal squadron. Once you finish your Constabulary training, of course."

The boy's face lit up as though she had offered a hundred solidi. Melissa gave him a broad smile, then climbed through the manhole and disappeared into the streets.

CHAPTER IV

The next several days dragged by in a haze of nightmares and nothingness. Whenever Charlotte closed her eyes, she saw it: the blood, the flying chips of stone as bullets collided with walls. Then came the screams. They ripped through her, as shrill as fingernails dragging over chalkboard.

She remained on her front until the wounds closed, and when she was finally allowed to turn over, she fixed her attention on the window and didn't move. She didn't even think. She refused to allow herself to. Whenever her mind felt as though it was drawing too close to the surface, she pushed it back down.

She waited for tears, but they refused to come. They built inside, exhausting her. She even forgot about her injuries. They didn't hurt at all compared to every blink, every breath, every moment her heart continued to beat. She was a lost bird in an endless night, and the only stars which had ever guided her had fallen.

The snow didn't cease. It seemed the City was trying to cover itself with its very own spell. Perhaps, if it was thick enough, everything would be hidden and beautiful again.

Charlotte wondered, what did snow sound like, when it hit the cobblestones? She couldn't hear anything, but she supposed that was because she was a human. Felines could hear a lot more than her. If she was a lunafauna, would she be able to pick it up? It would be a gentler sound than rain, she decided — like sugar perhaps, falling onto a very hard surface. She thought of last Midwinter, when the cook had made a house out of gingerbread, then invited her to shake the sieve and sprinkle icing sugar over it.

If only real snow tasted like sugar. If only it could stay white, and not turn red. Midwinter was coming round again soon. Charlotte had been looking forward to it, but not now. Last year's really had been the last.

Malcolm came to the hospital every evening after he finished work. He was the same age as her father, in his early thirties, with wiry limbs that reminded her of the stick figures she drew in her exercise books. His aquiline nose was crooked from being broken in several places, and his ears stuck out from his head like open carriage doors. All the times he had visited the manor, he'd worn a simple everyday wig, but now he hadn't bothered, and Charlotte saw his receding brown hairline.

He told her that he had been talking to a person called a magistrate.

"Do you know what that means?" he asked.

Charlotte thought it might be somebody who could do magic, but she was sure if that was the case, she would have met one before now. So she shrugged her shoulders apathetically.

"It's a person who's in charge of the law," Malcolm explained. "You see, you don't have any next of kin."

"What does that mean?"

"Other family. Grandparents, aunts, uncles… you know."

"I have an uncle," Charlotte protested. "Uncle Leo. You know that."

"Your Uncle Leo died a long time ago. He can't look after you," said Malcolm softly. "See, your Papa left a will, which said that if anything should happen to him or your Mama, you'd have someone to take care of you. That person was me. He — both of them — wanted it to be somebody you knew."

Charlotte looked at him. "So, I'm moving in with you?"

"Yes," said Malcolm. "I promise I'll do everything I can for you. Your Papa and I were like brothers. He trusted me. You trust me too, don't you?"

Charlotte gave a wooden nod.

"Good," smiled Malcolm. Then he reached inside his coat and produced a tiny parcel. Each time he visited, he had brought her something: a slice of pie, a paper snowdrop. Today, he revealed a little handheld music box.

Charlotte knew at once that he had made it. It bore the same delicate craftsmanship as all the other toys he'd created for her. It hurt to think of them now: their polished metal covered with soot, warped by heat into something only fit for a garbage heap.

She closed her eyes. Malcolm noticed her struggle, and held her hand until the medics quietly asked him to leave.

Only when Charlotte was alone did she finally bring herself to inspect the music box. The mechanism inside was simple, yet beautifully intricate. The bumps in the cylinder were the size of pinheads, and the teeth of the comb were so small, she could scarcely make them out individually. She turned the crank long into the night, listening to the delicate tune over and over. It sounded like spiderwebs floating on air. Every note was a tear which she couldn't shed.

The doctors tried to make her eat. The food was wholesome, but bland, and she only swallowed it because they wouldn't leave her alone until her plate was clear. The water wasn't much better. When she held the glass up to the light, she saw particles floating in it. There were purification tanks all over the City, but the best ones were only for the upper four Levels, where the aristocrats lived. Not here, in the Fifth.

On the morning of the twelfth day, Malcolm arrived,

followed by Doctor Kelley. She checked Charlotte's pulse and slid a thermometer under her tongue.

"You're ready to go now, dearie. Make sure you mind her stitches, Mr Godwin. She'll have to come back in a couple of weeks to have them removed, so until then, she needs plenty of rest. No extreme movements."

"I understand. Thank you so much for taking care of her," Malcolm replied with a grateful nod. He perched on the edge of the mattress. "You'll be safe with me," he said. "I promise."

"How long will it take to get to your shop?" Charlotte asked.

"Not long. I'll find a cab, save you walking. Now, go and get changed. I'll wait for you here."

Charlotte was led to a side room and helped into a faded grey dress. It wasn't one of her own; it had come from a charity collection within the hospital. Doctor Kelley tied the laces on her boots, handed over her hat and coat — the bullet-holes neatly stitched — and returned her to Malcolm. She clutched her doll in one hand and held onto him with the other.

As they walked along the corridors, medics and alchemists nodded at her, or patted her head as they passed. Charlotte only recognised a few of them, but they all seemed to know her.

"Why are they looking at me like that?" she hissed.

"It's just because of what happened in Rene," replied Malcolm. "Don't worry. It will stop soon."

Outside, crisp morning air flooded Charlotte's lungs. She shielded her eyes. The sun was masked by pale clouds, but the light reflected off the thick snow in every direction. No matter where she looked, it seemed flat, like someone had started drawing on a blank sheet of paper, blocked in a couple of windows and doors, then given up.

A cab arrived: a simple three-wheeled carriage with the

driver on a raised seat. Suspended below him was the drive mechanism: a series of gears and pistons connected to the front axle.

Charlotte swallowed anxiously. It looked exactly like the one which had been waiting on the other side of the square. She thought about the young cabbie whose neck had exploded in a fountain of blood. And her parents, lying lifeless on the ground...

She forced it down, wrinkled her nose as she climbed inside. The seats smelled of cheap tobacco and stale sweat.

"Where to, mate?" the cabbie asked through a peephole.

"Renshaw Street, Fifth West," replied Malcolm. "Go as smoothly as you can, please."

There was a jolt as the gears clicked into position and the carriage trundled away.

Charlotte gazed out of the window. The City built itself up slowly as her eyes adjusted to the glare. First came the sounds: the rumble of traffic; vendors advertising their ways in strange singsong voices. It was too cloudy to cast shadows, yet they still formed, as though every stone and brick were laced with the absence of light, and tried to hide it behind their elaborate moulded facades. On the main thoroughfares, vehicles had pressed the snow into slush, stained black at the edges from oil. Pedestrians bent their heads against a wind which screeched between the buildings like a living thing. Many people were queuing at a newspaper stall on the corner.

Charlotte read the headline emblazoned across the kiosk's front.

RENE SQ. MASSACRE: CASUALTIES CONFIRMED AT 23
LORD & LADY BELLAMY FOUND AMONG DEAD
ESCAPED LUNAFAUNA CONVICT R. CUNNINGHAM NAMED
RESPONSIBLE

The cabbie noticed it as well, and spoke up.

"Hey, bloody awful, that shooting. Unprovoked, they're sayin'. Some lunatic feline got out of gaol, shot everyone and then himself."

Charlotte leaned forward in affront. "That's not—"

"Quiet!" Malcolm hissed. He gave her a firm look and she shut her mouth.

"So much for all that early gossip about it being premeditated," the cabbie continued. "It was an accident, what I heard. Some idiot copper hadn't locked Cunningham's cell properly." He spat in contempt. "Bloody filth, lunafauna are, living in their own piss. I don't know why the Potentate puts up with 'em. We figured out magic ages ago, we don't need 'em anymore. They're no better than the animals we actually eat."

Malcolm's lips twisted into a grimace.

"It's very sad," he said simply.

His piece finished, the cabbie fell silent.

As they descended the Interlevel, Charlotte replayed the conversation in her head. She wasn't sure what a *convict* was, but from the sound of things, it was someone who killed people on their own. But she had seen that group of men, dressed in dark blue. There were about ten of them, including the tall woman with the black hair. *They* had been behind the shooting, not some lone lunafauna. She knew it. She remembered. She would never forget.

Eleven people, who had killed over forty. The square had trapped them. They couldn't get out…

It was all a lie. But why? What was going on?

Before she could think any more about it, the carriage stopped. The street was large, but scarce — the amount of snow still left on the cobbles told Charlotte that not much traffic had been this way. The terraced buildings were old and leaned close to one another, giving the strange impression they were stretched thin.

"Here we are," said Malcolm, his voice tight with embarrassment.

Charlotte gazed upon a shop frontage, pale from a fresh coat of whitewash. A sign protruded above it, reading:

GODWIN & SON WATCH MECHANICS, 5TH W. QTR.
FINE CLOCK AND GEAR WORKS FOR A FAIR PRICE

Malcolm unlocked the door. Charlotte hovered on the threshold for a moment. Once she moved, it would be the point of no return. The furthest, both figuratively and literally, she had ever been from home.

She took a deep breath, and stepped across.

She couldn't contain her surprise. The space was large, furnished in a way that made the most of what it had. There was a workbench, littered with boxes of parts and tools. Clocks and other devices lined the room, and a few chairs stood by the window for clients. In the corner, a spiral staircase led to a mezzanine, which Charlotte presumed was the living quarters.

Malcolm approached a wall, practically invisible from the number of clocks hanging on it, and wound each with a key. At once, the place filled with ticking. It was so loud, it echoed inside Charlotte's head, and for a moment, she worried she had turned as hollow as the doll she was holding. She was used to that sound, everyone in Forest was, but not like *this*.

Malcolm, however, didn't bat an eye. How long had he listened to those clocks? How was he not crazy from it? Had it been so long that he couldn't even hear them anymore?

"I've put you up in the back bedroom," he said. "It used to be mine when I was your age. There's not much there at the moment, but it's market day on Monday, so we'll go and get you some stuff. You'll need some new clothes, at any rate."

He cleared his throat awkwardly, one hand creeping to his pocket. Charlotte knew he was after his watch.

She twisted her fingers together and mumbled, "Thank you, Malcolm."

Malcolm left his watch alone and knelt so he was at her height.

"Listen, I know this is really different from what you've known, kiddo," he said. "But I'm going to do everything I can to make sure you're comfortable and cared for. You know that, don't you?"

A frown stole across Charlotte's face. She did know that. She would have chosen to be with Malcolm any day over some stranger who she'd never met. But she still couldn't shake her unease. It crawled under her skin like insects, tried to dive deeper, burning as though she had swallowed a live coal.

"Why did you tell me to be quiet?" she demanded. "That cab man had it all wrong! Why did you lie and say it was a *conny-vict?*"

Malcolm blinked in surprise. "You mean it wasn't?"

"No! There were loads of them! And they were all dressed like constables. And there was a woman…"

Charlotte's voice trailed off. The horror flashed before her again; she smelled the hot blood on the air. She glanced away, tried to focus on something else, and found a piece of exposed brick where the plaster had broken off. But it was too pink: the colour of raw meat. Was that what everyone's insides looked like?

"Why did they do it?" she whispered. "Are they going to come back for me?"

"No," Malcolm said at once. "I promise. I won't let them."

"But what if they shoot you, too?"

"Don't be silly. Of course they won't."

He tried to be nonchalant, but his tone didn't fool her. Charlotte remembered her father's expression when they had reached the square. She thought of her mother's lips, redder than any rouge she'd applied for the grand Parliamentary events.

The wounds twitched, blazing right down to her bones.

"Mama and Papa really are dead, aren't they?" she breathed. "They're not coming back. That's what a *cassul-ty* is."

Malcolm didn't look away. Pale light fell behind him like spilled milk.

"Yes," he said.

Charlotte waited for tears, but they still didn't come. Guilt crumpled her stomach as though it were paper. She should be crying — she should have cried from the moment she saw the tall woman. She saw that chiselled face float in her mind: a little younger than her parents, sharp eyes with sparks in their depths.

"But why would the constables shoot them?" Charlotte asked instead. "They did nothing wrong!"

"I know," said Malcolm. "Your parents were very good people. Your Papa was amazing; all the charity work he did. But… They are gone now, Charlotte. And the details around what happened must have been changed."

"But it's a lie!" she protested.

"Maybe the Constabulary decided to cover it up to shelter you. Sometimes you need to lie in order to protect people."

"Then why would they have shot me as well, if they wanted to protect me?"

"I don't know. But you're still here. And as for Rene, whatever the reason is, it must be for the greater good."

Charlotte fell silent at that. It was something her father had said often: the greater good always had to come first. It was why he'd devoted so much time to helping the poorer areas of the City, even though it earned sneers from his colleagues. The other Lords only parted with their coins under pressure, never because they felt it was the right thing to do. And even though she was only a child, Charlotte had always admired him for that. Even now, she felt a flicker of pride in her chest. It was faint, a tiny ember dulled by ash, but it was there.

A bell jungled above the door, and a canine lunafauna peeked through. Her floppy ears hung down below a wide-brimmed hat. A threadbare skirt and shawl covered her thin body, and her bare paws tracked snow behind her. She stood upright like a human, but fur ran along her jawbone and the backs of her front paws, in which she clutched a small mantel clock.

She sniffed the air and said meekly, "I beg your pardon, are you open?"

Malcolm smiled. "We certainly are."

The canine still didn't move. She held herself like a taut spring, shoulders hunched, tail between her legs, as though expecting a blow.

"I heard you… accept us here?"

"I accept all honest people here," Malcolm replied warmly. "Please come in, out of the cold."

The canine relaxed. Malcolm steered Charlotte towards the stairs and leaned close so he could whisper.

"Just leave me while I deal with this customer. Your room's the last one on the right."

Charlotte clung to the iron banister until she reached the mezzanine. It felt cold under her fingers. It was well made, but simple and spindly. There was no wood in it, like the one at the manor. She knew Malcolm wouldn't be able to afford anything like that. Would she ever see wood again?

She didn't go straight to the bedroom. Instead, she paused and listened.

"You've come a long way from Faunatown."

"It's nice to find someone this high up the Levels who'll have anything to do with us," the canine admitted. "I knew about this place, but I could hardly believe it. So many humans don't want us outside."

"Then they need to check their priorities and privileges, if you ask me. You're all residents of this City as much as anyone else."

"I wish others thought the same, Mr Godwin."

Malcolm let out a humble chuckle.

"One day. I'd like to think that, one day, things will change for the better around here. Now, let's take a look and see what we can do…"

He set about opening the clock. Charlotte tried to peer over the mezzanine, but Malcolm moved out of sight, and she didn't want him to spot her. Her mother had always insisted on the importance of good impressions. Not doing as she was told on her first day in the shop wouldn't be a welcome start.

She went to the door Malcolm had indicated, but it hadn't been fitted well in the frame, and jammed. She aimed a kick at the corner. It swung open, revealing a tiny box room. The bed was at least a foot narrower than what she expected, with a single flat pillow which Malcolm had done his best to fluff up. Thin wintry sunlight streamed through a window over a dented copper dresser. The air smelled of old dust recently disturbed, overhung with damp mortar and cheap waxy soap.

Charlotte's heart flipped as she looked around. It was all familiar enough, with everything it needed. But didn't feel right, like a well-worn glove belonging to any hand except her own. She hugged her doll, slid down the wall until she was huddled in a ball on the floor. And, completely unwilled, tears finally ran from her eyes.

The spell was broken, and it would never be remade.

CHAPTER V

The South Quarter was an intermediate area: not as affluent as the East and West, still able to stand above the more rampant poverty of the North. But it was also the place where the divide was most clearly seen, because it also had Faunatown.

Spreading from the Fifth Level to the Twelfth at the very bottom of the City, Faunatown held the look and feel of a community fused onto the rest of Forest like a tick. The streets were barely more than dirt tracks lined with cracked cobbles. Only a handful of buildings bore the ornamental façade of the no-tail areas, and most windows were shuttered in an attempt to save money. The men in power, long ago, had insisted that glass wasn't a necessity when the residents had fur which could keep out the cold. That attitude had never changed.

The lunafauna had been resident in Forest for almost as long as the no-tails, but it quickly became apparent they were second class citizens. The line of value was drawn at their magic. Nobody could take anything more than a menial job, or strive to make a life beyond their station. The lucky ones became teachers or lightsmen. Those who fortune truly blessed might join the Constabulary and earn the right to good accommodation. But for most, they had no choice other than scraping by, trying to maintain their dignity along the way. And some, like many other poor souls, turned to thievery. Everything from pickpocketing to the organised gangs of Forest's underbelly.

In the tavern area, Phoebe Feline pondered it all, as she

often did when the night was long and the time slow. She was in her cat form, perched on the bar of The Three Cogwheels. Grime coated the stone walls. Portraits of old patrons hung alongside tobacco-stained flowers made from the cheapest paper. Above the smell of beer, smoke and unwashed bodies, she noticed other scents: despair, poverty, and the quiet, creeping acceptance that neither would ever change. As the only one with any kind of power, Phoebe did all she could to help. But even she was limited. Like for many of her neighbours, the only medicine was alcohol.

And now there was the news of the massacre in the Fourth West. She had done her best to assist August, to stand by his side when she knew all the others would forsake him. As usual, whenever she tried to make things better, it led to nothing but pain and death. And, of course, it was never her own.

The Tower bells rang one o'clock in the morning.

"Closing time," said the barkeep.

Phoebe flicked her whiskers and drank the last of the wine from the dish in front of her.

"Thanks, Timmy," she said. "Happy transnight. May magic shine on you."

"The same to you," he replied. "The next bottle's on the house. Get home safe, now."

"I will. Take care of yourself."

Phoebe rubbed herself against him, then jumped off the bar and walked outside. The world swam and warped, and she shook her head in an attempt to see straight. The road was empty, save for the other tavern-goers like her. All were drunk, either in their taller forms or down on all fours, and some in the process of transitioning from one to the other.

On transnights like this, whenever the moon was full, every lunafauna could change their shape. It was the one aspect of magic they were still permitted to use, and even that was controlled in insidious ways. Nobody dared to keep their animal form for too long, in case they were left stuck in it for a month and unable to perform their jobs.

Phoebe took the long way back to her house, so she could feel the moonlight. It was music without sound; something deeper and truer than any of the stone buildings which fenced her in. Under it, she could almost smell the sweetness of the ancient trees.

What she wouldn't have given for absinthe. At least it was green. And strong enough to truly incapacitate her.

She let herself in through a small door. Her home was massive for Faunatown, to mark her as the single Parliamentary Fellow in the area. But the grounds were strewn with old bottles; the gate left open so struggling souls could help themselves to whatever came into her possession. She would have renounced it all in a heartbeat, if only she could.

Unlike all of Forest's inhabitants, Phoebe remembered what it had been like to *come* to the City. Back then, it was a jewel in the landscape: a destination of promise, coursing with innovation, surrounded by bounty and life. Phoebe had rejoiced when she and her fellow lunafauna had arrived, and had been given a whole area to themselves. But then, slowly, the days had turned darker. The place became a mockery of what it once boasted. Order, advancement and respect were lost beneath hierarchy and intolerance.

And then she had found out what went on beneath the streets. Something right under the peoples' noses, so obvious yet so obscure, which ate at her from the inside like maggots, until all she felt was disgust. Not only for them, but for herself. And now, there was no way out.

Phoebe sat down, scratched with her back foot. One of her claws caught the hoop in her ear. The ruby it held was small, but that hardly made any difference to the weight. For the thousandth time, she considered ripping it out, but the fancy died in her mind like smoke escaping into air. There was no point. Never would be.

She froze. A soft tapping cut through the silence. Fingernails on a table.

Her tail swept from side to side. The grounds were open to everyone, but nobody came *inside* her house. And those weren't the nails of a lunafauna.

The sound was in the drawing room. She hurried towards it, and no sooner had she stepped through the doorway, a lighting mechanism burst into life.

She immediately spotted a woman reclining in a chair. A long black braid cascaded over her shoulder.

"You're home rather late," said Melissa Spectre. "Or, should that be early?"

Phoebe flattened her ears against her skull.

"Get your skinny ass out of here, Vixen."

Melissa raised an eyebrow. "Not as slurred as I thought you'd be. Good."

A hand suddenly grabbed Phoebe by the scruff. She yowled, tried to twist around, but was lifted clean off her feet before she had the chance. Whoever held her moved closer to the window, so the moonlight hit her.

"Don't let go, Copley," said Melissa. "She might be a Lady, but she's as rabid as the rest of them."

Phoebe hissed. "Put me down!"

"Put yourself down," Melissa said, very calmly. "I know it's a transnight. So transform."

She got to her feet and approached, her boot heels clipping the floor with every step.

"You killed them," Phoebe snarled. "August, Lena... all those innocent people..."

"May they rest in peace," Melissa said. "If you're going to

lay blame, then you need to look in the mirror. *You* tried to help him escape. *You* organised a carriage for him. *You* were willing to break all that the Aeternum stands for, our most basic rule. Ensure the Keeper remains safe."

"You haven't got a clue what the Aeternum stands for," Phoebe snapped.

"And you do, because you're *so much older* than all of us," Melissa said, voice dripping with sarcasm. "My Lady, you look terribly uncomfortable up here. Just shift your form and I'm sure you'll feel better."

She was right. Copley's thin fingers were digging into Phoebe's flesh, and hanging suspended in the air was making it difficult to breathe.

She glanced around. There was another officer standing behind him. Like Melissa — and Copley; Phoebe could feel the hard ridge of it below his knuckle — the second man wore a ruby ring. And Melissa had only lit one lamp, but it was wound to full capacity.

The Vixen didn't need much light when she paid unexpected visits. Something intricate was intended tonight. Something which required no shadows and no room for error.

"Why's it so important to you that I do?" Phoebe asked instead.

"Your wellbeing is important to me."

"Piss off. I wish I was drunk enough to even find that amusing."

Copley shook her.

"You can't talk to the Chief Officer like that!"

"Oh, shut it!" Phoebe snarled, then threw an expectant look at Melissa. "Is he a new one? I hope you know what you've let yourself in for, kid."

Melissa's lips twisted into a smile which didn't reach her

eyes.

"Relax, Copley," she said. "Dealings with Lady Feline often take a rather blunt turn. It's up to us to not descend to her level."

Phoebe spat out a laugh. "Choice words. What *dealings* did you have in mind, then? You obviously need to see what you're doing, so… something slow? Not your usual style. And I know Daniel hasn't ordered you to kill me. I'm worth more to you alive, or where would Faunatown be? So quit wasting my time and get to the point."

Melissa moved closer, not breaking her composure for a moment. Nausea sank through Phoebe's belly and she fought the urge to grimace. A look like that, so strong, unrelenting… it was a threat. Dominance. The only respite was to turn away, and she refused to do that.

"Transform, and I will," said Melissa. "Otherwise, we'll all be here for a lot longer than any of us would like."

Phoebe twitched. She wanted nothing more than to lunge forward and rip Melissa's sly eyes clean out of her head. But the skin around her chest and throat was too tight. Each breath took less and less air into her lungs.

She reached for the moonlight and drew it through her body. Magic rippled across her in a thousand tiny caresses. Her front paws protruded to form fingers. Her fur withdrew until it was only a fine covering, still scattered with the brown stripes of her tabby markings. She grew to human size, and as soon as her feet touched the ground, she wrenched herself out of Copley's grasp and swiped her claws at him.

Melissa sneered in disgust. "Your kind's true colours never fail to shine through, do they?"

Phoebe scoffed. "Neither do yours."

Melissa looked over Phoebe's shoulder. Phoebe didn't

bother turning around, just listened as a pair of shoes tapped across the floor. How many officers were in here? Had she truly drunk so much that her hearing had betrayed her?

A thin man in his late fifties emerged, with a curled wig on his head and a hooked nose that seemed too large for his face. Professor Victor Paley: the leader of the small company of alchemists who had pledged their services to the Aeternum. His cheeks were lined and hollow, but his intelligent eyes were sharper than needles. Even from across the room, Phoebe felt them pricking at her.

"Lady Feline," he said. "I'm deeply sorry to have to meet you like this."

His mouth was turned down a little, as though in regret, but Phoebe wasn't sure if she believed it.

Her gaze moved to the bag he carried. He opened it and drew out a length of leather. At first, Phoebe thought it was a belt, but then she looked again. It was too short for that.

Her stomach turned over with disdain.

"A *collar?*"

Paley took a step closer, and she noticed something else. In the middle of the strip was a mechanism, no larger than a thimble. And attached to it was something even smaller: a tiny orb, practically invisible save for its faint white glow. That added power source wouldn't be there, save for one reason. The mainspring wasn't intended to be wound for a very long time. And, protruding from the metal plates, something sharp glinted in the light. A curved needle.

Phoebe's ears twisted back again. Now she finally understood why Paley was there, and why Melissa had cranked the lamp up to full power. It was a suppression device.

"Those things are illegal," she said. She cursed herself when she heard her voice wobble.

Melissa gave her a condescending glance.

"You're too important to lose, so think of this as a compromise," she said, with such cool indifference, Phoebe shivered. "You won't be hurt. You will continue running Faunatown. You will keep your title, your station, your house, everything. But you will have no voice. The magic attached to this means you will never be able to communicate about the Aeternum with anybody, or anything about the incident with August Bellamy, until the Potentate decides to trust you again."

Phoebe scowled. "And if I refuse?"

"I'll cut out your tongue. Would you rather not speak at all, ever again? Or just certain words, for a little while, out of your *very long life?*"

Phoebe's eyes flashed between Melissa, Paley, and the two officers. All were watching her, warily, but intently. They wouldn't leave until it was done.

The mere sight of the collar almost made her vomit. But she straightened her back, summoned whatever pride she could, and fixed Melissa with a glare colder than steel.

"Get on with it, then. But it won't matter in the end. You think I haven't put up with shit from no-tails like you before? A hundred years from now, I'll be dancing on your grave."

Melissa smiled. The officers snatched Phoebe and forced her over the table beside the lamp. She smelled the sweat on Melissa's trousers as she held her head in position. It wasn't just her own. There was a man's there, too. Daniel's.

Paley's breathing grew heavy with concentration. Phoebe braced herself, but the scratch of the needle still tore out a shriek. She tried to get free; Copley pinned her down harder. The point dug into the skin at the back of her neck. She couldn't even tell how deep. It hadn't been long enough to reach her spine, surely...

The mechanism clicked. Then Melissa wrapped the collar

tight and locked it.

Whole seconds passed before Phoebe realised the hands were gone from her shoulders. She forgot about her body, about everything except the needle.

Her blood felt slower, cloggy, like mud, moving just enough to do its job and nothing more. The sweet silvery power of the transnight leached out of it. She tried to draw it, to change back into her smaller form, but it was no use. The sharp point pinched and stung her until she stopped.

Gasping with pain, she forced herself to stand. The collar pressed against her skin and bent her fur in all the wrong ways. She curled her fingers so her claws were on full display.

She spoke. Each word scrambled against her throat as she tried to give it purchase.

"There wasn't just a vocal restriction in this thing."

Melissa stayed exactly where she was, just out of arm's length. The sly smirk lingered on her lips.

"I forgot to mention. You won't be able to shift until it's removed. Maybe it will help you to remember to *act* a little more human, even if you can never be one. It might take some time to get used to. But, then again, you have all the time in the world, don't you?"

Phoebe wheeled on Paley. He was an alchemist: a master of the discipline which had succeeded the ancient magic of the lunafauna. Only he would have known how to create the restrictions on a device like this.

"You bastard," she snarled, trembling with anger.

"I'm sorry," he whispered.

Phoebe thrashed her tail like a whip.

"Get out."

Melissa smiled at her reaction.

"I believe that will be all, gentlemen," she said. "Thank

you for your cooperation, Lady Feline."

She led the officers away. Phoebe stayed still until she heard the latch, deep in the bowels of the house. Only when she was sure she was alone did she sink onto all fours, and scream.

CHAPTER VI

Charlotte awoke to the Tower striking eight, then the chimes faded into the new plethora of noises she was still becoming used to. In the manor, the large grounds and thick walls meant it was harder to detect the day-to-day sounds of the City. But here, there was no escaping them. The incessant clocks downstairs were the least of it. She heard the loud rattle of wheels on the road, the steady clicking of a light mechanism in the street near her window, the hubbub of a crowd heading to market.

She groaned. Today, Malcolm was taking her for new clothes.

She tried to go back to sleep, but couldn't get comfortable again, so she made her bed as best she could. She'd never had to do it before. There were always servants who did it much nicer. She tried not to think about them.

Malcolm knocked on the door. "You awake?"

"Yes," she replied glumly.

He entered with fresh bandages and a bowl of warm water. Charlotte hesitated when she saw it. He had cleaned her stitches since she'd left the hospital, but it wasn't the pain which she dreaded. Before, her mother and the maids were the ones who had helped her get changed. Not even her father had seen her in a state of undress. For as much as she trusted Malcolm, awkwardness weighed on her chest like a rock.

Deciding to get it over as fast as possible, she dropped her nightdress to just below her shoulders. Even bearing that amount of flesh made her feel as though something was stuck in her throat. She fixed her eyes on a spot on the wall and challenged herself not to blink, not to think too hard, as Malcolm peeled off the previous day's gauze. He worked quickly and gently, but the softest touch still stung. As soon as he was done, he wrapped new layers over her stitches, then took the grey dress from the end of the bed.

"I bet you'll be happy to have something different to wear," he said, flippantly.

Charlotte crossed her arms. She hated when adults talked like that.

"I don't want to go."

"You can't live in this all through winter."

"Well, can't *you* go and get the clothes, and come straight back?"

"No, because I need to buy more than just clothes. Anyway, it will do you good to get some fresh air. And you can pick something you like."

Charlotte stayed quiet. That was tempting, but fear stabbed her heart like an icicle. She didn't want either of them to go out there. It was so noisy — anyone could hide. Anyone could do *anything*...

"Alright, my eyes are closed," said Malcolm.

Charlotte checked, then eased herself out of her nightgown and into the dress. She cleared her throat, the way her mother had done sometimes, to let him know he could look. With a kind smile, Malcolm turned her on the spot so he could fasten the button at the back of her neck.

"I know what you're thinking," he said. "Don't worry. It will be safe."

"It might not be."

"It will. I promise."

He did his best to work a brush through her unruly long hair. The teeth snagged and she yelped in pain. He muttered an apology, then attempted to pin it into a bun, but tendrils worked loose, so he stuffed it under her hat.

"Sorry," he said. "I know I'm rubbish at this. I've never had to do it before."

Charlotte glanced at him. "Why aren't you wearing a wig? Papa never went out without a wig."

"Because your Papa was a Parliamentary Fellow," replied Malcolm. "Some folks around these parts wear wigs, but not all. I just prefer not to, unless I have to make an impression. They make my head itch. Anyway, enough about that. Can you try to put your boots on by yourself?"

Charlotte frowned. "By myself?"

Malcolm gave a half-smile. "I can't do this for you forever. You'll have to learn quick how to look after yourself."

"But…" Charlotte glanced at her boots, strewn on the floor where she'd left them the day before. "I thought that was your job."

Malcolm chuckled. "I'm a watch mechanic, kiddo, not a nanny. Sit on the bed."

He slipped her feet into the shoes. When he held the laces, Charlotte's stomach twisted with nerves, but he just told her to tie a simple knot. She did, and he finished off the bow, slowly, so she could watch what he was doing.

"See?" he said. "It's not so hard, is it?"

"Well, you know how to do it," she replied in a dour tone.

Malcolm smiled. "You'll pick it up soon enough. Now, shall we go and see what we can find?"

Before she could protest further, he led her down the staircase, pulled on a thin jacket and top hat. Then he buttoned Charlotte's coat and they stepped onto the pavement.

She shuddered as the icy air pressed on her face. This was the first time she'd been outside since leaving the hospital. Spikes of hardened frost crowned the thick snow. Some children tried to play in it, but it was too cold to hold any structure. It crumbled as soon as they touched it and powdery snowballs fell apart in mid-air.

But they weren't what caught her attention. Bunting dangled across the street like clothes lines, every small red triangle embroidered with a golden *C*. Even that innocuous sight made her heart race. So much red, against white snow and drab stone…

"What's all this for?" Charlotte asked, desperate for something to break the connection. If she knew why they were there, then surely, they wouldn't seem threatening.

"Potentate Carter and the High Lady Elisabeth have had a son," Malcolm explained. "It was in the paper yesterday morning. That's why the decorations are all red, you see. That's the colour of the Potentates. And the *C* stands for Carter."

"I know that," Charlotte snapped. "Everyone knows that."

Malcolm didn't reply, but he breathed in hard through his nose and gave a small cough. Worried she had upset him, Charlotte spoke again, softer.

"I'm sorry. What does *Potentate* mean though? The word, I mean. Papa never told me."

Malcolm shot a fleeting glance in the direction of the First Level.

"It means someone who is potent. Powerful," he replied. "And the Carters are powerful because they're the ones who look after us. So that makes Daniel Carter the Potentate of Forest."

He sounded distracted, so Charlotte let the conversation drop as they walked away. No matter where she looked, her eyes couldn't settle. There were so many people, heaving against each other like swirling water.

Were any of them the tall dark-haired woman? Could they have guns hidden under their coats?

"Easy," Malcolm said. "You'll break my fingers!"

Charlotte quickly loosened her grip. "Sorry."

"Don't worry. I've got you," he assured. "Everything's fine."

They turned a corner into Godstall Square. As soon as Charlotte saw it, anxiety pooled thick and heavy in her belly. It was larger than Rene, with more roads leading in and out, but the buildings still towered on all sides like the edges of a huge stone box. And the entire place thronged with people, moving in a hundred different directions; a tangle of heights and colours and sweeping skirts.

A web of bunting criss-crossed overhead in a bizarre fabric ceiling. Charlotte caught glimpses of the Tower in the gaps between the flags. Now she was in the Fifth Level, it was another hundred feet further away than what she was used to, but even so, it seemed more imposing than ever in the early daylight. The giant glass faces reflected the sun, so even if it hadn't been so high, it was impossible to see into the chamber beyond.

She shivered. She had gazed upon that enormous structure every day, heard its bells ring every hour of her life. Now, she felt as though someone was up there, staring at her.

Malcolm guided her between the stalls. The air filled with the smell of fresh bread. Charlotte's stomach grumbled as she noticed a golden pot pie on a bakery stand. She tugged at Malcolm's sleeve, and he rolled his eyes teasingly before handing over two solidus coins.

The baker cut a couple of slices. He was a skinny and balding middle-aged man, whose eyes skimmed everywhere, never settling for more than a few seconds. The skin on his hands was so thin, every bone was visible, and veins ran under it like blue ropes.

"Morning, Samuel," said Malcolm.

"Mm," grunted the baker. He jabbed his chin at Charlotte. "Who's that?"

"A friend's daughter. She's staying with me," Malcolm replied. "Charlotte, this is Samuel Tiffin."

Charlotte stayed quiet. The fitful way the baker moved reminded her of her father on the night they had run.

"Whatever," Tiffin muttered. "You want bread, too?"

"Yes, please."

Tiffin wrapped a loaf with a derisive sniff. As soon as Malcolm had paid, he turned away and started humming tunelessly under his breath

Charlotte frowned in alarm. Malcolm noticed and whispered to her.

"Don't mind him." He tapped his temple. "Samuel's not all there, but he's harmless."

"What's wrong with him?"

"Nothing, really. He's just a bit strange. Not very good with manners."

Charlotte peered at Tiffin again. Her mother would have thrown a fit if anyone spoke to her without saying *please* and *thank you*. Etiquette was boring, sitting straight in a chair and knowing the intricate ways of accepting a cup of tea; but courtesy was simple enough. How could anyone, especially an adult, not know it?

She decided against mentioning that, and instead said, "He's got a funny name for a baker. Why's he named after a cake?"

"Maybe that's why he's a baker," Malcolm said with a smirk.

He passed a pie slice to her. It tasted surprisingly good for the Fifth Level: the chicken was tougher than Charlotte was used to, but the pastry was flaky and light. As she ate, her attention wandered to a gang of older boys, tossing a battered leather ball at the edge of the square. Their trousers were faded, hems only reaching half-way down their shins. They must have been from an orphanage. Only children with no parents wore the same clothes for years on end.

Charlotte stopped chewing as she thought of that. *She* had no parents either.

The crowd drifted into a flat current of dull noise and movement, stepping around her without seeing her, as though she were a ghost trespassing into their world. The only thing she was aware of was the bunting. It was no longer blood on snow. Now, each triangle seemed like a scarlet arrowhead pointing straight at her, singling her out in her well-made coat over a donated dress. The one who was different. The one who got away.

Malcolm's voice swam through the fug.

"What's the matter? Don't you like the pie?"

Charlotte glanced at it. The crust suddenly looked soggy and colourless, as if she had dropped it. She shook her head.

"Alright, give it to me. I'll heat it up for you later. Let's get your clothes, and then we can go."

Charlotte didn't reply. Her mind felt smaller than her skull, as though it had crumpled like paper into a ball. She tried to open it, but couldn't read the words written there. *Get clothes.* That was what Malcolm had said. Yes, that was what they needed to do.

A group of women muttered near the news vendor. Charlotte focused on them. They sounded like excited geese, but that didn't matter. She just needed something to distract herself.

"Isn't it wonderful news about the baby? The Carters must be so proud. When do you think Presentation Day will be?"

"Oh, come on. How many people do you think will show up? Who gives a toss about the Potentate anymore?"

"*I* do! Gosh, Winnie, always so negative!"

"To be honest, it's what everyone needs right now. Has your power been going down, too?"

"Yes. My lights went off for an hour last night! At least it wasn't the heating."

"*At least?* Are you forgetting everything else? Body-snatching, thieves, lunafauna getting mouthy... What's this place coming to? And now there's Rene."

"Did you hear though? The Bellamys were there, but their kid wasn't. I bet she was caught in the fire. Poor thing."

"I don't know. They found all the other bodies in the fire, what I heard. But not a kid."

The ground lurched under Charlotte's feet. She stared at her boots, the dirty snow, cigarette ends crushed into the space between the cobbles. The plan for distraction fell apart like ash. Why did Malcolm think it was a good idea to bring her out here? He wasn't stupid, he *must* have known there would be gossip. But he didn't react to anything the women said. Was he not bothered? Or had he just not heard them?

Charlotte tried to imitate him, right down to placing her feet at the same time as him. There was a rhythm to it, oddly comforting. It reminded her of the swing, moving back and forth like a pendulum. Tick tock.

She thought of the clocks back at the shop. Had he wound them that morning?

Malcolm led her to a stall lined with dresses and suits. Most were cheap drab colours, but some bore a hint of pastel for the richer customers.

"Good morning," the vendor said, in such a forced merry tone, Malcolm winced. "Quality garments here, mate. Nothin' like that rubbish you'll find over in Clayton Square. Feel this wool! See, that'll get you through winter quite nicely! And I have a sale on wallets, if you're interested."

"Thank you," Malcolm smiled politely. "You pick first, kiddo."

Charlotte pointed at a pair of dungarees.

The vendor gave her a patronising smirk. "They're for boys, sweetie."

Charlotte didn't blink. "I'd still like them, please, sir."

The vendor arched his eyebrows in surprise. He laughed: a dull empty sound which seemed to cut itself off mid-breath.

"Civil little thing, ain't she?" he remarked.

Malcolm shrugged. "She just knows what she likes, that's all. And girls wear trousers sometimes if they have hard work to do. But you'll need some dresses too, kiddo."

The vendor ran his watery eyes over Charlotte to measure her up, and presented two frocks: one dark blue and the other black. Malcolm bought both, along with the dungarees, then steered Charlotte towards the grocer. She gasped at the sight of so much green. It was only vegetables, grown in glasshouses outside the City, but food like this was the only way anyone ever saw such a colour.

"I wasn't expecting you to go for boy's clothes," Malcolm muttered.

"Mama always made me wear dresses whenever we had guests," said Charlotte. "But when it was just us, she let me wear things like that. In case I fell off the swing or something…"

She forgot what she was saying. A crafts stall had set up in the next aisle. Malcolm noticed her looking.

"Go on," he smiled.

Charlotte hesitated. "But…"

"I'll be right here. I'll come and get you in a minute."

Charlotte swallowed her nerves, then picked her way through the crowd and stood at an angle so nobody could jostle her. The vendor had claimed a spot beside a lighting mechanism, and was using it to his advantage: marionettes and dolls hung off the grooved teeth so they were in plain sight. But what truly captured Charlotte's attention were the paper flowers: folded into artistic petals, some coloured with inks, the leaves scored with a knife to give the impression of veins.

Scented paper bouquets used to fill the Bellamy manor. Charlotte had always marvelled at them, how they managed to evoke the image of things that couldn't grow anymore. She remembered being told that hundreds of years ago, when Forest was founded, it had been surrounded by woodland. It was after such beauty that the first people had modelled their new City: mimicking nature not only in name, but in design. The streets twisted like branches and the stone decorations on the buildings echoed foliage. The artificial rivers were called that on purpose, even cascading in manmade waterfalls from the grounds of the Potentate's Pavilion on the First Level. And at the centre, the Tower rose like a tree trunk: the life-giver of everything which surrounded it.

Now, the true trees were gone, as was the original forest. All that was left was a barren wasteland called the Meadows. Out there, miles beyond the City walls, the only plants thrived in glasshouses, for crops and paper and livestock food, specially tended by experts under artificial suns. In the wild, the soil was dead. It had been for centuries. Like everyone around her, Charlotte had never seen a real flower, and knew she never would.

Suddenly feeling watched, she raised her eyes. The boys had stopped playing with their ball and looked straight at her. They huddled close together, whispering and nodding their heads.

Unease settled on her like a cold mist. She needed to get

back to Malcolm. She turned around, but spun straight into another boy. He snatched her arm and dragged her towards the group.

A flare of panic mounted inside her. If he pulled too hard, he'd break her stitches…

"Alright, I did your stupid dare, Edgar," the boy barked. "Give me that solidus."

"Not so fast," said the tallest. He bent so his head was level with Charlotte. "You're that Bellamy kid, ain't you?"

Charlotte tried to run, but Edgar thrust his face close. He smelled rancid, like old onions, and the edges of his fingernails were coated black with grime.

"I heard you got shot," he pressed. "It hurt?"

"Take your hands off me!" Charlotte snapped, with as much authority as she could. But that only made the boys snigger.

"Come on, it's her," insisted a third. "I told you it was. Look at her boots. And listen to the way she talks: all hoity toity!"

"Dare's not over yet, though," Edgar said. "Let's see 'em."

Before Charlotte could react, he spun her around and wrenched open the button on her dress. He caught the edge of her bandage. Fright and anger surged; all her politeness flashed away. She turned, eyes blazing, and slapped him.

Edgar paused, stunned. Then he shoved her. Charlotte barely realised she had fallen before a foot ploughed into her gut.

"You're not in your manor here, Bellamy!" he snarled furiously. "You're no better than us here, you got that? You can't hit us!"

Charlotte threw her arms up to protect her face. But then she noticed how close Edgar was to her own feet. She flung her leg out and caught him behind the knee, scrambled away towards Malcolm. When he saw her, he leapt between her and the boys.

"That's enough, you hear?" he growled. "You lot get out

of here! Go on!"

They backed off nervously. Edgar glared at Charlotte for a moment longer before stalking down an alley.

A low hum of whispers spread through the watching crowd. Malcolm ushered Charlotte into a side street to escape, then knelt in front of her. She clung onto his arms and tried to breathe, but it felt like she was dragging water through her lungs, not air.

"You alright?" Malcolm asked.

"They kicked me! And my dress…" Charlotte wheezed.

She paused. Now the fright was over, she felt pain in her back, and something wet.

"Is it bleeding?" she cried.

Malcolm peered down her collar to check. "A little. I'll clean it when we get home. Come on."

He took her hand, gently, as though she was made of thin porcelain. As they walked away, Charlotte sensed eyes on her again, and shot a quick look over her shoulder.

Halfway down the street, a dark-haired boy lounged in a doorway. To her relief, it wasn't Edgar; too old to be him. The long shadows turned his clothes black, but she recognised the cut of them. A Constabulary uniform.

Her pulse burst all over her body like a firework. Every muscle prepared to bolt; whereabouts didn't matter, so long as it was away from him…

But the officer turned in the opposite direction and strode off. Charlotte swallowed so hard, her ears popped. Just a regular constable, on his duties, nothing more.

Not all of them were murderers. She needed to believe that.

CHAPTER VII

Malcolm replaced Charlotte's bandages and left her to put her clothes away while he opened the shop. Luckily, no stitches were broken, but her stomach ached from where Edgar had kicked her, as though the front of her body had been shoved to the back. She flung herself on the bed, buried her face in the pillow and cried.

She wasn't sure how long she lay there, but when she looked up, the sun had shifted and the last of the clouds had drifted away. Dust motes danced in the window, appearing and vanishing in a matter of seconds. The distant sound of ticking clocks reached her ears, all overlapping each other. The tuneless symphony was comforting in a way, like a warm bath.

But that was all she could hear. Whatever Malcolm was doing, it wasn't making any noise.

Curiosity tugged at her mind like a string. What *was* he doing?

Charlotte headed onto the landing, pressed her face against the banister slats and peered at the shop floor. Malcolm sat at his workbench, an array of tiny components spread before him on a length of black material. He was so lost in concentration, he had let a cup of tea go cold.

Charlotte remembered a show her parents had taken her to at the Second West Theatre. Among the acts was an illusionist, and she had looked on, captivated, as he brandished his cards like they were an extension of his own body. Now, Malcolm's rough hands were doing the same thing. They assumed an elegant confidence which made her feel as though she were watching a dance. Screwdrivers pirouetted and cogs spun, each smaller and more intricate than the last. She'd never seen him move like that.

Fascinated, she made her way downstairs. She thought of all the toys he had made for her; imagined him putting them together right here.

"What are you doing?" she asked.

Malcolm blinked rapidly as if she had woken him. Lines shone on his cheeks, from where tears had run and then dried.

"Just working," he said, tightly, like he'd forgotten how to use his voice. "It helps me deal with things if I focus on something else. Is your back still hurting?"

Charlotte shook her head. "Did you... hear me crying?"

Malcolm's face softened. "Yes, I did. But sometimes it does us good to cry."

He wiped his face, then dipped a stick into a tiny bottle. The liquid smelled sharp and Charlotte wrinkled her nose.

"What's that?" she asked.

"Cleaning solution," Malcolm replied. "The gentleman who brought this in only wanted me to fix the mainspring. But everything needs cleaning before I replace it, otherwise it won't run smoothly."

He pulled the stick out. The end was wrapped in a ball of material, and he wiped it over a cog, so carefully, it hardly looked like he was touching it. It was then that Charlotte noticed the components came from a pocket watch. Just the thought of every single piece fitting into the empty case was astounding. The gears and screws were so intricate. She stared at the miniature teeth, imagining them all being cut by hand. It must have taken months to create from scratch. The only thing anyone could see, or was meant to see, was the sleek face which told the time, but hidden behind it lay this elaborate moving puzzle.

"What's a *mainspringy?*" she wondered aloud.

Malcolm brought his finger to a thin metal ribbon. "This. It's the part which makes the whole watch run."

Charlotte peered at it. "But it doesn't look broken or anything."

"It's just worn out, so I need to replace it," Malcolm explained. "Did you ever see your Papa twisting a little knob on the side of his watch?"

"Yes."

"Well, that connects to a mainspring. When you twist it, the mainspring gets tighter and tighter, in a spiral. Then it slowly unwinds around itself, and that's the power behind all the other pieces: the gears, the escapement, the turning hands. But when it's not wound, it won't run. See?"

"I think so," said Charlotte. "Do the lighting mechanisms have a mainspringy as well?"

Malcolm smiled. "Lighting mechanisms, heating systems, carriages… If it needs power, it will have a mainspring or pendulum somewhere in the movement, and either a knob or a crank to wind it up."

"But what about the Tower?" Charlotte asked.

"What about it?"

"Well, the big lighting mechanisms have lightsmen, the omnibuses have cabbies. Who winds up the Tower clock? That must have the biggest mainspringy of them all, right?"

Malcolm laced his fingers together. "You must have heard about the Keeper?"

"Papa mentioned it once," Charlotte said. "What is it?"

"Well, that's the funny thing. Nobody really knows. All *I* know is that he's someone who keeps the Tower clock working. Officially, he's called the Timekeeper, but that's a bit of a mouthful. I suppose only the Potentate knows who he is."

"Well, if no-one's ever seen him, how do we know he exists? Mama told me stories about the Fabric of Time, but that doesn't exist, does it?"

"No, kiddo, it doesn't. That's just a story. But it's meant to be a kind of magic, and we know magic exists, don't we? The ancient magic? It's how the lunafauna can change their shape, after all. But we can tell the Keeper exists because no mainspring runs forever. It will always need someone to wind it and maintain it. So he's got a very important job, whoever he is. We all rely on the Tower. It's connected to every other mechanism in the City. It's the heart of Forest. So imagine what would happen if *that* ever stopped."

Malcolm pressed a magnifying loupe to his eye and picked up a pair of tweezers.

"Now, do you want to see how all this fits together?"

Charlotte nodded eagerly. "Yes, please! It looks so complicated."

"It isn't, really. It's just all about reassembling the pieces in the correct order."

Malcolm placed the gears into position and secured them with a screwdriver. He handled everything with a sureness that could only come from years of practise. This was better than the illusionist, Charlotte decided, because there was nothing fake about it. It was solid, real, something so integral that its beauty was all around her, in every aspect of life.

"It's a shame I can't show you orbs, kiddo," Malcolm said. "Do you know what they are?"

She shook her head, entranced.

"They're special globes made by the alchemists. I don't see them often around here. Most people can't afford them. Your parents had some, though. They gave each other a wristwatch on their wedding day, fitted with orbs. Gorgeous things."

Charlotte knew the watches he meant. Her mother and father had always worn them. Were they still on her parents' bodies as they laid in the undertaker's studio?

Blood on snow. She forced the memory away before it could strangle her.

The ticking clocks cut through and she latched onto the sound: steady, unbroken, ceaseless. Back and forth, like the feeling of being on the swing and her father pushing her.

It worked. She breathed in, filled her lungs, and let it all out slowly.

"What do they do? The orbs?" she asked instead.

Malcolm picked up the mainspring.

"They're placed here, at the centre. Then the orb and spring can work together, and the watch will carry on ticking for a whole lifetime. There's no need for them to be wound at all. I think the longest one has ever run is fifty years."

Charlotte's mouth opened in awe. "How does that work? What are they made of?"

"Only the alchemists know that," said Malcolm, a hint of mystery in his voice. "They have to take a special oath before they can work with orbs. There's definitely magic involved — alchemy grew out of the ancient magic, after all. But nobody's ever revealed what they actually are. I wanted to train in alchemy once, you know, but I couldn't. Life got in the way."

A strange gleam came into his eyes. He let the loupe fall, caught it in his hand without looking.

"Since we're on the subject of orbs, do you want to know a secret? You can't tell anyone, alright?"

Charlotte leaned forward. "What?"

"I'm not completely sure how the alchemists fit orbs to mainsprings, but I had a peek at your parents' watches, and it looks like they're sliced open. Like a boiled egg cut in half, but with the yolk still intact. They have a central bit that pulses, and that's where the power comes from. But what if we could fuse that centre to the spring itself? Make it a part of the mechanism in every way? Then, I think — no, I'm certain — it wouldn't have to be rewound, *ever*."

Malcolm smiled broadly. He looked like a little boy at Midwinter.

"Imagine it," he whispered. "No more turning cranks to power everything. It would be a graft to change the whole City."

"You mean, everything would be over?" Charlotte asked.

"No, it would be *better*."

"How? Aren't people already coming up with a way to do something like that? Papa said some alchemists are trying to use the sun and moon to power stuff."

Malcolm heaved a rueful sigh. "That's right, but it won't happen. The Potentate says it's too similar to the way the lunafauna do things. He'd rather keep things as they are."

"So, we're sticking with clocks?" Charlotte asked. "Doesn't that mean your graft-thing would work, if they used it?"

"Absolutely," said Malcolm. "It would save so much money in power, everything would run smoother. An omnibus wouldn't need a cabbie to pedal it everywhere. It could take itself, under its own power. Do you understand?"

"That sounds silly," chuckled Charlotte. But she saw how earnest Malcolm was about the subject, and pulled her grin under control. "Are you going to try and make it work?" she said instead.

A door seemed to close behind Malcolm's eyes. "Probably not. I'm no alchemist."

"But you said you wanted to be one."

"A long time ago. It's too late for me now. I know it could work, and if people had the guts to trust me and let me try it, it would definitely happen. But they won't. That's just the way things are."

His voice changed, became lower and melancholy. The sound tugged at Charlotte's heart. Why did adults give up so easily? They all seemed to enjoy nothing more than complaining about whatever could have been.

Malcolm rolled the pocket watch's old mainspring between his fingers.

"Our secret, remember? Don't tell anyone. Let's say I do manage to try it out someday, and someone else got wind of my idea and beat me to it!"

"I won't," said Charlotte. "I promise."

Malcolm smiled. He put the mainspring down, fetched a new one, and wound it into a tight coil to fit inside the watch. Charlotte kept her eyes on him, but in her mind, all her thoughts flashed and tumbled around each other.

Forest running under its own power? Could such a thing be possible? She tried to picture a life without station masters cranking up the trains, or walking along a street and not seeing any lighting mechanisms. How would heating systems work without cogs to warm the coils?

And wouldn't it also mean the end of the Keeper?

"Malcolm?" she said slowly. "Do you suppose the Keeper is inside the Tower? Lives in it, I mean?"

"Maybe," he replied. "Why do you ask?"

She twiddled her thumbs. "When we were in the square today, I thought someone was watching from up there. I mean… I didn't see anything, but I felt it."

Malcolm raised his brows. "Well, you never know. It might have been him."

There was an airy humour in his tone, like he wasn't taking her seriously. Heat rose to Charlotte's face. It was the same way of speaking which her governess had used whenever she was indulging a silly story.

"I'm telling the truth!" she snapped. "I can tell you don't believe me. Like nobody believes it wasn't a conny-vict!"

Charlotte crossed her arms so vigorously, she winced. She could still feel Edgar's foot driving into her stomach. She recalled the stink of his breath and ferocity of his voice, as if *she* was responsible for all the misfortune he had known. And beyond him, eyes, bearing down as forceful as gravity, even from above, somewhere invisible in the wintry sky.

"Those boys started it, you know," she mumbled. "I wasn't doing anything wrong."

"That doesn't surprise me," said Malcolm. "I know them. They're troublemakers. The only reason they do it is because they see something in you which they don't have. And that makes them feel like they're less than you."

"But I didn't have anything," Charlotte insisted. "I didn't have any money or food or…"

Malcolm shook his head gently.

"Most of the time, it's not something physical. You're different from them, and that's a good thing: it makes you who you are. But sometimes, different can be dangerous. It lets people see you. And at the moment, I'm not sure how dangerous things will be. People might want to use it against you."

Charlotte nibbled her lip. Edgar and the others had recognised her so easily. They had seen it in her boots and coat; heard it in her voice. Maybe she even held herself in a way that set her apart: shoulders pulled down and back straight. Had her mother's insistence on posture branded itself onto her skin? How was she supposed to hide something like that?

"I've got an idea," she said. "I once read a book about a man who could turn himself invisible with a special mechanism.

Can you make me one of those? Then they'd never see me again and couldn't come after me."

Malcolm chuckled. "I think that can only happen in a story, kiddo."

"Oh."

Charlotte fiddled with her sleeve cuff. A thread had broken on the inside. She tugged at it, watched the fabric ripple as it pulled taut.

"So... I shouldn't be me?"

"That's not what I mean," Malcolm said. He took hold of her hands. "You should always be proud of who you are, and never forget it. Just mind what you say. There's a time and place to be all who Charlotte Bellamy is, but it's not now."

Charlotte lowered her eyes. She didn't want to cry again. Something told her that she had no tears left, and that would only make it hurt even more.

"I just thought, am I not a Lady now?" she asked. "Now that... well... you know."

Malcolm shook his head. "You're too young. You need to be at least fifteen before you can take your title."

"How do you know that?"

"Do you remember when I had to see the magistrate? He told me about your parents' will. They had a lot of money, and when the bank found out you were alive, all that money was frozen — kept safe until you're old enough to use it. I'm allowed to take a little stipend out of it to look after you, but it's yours. You'll get it when you come of age, when you're twenty-one, or if you choose to become a Lady when you're fifteen."

Charlotte hesitated. Malcolm's face was guarded, like he was looking at her through a sheet of glass.

"But you don't think I should," she said.

"That's a choice you can make when you're older, and

when it's safer," Malcolm said. "You'll get your parents' money either way. But you've had a good life so far, and you will again. It's not the same for most other children. The reason your Papa used to help the orphanages was because of kids like those in the square today. He set up his sanctuary building for them, you know. He didn't want the thief gangs to get their hooks in them. But nothing he gave will ever be the same as what you've had every day."

Malcolm rubbed his face with one hand and left a streak of grease behind. He sucked his lips into his mouth, as though tasting words he hadn't said yet, trying to decide whether it was a good idea to let them out. Then he offered a smile. It was so sincere, so beseeching, that Charlotte's heart melted.

"I know I can never take your parents' place. I wouldn't want to," he said. "But I hope the two of us can make some good out of all the bad. What do you think?"

Charlotte regarded him. There was no way back now, she knew that already. The old life was gone, ripped away, cold air blowing into an open wound. The new one which laid before her leered in shadows, bled itself out of the lines, spoke and moved in ways she couldn't understand. But she would learn them, accept them, and he would help her. She wouldn't be alone.

She put her arms around his neck. It was the first time she had embraced him since the shooting. Something in the touch cut through the darkness, like the sun burning away a cloud. She didn't let go. This was a new spell — she could feel it weaving around her with every moment. She drank it in: the smell of the cleaning solution and soap on Malcolm's clothes, the ticking clocks, the touch of his hand as it rested on the back of her head.

"Did you like what I was doing with the watch?" he asked.

"Yes. A lot," she said.

"Would you like to learn how to do it?"

"Yes, please. Would that be alright?"

In response, Malcolm rummaged under the desk and emerged with a battered mantel clock. The glass in the face was missing and the numerals were dirty with age, but when he opened the back, it revealed a near-complete movement.

"I've been keeping this for spare parts," he explained. "You can have it to tinker with, get to know how things fit together. Just don't try to take the mainspring out without my help. If you don't know what you're doing, it can snap back and hit you in the eye."

Charlotte beamed as though he had presented a beautiful new toy.

"I can have it?"

"So long as I don't find gears all over your bedroom floor, yes," smiled Malcolm. "Careful, now. It's heavy."

"Thank you!" Charlotte said. Then she rushed upstairs, almost tripping over her own feet in her haste.

CHAPTER VIII

Oscar walked through the Roots towards Melissa Spectre's headquarters. His colleagues said the Chief Officer had her base here so she could easily get to any area of Forest — no entrance to any Level was too far away. He thought of her derogatory nickname, Vixen. He recalled hearing, as a child, that was the word for a female fox. There were no foxes in the City itself, but far out in the Meadows, he'd seen their burrows. The building itself reminded him of those: a secret structure, deceptively large, hidden under the earth.

A couple of officers in the foyer threw him a curious glance. Oscar was tall for a fourteen-year-old, but they still towered over him.

"What are you here for, kid?" one of them asked scornfully. He wore a ring with a red stone, and a circle was sewn over his left breast. That was the sign of Melissa's personal squadron: the Circulus.

Oscar looked at his badge and saw that his name was Copley. He wasn't even into his twenties, yet he held himself like the crowning jewel of a tiara. His acme-riddled face twisted into an elusive smirk of self-confidence that grated on Oscar's patience. He had seen this before: youngsters who flushed in their own arrogance simply because an ounce of power had been handed to them.

Oscar kept his composure and answered politely.

"I have a report for Madam Spectre about the Rene incident. Important, as I'm sure you're aware."

A muscle twitched in Copley's jaw. Oscar didn't look away, didn't even blink. This was as much a pecking order as anything else he knew, and the worst thing for a weakling was to be stared down. And he had a natural advantage. Everyone was always fascinated by his multicoloured eyes at first, but after a couple of seconds, the curiosity turned to discomfort.

Sure enough, Copley started to glance between them, unsure which one to focus on. Then he tossed his head, and Oscar followed him along a corridor lined with pilasters and flowery festoons. Copley knocked on the door at the far end, and Melissa opened it, a wad of papers under her arm.

"Hargreaves," she said. "Come in, please. Thank you, Copley, that will be all. Close the door behind you."

"Yes, Madam Spectre," Copley replied in a small voice.

Melissa laid the papers on her desk, reading-side down.

"Excuse me," she said, tapping the topmost sheet. "One can't carry out sensitive duties without an obscene amount of paperwork."

"I understand, Madam," said Oscar. He suddenly remembered he was still wearing his cap and whipped it off.

The overhead light fixture flickered. For a brief second, both the room and outside the windows plunged into darkness. Then the blubs flashed back into life as though nothing had happened.

Melissa glanced towards the Tower with a flinty expression.

"We'll need to get someone to look at those bloody mechanisms again," she said. "Anyway, what do you have for me? How's Charlotte Bellamy?"

"I followed her and her new guardian to the Godstall

Market. That's where I've just come from," replied Oscar. "She's better than the last time I saw her."

He winced as he thought of the last time, when she had been frozen and broken in his arms, whimpering for her mother. He'd scrubbed his uniform and body, but he could still feel her blood running down his chest.

Melissa perched on the edge of her desk. "Anything I should be concerned about?"

"Not that I could see. Or hear."

"That's welcome news. Thank you. I knew I could trust you to do a good job."

Oscar quickly hid a smile before it could break over his face.

"Is there anything else I can help with?" he asked.

"Now that you mention it, yes, there is," Melissa said. "You came to us from the Ninth North, didn't you? A ripe place for Rats to go scurrying."

The secret smile vanished and a chill ran down Oscar's spine. Melissa's tone was civil, but he could tell she knew everything about him. She knew everything about everybody.

"Yes, I did. Thanks to Lord Bellamy's sanctuary house."

"Ah, Bellamy," Melissa sighed dramatically. "We can't seem to get away from Bellamys lately, can we?"

Oscar stayed as still as he could. "It wouldn't seem so, Madam."

"Well, we must put a pin in Bellamy matters for now. I have need for you tonight, back in your old scurrying ground."

She picked up a letter from beneath her ashtray. The words were scarcely legible, and had run in places where something had spilled.

"This tipoff was left for me this morning," she said. "It's anonymous, but says the Shadow Rats are planning a raid tonight at the Balm Street Orb Works. Do you know it?"

"Yes," Oscar replied, but he couldn't keep a frown from stealing across his forehead. "It seems like a strange mark, though."

"Why? Orbs are valuable."

"Not from there. The Ninth North... That far down in the Levels, those orbs will only be sub-market. I can't see why King R — Dawkins — would want them. He'd barely get five solidi for each one."

The more Oscar thought about it, the more his gut twisted, but he tried to ignore it. It was just nerves about his past being brought up, that was all.

Melissa flicked a corner of the letter between her fingers.

"Well, he must have his reasons. And I have my orders. Potentate Carter wants me to catch the Rats before they can take anything." She looked straight at Oscar. "And I dare say nobody will know their movements better than one of their own."

"With respect, Madam, I'm not one of them anymore."

"I know you're not," Melissa said. "I only mention it because you and your friend aren't the first youngsters Lord Bellamy plucked from the thieves, but you're the first in a while to join the Constabulary. I wanted to have Irving with me tonight, but he's taken ill, so that leaves only you."

"Richie's ill?" Oscar repeated in alarm. "What's wrong with him?"

"Food poisoning, I believe. Don't worry, nothing he won't recover from. It just means he can't be running around the streets when I need him most."

"But... I thought you wanted me watching Charlotte Bellamy?"

"I do," Melissa said, a frustrated growl in her throat. "I don't want you on this mission, Hargreaves. You're too important to a greater cause. I need to know if she says anything and who she might say it to. But I have no choice. This order has come from above me. My officers know the job, and I know some of the lower Levels well enough, but you know the Ninth North and the Rats. You were closer to them than any of us. You'll be able to read their movements, hear signals which we might not recognise. So, you help us get in position for an ambush, then go back to the Fifth West."

Oscar planted his feet firmly so he couldn't shuffle his feet. Something didn't feel right about this. He and Richie had come to the Constabulary so they could move on from their past. And, now he thought about it, Melissa's words about the Bellamy girl weighed uneasily on his chest. All she had done was survive a horrendous event. Why did she need to be watched so closely? She was only eight. She couldn't know anything dangerous. Could she?

"Madam," Oscar said carefully, "may I please ask a question?"

Melissa didn't blink. "Of course."

Oscar licked his lips. "Why's it so important to know what she says and to whom?"

"Because she's the daughter of a Lord," replied Melissa at once. "That has many connotations. I have to make sure she's safe. And that includes whether she's privy to any sensitive information."

"Like what?" Oscar pressed.

"That's not your concern at the moment," said Melissa firmly. "But it could be, if you impress me tonight. I've already spoken to you about joining the Circulus. Promotion comes with its own benefits, the least of which is intimate knowledge. And you would receive a house of your own, a pay rise, a pension."

She rocked forward a little so she was closer to him.

"And I'm willing to grant you early access to all that, in exchange for your help. It will be beneficial to both of us."

Oscar's heart fluttered. He thought of Copley's smug smirk; of how *he* could be standing beside him, equal. He glanced at his hand, imagined a red ring on his finger, just like Melissa's. Acceptance, progress... Finally, a line could be drawn under everything he had endeavoured to escape.

And Charlotte's guardian had been putting her to bed at nine o'clock. There would be no need to watch her when she was asleep.

He swallowed his anxiety and nodded. "When do we leave?"

Melissa smiled. "Midnight."

The rest of the day disappeared quicker than Oscar imagined possible. Time seemed like smoke, incapable of containment, integrating itself with the frigid air until both were one and the same. Before he knew it, he was walking with a small team of Circulus officers, Melissa at the helm, into the bowels of the Ninth North.

The streets twisted in every direction like a tangled skein of wool. Huge factories crammed the sides, some still operational and others abandoned, chimneys towering into the dark sky. Feathery frost clung to gutters and extended off windowsills in long thin fingers. But despite winter's beauty, Oscar could still catch the unmistakable odours of urine, something dead down a nearby alley, overflowing bins and old oil dripping from the lighting mechanisms.

The smells never went away in the Ninth North. Every inhale brought a jolt of equally cold reminiscence. He knew these routes. The ways of this part of the City were imprinted on him like a stain. He could have run the paths blindfolded: through the alleys, across the rooftops and everywhere in-between.

He would have given anything to be at the barracks, climbing into his bunk. Or even still lurking by the watch shop, listening to Charlotte Bellamy. Anywhere but *here*.

"Does it feel nice to be home, kid?" Copley hissed at him.

"Once a Rat, always a Rat," another officer smirked.

Oscar was tempted to drive his fist into Copley's face. But he controlled himself and kept his attention on the road. They could poke fun all they wanted. *He* was the most important member of the party tonight.

He directed them close to an Interlevel. The road was almost empty — only a few homeless figures huddled in doorways. Clouds of breath misted before them, their hair already laced with ice. Oscar's heart sank at the sight. More than one would be dead by morning.

A young woman, no more than skin draped over a skeleton, raised a feeble hand. With the other, she clutched a bundle to her chest.

"Any… change?" she whimpered. "Please, kind sirs. My baby…"

To Oscar's surprise, Melissa pulled a solidus from her pocket and dropped it at her feet. The woman scrambled for it, crying with gratitude. But Melissa didn't speak, didn't even pause to meet her eyes.

"Uh… Madam Spectre?" Copley whispered.

"What?"

"Look."

Copley pointed at a nearby wall. It was painted with graffiti, in whitewash: easily read despite the low light. Some of the words were familiar obscenities, condemning lunafauna and cursing taxes. But others slashed against Oscar's mind like a razor. Even the lettering seemed sharp and rushed, as though it had been written with a blade rather than a brush.

PROGRESS — THE KEY TO THE FUTURE!
AD MELIORA!
FREE KNOWLEDGE, FREE YOURSELF!

Oscar had seen those before. They were toted by some of the purist alchemists who claimed to be hard done by. He'd watched them on their marches, raising their voices against the Potentate in a desperate bid to be heard.

But their slogans weren't what Copley had noticed, either.

RENE SQUARE – JUSTICE FOR THE 23!
BELLAMY: MURDERED FOR TRUTH!

Melissa's shoulders tensed. It was barely noticeable, but Oscar saw it. He suddenly remembered standing outside the burning manor, and how her pistol had moved in its holster.

His eyes strayed to that same pistol as she ushered the team onwards. She didn't know something, did she? She came to Rene afterwards, and she hadn't been carrying a rifle…

"What do you think that's all about?" one of the officers whispered. "People think it wasn't a convict?"

Copley shrugged. "Sure looks that way."

"Silence!" Melissa snapped.

Oscar pushed the concerns from his mind. He needed to concentrate. This was one of the worst places to let his guard down.

The last time he had been here, he was on the other side. If he hadn't left when he did, he might very well be on the raid he was now waiting to ambush. He thought of the youngsters who had entered the gang at the same time as him and Richie. Would any of them be coming? Would they recognise him? He might look different now, in uniform, clean-shaven with his hair cut short, but nothing could disguise his eyes.

The orb studio appeared and he pointed it out. Melissa led the team into a narrow street opposite the entrance.

"And now we wait. Be ready," she whispered, so softly, even Oscar struggled to hear her.

He peered at the locks on the studio door. There were three: large and well-made, but even from a distance, he could tell they were rusted. They wouldn't take much effort to pick. He had opened locks in similar states in just a few seconds.

But his unease returned, cramped his stomach and pulled at his guts like a hook. Balm Street was one of only three orb studios in the entire Ninth North. Most of the studios were higher up the Quarter, closer to their intended clientele: those rich enough to actually afford the wares. This old workshop was hardly worth an entire raid.

The surrounding buildings were warehouses, close together, draped in shadows. Alleys veined off the main road like the threads of a web. Old lighting and heating mechanisms ticked on the pavements nearby. Their huge tangles of gears could have filled a room, but the bulbs gave off barely enough light to see by. The whole place was both exposed in the wrong way and secluded in the wrong way.

The hairs on the back of Oscar's neck stood up.

"This isn't right," he hissed.

Melissa glanced at him. "Why?"

"Who gave you the tipoff?"

"I told you, it was anonymous."

There was a sudden crash from a backstreet. Some of the

officers jumped, but it only confirmed Oscar's suspicions.

"They're already here! They're waiting for us!"

The mild annoyance on Melissa's face immediately snapped into concentration.

"Get out of here and back to your post," she said.

"Too bad you can't all get out, Vixen."

A group of figures swarmed from the alleys. Dark clothing easily disguised them against the darkness. There weren't many, but they still outnumbered the team, and guns and knives glinted in their hands. Even through the grease smeared on their faces, Oscar recognised most of them.

His mind turned blank with fright. He grabbed his own pistol, readied it to fire. The air filled with the clicking of flintlocks as the other officers did the same.

Then an imposing mountain of a man emerged, and his blood ran cold.

It was Jon Dawkins, leader of the Shadow Rats, but Oscar knew him by another name: King Rat. He was the most formidable boss the gang had known for years, notorious for his stealth and ruthlessness. Authority hung around him, so heavy, Oscar thought he could physically feel it.

Melissa took aim straight at Dawkins.

"Stay where you are and lower your weapons," she ordered.

Dawkins laughed. It was humourless — a cruel, harsh staccato sound. He stroked one of his coal-black sideburns with a finger as thick as a cigar.

"How funny to think Mister High-and-Mighty Potentate will listen to the lowest scum, so long as they send an unsigned letter," he said, icy vitriol in every word. "And look at *you*, hiding behind *her*, Oscar Hargreaves. You traitorous little shit."

Oscar's fingers trembled on his pistol. Melissa moved so

she was in front of him.

"Lower your weapons, Dawkins," she snarled.

"Or what? You'll do us like you did those poor bastards in Rene?"

Oscar's heart jolted. So he'd been right: the Rats didn't have anything to do with the massacre. He glanced at Melissa to gauge her reaction. Not a single muscle twitched.

"This is your final warning," she said.

"You're in no position to warn me against anything. Your lackeys killed one of my favourite girls in that square. You've walked right into your own grave tonight. An eye for an eye, and all that. It's been a long time coming, believe me."

A thousand feet above, the Tower clock chimed midnight. Dawkins didn't blink.

"Take Hargreaves and kill the others. This bitch's head is mine."

CHAPTER IX

The Rats sprang forward. Melissa's pistol fired in a shower of sparks. The other officers began shooting too, and the alley filled with smoke.

Oscar took aim at one of the Rats. She was too quick and swept at him with a knife. Oscar sidestepped; muscle-memory overtook him and he kicked the blade away. The Rat was older than him, but Oscar hadn't spent the last few weeks living off scraps. He overpowered the girl with ease and slammed her head against the bricks.

She slumped in his arms, still alive. Oscar laid her down as gently as he could. No matter that he wasn't one of them anymore, he couldn't kill them.

Powder burned the back of his throat. Chips of stone and mortar flew about his face. The Rats came from every angle — some even leapt from the roofs, disguised by the smog. Blood splattered the walls. All around were screams and the thuds of bullets meeting flesh.

One whistled past Oscar's ear and he threw himself to the floor. Something wet seeped into his shirt. Panicking, he checked himself, but there was no blood — he had just landed in a puddle. He didn't want to think about whether it was water or not.

A shot hit the lighting mechanism and shattered the bulb. The entire alley turned black. Only the bursts of flintlocks flashed through the smoke. Oscar caught a glimpse of Melissa, still on her feet, firing with practised precision. But now he was on the ground, below the haze, he also noticed the bodies. There were some thieves, but most were officers. How many were dead?

A weight fell on top of him. He scrambled away, fist drawn back in case it was a Rat. But it wasn't. Copley stared through him, a lifeless bloodied mess in place of the smirk.

Oscar fought to breathe. Copley was an obnoxious buffoon, but he shouldn't have died like *this*...

The Circulus were skilled — anyone wanting to join it had to be highly-trained. But the thieves worked in a different way. They fought dirty and used the environment which they knew so well. They were picking the officers off like flies.

Oscar pushed Copley aside, staggered upright. The smoke parted, and his panic gave way to terror. He was looking straight into the face of King Rat.

"Nice to see you again," Dawkins snarled. "You're going to answer for this, Hargreaves."

He snatched Oscar's jacket in one massive hand, tore his pistol away with the other, and tossed him into the clutches of two waiting Rats.

"Sinclair, Rowland, get that boy out of here!" he ordered.

"No!" Oscar cried. "Let go of me!"

One of the Rats pushed a blade against his throat.

"Thought you could leave us that easily, did you? You were one of our best, you little son of a bitch."

The heating mechanism suddenly broke apart and hurtled towards them. The Rats jumped aside, and in their distraction, slackened their hold.

Oscar flung his head back and felt a nose break like a matchstick. The knife dropped; he wrenched himself free and kicked the second Rat in the groin. The man fell with a scream. Before either could seize him again, Oscar ran to one of the collapsed gears and crouched behind it.

He waited. Adrenaline surged through his veins like acid. Had they seen where he'd gone?

After a few awful seconds, he realised they hadn't. But he didn't relax. Bullets ricocheted off the broken mechanism. He laid flat on the ground, hardly dared to breathe for fear of coughing on the smoke.

How was he not dead? He felt like Charlotte Bellamy, trapped under her unorthodox metal shield in Rene.

He had a mind to flee, but decided against it. If he moved, they might spot him, and he was unarmed. They would kill him, or drag him back to the nest. Oscar didn't know which prospect was worse.

Then he saw Dawkins, grappling with someone — Melissa. She snatched a broken bottle from the floor and slashed him across the face. Dawkins fell onto his knees with a howl.

Melissa aimed her pistol at his head.

"You're under arrest!" she shouted.

Oscar hurriedly took stock of what he could see. Bodies were sprawled over the cobbles. Blood ran into the gutters at the side of the road. Injured thieves staggered in the shadows, but of the officers, there was only him and Melissa left.

It was impossible to bring down King Rat without backup. Oscar had seen him walk away after being stabbed in the leg. He could bundle both of them under his arms as though they weighed no more than children. At any moment, he and the others would be upon Melissa and tear the flesh from her bones…

Oscar did the only thing he could think of and jumped up.

"Madam Spectre, we need to go!"

Melissa glanced at the scene around her. Then she sprinted towards Oscar; allowed him to take the lead as they vanished into the streets. The twisting maze of walls and pavements blended together like mud in the rain. He had never been so glad to know an area so thoroughly.

As they drew near an abandoned warehouse, Melissa snatched Oscar's wrist, pulled him into a small courtyard. A manhole sat in the centre and she stomped on it five times. As soon as it opened, she threw Oscar down it and jumped after him.

A guard heaved the cover shut behind them. Melissa kept still, listening. But after several long moments, she let out a great sigh and shoved her pistol back into the holster. Blood and dirt splattered her uniform, and her eyes shone, but Oscar couldn't tell if it was from fright or anger.

"Madam Spectre, what happened?" asked the guard.

"A close shave, Price," Melissa panted. "I'll send backup here, to every entrance in this area. Just in case. Hargreaves, are you alright?"

Oscar nodded. "I think so. Are you?"

"A little scratch on my arm. Nothing serious," Melissa answered. She ushered him into the elevator and turned the crank with a shaky hand. "Go to the infirmary. Have someone check you over."

"I'm not hurt."

"Go anyway. How did you know it was a trap?"

"I had a feeling," admitted Oscar. "I'm sorry I didn't realise earlier."

"That wasn't your fault. It was mine," said Melissa. Shame grated in her voice.

Oscar wanted to console her, but he held himself back. She wasn't the type of person who would take kindly to sympathy. So instead, he asked, "Are the others all dead?"

Melissa closed her eyes.

"Probably. I'll send a stronger force out to gather them at first light." She made a fist, so tight, her knuckles cracked under her glove. "Why did Dawkins try to take you?"

"I must have been more of a loss than I thought."

"What would he have done to you?"

Oscar swallowed. He had heard his fair share of screams from those who displeased King Rat.

His silence was as good an answer as any. Melissa kept quiet until the elevator reached the Roots, then guided him onto the walkway and put a hand on his shoulder. The smallest hint of a smile fleeted across her lips.

"Well done," she said. "You're sharp. More so than I was expecting, if I'm honest. You did your job well."

"Thank you," Oscar said, as solidly as he could. But beneath the thin skin of the words, he struggled not to tremble. He felt like a terrified child. He had thought himself so secure and safe and ready to do better... and if a single thing had happened differently tonight, he would have lost it all.

Melissa's voice pushed through to him: quiet, but firm.

"Infirmary first, then get some sleep. Can you be back in the Fifth West at eight o'clock tomorrow?"

"Of course."

"Good. Thank you."

Melissa walked over an adjacent bridge. As soon as she was out of sight, Oscar snatched a railing and let himself hunch over it. He'd held his posture and nerve for long enough.

He couldn't believe what had just happened. All those officers, dead... the writing on the walls... the smell of piss and winter mixed with blood and gunpowder... He felt King Rat's giant fingers around his arm, the knife on his throat...

"Get a hold of yourself," he muttered. The infirmary. Yes, that was where he needed to go.

He approached another elevator, went to wind the crank, but then noticed a team of construction workers balanced precariously along the shaft.

One of them called down to him.

"Sorry, mate! Out of order! The power's gone! You'll have to take the stairs!"

"Oh, come on!" Oscar groaned. A lifetime of moving up and down the Levels meant everybody had legs of iron, but after tonight, the last thing he wanted was to climb.

He dragged himself to a staircase. It was divided at the same places as an Interlevel on the surface: every hundred feet, a shaft branched off and connected to a secret entrance. It was the size of a regular Interlevel, too: large enough for several people to walk abreast. But tonight, Oscar was alone, a tiny bee stumbling through the tunnels of a giant hive.

By the time he came to the next Level, his calves were burning, and he took a moment to catch his breath. The infirmary stood before him: a huge building held by several pillars and set into the wall for extra support. It protruded like a tumour — even the cables securing it to the rock reminded Oscar of tendons. Around it, shimmering brighter than the sun on spider silk, hung the ancient magic which kept the Roots from collapsing upon themselves.

The medics checked him, but as he suspected, there wasn't a scratch to be found. And now the adrenaline had subsided, he could tell from the smell of the brown stain on his shirt that it definitely wasn't water. One of the doctors wrinkled her nose at it.

"You'd best get that washed, Constable," she advised.

"I will," Oscar said. "But... before I go, can you please tell me where Richard Irving is?"

The medic pointed to a map of the building on a wall.

"First floor, room six. I took him up myself. Food poisoning."

"That's right," muttered Oscar. "Thanks."

He walked there as fast as he could, and peered through the window in the door to check Richie was awake. Seeing that he was, he let himself inside without knocking.

The room reeked of vomit, but Oscar was hardly bothered. His nose was still overwhelmed by the odours of the streets. He could almost feel it clinging to him, trying to creep under his skin like maggots.

Richie looked over in alarm. His face was as white as milk.

"Damn it, Oscar! I could have been taking a crap for all you knew!"

"I've slept next to you since we were born. What *haven't* I seen you do at this point?"

Richie smirked. "Aside from a girl, nothing much, I suppose! Hey, what's wrong? Where did all that blood come from? And what the hell's that on your shirt? It stinks!"

"You don't smell much better," Oscar retorted. He perched on the end of the bed and massaged his temples.

Richie shuffled closer. "You hurt?"

"No. How did you get food poisoning?"

"It was that cheese, from yesterday. I'm sorry. I heard you had to go along on something I should have done."

Oscar regarded his uniform. Less than a month had passed since Rene Square, and he would need to wash blood out of it again. The blood of other people.

"Yeah," he muttered. His own voice sounded thin and detached, as though his mouth had dropped to between his feet. "I'm glad you weren't there, though. King Rat set a trap to kill Madam Spectre. We were the only two who made it out."

Richie's cheeks turned even paler. "Are you alright?"

"I'm fine. He was so mad when he saw me… They tried to take me back. A heating mechanism fell apart and I managed to hide behind that. But all the others, the officers…"

Oscar's words trailed off. He and Richie had been with the gang for four years, but in that time, no defectors had been recaptured. Nobody had even dared to flee since Dawkins assumed power. Everyone was too terrified of him.

Until the day the two of them had run away.

Richie laid a hand on Oscar's shoulder.

"I'm glad you got out," he said. "But... don't worry. They're never going to take us back. We're better than that, remember? That was what Lord Bellamy said to us."

The mention of Bellamy twisted Oscar's throat like a cord.

"There's more. I saw graffiti everywhere, claiming Bellamy was murdered. And King Rat said Madam Spectre was responsible."

Richie shook his head. "She wasn't. You know as well as I do, he just hates her. He'll look for any excuse to bring her down."

"Any excuse? Including taking part in an ambush himself? Come on, Richie, you know he never leaves the nest. Not unless it's personal, and apparently one of his girls was in Rene."

"I didn't see any Rats I recognised when *we* were in Rene," Richie insisted, but he knotted his fingers together anxiously and discomfort stole across his face like mist.

Oscar felt the same. He recalled the burning Bellamy manor, the sharp sound from inside. Melissa had claimed it wasn't shots. He believed her... and yet a stone of doubt formed in the pit of his stomach.

"Please keep this between us," he said. "I'm not sure what to do."

"Of course I will," Richie replied. "But what aren't you sure of? Madam Spectre saved us just as much as Bellamy did. Where would we be if she hadn't let us train? And we've got prospects here. Imagine how things will be if we get into the Circulus! We'll never want for anything again, and King Rat won't dare come near us!"

"I was with Circulus officers tonight. He took them all down," Oscar said darkly.

Richie's head remained high with assurance. "They weren't us."

It was wishful thinking, and Oscar hoped Richie knew that, too. But there was also a shred of truth to his friend's words. Without Melissa, they would still be stuck in the Ninth North, living off the grace of dishonest men, constantly thinking of the next meal and hoping the winter wouldn't be too cold. Constabulary life was hard, but nothing compared to what they had come from.

And Oscar had already been offered that next rung in the ladder, with all its promises. It was hovering before him: a tantalising silver platter after a life in the gutter. All he needed to do was reach out and take it.

For the second time that evening, he visualised a ring on his finger, with the polished ruby shining like a drop of blood. He thought of Charlotte Bellamy, her white nightgown turned crimson, flames dancing against the snowy sky...

"I need to sleep," he muttered. "I'm back in the Fifth West tomorrow."

"I wish I could go with you," Richie said. "Thanks for coming to check on me. Nobody else bothered to." He grasped Oscar's hand. "I'm glad you're alright."

Oscar tossed him a smile, fetched the basin from beside the bed and emptied the vomit down a sink. Then he replaced it on the nightstand and slipped out of the door.

CHAPTER X

Two nights later, the snow transformed to bitter rain. Lightsmen roamed in force to keep the lighting mechanisms from freezing. Inside the warehouses, workers walked treadmills and turned cranks, drawing power from the Tower into the heating units around the higher Levels. Those lower down had to make do with decade-old mechanisms, rusted and rickety. In Faunatown, the lunafauna fluffed up their coats and huddled beneath blankets, some sleeping close together in packs.

The watch shop was among the lucky places. Such a trade was lucrative enough for Malcolm to afford quality heat coils in both floors of the building. So despite her draughty window, Charlotte was warm: a simple luxury which she knew not to take for granted.

Malcolm had said that keeping busy helped him, and she found the same was true for her. With every cog she removed from the mantel clock, her curiosity bloomed. It amazed her to think the entire City ran on these little grooved circles and spirals of metal. The concept was so humble, it was scarcely believed.

Malcolm entered her bedroom and peered at the gears she had laid out on the dresser.

"Very good," he remarked. "But have a closer look at these two. The teeth on that one are slightly bigger, see?"

She moved it further up. "So, it goes here?"

"That's it. You're learning fast," Malcolm beamed.

"Actually, learning is what I want to talk to you about. You know that phonograph I've been working on? A gentleman from the Second East brought it in. He said word reached him about me, and he came specially."

Charlotte's eyes widened. The Second East was one of the most opulent areas in the City. The only place greater was the First Level, directly above it, where the Potentate's Pavilion stood.

"He collected it this evening," continued Malcolm, "and he's paid me five hundred solidi. More than I usually make in two months. And more than enough for me to enrol you at the Academy."

Charlotte's grin dropped into a scowl.

"*School?* I don't want to!"

"Well, tough," Malcolm said, in a tone which revealed he'd been expecting such an argument. "It's near the end of term now, but we'll speak with the principal tomorrow, and you can start after Midwinter. I was going to send you there as soon as I could, anyway."

"But I never had to go to school before. Mrs Parslow taught me!"

"I can't afford a governess. It's the Academy or nothing."

"Then I choose nothing," Charlotte huffed. "I want to stay here and help you. Anyway, I already know the three Rs. Reading, writing, and 'rithmetic. So why do I need to go?"

"There are bigger words to learn, that's why," Malcolm chuckled. "Alright, let's make a deal. I'll take you on as my apprentice in the shop, but only if you go to the Academy. I know a lot has changed, but you're still the daughter of a Lord. You need a proper education."

Malcolm held out his hand. Charlotte pouted, but rolled her eyes in defeat and shook.

"Alright," he smiled. "Put the clock away and get into

bed."

"It's only a quarter past eight! It's not time for bed yet!" Charlotte protested.

"It is when we're getting up early," Malcolm said.

He punched her pillow a few times to force it into shape. Charlotte climbed between the sheets and fixed her eyes on a spot on the wall, pointedly not looking at him. Bedtime before nine o' clock seemed an even bigger insult than school.

Her feet pounded on the cobbles. They were covered with snow. She couldn't run too fast, or she would slip. But it didn't matter, because nothing was *too fast*. Time slowed to a crawl as bullets flew around her. She watched her father hit the floor, his skull blown open, brains and blood leaking across the square. The tall woman came closer...

Charlotte flung herself away, and awoke. The nightmare vanished, the buildings flashed into a bedroom. Not *her* room; Malcolm's childhood room, which was now the one she slept in...

No. It *was* her room. Her old one didn't exist anymore.

Charlotte clutched her doll until the sun rose. Malcolm helped her to dress, they ate a bowl of porridge, then emerged from the shop into a haze of freezing rain. Carriages rolled out of it like shadows, took solid form for a moment as they drew close, only to disappear again in the opposite direction. The drains had overflowed and sent filthy streams towards the crossroads. A puddle splashed up Charlotte's boots and soaked her calves.

"I'm all wet!" she snapped.

"It will dry," said Malcolm. "I bet if we wring out our coats when we get home, we'll have enough water for a cup of tea each."

He hailed a cab and helped her inside.

"Bold Street, Fourth West, please," he called through the peephole, then took off his hat and ran an anxious hand across his wig. It was the one he'd worn whenever he came to the Bellamy manor: a simple off-white with a black ribbon at the back. Charlotte remembered what he had said on market day, that he only used it when he wanted to make an impression. And, she supposed, when he was going among those above his class.

"Malcolm?" she asked, "how did you and Papa become friends?"

A soft smile crept over Malcolm's lips.

"By accident," he said. "My father was your grandfather's personal watch mechanic. You don't get that as much these days, but twenty years ago, it was quite common. He used to be the watch mechanic for the Pavilion, too. Anyway, one day when I was about your age, I went to the Bellamy manor with him, as his apprentice. There were three boys playing in the grounds — your Papa and Uncle Leo. They asked me to join them, but I couldn't. I was there to work. But they told me to sneak back later. So I did. They made me welcome, and that was how it went."

"Who was the third boy?" Charlotte pressed.

Malcolm cleared his throat. "Daniel Carter."

She gasped. "*The Potentate?* You know the Potentate, like Papa?"

"*Knew* him, once," Malcolm said curtly. "We fell out a long time ago and haven't seen each other since. I don't want to talk about that."

Charlotte watched him under her lashes, but she couldn't read his face. His eyes were glazed, like he was looking at something far away.

The new information swayed inside her head like a pendulum. Not only that Malcolm had played with the *Potentate*, but her *father* had as well, before either of them stepped into a Parliamentary Moot. The only images she had ever seen of Daniel Carter were drawings on flyers and newspapers: an austere man in a frilly collar. It was difficult to even imagine him as a child. How could somebody like that have run around and laughed like anyone else?

The carriage ascended the Interlevel and rolled into the Fourth West. As soon as they emerged from the tunnel, Charlotte's attention shifted to the streets. They weren't unlike where she had just come from, but the glass in the houses was more refined and the pavements were clear of rubbish. The bunting was larger, too, though it had darkened in the rain and the dye had run, dripping off the edges in a red stream.

Her stomach lurched. Why did everything red have to look like blood now?

A sign for Bold Street appeared. Halfway down, a large building stood in the centre of a flagged yard. On every wall, graceful lines and curves arched toward the sky in a majestic asymmetrical pattern. A wrought iron fence encircled the campus, and set into the gate's pillar was a plaque:

4TH W. QTR. ACADEMY OF EDUCATION FOR THE YOUNG
SPECIALIST SCHOOL IN ALCHEMICAL AND MEDICAL SCIENCES

Malcolm paid the cabbie and led Charlotte inside. Exposed mechanisms ran along the ceiling. Mouldings lined the classroom doors, carved to mimic leaves and ferns. Each detail was outlined in cheap gold paint that had flaked in places to expose the plaster underneath. It was pretty, but Charlotte could tell it was an imitation when compared to the true craftsmanship of the Bellamy manor.

They ascended a staircase into the staff quarters, and

Malcolm knocked on a door which read:

DOCTOR BRIDGET DICKINSON, MALC. (HONS):
PRINCIPAL

"*Dickinson?*" Malcolm gasped. "Oh, you're in good hands! The Dickinsons are one of the greatest alchemy families in the whole City. Ages ago, they basically invented orbs. You'll be learning from the best. I had no idea a Dickinson had taken over this place!"

Charlotte threw a sideways glance at him. She hadn't seen him so excited since he'd told her about the graft.

"Enter," someone called.

The room seemed to be made entirely of metal shelves, each crammed with books. Many were so thick, Charlotte imagined they could have been wedged behind a carriage to keep it from rolling away. Overcome with curiosity, she squinted at the spines.

Theatrum Chemicum; The Use of Alchemy in Medical Contexts; Origins of the Orb-Mainspring Symbiosis…

"Do you find my reading material interesting, miss?"

Charlotte jumped. She hadn't even noticed the desk in the corner. A middle-aged woman sat there, her hair pinned into a high bun, its natural colour lost beneath a copious application of white powder. Her dress was pale too: thick grey wool that managed to be opulent and practical at the same time. Her eyes shone with intelligence, like polished glass, and she pursed her thin lips as though sucking lemons. Charlotte wondered if she ever smiled at all.

"What's a *symbissy?*" she blurted, the last book title still in her mind.

Doctor Dickinson arched an eyebrow. "A *symbiosis* is

something working with another. I would appreciate it if your manners could do the same with mine, miss."

Malcolm quickly stepped in.

"Good morning, Ma'am," he said. "My name is Malcolm Godwin. I was hoping to enrol her here."

Dickinson threw a critical glance at Charlotte. "She's a little old to be starting school."

"She was privately educated," Malcolm explained. "But that's no longer possible."

"Are you her father, sir?"

"Her guardian. Her father was Lord August Bellamy."

Dickinson's lips tightened even more and she raised her chin in newfound interest.

"I see," she said after a long pause. "How old are you?"

"Eight and a half," Charlotte said.

"And what did your governess teach you?"

"The three Rs, music and needlework."

"Playing the harpsichord won't be much use below the Third Level, Miss Bellamy," Dickinson said. "You need to learn mathematics, science—"

"Can I do alchemy?" Charlotte asked.

Dickinson's expression hardened. "You'll also need to learn to not interrupt. And yes, you can study alchemy, but not until you're older. You must have a grounding in other subjects before you can even attempt it."

Charlotte gripped the sides of her skirt. She felt like a worm on a hook. But, she reasoned, it would be worth enduring. If she complied, she could become Malcolm's apprentice, and at some point, learn the mysteries of alchemy. Then maybe she could teach it to him. Maybe the two of them could even create his special graft together.

Dickinson removed a sheet of paper from a file.

"Fill in all the details, please, Mr Godwin."

Malcolm's face lit up. "Thank you so much, Ma'am! Will you be teaching her?"

"I'm afraid not. I only teach advanced academics: the optional classes after one reaches seventeen. For now, she'll be with Evelyn Gilbaut. One of the finest in my employ."

Malcolm scribbled across the form, pausing every few lines to dip the nib into an inkwell. He signed with a flourish, then handed over a wad of solidi notes, which Dickinson locked inside a drawer in her desk.

"Perfect. Come, I'll introduce you to Miss Gilbaut and her class. Then you'll know where to go."

She led them to the ground floor and knocked on a door close to the entrance. She didn't wait for an answer before letting herself in.

Charlotte swallowed as twenty children turned to look at her, all dressed as smartly as their parents could afford. She drew her shoulders back, the way her mother had taught her, but stopped herself before she could stand too straight. She didn't want any of these new faces to see through her and turn fierce, the way Edgar did.

She glanced at a boy in the front row, about a year older than her, with dark blonde hair and rounded spectacles. He gave her a smile, and she tentatively returned it.

"Good morning, Doctor Dickinson," the teacher said. She was a feline lunafauna: her cheeks and flat nose were sprinkled with snowy fur, and a pair of cat ears protruded through her hair, so blonde it looked almost white.

"Miss Gilbaut," said Dickinson, with a nod of appreciation. "You have a new student as of next term."

Miss Gilbaut beamed at Charlotte, and she immediately felt more at ease. This teacher seemed much nicer. And, despite her initial reservation, she now felt a shred of respect for Dickinson. The principal could have refused to let lunafauna work for her — many skilled places did. The fact that the feline was here made Charlotte's heart flutter. Her father would have been proud to see it.

"What's your name, dear?" asked Miss Gilbaut.

"Charlotte Bellamy,"

The class gasped. Even Miss Gilbaut seemed taken aback. Her whiskers twitched as she composed herself.

Charlotte's belly turned over. Shouldn't she have said it? No, everyone would have found out eventually. But logic didn't make her feel any better.

"Well, it's lovely to meet you," Miss Gilbaut said, then turned to the children. "You all remember how scary your first day was, so make sure you're nice to Charlotte when she joins us. We want her to be welcome."

A boy at the back leaned forward.

"What was it like?"

"Tobias!" Miss Gilbaut warned.

Charlotte glared at him. Malcolm's hand came down on her shoulder. She could almost hear him encouraging her not to respond.

"Clark, you're to report to my office at recess," snapped Dickinson. "I will not tolerate behaviour like that in my Academy. Do you understand?"

"Yes, Ma'am," replied the boy demurely. Dickinson gave him another scowl, then led Charlotte and Malcolm to the exit.

"I'm sorry about that. It won't happen again," she said, gentler than before. "Miss Bellamy, I realise this is hard for you, and I have high expectations for students. But things will be fine. This is a safe place. I want you to know that."

"Thank you," Charlotte muttered.

Malcolm shook Dickinson's hand and wished her a pleasant Midwinter. She saw them out, then Malcolm paused briefly to adjust Charlotte's scarf. The temperature had plummeted while they had been inside, and sleety rain bounced off the flagstones like coins.

Cries and angry voices suddenly rose on the air. Charlotte looked around in alarm. Two young men stood outside the Academy, dressed in smart but faded clothes. They were the kind of people who she had seen pretending to be kingpins until they noticed her father walking past.

They had a lunafauna on the floor between them. He had curled up into a ball, was begging for mercy, but they didn't listen. A hail of blows came down on his head.

"Damn fleabag!" one of them snarled.

At once, Malcolm sprinted over and shoved himself between them.

"What are you doing? Stop that!"

"This doesn't concern you," the second man snapped.

"It's my concern if I say it is! How dare you!"

Malcolm angled himself in front of the lunafauna. His normally placid face turned red with rage.

"Filth like that have no place this high up the Levels!" yelled the first man. "Didn't you hear about the shooting? One of them did it! Let those things out of where they belong, and what else do you expect?"

The second man took a step closer. Malcolm squared up to him, with a defiance that told Charlotte it wasn't the first time he had intervened like this.

The sight made her heart race. She was barely aware of the rain anymore, only the adrenaline firing through her veins. Malcolm's stance was identical to the pose her father had taken, when the tall woman came towards him and pointed a gun at his head…

A hint of phantom pain shot across her back. She couldn't halt the panic. It pressed on her, pinned her in place. Like the weight of the lighting mechanism as it fell on top of her…

"You're seriously defending *that?*" the man snarled in Malcolm's face. "It's not even human."

"I could say the same about you," Malcolm said coldly. "Get out of here before I call for the police!"

The first man threw Malcolm a disdainful sneer and pulled his comrade away.

As soon as they were gone, Malcolm helped the lunafauna to his feet. He was a canine, with spaniel features: upturned nose, large dark eyes, tousled ears hanging either side of his face. A thin lightsman's smock covered his body and his paws were darkened with oil. He must have just left maintaining his mechanism.

Malcolm held a handkerchief to a cut on the lunafauna's lip.

"You alright?" he asked.

"I'll be fine. How can I repay you?"

"By going to the hospital. Then speak to the Constabulary. Can I call you a cab? We can come with you, if you need help?"

The lunafauna shook his head. "No, I can manage. Thank you, sir. Not many no-tails would do what you just did. The Constabulary, least of all."

Malcolm closed his eyes. Charlotte couldn't tell if he was more upset or angry.

The canine limped towards the Interlevel. His tail hung between his legs and the rain ran off it like a waterfall. Malcolm watched with a shadowed expression.

"Charlotte," he said, "I know August taught you this, but I'm going to repeat it. *Never* think you're better than anyone else. Where we come from means nothing. It's how we live that means everything."

All the muscles in Charlotte's chest tightened. She had never seen such brutality against a lunafauna. It left her bones shaking. Was it always this terrible? Or was it worse because of that horrible lie about...

The memory invaded again: gunshots followed by screams, then awful silence...

Her heart pounded. The pressure in her ribs grew. No matter where she looked, she couldn't focus. The entire world felt huge and sharp, closing in around her like the walls of a nightmare.

She noticed blood on the floor where the lunafauna had been lying.

The panic exploded. She bolted down the street. She heard Malcolm shout after her, but she didn't look back. He sounded as though he was underwater. She scurried around the corner, past a young constable, and into a nearby Interlevel.

It was busy. The iron steps groaned under the weight of pedestrians and commuters. No matter how fast she moved, she couldn't outrun the terror. It just became worse and crammed her lungs together. Every breath brought a wave of pain. Was she having a heart attack?

No, she wouldn't still be standing if she was. She wouldn't still be alive.

She climbed to the next Level and took a random route. This was the Third West, *her* Level: the place where she had lived all her life. But while she recognised the majestic buildings, everything seemed empty. It tugged at a strange sentiment, somewhere deep and far away. She was gazing upon a scene from a story which wasn't her own anymore.

A tower of blackened walls appeared ahead. The rafters were exposed, opening a charred attic to the sky, like the chest of a disembowelled creature.

Charlotte walked towards the remains of her home. The only thing she recognised was her swing, still hanging from its frame amid heaps of debris. She had a mind to sit on it, to try and glean some semblance of the familiar, but it was impossible: the entrances to the grounds were fenced off by iron barriers. But she peered into the side alley, and realised they had missed the crack in the wall which led to the hidden tunnel.

Something caught her eye. In the shadows of the hole, partially buried beneath a bookcase, lay a golden strip. She picked it up, and gasped.

It was her mother's wristwatch. The glass was smashed and the pearlescent face stained, but it was otherwise undamaged.

How had it gotten here? Charlotte remembered her mother wearing it the night they ran away. It must have snagged during. Had she not noticed it was missing, or just been in too much of a hurry to go back for it?

It didn't matter, either way. She had still lost it. And she was still dead.

Charlotte sank down the bricks. Her wounds flared with pain as they scraped against the wall. She thought of the snow on her skin, the sound of gunfire and strange Latin words which she didn't understand. *Ad maius bonum* and *Cor Aeternum.*

She wanted to come apart at the seams like an old garment. Why was everything so cruel? Her father had always told her to look for the good in everyone, that there wasn't a single human or lunafauna in the City without it. How could he have been so terribly wrong?

"Charlotte!"

She recognised Malcolm's voice immediately, but couldn't bring herself to call back. She felt as though all her strength had seeped into the puddle underneath her.

He ran towards her. His wig hung in soaking ruins around his cheeks.

"Charlotte, what were you doing?" he shouted. "You could have gotten yourself lost, or kidnapped, or something! Don't *ever* do that again, do you hear me?"

Charlotte just looked up at him blankly. Realising her distress, Malcolm lifted her to her feet, and she wrapped her arms around his waist. She wasn't sure if she would be able to take her own weight if she let go.

When Malcolm spoke again, his voice was softer.

"I had a feeling you'd come here. You certainly beat me to it!"

Charlotte sighed. She knew what he was doing. He was trying to get her to talk about something, anything, just to make sure she *could* still talk. She had always hated when adults did that.

In the end, however, she relented, and said, "I found Mama's watch."

She held it up.

"That's the one I was telling you about," Malcolm smiled. "The one with an orb inside, so it never needs to be rewound. Oh, look at the face… Don't worry, I can fix that, no problem. I'll do it as soon as we get home."

"Could you put it on me, please?"

Malcolm slipped it around her wrist. As relieved as Charlotte was that her doll had survived Rene, this little piece of jewellery was something not hers. It had been bought by her father, worn by her mother. Lena Bellamy's skin had rested where hers did now.

Malcolm coaxed her away, towards the main road, and whistled for a passing cab. As soon as they were inside, he began rubbing her arms to warm her.

"You're freezing. Hopefully you won't catch a cold. And look at your dress!"

"It's just clothes," Charlotte said sullenly.

Sobs caught her before she could fight. They tore out of her throat with such ferocity, she struggled to breathe.

"I miss them, Malcolm!" she cried. "I want them! I want it to stop, all of it!"

Malcolm pulled her into a hug.

"I know," he said tenderly. "I miss them too. But it will be alright, I promise. I've got you, and you've got me. We'll come through this together."

"It's not fair! Why is it all so mean? I don't understand any of it!"

"Life isn't fair very often. And what we can't understand... Well, we just need to accept. It's not a great solution, but for the most part, it's the only one we have."

He stroked her hair away from her face. The cab bounced relentlessly along the roads, but he did his best to rock her back and forth.

"Hey," he whispered, "I've got an idea. Whenever you feel overwhelmed like this, I want you to tell yourself something until it feels better. Say it with me, alright? Twenty-three people were shot in Rene Square, but I survived. I miss my parents, but they live on through me. I can't reverse the past, but the past can't hurt me. Nobody controls my life but me."

CHAPTER XI

Daniel stared at the canopy above the bed. Nobody in Forest had finer sheets or a softer mattress, but he couldn't settle. He just listened to the Tower; felt the hours slip by in fifteen-minute pockets, one after another.

He turned his head to the side. Elisabeth was facing him, eyes closed. Even in the gloom, he could see her red hair, the pale fabric of her nightgown, the shapely line of her jaw. She was pretty, that was true, but nothing more. In one respect, that was exactly what Daniel wanted: she knew her place and didn't try to test the boundaries. And yet he found himself wishing she could be *more* — more forthright, more outspoken, more challenging. The way Melissa was. It felt like spiteful irony that out of all the Dickinsons, renowned for their stubbornness and intelligence, he'd gotten the runt of the litter.

He slipped out of bed and dressed hastily in a suit and jacket.

Elisabeth sat up. Daniel winced, but didn't stop. It didn't matter that she had spotted him. It never did.

"Daniel?"

"Go back to sleep."

"But… it's cold," Elisabeth said in a tiny voice. "Daniel, please. Don't."

He gritted his teeth, fumbling to fasten the buttons.

"Please," she said again.

"Go back to sleep."

Daniel walked out and shut the door. He hovered there for a moment, wrestling with his conscience, but he beat it down and carried on his way. He only paused for long enough to peer into the nursery at his slumbering son.

He opened a hidden entrance, to a spiral staircase which connected the Pavilion to the Roots, and took the shortest route to Melissa's house. It was a small abode, which she had insisted upon, since she spent too much time away to appreciate it as anything more than a place to sleep. He opened the back door with a special key, of which Melissa herself owned the only counterpart.

He found her in an armchair, a lap desk on her knee, working through a pile of paperwork. A cigarette smouldered from the edge of a full ashtray. Gauze encircled her right forearm: the memento of her battle with Jon Dawkins.

She didn't look up when he entered.

"How's the baby?" she asked.

Daniel smiled. "Nice and healthy. His mother's recovering well, too."

"Have you chosen a name yet?"

"Nicolas Alastair."

"I like it. Do you intend for the presentation ceremony to go ahead?"

"Yes. It's a perfect chance to reinforce support for the Potentates. Our bond's secure."

"Especially now you've settled matters with Samuel Tiffin." Melissa raised her eyes and pressed her pen against her lips. "I forgot to ask, last time I saw you. How did he take your proposition?"

Daniel fought back a scowl. "Poorly. But I explained things to him in a genteel manner and he seems to have come around."

"What did you offer him?"

"The best life a child could ask for. His daughter will want for nothing. It's the least I can do, without drawing too much attention. And she won't be missed."

Melissa paused.

"Have you told the Keeper?"

"Why bother?" replied Daniel. "He knows everything already. And he has no choice in the matter."

"He still has agency."

"Not enough to be of any concern. Look, I hate the idea of this. Repeating what was done to me. But it's the only way, and you know it. The things we must do for love."

"Love for your son," said Melissa, "or everyone else?"

Daniel looked straight at her.

"Both."

She held his eyes for a long moment, then turned back to her papers. Daniel glanced at his watch.

"You do realise it's almost one in the morning?" he said.

Melissa continued writing. "A perfect time to not be distracted. What happened the other night... It's worrying. There's evidence of unrest."

Daniel took the pen out of her hand and laid it down.

"It's not the first time people have graffitied," he said. "We've been dealing with lunafauna and alchemists protesting their lot for years. So just let them moan. Everyone needs to pass their spare time in some way."

"I can deal with *alchemists*," Melissa insisted. "They're just frustrating. They're easy enough to manage, because I know who they are. But someone — or some people — don't believe the cover story about Bellamy, and that concerns me."

Daniel shook his head. "Rumours and conspiracies. You worry too much."

"I know," Melissa said. "That's why I'm good at my job."

She put the lap desk on the side table, still open, then leaned back in her chair.

"But evidently not good enough to know I was walking straight into a trap. I lost officers, led them right to where Dawkins wanted us. It's getting dangerous out there. I can feel it, even if I can't pin down all the details."

"Melissa, if you're still punishing yourself for Rene—"

"No, it's not about that. You don't understand," she snapped. Her composure broke a little: hairline cracks in fine porcelain. "I know I've had to do terrible things, to keep the City safe, in order, preserve the Aeternum ... call it what you want. I'm a killer. I'm still willing to kill Bellamy's daughter if it comes to that. But I've never led my own people to their doom. People who I care about."

Daniel knelt before her. He thought he saw tears in her eyes, but she blinked them away and forced a flinty mask into their place. She *never* cried. It was something beyond her — he would have sooner believed her capable of flight than of weeping. But that was who she was and why he respected her so much. She could do what he could not.

"It wasn't your fault," he said. "You and that youngster who escaped, you were both able to do that for a reason. You are the Chief Officer, not just of the Constabulary, but of the Circulus, for a *reason*."

Melissa sighed. "The greater good."

"Exactly," said Daniel. "I'm just glad *you* got out. I was so worried."

"And the officers?"

"Will be put to rest with full honours. Their families will receive compensation. And the Tower will tick on, the way it always has, and take everything else in its wake. We just need to endure with it."

Melissa listened to him intently, then nodded.

"I'll see to it myself. I was responsible for them. I will honour them," she said. "I'm sorry, Daniel. I was weak. I've been weak ever since this damn thing started."

"You are anything but weak. That's only tiredness talking," said Daniel. "When was the last time you had a full night's sleep?"

"I can sleep when I'm dead."

"We'll just ease the taxes on the alchemists until they find something else to cry about. Will that make you feel better?"

"And make up the difference, where?" asked Melissa. "Shifting it onto Faunatown would be very unwise, especially after we used that lunafauna convict in Rene. And if Dawkins is so keen to kill me, the other thieves won't take long to follow his lead."

"So the only ones we can trust are in the topmost Levels, but we've always known that," Daniel said. "This doesn't change a thing. The slums might be larger in number than the higher people, but they're spread out, contained. They complain because that's all they *can* do. And it doesn't matter in the end, because we have the Invisible Law, and we have *you*. You and the Circulus are the rivets which keep everything together. Just as much as the Keeper does."

Melissa scoffed. "I'm sure people would be happier to see me out of the picture than him."

Daniel took her hand. "How can you say that? He's not human."

"And I am? Are any of us, truly?"

Melissa sat very still, not even blinking. Her face was drawn with fatigue, but held the sharpness which never faded.

Daniel remembered the day he had met her. It was before

he was due to marry, but she had struck him deeper than anything he felt for his fiancée. She was strong, different, and unafraid to show it. Her ferocity spoke to him in a way Elisabeth's decorum couldn't. She was his true equal.

Melissa didn't wait for him to kiss her. She got to her feet, grabbed his waist and spun him down into the chair. She straddled him, unbuttoned his trousers, and brought her lips to his. He tasted her desperation, felt her shaking as she moved against him. He wrenched open her shirt. His ring caught the lamplight and set a dozen red facets reflecting in her eyes.

The Tower clock chimed one. Daniel let his head fall back as she nuzzled his neck. They had all night. It might as well have been all the time in the world.

Melissa knew she was waking up, but she didn't open her eyes straightaway. Every part of her body was made of light, still spinning in the aftermath of pleasure. Was it hours ago? Minutes? Heartbeats?

Bedsheets formed underneath her, as softly as though she had drifted onto a cloud. They were warm and smelled of Daniel. She felt him, pressed against her back, one arm encircling her waist.

She disentangled herself from him and turned a crank in the wall to activate the overhead lighting mechanism. She only gave it a single rotation: enough to cast a glow without dazzling the eye. The clock on the nightstand read a quarter to six. She washed at the basin, braided her hair, and laced her stays.

The Tower struck the hour. Daniel didn't stir. He had spent his entire life in the Pavilion, closer to the bells than anyone else in Forest. The skill to continue sleeping despite their ringing was one all Carters acquired early.

Melissa dressed in a fresh uniform and picked out her boots from the clothes strewn across the floor. Then she kissed Daniel on the mouth. Finally, his eyes fluttered open.

"You don't have to go yet," he whispered.

Melissa moved back. "Yes, I do, and so do you. Take a bath, then go and see your son."

Daniel scowled, but a wave of pride came over his face at the mention of Nicolas.

"Everyone's going to be so happy," he said. "This place needs some good news after everything that's happened. What's better than a baby?"

"I can see how much you love him," said Melissa. "You've waited long enough."

Daniel smiled. He pulled on his trousers, then stepped in front of her, blocking the door. He ran his hands around her hips.

"I'll come back when I can," he murmured in her ear.

Melissa snatched a breath. It would be so easy to climb back into bed. Both of them were the leaders of everything — nobody could tell them what to do or chastise them for being late…

But, no. Logic elbowed its way through her lust. She had to catch Hargreaves.

She pulled herself out of Daniel's arms.

"When you can," she said. She kissed him again, and left the house before he could convince her to stay.

As usual, there was little change in the light levels in the Roots. No sun could permeate this deep, but to grant some semblance of normality, lightsmen worked the mechanisms to mimic the hours of day. Now, it was still dark, with only enough of a glow to see by, so those heading to street-level could adjust easily.

Melissa made her way to the nearest entrance: the old bookshop in the Fourth South's Hamilton Street. But she didn't go up into the fresh air. Instead, she waited. This was the closest doorway to the aboveground barracks, and she had learned quickly that Hargreaves used it as a shortcut to the Fifth West.

Sure enough, at half past six, he emerged. Even though Melissa wasn't in plain sight, Hargreaves spotted her immediately. She smiled. He had the same sharp perception she saw in herself. Maybe it was from his time with the Shadow Rats, or just a natural disposition, but it was valuable nonetheless.

"Madam Spectre," Hargreaves said in surprise. "Good morning."

"Good morning," she replied. "I wanted to speak to you before you reported to your post."

"Is something wrong?"

"Not at all."

Melissa beckoned him over. She noticed a tiny red line on his jaw — he had cut himself shaving. She smelled the cream he had used: the cheap and unperfumed staple of the barracks, and made a mental note to replace it.

"I wanted to personally congratulate and thank you," she said. "Your bravery a few nights ago was unparalleled. You stood in for your comrade, and then you saved my life. Not many can claim to have done that."

Hargreaves lowered his gaze.

"I wouldn't want to claim anything, Madam," he said humbly. But beneath his tone, Melissa heard the warmth of delight. It was faint — he would have known little praise in his life — but it was definitely there.

"You're strong," she continued. "And you're valuable to me. So I want you to keep training, work hard, and carry on watching Charlotte Bellamy. But you're not to step foot in the

Ninth North again. I won't give Jon Dawkins another chance to carry you off."

"With pleasure, Madam," replied Hargreaves.

Melissa waited until he looked at her again.

"I've decided to speed up your induction into the Circulus."

Hargreaves's cheeks took on a pale cast.

"It would give you more protection," Melissa said. "You would have a connection to the innermost circle of the Parliamentary."

She moved her hands so the ring on her finger was visible. Hargreaves glanced at it with a guarded expression.

"Might I… have some time to think it over?" he asked.

Melissa didn't blink. "I'll have fewer powers to guard you."

"I don't understand."

"If you remain only a part of the regular Constabulary, you'll still have to do your rounds in all the Levels in every Quarter. I can't make an exception to that just because I like you. But if you take my offer, you can stay in the Fifth West. Or wherever Charlotte Bellamy goes. And I'm sure that will always be far away from the Rats."

Melissa watched Hargreaves carefully. She could see him piecing together the information and balancing the benefits, but there was a shred of suspicion in him, too. Very few were brought into the Circulus so young, and even fewer from a background such as his. And then there was the small matter of him being one of the first responders at Rene, hearing Dawkins's claim that a convict hadn't been behind it.

He wasn't to know, but he was a liability as much as the girl she had told him to watch. The difference was that she could make use of him. And she would mould him into a fine, strong example in time. For now, all she needed to do was make him accept.

"I can see you want to leave your past behind," Melissa said in a silken tone. "Let me help you. Be my protégé. It's the least I can do to show my gratitude."

Hargreaves swallowed. He stood perfectly still, but his lips pursed slightly, and Melissa could tell he was gnawing on his tongue behind a composed face.

Yes, he was very much like her. He knew not to let his emotions show.

She extended a hand. Hargreaves looked at it and back to her, in one fluid motion. His fingers twitched. Then he reached out and shook.

"Thank you for the honour," he said.

Melissa smiled. It was like watching a moth fluttering toward the light. Once ensnared, it would never be able to turn away. And even if it did, the brightness would be branded onto its vision forever.

"Come and see me after the girl goes to sleep," she said. "I'll want to hear your report, as usual."

Hargreaves nodded. "Yes, Madam Spectre."

CHAPTER XII

Evelyn Gilbaut lived on the outskirts of Faunatown, at the corner of the Fifth South. It was the highest Level of the lunafauna community, and it suited her well. She was close to an Interlevel which granted access to the Academy in the Fourth West, but she wasn't too far from the tavern area, either. Like many around her, alcohol was always a welcome respite.

On every wall, flyers and graffiti were plastered over the newspapers. Several had been torn down by the Constabulary, but as soon as one was removed, five more would appear elsewhere. In front of the Town Hall in Aspinall Square, Evelyn passed a group of youths painting in sloppy red letters:

CUNNINGHAM INNOCENT!
FIAT JUSTITIA RUAT CAELUM!

She swept her tail back and forth in agitation. Ever since the Rene Square incident, a horrid tension had lingered over the heads of all lunafauna, like ripples on a pond, refusing to subside. The named convict had been one of their own. Evelyn had even known him, back in her youth: poor and troubled Roger Cunningham. He was put away in the Seventh North Gaol years ago for killing his siblings, but everyone in Faunatown knew it was in self-defence. And he was only twelve months away from completing his sentence. Why would he break out and murder twenty-three strangers?

It didn't seem right, and the tremor was far from over.

Evelyn ordered a glass of gin at The Ring O' Bells and settled in the corner. It was early, but the place was already beginning to fill up. Many patrons were in their larger forms, but the occasional person walked on four paws rather than two. Instead of glasses, they were given dishes. Here, they were safe. This was *their* part of the City; had been for as long as Forest had stood. No matter that it was forced upon them. Any home was better than none at all.

A feline woman strode through the door, dressed in only a shawl: the bare minimum that lunafauna were permitted to wear outdoors. It was bunched around her neck to keep out the cold. A small gold hoop, set with a ruby, hung from her left ear. The other patrons waved at her; tails wagged and the air filled with friendly purring.

"Hello, Phoebe," the barkeep smiled. "Aren't you freezing?"

"I've had worse," Phoebe replied. "Can I get a red?"

"A glass?"

"Don't be dumb, Simon. The whole bottle," said Phoebe. Then she noticed Evelyn and added, "Actually, throw in two glasses."

Phoebe tossed several solidi onto the bar, ambled towards Evelyn and sat opposite her. She squinted her eyes in greeting and flicked the edge of her nail against the gin glass. It was long and curved: an oversized cat claw.

"Why do you bother with this cheap crap?" she asked.

"I like it," Evelyn said.

Phoebe shrugged. "Fair enough. Well, put it aside for now. We've got better stuff on the way."

Her tone was warm, the way it usually was, yet Evelyn sensed stress beneath it: the kind which often crept into her voice after a Parliamentary Moot. But there hadn't been any Moots today — the next one wasn't until next month. Phoebe was holding herself differently too, as though she was in pain and trying to hide it.

And she had known true pain. Evelyn could see all the scars distorting Phoebe's fur. No lunafauna was without them, but her collection was horrifying, covering her entire body in a map of old wounds. Evelyn knew the stories behind some: whippings, drunken fights with the Constabulary... But the one on Phoebe's chest, the deepest of all, was a mystery. It was so terrible, the pattern of her coat hadn't even grown back over it.

Simon approached with a bottle and two glasses. He had barely a chance to lay them down before Phoebe popped the cork and poured.

"Not too much," Evelyn protested.

In response, Phoebe kept the first glass, full to the brim, then stopped halfway with the second.

Evelyn shook her head despairingly. "You're going to kill yourself."

Phoebe snorted a laugh. "Don't worry, not for another decade or so."

"How many will it be this time?"

"What, lives or deaths?"

"Deaths."

"Four. Five more to go. What joy." Phoebe took a large mouthful of wine and scratched her neck through the shawl. "I don't want to talk about that. Your day must have been more interesting than mine. It was the last one of the term, wasn't it? Did the kids give you any Midwinter gifts?"

"Julian brought me a new pen. Sweet boy."

"Julian? He's Bridget's nephew, right?"

"Yes, with the spectacles. And I've got a new student once

the new term starts." Evelyn lowered her voice. "Charlotte Bellamy."

Phoebe's glass paused halfway to her lips.

"What's the matter?" Evelyn whispered.

"Not here," Phoebe replied. "Simon, can you watch the table for us, please? We'll be back in a minute."

She pulled Evelyn into the small courtyard at the side of the tavern. It stank of old vomit and the overflowing gutter spewed its bowels across the wet cobbles. Evelyn wrinkled her nose. Her sense of smell might not have been as strong as her canine neighbours, but it was still enough to flip her stomach.

Phoebe turned her ears, listening to make sure they were alone. Her tail puffed up and flicked from side to side. She was frightened.

"I heard the girl survived. How is she? Is she managing alright?"

Evelyn nodded. "Yes, she's with a new guardian. Why? What's wrong?"

"I just… want to make sure she's safe," said Phoebe. She sounded strained and hurt, and scratched incessantly at her neck.

Evelyn frowned. She had never seen Phoebe this restless. It was as though something had stung her, or if she had a splinter in a place she couldn't reach.

Then her shawl slipped. Phoebe tried to pull it up again, but Evelyn yanked it away.

A horrified hiss grew in her throat.

"Phoebe… What happened? Who put that on you?"

"It's fine," Phoebe answered flatly.

"It's *not* fine!" Evelyn cried. "That's…"

She was too appalled to finish. The collar was well-made, with some kind of mechanism at the back — so small, she hadn't noticed it at first. And there was magic on it. She could sense that as easily as rain on a summer day.

Centuries ago, collars were forced on the lunafauna during their enslavement in the higher Levels. Some had been like this, infused with the warped kind of magic which the alchemists had mastered, to keep even tighter control. Then Phoebe herself had become a Lady, and her first act was to overturn the servitude and dispose of the collars. To now see *her* with one of those disgusting relics made Evelyn feel sick.

"Did someone in the Parliamentary do that?" Evelyn asked. "You *can't* wear that thing… it's just—"

"It's not something you should concern yourself with," Phoebe said quietly.

"You're my friend! You are my concern!"

"I can't tell you. Irony is sweet, isn't it?"

"I don't understand."

"You don't want to. But let's just say that it will be like this for a while."

Evelyn swallowed. "Tell me."

"I *can't*," snarled Phoebe.

Evelyn reached towards her. "Stay still. I'm getting it off you."

"*No!*" Phoebe cried, and threw herself against the wall. Her fur stood up in warning. "Please, Evie, don't. It will hurt too much. I've already tried. And there's metal inside it. You can't even cut it off."

"Alright!" Evelyn said. "I won't touch it."

Phoebe closed her eyes, as though bracing herself for tears, but none came. No matter what she went through, Evelyn couldn't remember ever seeing her cry.

"I'm sorry," Phoebe muttered.

"I'm not offended. I'm just worried about you."

"I'll survive. You know that."

A tiny crack appeared at the corner of Phoebe's mask. For the briefest moment, Evelyn saw through the boldness to the individual underneath. An old woman and a little kitten in equal measure, who only drank to suppress the immense weight on her shoulders — and to keep her backbone as straight and powerful as it could be.

"You shouldn't be friends with me," Phoebe said ruefully. "It would be for the best if you—"

"Rubbish," Evelyn said. "You can't go through life without having someone to rely on."

"I've managed it for long enough."

"And you've been alone for long enough, too. I'm not going anywhere."

Phoebe met her eyes steadily. "This will only hurt both of us. You know that, right? *I* should bloody know it by now."

"Phoebe—"

"I'll do what I've always done, and do my best to look after everyone. In return, I need people to not get close. That includes you. I'm sorry."

She wrapped the shawl around her neck and walked towards the mouth of the alley.

"Take that red home," she said. "My treat."

Evelyn went to grab her, but froze. The sound of crashing and angry shouts filled the air.

Phoebe's ears swivelled. At once, the haziness vanished from her eyes, leaving only razor focus.

She ran into the street, with Evelyn in hot pursuit. The noise grew louder: breaking glass, raised voices, cries of pain.

They rounded the corner, into Aspinall Square. Phoebe flung out an arm to keep Evelyn behind her. The entire area had erupted into chaos. It was clear something was happening, but the wall of people was too thick to see. Lunafauna thronged, in both tall and small forms, throwing stones, biting at no-tail constables who were beating them back. Behind them were the red letters which Evelyn had seen the youths painting. But now, they had been smeared with black.

"Stop this!" Phoebe bellowed. "Stop! Enough!"

The mob didn't listen. Phoebe snarled in frustration. She climbed up a lighting mechanism and ran along a wall, towards the fray, her tail stretched out to keep her balance.

Evelyn scaled a nearby lightsman's hut to avoid being crushed. Her heart skipped a beat. The officers had one of the youths, a feline lunafauna, on his knees with his wrists cuffed.

"Let him go!" a nearby woman shouted. "He's just a lad!"

"He was inciting discord!" replied the nearest officer, and pulled on the boy's tail until he yelped.

Evelyn winced. Even from this distance, she spotted the man's name badge: Reece. A red ring and embroidered circle marked him as one of the Vixen's personal squadron.

"Stand down, all of you, or you will be arrested!" Reece ordered.

"Or you'll shoot us like Bellamy, more like!" a canine lunafauna flung back.

"Or are we not good enough for that? Us *animals?*"

"Cunningham was innocent!"

"Wasn't it good enough that you've pushed us down, you murderers?"

Reece drew a pistol and fired it into the air.

"This is your final warning! Remember your place!"

Phoebe seized her chance. She leaned down the wall and snatched the gun out of Reece's hand.

"I said, that's enough!" she shouted, then cracked the pistol open and tossed the bullets away.

The effect was instantaneous. The lunafauna lowered their

paws and backed off. Those in their canine forms let out a low whine. The anger still hung like a heavy gas, but something else rose from beneath it. Respect.

Phoebe hissed at the officers, lips drawn back to expose her teeth.

"How dare you threaten my people! Let the boy go!"

Reece sneered. "That's not your order to give, Lady Feline!"

Phoebe bent so she was closer to him. Her eyes grew huge, the pupils completely dilated.

"This is *my* part of the City, not yours. If I tell you to let that boy go, you will let him go."

"You can't tell us what to do."

"Do I look like I care, you little shit?"

"Madam Spectre will hear of this!"

"I'm sure she will," said Phoebe coldly. "But do you honestly think she'll appreciate you adding to her mountain of mess? No. So just leave him alone and let me deal with it. Then you go home and crawl into bed, like the good little children you are."

She jumped off the wall and faced Reece. He was taller than her, but Phoebe puffed out her fur and stood her ground with all the strength her years allowed her.

Reece scowled. "You really think I need to listen to *you?*"

Phoebe didn't move. "You damn well know you will."

For a horribly long time, neither of them moved. Time seemed to freeze across the square. Even the most incensed lunafauna in the mob flattened their ears and crept away.

Evelyn held her breath. She had never seen Phoebe look so intimidating. Rage billowed off her, like the charge in the air which heralded a coming storm. Her claws slowly extended. Would she attack him? Surely not...

Reece's shoulders slumped. He uncuffed the boy, then held out his hand, and Phoebe slammed the empty pistol into his palm.

"So now we understand each other," she growled, "you can piss off."

Reece gave a sharp sigh. "This isn't over."

"Yes, it is," Phoebe replied dangerously.

The officers glared at her as they passed, but she stared straight back until they couldn't bear the weight of her eyes any longer. Finally, when they had disappeared, she helped the boy to his feet and turned to the crowd.

"Alright, everyone, listen," she said. "I know you thought this was a good thing. Damn, I might have joined in if the circumstances were different. But this isn't going to help right now. I need you all to go home. Keep yourselves safe. Don't give the no-tails any excuse to victimise you."

A nearby man stepped up. He was in his dog form, ears drooping and tail between his legs.

"We can't deal with it anymore, Phoebe! They treat us worse than dirt! We can't say or do anything! And Roger Cunningham was innocent! You know that! He wasn't even in Rene! He *never* would have killed all those people! Something's got to give!"

Phoebe scratched her neck.

"I… I'm trying to do what I can for everyone right now," she said. "No-tails hate what they don't understand. They always have; always think they're better than us. And I know this is hard, I really do. But *we* make things harder from *them* just by existing. I've seen our people through the wasteland to this City. I've watched Faunatown rise, our community grow. I might moan and get pissed, but I've always been with you, from your forefathers right down to your children. I've seen our slavery. I saw no-tails stealing from our graves. We've had hard times since the start, but every single time, they passed. This will, too. So please, do what we've always done, and endure with me. It's not today, but our day *will* come. And I will be there marching with you when it does. I promise."

The gathering fell silent at her words. The Potentate had delivered so many ostentatious speeches from his balcony, but all were filled with falsehood. He was too separate from his own people to know them. But here, now, as though a switch had flipped, Phoebe became the leader Evelyn remembered from childhood. A leader who even the oldest lunafauna could look upon in adoration. But beyond that, Phoebe was something more, standing naked save for her purse and shawl. Something no human or all-powerful Potentate could ever be.

She was one of them.

Slowly, the crowd dispersed, supporting their neighbours or carrying them in their arms. The cobbles were littered with bullet casings and scraps of fur which had been torn out in the chaos. Evelyn snarled under her breath, but refused to let the anger rise. She was better than that. All the lunafauna were. And this could have been far, far worse.

Phoebe drew the boy close, and pressed her nose to his.

"May magic shine on you," she whispered, then sent him down a nearby street. Her ear swivelled as Evelyn slid off the lightsman's hut. "Silly kid. He was just trying to do something honourable."

Evelyn drew a shaky breath. The adrenaline was receding now, but that only left room for nausea. It twisted her guts, and crawled across her skin so intensely, she worried for a moment that she had caught fleas. On instinct, she parted the fur on her arm, but to her relief, found nothing.

"Does anyone ever thank you?" she asked.

Phoebe rolled her eyes. "They can thank me by not sticking their necks out when I do it for them."

The choice of words sent a shiver through Evelyn. She glanced at Phoebe's shawl, pictured the awful collar underneath it.

"Why does that hurt you?" she asked gently. "The no-tails put something in it? One of the alchemists? I can feel the magic."

Phoebe sighed.

"You can't talk about it," Evelyn realised. "That's what it does, isn't it?"

"Let's just say," Phoebe uttered scathingly, "that this isn't the first time I've worn one of these. And this one's better made than the last."

"The Vixen did it. She'll punish you for this, won't she?"

Phoebe scoffed. "What more can they do to me?"

Her tone broke something inside Evelyn. It was both triumphant and indifferent: a mixture which could only come from living as long as Phoebe had. And knowing she would still outlive them all.

Evelyn rubbed up against her. Phoebe stiffened in alarm.

"You shouldn't," she said cautiously.

Evelyn squinted her eyes and closed them completely: the ultimate mark of affection among felines.

"Who gives a damn?" she replied. "You'll always be here for us. Let *me* always be here for *you*. Or, at least, as long as I can. That's what friends are for."

Phoebe went to argue, but then a purr rose in her throat. She licked Evelyn's ears and pulled her into an embrace. The desperation of it pressed the breath from her lungs. How long had it been since Phoebe had hugged anyone? A year? A decade? An entire century?

"In that case," Phoebe said, "you can buy me the next

bottle of red."

When the two of them drew apart, Evelyn glanced at the graffiti. The black paint which the officers had thrown over it hadn't completely hidden the words beneath. Under the flickering streetlamps, it looked as if it had been daubed in blood.

"What does it say that made them so angry?" she asked. "I've… never really had a good grasp of Latin."

Phoebe's back was to the graffiti, but she didn't turn around. She had already seen it.

"Let justice be done though the sky falls."

Hundreds of feet above, the Tower clock chimed twelve times.

CHAPTER XIII

Midwinter came and went. Gifts were exchanged and meals eaten. Lines of people danced through the streets. Phoebe barely remembered it. As on every solstice, she had been too intoxicated to recall anything.

Twelve days later, the garlands came down. But the red bunting stayed exactly where it was: first soaked with rain, then crystallised by frost. Phoebe looked at it scornfully through her bedroom window. Today was the one so many people had been waiting for. Crowds would be flocking to the Second Level to catch a glimpse of the Pavilion, for the infant Carter boy to make his first public appearance. It was a ceremony which had been held for centuries, and Phoebe had attended all of them.

She wondered how much smaller this one would be than Daniel's. In his thirty years of life, he hadn't garnered much favour.

Phoebe pressed herself into a stuffy dress she reserved only for Parliamentary meetings, and hid the atrocious collar under some lace. She didn't bother with a wig. Instead, she brushed the fur on her face and tied her longer humanlike hair into a bun. Usually, she left it hanging loose like a mane, but Daniel's father had loudly warned her to take more pride in her appearance. The next best thing was to put it up as high as possible, so her large feline ears could be seen. Yes, indeed she would be proud.

Outside, she climbed into a waiting carriage. The seats were comfortable, but the perfume on the upholstery made her eyes water. She distracted herself by following the route in her mind. It wasn't difficult. She knew every single turn and the bump of every manhole.

This City, once so full of promise, had made itself from nature, sought to understand and control it, without appreciating the truth of it. The no-tails claimed their intentions were to build a paradise, but from the beginning, it had been occupied by horrors. Nothing was good, or bad. Such black and white thinking was lost on every generation of young powerful idiots who tried to make gold from garbage.

One day, Phoebe thought. One day, when the world was older, everything would fall into place. Life always found a way to keep the balance. She had to trust that.

The carriage reached a private Interlevel leading straight to the Pavilion: a steep tunnel, sealed off from the Second Level by a thick metal door. The driver groaned with effort as he hitched the wheels onto a chain mechanism in the ground. After several minutes ascending the shaft, they entered the Pavilion grounds.

The entire expanse boasted elegant metal sculptures, paths paved with limestone so they shone in the sun. Fountains were fed by the artificial rivers, which then spilled over the balustrades as sparkling waterfalls. Here and there lay mechanisms for lighting, heating and water, expertly disguised so as not to be an eyesore. And the building itself was even more impressive. Every white wall bore swirling green moulding to echo vines and branches. Flying buttresses and oriel windows stood below a roof crowned with twisted spires. Slicing through the centre was the Tower, its southern face just one hundred feet above the highest chimney pot.

Phoebe didn't wait for the footman to let her out. She opened the door, tossed a few coins over her shoulder, and stepped into the Pavilion foyer. A wooden staircase swept along the walls, and mirrors stood everywhere, to make the gigantic space appear even larger.

"Lady Feline," said a well-dressed servant.

Phoebe glanced at him. "Expecting many tips today, Terence?"

Terence didn't react, too used to her demeanour by now.

"One would hope so, My Lady. Today is an important day after all."

"Mm. Woman has baby, father shows it off. Astounding," Phoebe said. "Well, you can earn your first tip right now. Fetch the strongest liquor in this place and you'll get forty solidi off me."

Terence immediately disappeared down an adjacent corridor, which Phoebe knew led to the wine cellar.

She climbed the staircase and made her way to the Great West Suite. A detailed fresco of clouds and birds coated the ceiling. Every horizontal surface held some kind of gaudy ornament. It was supposed to be modelled on foliage, but Phoebe couldn't help scoffing. It was clear none of those pompous artists had ever seen a real leaf growing in the wild.

The other Lords and Ladies were already assembled. They sipped wine from crystal glasses and wore their customary high fashion wigs in a plethora of pastels. The powder in them got up Phoebe's nose and she struggled not to sneeze. Even though her own attire was covered in ridiculous ruffles, she was underdressed compared to the rest of them.

Good. That was what they wanted. She was a Fellow, a Lady, yet still an *animal*, after all. But she refused to see it in the same light. She would miss no opportunity to remind these highbrow fools that she was not like them.

Daniel spotted her. The faintest hint of danger shone in his eyes. The unrest in Faunatown had been kept quiet, but he knew. Phoebe wasn't surprised. Everything got back to him and the Vixen. But she had her own armour-piercing strike ready, should she need to use it.

"I was beginning to worry you might not be joining us," Daniel said. His tone was smooth, but veiled a deeper sharpness, like a hidden blade.

"I wouldn't want to disappoint you," Phoebe replied. After a moment — just long enough to not be disrespectful — she curtsied.

As soon as she straightened up, Daniel steered her to a sofa where Elisabeth was sitting. Phoebe offered her a sincere smile. Aside from August and Lena Bellamy, the High Lady was the only member of this class whom she genuinely respected.

An infant was nestled in Elisabeth's arms. He had Daniel's intense green eyes and rounded chin, and a tuft of carrot red hair covered his head. Phoebe knew that was the same shade as Elisabeth's, concealed underneath her massive lilac wig.

"My Lady," Phoebe greeted. "How are you?"

"I'm well, Lady Feline. Thank you for asking," said Elisabeth. "This is Nicolas. Isn't he beautiful?"

Phoebe regarded him. The Carters had tried for a child for years, never with any success, and Elisabeth's love for the tiny boy radiated like the sun. But Phoebe was careful to hold her tongue. She didn't like babies. All they did was scream and smell.

With practised poise, she excused herself and retreated to the window. She didn't need to wait long before Terence appeared, balancing a goblet and bottle of red wine on a platter. Ignoring the glass, Phoebe took it by the neck.

"*This* was the best you had? Biggest cellar in the whole City, and all you found was sugary rubbish? Is your absinthe off limits to fleabags?"

Terence floundered, but Phoebe handed over the forty solidi, then uncorked the bottle and drank straight from it. A few of the nearby Lords threw her a disapproving glance. She responded with an exaggerated grin, and moved further away for some peace.

"A little early in the day for that, isn't it?" a sleek voice asked from beside her.

Phoebe recognised who it was instantly. She had known it wouldn't be long.

"Please, Vixen," she said. "What's the difference between wine and whatever else is on offer? You could use some. Might loosen you up a bit."

"I don't think so," Melissa said coldly.

"Of course you don't," Phoebe muttered. She raised the bottle in mock salutation.

Melissa was still wearing her Constabulary clothes, but with a longer formal jacket, trimmed in lace. She had also tied her hair into a bun and powdered it: something she only did for special occasions. It softened her face a little, but her eyes were as fierce as ever.

Phoebe didn't look away. She had known many Chief Officers in her day, but none as obstinate as this woman. In different circumstances, she might have found herself admiring it.

"Rather upsetting about Aspinall Square, isn't it?" Melissa said. "It seems squares are rapidly becoming places of unrest."

"They always have been," Phoebe replied. "It's just unfortunate you've seen it twice in quick succession. Your hair would have curled a few hundred years ago, when the lunafauna realised the change had been limited to just one day. Every square in Faunatown was on fire."

Melissa rolled her eyes. "I know you like to blame us for everything, but what our ancestors did is rather out of our control. Not everyone is as blessed as you when it comes to longevity."

"If you think it's a blessing, you're dumber than I gave you credit for. And while none of you caused it, you've done no favours for breaking it."

"It's unnecessary, that's why. Just like what happened two weeks ago."

"It's dealt with," Phoebe snapped. "You don't have to concern yourself with it. Or my people."

Melissa's expression dripped with venom. "I concern myself with everything, My Lady."

"So I'm aware," Phoebe said curtly.

She could have laughed. These fools were all the same, happy to bask in their own filth simply because it was prettied up and smelled of sugar. They thought themselves so untouchable, so immortal. If they knew the truth of that, they would hardly be so arrogant about it.

She drank again. Melissa watched with wordless disdain. Her face was as stoic and unreserved as always, but Phoebe had been around her long enough to know when her blood was boiling. It would be betrayed by small involuntary twitches at the corner of her mouth, the way her eyes sparkled with warning.

"I want you to know I won't stand for that sort of behaviour in Faunatown again, and neither will the Potentate," Melissa said. She moved her hands so the one with the red ring was resting on top.

Phoebe didn't even flinch.

"Maybe if you had the grace to treat them with equality, you wouldn't have to worry about anything."

"And if they had the grace to behave any differently than livestock, such a proposal could be considered."

"Then let's make a deal, shall we?" Phoebe said icily. "Your ancestors appointed me the lunafauna leader. We all know I do a damn better job of running the show than your people do. So you keep your nose out of Faunatown, and I'll make sure it stays running."

Melissa gave her an acidic smile.

"My officers will be sent wherever there is discord, Lady Feline. If you obstruct me, or them, then you're facilitating that discord. You're in no position to threaten me."

Phoebe glared at her. "Likewise."

"And you're lying to yourself," said Melissa. "You might be the leader of Faunatown, but you are still subservient to the Potentate, just like all your kind. You *will* remember that."

"Of course," said Phoebe, "because who else can allow me to shift again?"

"Exactly. Which reminds me: how comfortable is your collar? I was meaning to ask. Is the magic tight enough for your liking?"

Phoebe knew that remark had been coming. But she parried the blow with a pleasant grin, which showed her pointed canines just enough. It was time to play her trump card.

"It's about as comfortable as your own little secret, I'd imagine."

She cast a deliberate glance towards Daniel.

Melissa's eyes widened. It was subtle; most no-tails wouldn't have noticed. But Phoebe's vision was twice as sharp as any others' in the room. And she recognised the emotion behind it, too. The Vixen was afraid.

"I don't know what you're talking about," said Melissa.

"Yes, you do," Phoebe replied, lowering her voice. "Feline ears are sensitive things. And what mine have heard has come straight from the gutter."

"Who told you?"

"Nobody. I'd simply advise you to be a little quieter whenever he pays you a visit in the Roots. You're lucky it was only me who was passing by."

"And how long have you known?" Melissa hissed.

Phoebe smiled. She was enjoying this joust far too much. "Would you prefer a lie or the truth?"

Melissa swallowed. Then she drew closer, danger in her eyes.

"I trust you know how to hold your tongue better than your drink."

"Don't insult me," Phoebe said dramatically. "You'll be hard pressed to find anyone who holds their drink better than me. If you *did* ever dare to down a few, I'd run you into the ground."

Melissa gripped Phoebe's shoulder.

"Let's keep this between ourselves, shall we? I wouldn't want us to stop being friends."

"Oh, neither would I," said Phoebe.

"So keep your mouth shut."

"Don't worry. Your secret's safe with me. Potentates have always been able to do whatever they want. And let's not forget Daniel has work to do yet. He still needs one more child. One to rule and one to run. And after the hassle he and Elisabeth had with Nicolas… Well, he needs all the *practise* he can get."

Melissa opened her mouth to retort, but was cut off by the chime of a glass being tapped. At once, everyone rose to their feet. The Ladies hovered beside their husbands, and Daniel helped Elisabeth off the couch.

Phoebe gave a sarcastic pout. "Oh, dear. Looks like we'll have to end our little chat prematurely."

Melissa shot Phoebe one final scowl, then strode away to stand sentinel at the balcony doors. Phoebe watched her go. The blow had landed just as she'd known it would. It was a small victory, but valued nonetheless.

The needle twitched under her skin. She scratched at it, took another quick gulp of wine, then waited as the Parliamentary Fellows lined up. This end of the Pavilion backed straight onto the

West Quarter, and a special wide balcony fanned out from the suite, visible to many streets in the Second West. Even from where she stood, Phoebe could see that the Level below was packed with people.

But she'd been right. There were fewer than thirty years ago. All the bunting hadn't worked as well as it should have done.

The Tower clock struck noon and reverberated through the building. The doors opened, and a wave of cheers erupted as the company moved onto the balcony. Daniel and Elisabeth went straight to the front centre with Nicolas, while Phoebe kept to the far end, glad to be left alone at last.

The heating mechanism groaned and the light fixtures flickered. Phoebe turned her eyes skyward, imagining the Keeper a hundred feet above her head. And all these people around her… So oblivious, like children playing pretend.

If only they knew.

CHAPTER XIV

The crowds made Charlotte feel sick. There was too much movement, too much noise. She clung to Miss Gilbaut's skirt and imagined she could see the baby that everyone was cheering for. It was difficult enough to make out individual adults up there, let alone a tiny infant, but she tried.

She was glad when it was over and the class returned to the omnibus. But as she climbed inside and sat next to Julian — the bespectacled boy who had smiled at her on her first day — a darkness settled over her like cold rain. The presentation had been a welcome distraction, but now there was nothing to shield her from what would come the following day.

Tomorrow, her parents would be laid to rest.

Malcolm was waiting at the Academy gates. Charlotte bid a hasty goodbye to Julian and Miss Gilbaut, and ran straight to him.

"Was it good?" Malcolm asked.

"I couldn't really see anything," Charlotte replied. "Why didn't you come?"

Malcolm shrugged. "I'm not that interested. And I had work to get on with."

Charlotte heard a tightness in his voice, remembered how he and the Potentate had used to be friends. It made sense that he wouldn't want to get involved with anything.

When they returned to the shop, Charlotte immediately

began taking the mantel clock apart. She didn't care that she had already reassembled it. She needed something to occupy her mind against the barrage of emotions threatening to engulf her. Even the ceaseless ticking from downstairs held something of a comfort now. It was steady, constant, never doing anything except exactly what she expected. The sound encircled her, safe and secure. And, as Malcolm had said, work helped to chase away the internal noise, until only blessed silence remained.

Her wounds ached. At the weekend, her stitches had finally been removed, but the skin was still tender. She supposed, in some form, she would feel the bullets forever.

She awoke early the next morning, but stayed huddled in bed, listening to the Tower's chimes. She wasn't sure if she wanted them to speed up or slow down. She pulled the blankets tight and tried to imagine her mother's spell. But it felt wrong and empty, like a thin sheet over a great dark pit.

Malcolm helped Charlotte into an austere dress that fell straight to her ankles. Then he pinned her hair, with markedly more ease than his first attempt weeks ago, and tied the top with a cascade of black ribbons. Finally, he handed her a bonnet, which she put on herself.

She glanced at her mother's wristwatch. Malcolm had replaced the glass and cleaned it, so it looked as perfect as the day it was made.

"Are you ready, kiddo?" he asked quietly.

Charlotte's stomach churned. "No."

Malcolm grimaced. "Me, neither."

He took her hand, locked the shop and called for a cab. Charlotte tried to block out her senses as she climbed into the back. All carriages were black, but now, wearing black clothes, with no pastels or even browns in sight, she felt as if she herself were entering a hearse.

A horrible thought flickered through her head. She *should* be in the hearse.

She dug her nails into her palms, focused on the pain, and stared out of the window. The cab made its way around the Fifth Level until they reached the East Quarter, then began descending through the Interlevels. The surroundings transformed from smart clean buildings to dilapidated shells. Grime-coated chimney stacks towered against the smoggy sky. Cracked plaster exposed the bricks underneath, caked with so much dirt, they looked as though they were made of coal. People staggered about, begging so feebly that the wind snatched the words straight out of their mouths. The sour stench of human waste hit Charlotte's nose and she held her breath to avoid smelling it. Something else lingered underneath it: cold and heavy, which dragged over her skin like slimy fingers. Despair.

She had never seen the slums before, had never been below the Seventh Level. Was this what her father had been trying to make better? By the time the carriage reached the Twelfth East, she barely believed she could still be in the same City.

She noticed a wall, thirty feet tall and almost half as thick. It ran around the entire Twelfth Level on all sides, to keep it from sprawling into the Meadows like a festering wound. Every few miles, a tunnel gouged through it, decorated to resemble gates as some kind of aesthetic afterthought.

The carriage halted outside one of them, and Charlotte and Malcolm walked into the emptiness beyond. A depressing void of grey land stretched as far as the eye could see. The ground was bare earth, studded with old bricks and discarded rubbish. Charlotte tried to imagine the entire space filled with living trees, or even flowers, like the paper ones she admired. But it was impossible. Nothing could ever grow here, and she had only ever seen drawings of trees in old books. How could a plant grow to be taller than a house?

Thinking about it was too much work, so she turned her attention to the graveyard in the distance. The Meadows were also divided into Quarters: the South and West contained the farms and glasshouses; the North had the wells, which fed the artificial river systems; and the dead occupied the East. A single road snaked towards it, cobbles half-buried and broken.

A crowd of mourners approached. Charlotte recognised a few of the faces: Lords and Ladies who her mother had entertained in the drawing room. Others, she didn't know at all, but she gathered by their cheaper clothes that they were the people her father had helped. The aristocrats sniffed when they saw them. Some muttered in disgust and brushed at their sleeves, as though even the sight of the commoners soiled them.

Malcolm's nose twitched with irritation. And, for the first time in her life, Charlotte felt the same. These people were *her* people. Even their mourning clothes were ludicrously elaborate, made to the height of fashion, and would likely be thrown away at the end of the month. How many had ridden through the slums with the curtains drawn in their carriages?

Some might be there because they had loved her parents. But they were also there to save face. It was all just a show.

Then Charlotte noticed the hearse, and her throat turned to ice. Inside lay two plain metal coffins.

Her mind shrank away from her body, like the final glow of a bulb before it faded to nothing. Her parents were in there. But as quickly as the thought became real, another slammed into her, as hard as if she had been punched. The coffins were too small. They were the correct size, of course, but was *that* all her mother and father had been? Enough to fit into a box narrower than the bookcase in her old bedroom?

Someone moved on the other side of the hearse. A boy was

looking at the coffins too, his face dark with respect. He was older than her, maybe fourteen or fifteen, hair as black as his clothes. Had her father helped him as well?

He glanced at Charlotte, and her heart raced when she saw his eyes. One was blue, the other brown.

She hesitated. Should she speak to him? Her tongue sat heavy in her mouth like a slug. She couldn't think, couldn't do anything…

The boy turned away.

"Come on," Malcolm whispered to her, choking on tears. "It's time to go."

The procession moved out, and the graveyard built itself around them with the creeping advance of slipping into a dream. First came the mass and pauper graves, the bodies coated with a thin layer of quicklime. Some were defaced: a result of robbers coming to take the corpses. Others had been recently exhumed so the remains could be stored in the Cavern of Skulls: the massive ossuary beneath the Eleventh and Twelfth Levels. No matter how large the East Meadows were, they couldn't contain everyone forever. Only the rich stayed indefinitely.

The graves grew more elaborate, and reared higher, like shadows made solid. Charlotte had never seen anywhere so completely abandoned by life. The mausoleums clustered together in a windowless ghost town. They were all closed, save for one, with BELLAMY carved upon the lintel. Charlotte looked down the corridor, lined with tiny doors.

Malcolm stepped forward and, with the help of a couple of other men, lifted the first coffin onto his shoulders. They walked to a hole in the wall and slid it into the dark. Then they did the same with the second one.

The scene blurred as tears spilled from Charlotte's eyes. This was too real, too close. She twisted her fingers together until they hurt. Quiet sobs rippled through her body and threatened to shake her into a million pieces.

She wanted to run, like she had from the Academy, and never look back. But she stood still, and turned her attention on the other doors in the wall. Some were unclaimed, but most were already sealed and named. She recognised a handful from her father's old stories.

KATHARINE M. BELLAMY
THOMAS V. BELLAMY
LEOPOLD R. BELLAMY

Charlotte let out a deep breath. She supposed she herself was undergoing a kind of death. She might not be alongside her parents, but her earlier thought of belonging in the hearse wasn't far from the truth. A part of her had died in Rene too, and she had been mourning that just as much as them.

She let the moment consume her like a black cloud. It had been there all the time, always felt, rarely seen. It was the opposite and final remnant of the spell: the realisation that blankets were not shields, and the world hid an ugly face beneath virgin snow.

Her memory settled on the tall police officer's face, with her glassy face and dark braid like a hornet's sting. It was all *her* fault. *She* had chased them, given the order, pulled the trigger. Charlotte would never forget her, and never forgive her.

When the ceremony was over, the attendees approached to offer their condolences. Several of the Counts reminded Charlotte that she would always be welcome in the Parliamentary when she was old enough. She let the words roll off her. She could *never* be like them, not now. Not after all she had seen. She would keep her father's kindness and humility, apply it to her new life, and make it good.

A feline lunafauna walked over. A ring swung from her left ear and a long scar stretched over her forehead. She was clad in a black dress that even Charlotte knew was very old-fashioned; well-made, but faded around the hems. She caught the faint whiff of alcohol on the fabric.

"I'm sorry for your loss," the feline said. "Take care of yourself. You too, Mr Godwin."

Malcolm nodded and put an arm around Charlotte.

"Thank you. We'll take care of each other."

Charlotte looked around for the boy with the strange eyes, but he had disappeared.

Back in the City, over a thousand feet into the sky, the Tower bells struck midday.

The final toll clapped like thunder. The Timekeeper lifted his hand from the ringing mechanism, then climbed the spiral staircase to the topmost chamber. As he closed the trapdoor, his fingers brushed against the words he had carved into the floorboards so long ago. Sunlight streamed through the four clock faces set into each wall, and cast the soft shadows of their numerals across the ground.

He approached the eastern one, and peered through at the graveyard. The distance would have been too far for any human to see, or even a lunafauna with the keenest vision. But he was not human, or lunafauna. He was much more.

He spotted the two figures standing outside the mausoleum. A man and a girl. Malcolm Godwin and Charlotte Bellamy. They moved slowly, behind the congregation. They believed they had all the time in the world.

The Keeper touched his chest. They did, for now.

As he watched them, he saw the moments both had been born. Then another time, not yet realised, when the little girl would be a woman. She cowered in a bathroom and whispered a mantra to calm herself. She hid her hair, cut short, under a wig. A scalpel slid across an orb, followed by a bloodcurdling scream.

All relative. The turning wheel, wrapped in the Fabric of Time. People called it ancient magic, but like him, it was more than that. It was simply nature; manipulated, amplified: the threads of existence tied together in new ways to make the invisible visible. Or the living undying.

And only he could see them.

He heard the creak of ancient hinges, followed by footsteps.

"Hello, Daniel," said the Keeper. He didn't turn around, didn't even blink.

The Potentate approached cautiously, and stood several feet away. He was terrified of the Keeper touching him.

"You know why I'm here," Daniel said.

"Yes."

"You do realise—"

"This is all *my* fault."

Daniel screwed his eyes shut. "Please get out of my head."

"I'm not in your head," said the Keeper. "You are simply predictable, just like everyone out there. So emotional. What else would you do, but blame me?"

"Because you are to blame," Daniel snarled. "There are two bodies being put into that mausoleum today. There should have been three."

"Do you honestly want to argue about what should be? I know you considered killing Charlotte Bellamy, but I also knew you wouldn't. You don't have it in you. You feel you already have the blood of enough children on your hands."

Daniel's breath tightened in his throat. The Keeper heard it, sensed the contraction of every muscle and the flow of air into his lungs. But he couldn't *feel* it. That was beyond his power. He had no need for such functions, and so he had forgotten them.

Daniel's lungs… The Keeper saw them in so many ways. First, as a youngster, laughing alongside three other boys, decades ago. At the same time, he heard those lungs singing a lullaby to Nicolas Carter, crying over an infant child under a glass cover, moaning into Melissa Spectre's ear…

So many uses for a single breath, never ending or beginning.

Daniel raised his voice, louder than normal, so he could hear himself over the clicking mechanisms.

"I have no blood on my hands," he said.

"You lie to yourself, not to me."

"You will not speak to me like that."

"I will speak however I wish."

"And I'd hoped a few weeks of isolation would have taught you a lesson."

"They were no different to every minute," said the Keeper. "There's nothing you can do to punish me."

"Do you have any idea of the mess you've made?" Daniel snarled. "I still haven't finished cleaning it up!"

"Messes are a matter of perspective."

"Don't give me that crap. What were you even thinking, revealing yourself to August like that? How can someone as intelligent as you be such an idiot?"

Daniel's words were firm, but above them lingered the icy edge of unease. He was afraid, always afraid. This was, after all, the one part of Forest which stood higher than him.

The Keeper kept his eyes straight ahead. This chamber served a greater purpose than any insignificant human agendas which might play out in the streets below. It was more than Daniel could comprehend: a place where past, present and future ran alongside each other in a fluid dance.

So many threads, leading into so many strings, weaving together, connecting, spinning…

"Did you hear me?" Daniel snapped.

"I heard you," said the Keeper. He carried on watching Charlotte Bellamy. "All is as it should be."

PART TWO
ALBEDO
'PURIFICATION'

IF THERE WERE MACHINES
WHICH BORE A RESEMBLANCE
TO OUR BODY AND IMITATED
OUR ACTIONS AS FAR AS IT WAS
MORALLY POSSIBLE TO DO SO,
WE SHOULD ALWAYS RECOGNISE
THAT, FOR ALL THAT,
THEY WERE NOT REAL MEN.

CHAPTER XV

Twelve years later

Dawn light glinted across the rooftops, but the West Quarter remained in shadow, as it always did first thing in the morning. Icicles hung off the gutters like teeth. Saltmen walked the streets with bins of grit, shovelling it over the main thoroughfares. The winter had proved milder than usual, and the snow had melted early, but then frozen solid into treacherous sheets.

Charlotte was glad for it. She would always rather skid on ice than walk through snow. As treacherous as it could be, it never stained.

She pushed open the Academy gate and checked her wristwatch. There was time to catch her breath before class, so she sat on a bench and watched a group of younger boys trundling hoops with sticks. Today was the first of the new term, and her final year of advanced academics. By next Midwinter, she would be a qualified alchemist.

Someone tapped her shoulder. Julian was behind her, balancing on the wall with his arms outstretched.

"Good morning," he smiled.

"Good broken neck," Charlotte replied. "Get off there before Dickinson sees!"

"Ah, she won't cane me," Julian smirked, but he still leapt down. He perched beside Charlotte, checked nobody was looking, then revealed a pile of caramels.

Charlotte shot him a wicked grin. "Stopped by old man Kane's place on the way, did you?"

Julian winked. "He never saw a thing. Go on."

Charlotte took a caramel, and wedged it in her cheek so she could suck it and still talk. Julian flicked another into his mouth and pocketed the rest.

"Can I ask you a favour?" he asked.

In answer, Charlotte held out her hand. Julian passed over a sheet of paper. It was an essay which Dickinson had set them to complete before the first class.

"It looks fine," Charlotte said as she skimmed through it. "Oh, wait… there's one here. You've got the letters mixed up."

Julian growled under his breath. Charlotte fetched a pen and carefully corrected the mistake, then another couple while he wasn't looking.

"You're getting better," she insisted. "This time last year, your lines weren't even straight."

Julian shook his head. "I'm nearly twenty-one and I can't spell. What chance have I got of being an alchemist?"

"Well, *I* think you'll be fantastic."

"You're biased."

"I'm not! You're one of the smartest people I know. And Dickinson hasn't given up hope on you."

"Because my father would kill her if she did."

"Because she's your aunt, and she wants you to succeed," Charlotte insisted. "She wouldn't have fostered you all summer if she didn't want to help. And you know I'll always help you, too."

Julian slipped the paper back into his bag. He was the same boy who'd stood beside Charlotte on Presentation Day, with his spectacles and tidy blonde hair, but the years had been kind to him and left him oddly handsome. She had changed, too: her hair was still long and dark, but she had mastered the art of pinning it into a bun. A leaner diet had stripped away puppy fat and daily walks between the Levels had bulked out the muscles in her calves. Now both of them were twenty, only one year from legal adulthood.

The sound of the Tower bells floated on the air, followed by the smaller chimes of hundreds of other clocks within the Fourth Level. They rang three quarters: fifteen minutes until classes began.

"By the way," said Julian, "I've got a commission for you, if you don't mind?"

"Thanks," said Charlotte. "But what is it? If it's big—"

"It's not," Julian replied, and produced a small handheld music box. "This is my mother's. It broke a couple of weeks ago. She loves it, so I wanted to get it fixed for her birthday."

Charlotte inspected the box: a simple rectangle, with delicate leaf patterns on every surface.

"Malcolm made this," she said.

"Really? How do you know? His maker's mark?"

"Well, yeah, that too. But I can just tell. And he made me a similar one, a while ago."

She lifted the drum to expose the mechanism underneath. It was tiny: some of the cogs were smaller than her fingernail and the mainspring was like a strand of hair.

"When's your mother's birthday?" she asked.

"Saturday."

"Oh, you left me loads of time, didn't you?"

Julian frowned. "Why? Is it really bad?"

Charlotte jostled him with her elbow. "I'm only pulling your leg. One of the gears has slipped, that's all. See? The screw's come out. I can fix it now."

"I thought you'd have to take it home with you."

"No, it's an easy job. I've actually got that size of screwdriver with me."

"What? Why?"

"Force of habit. Malcolm always carries basic equipment, for emergencies. In case any mechanisms come apart, or something."

Charlotte rummaged in her satchel for her tool pouch, held a loupe to her eye, and quickly disassembled the music box. Then she extracted the loose screw, nudged the gear back into position, and twisted a tiny screwdriver against it. The blade spun in her hand with practised speed, never slipping. When it was tight, she fitted the drum back inside the casing and turned the handle. The comb plucked out a melody, as perfect as the day it had been made.

"There you go," she said. "You just need a ribbon now."

Julian grinned. "Thanks! I wish I could do stuff like this!"

"Well, you're practically ready to do surgeries," Charlotte countered. "There's no way I'd manage anything like that. The joys of coming from a medical family, huh? At least you won't get covered in grease."

"No, only blood and guts."

Charlotte shot a sideways glance at Julian. She could see the peach fuzz on his cheek, the small patch of stubble which he'd missed shaving that morning. His hair hung shorter than the other boys, just reaching his ears. His father had probably made him cut it before term started.

He wound the music box handle again. A few notes tinkled into the air.

"How much do you want for this?" he asked.

"Nothing."

The word was out of Charlotte's mouth before Julian had

even finished. She tried to shrug it off, but she knew she was blushing.

"Honestly?" Julian asked.

"Yeah. I'm not at the shop, so let's just call this one off the books."

Julian smiled, and Charlotte's heart fluttered. He shuffled a little closer. He'd been her friend for so long, but he was so sweet, and nobody had ever looked at her like that...

Nerves overwhelmed her. She wrenched open her satchel and thrust the screwdriver back into its pouch. One of her books tumbled onto the floor. She went to scoop it up, but Julian beat her to it, and his hand brushed hers.

Charlotte accidentally swallowed the caramel. She pressed her heel into the ground so she wouldn't kick herself.

The Tower struck nine. Charlotte snatched the book and made a show of straightening her dress. Julian didn't say anything, but she wasn't sure if that was a relief or not.

Two boys joined them on the way to the classroom. Tobias and Eugene Clark: the only others who had taken the third year of advanced academics. Tobias sat behind Charlotte and flicked her bun with his finger.

"Morning, *My Lady*," he sneered.

"Piss off," Charlotte snapped.

Dickinson strode through the door, her hair so heavily powdered, it seemed almost white. She was only in her fifties, but it made her look much older.

"Welcome back, everyone," she said, and began drawing a spherical object on the chalkboard. She didn't even pause to copy from a diagram; she pulled the image straight from her own memory. Charlotte recognised what it was, but said nothing. She had seen the same picture in a book which she'd read over the Midwinter break.

Eventually, Dickinson stood aside.

"Welcome to your final year," she said. "This is the time when you'll begin honing your theory into something you can use. From now on, we'll be covering practical alchemy. Or, in more simple terms, orbs."

Charlotte knotted her fingers together in excitement. This was what she had looked forward to for years.

"Am I correct in assuming you all know what orbs do, even if you've never seen them?" Dickinson continued, then glanced at Julian. "Don't you answer. You already have an advantage."

Charlotte raised her hand.

"They're little balls of light that can be attached to a mainspring, so a mechanism doesn't have to be rewound for a whole lifetime."

"Correct, Miss Bellamy," Dickinson said. "Take note: for a *lifetime*, not *forever*. And the reason they aren't seen very often is because they're expensive. But since you're going to study them, it's best if you see them up close. Tomorrow, we'll be visiting my family's studio: the Cropper Lane Orb Works. Transport will cost ten solidi a head, and it must be handed to me before we leave in the morning."

She picked up a long metal rod and pointed it at the Clarks. "And I will tell *you* right now. Do not, under any circumstances, try to access the restricted areas. Is that clear?"

They nodded. "Yes, Ma'am."

"Good." Dickinson gestured to the board. "Now, before you work with orbs in any advanced capacity, you'll need to take the Alchemical Oath. But we don't have to worry about that for a while. This year, you'll be learning about orb structure: the core, and how to weave magic around it. At their largest, orbs are the size of a fist, and at their smallest, more akin to a bead. But the latter is the only size you're likely to find nowadays. It means they may run for only a couple of decades as opposed to over a century, but they're still incredibly powerful objects."

Dickinson moved the rod into the centre of the drawing. It reminded Charlotte of the way Malcolm had described it when she was a child: *"Like a boiled egg cut in half, but with the yolk still intact."*

"Inside all orbs is the core," said Dickinson. "To tell whether an orb is spent or not, you need to inspect it. A working orb will emit a white glow, as Miss Bellamy mentioned. That comes from the magic bound into it. But if you cut it open, it should also pulse. Do you understand?"

"Yes, Ma'am," said the students.

"Now, to access the core, you must cut it down the centre. As long as the incision is straight and doesn't pass all the way through, you won't rupture it. This is the infinity incision, but in the oldest literature, you'll see it called the eternal cut."

Charlotte's blood suddenly felt as though ice had been shot into it. She'd spent the past two years reading about orbs. Every book mentioned the infinity incision. Never once had she heard the other term, and it stung her.

It sounded like something else, which she had spoken so little about. She had pushed it down, out of sight. Yet now, in a heartbeat, she heard her father shouting.

Eternal cut… *Cor Aeternum.*

"Miss Bellamy?"

Charlotte jumped so violently that she almost fell out of her chair. Dickinson stormed over.

"I'll remind you that your guardian scrimped and saved for you to carry on your schooling with me. I'd advise you not to waste his money by spending time inside your own head."

"I'm sorry," Charlotte said. The words shook their way out

of her mouth. The panic grew, pushing against her ribs. It felt as though somebody had grasped her lungs and was squeezing them to bursting point.

Dickinson's expression softened. She lowered her voice. "You're excused."

Relief tightened around Charlotte's throat. She walked outside as calmly as she could, then bolted into the girls' bathroom and locked herself in the end stall.

"Get a grip!" she snapped, but it didn't work. Every inhale brought a vision of stone chips flying through the air, blood pouring from her mother's lips, two bullets embedding themselves in her flesh…

Desperate, she switched to the old mantra Malcolm had given her.

"Twenty-three people were shot in Rene Square, but I survived. I miss my parents, but they live on through me. I can't reverse the past, but the past can't hurt me. Nobody controls my life but me."

She tried to time her breathing with the words. Just like the clocks in the shop, steady and sure, back and forth, to and fro.

Slowly, the pain began to recede. Then the door opened.

"Charlotte? I saw you come in here."

Charlotte didn't move. It was Miss Gilbaut.

"I'm fine," she said quickly.

"You're not. I can hear it in your voice," said Miss Gilbaut. "Please, come out. It's alright."

She spoke as though trying to calm a frightened animal. Shame burned Charlotte's chest. She steeled herself and unlocked the cubicle.

Miss Gilbaut stood by the sinks. Charlotte knew why she'd placed herself there: so she wouldn't block the door. Malcolm had once said that fear triggered the old part of a person which had once lived in the wilderness, and the natural response was always to run. If anyone would still understand that instinct clearly, it was a lunafauna.

"Oh, look at you," Miss Gilbaut said gently. "What's happened?"

"Nothing."

"Why don't you sit with me for five minutes? Do you want to talk? I'm not teaching this morning."

"I can't. I've got to get back to class."

"I'll tell Doctor Dickinson that you need to see me first. I'm sure she'll go over what you've missed if you ask her."

Charlotte closed her eyes despondently.

"She shouldn't have to. I should be over this by now!"

"There's no such thing as *should*," replied Miss Gilbaut. She took Charlotte's hand, directed her into her own classroom, then walked towards Dickinson's door.

Charlotte leaned against the wall with a groan. She hadn't been here since she finished her essential education two years ago. Midwinter streamers cascaded from the ceiling. They would be coming down in a couple of days.

Miss Gilbaut reappeared and opened the window.

"I know it's chilly, but let's have some fresh air for now," she remarked. "I've told Doctor Dickinson you're with me. She said it's fine. Just go and see her at recess."

Miss Gilbaut perched on the rim of her desk. She still wore the same patterned dresses, which Charlotte knew were expensive in Faunatown but simple elsewhere. Her face had sagged a little over the years, but her natural snowy fur hid those hairs which had paled with age.

Warmth ran over Charlotte as though she had settled next to a heating coil. In a way, Miss Gilbaut reminded her of her mother. Nothing had come close to recreating the spell, but she was so soft and kind, every word seemed like a miniature embrace. Charlotte knew she could speak to her old teacher about anything, and even if there were no answers, she would be comforted all the same.

"Are you having a good first day back?" asked Miss Gilbaut. She swept her tail to the side so it curled around one of the desk legs.

"So far," said Charlotte. "Until *that* happened. We're studying orbs."

"I bet you'll enjoy that. You've been looking forward to it for a while, haven't you? And I heard you're going on a field trip tomorrow?"

Charlotte looked at her feet.

"Something Doctor Dickinson said made me think back. It just came out of nowhere. And I don't know why."

"Memories can have a nasty habit of springing up when we least expect them. There's nothing wrong with that," said Miss Gilbaut. She clasped Charlotte's hand between two paws. The fleshy pads on her palms felt warm after the cold bathroom. "It's not a bad thing that you have these little flashes. If anything, it's good. It shows you remember, and that you've learned from it."

Charlotte swallowed. "Miss Gilbaut…"

"I've told you, you don't have to call me that anymore. It's Evelyn. I'm not your teacher now."

"I know, but it sounds strange. The same way I'd… never call Malcolm anything else."

Miss Gilbaut smiled. "Whatever makes you comfortable. What were you going to say?"

Charlotte looked at her. "Do you know what *Cor Aeternum* means?"

After carrying the words in her memory for so long, it was strange to speak them aloud. They felt like poisonous barbs in her throat: something sensed but not seen, an invisible illness spreading its malaise through air and blood.

Miss Gilbaut's ears lowered in concentration.

"My Latin was never the best, if I'm honest. But I think I know what those words are. *Aeternum* means eternal, and *Cor* is heart."

"Eternal heart?" Charlotte repeated. "But... that doesn't make any sense."

"What doesn't?" Miss Gilbaut asked.

Charlotte didn't answer straightaway. Malcolm had told her to be careful. She'd kept the details close, pressed them down to a place where they could stay numb. But with every passing year, their presence wore at her, like rain against stone. She felt it whenever she was alone, standing topless before the mirror in her bedroom, inspecting her scars.

This Midwinter had marked twelve years since she fled across Rene Square. It felt as though she had never stopped running.

"It wasn't a lunafauna, you know," she said. "That was a lie."

Miss Gilbaut's eyes widened. *"What?"*

A silent part of Charlotte screamed in protest, but she pushed it aside. Malcolm knew the truth. It was time someone else did.

"There was a carriage waiting for us. On the way, we were stopped by a woman in a Constabulary uniform. We got away from her, but she caught us in the square with some other officers. My father shouted those words, *Cor Aeternum*, and something about the Keeper. Then they started shooting."

Miss Gilbaut's ears went flat against her head and her pupils grew huge.

"Oh, dear girl," she breathed.

She pressed her forehead against Charlotte's, then hugged her. Charlotte didn't fight, just allowed herself to melt into the soft milky fur. There was no need to be afraid of a memory. For as horrid as it was, it was in the past, where it belonged.

The window wasn't open by much, but crouched underneath it, Oscar Hargreaves closed his eyes. For years, he'd climbed into bed with a light heart. He had watched from afar, listened through cracks, vigilant for those two fateful words. And now, after so long in silence, she had finally said them.

His entire body twisted against itself. Conscience and duty swung back and forth in his mind like a pendulum.

He crept away from the Academy, and hid behind the lighting mechanism near the fence. It ground its freshly-oiled gears together in a never-ending circle, slower than normal, just enough to keep the chain working until the evening. Oscar glanced at the mainspring at its centre, pictured its components extending into the ground, through the Roots, then up the Tower.

The Keeper's silhouette flashed in his mind. *Cor Aeternum.*

He slipped into the antechamber below the lightsman's hut. Every second of the elevator's descent felt too fast, and when it finally reached the Roots, he didn't move. A thought invaded his mind: was he hesitating so the subterranean lamps wouldn't dazzle him, or because he wanted to delay what he had to do?

He entered the Circulus headquarters, and knocked on the door to Melissa Spectre's office.

"Come in."

Oscar turned the handle with trembling fingers. Melissa sat behind her desk, organising a pile of papers. She took a drag of a cigarette and tapped the ash into a tray.

"Hargreaves," she said, then motioned to the documents with a snarl of disgust. "Look at this! Seventeen years leading everyone, not a page out of place. I have six months off duty, and my fool of an assistant leaves this mess!"

Melissa rubbed her leg with a grimace. Just after last Midsummer, she had broken it in two places during a mission to the Eleventh North. Potentate Carter had insisted she take leave for as long as she needed. So she'd disappeared into her house and refused all visits. She had barely been back for a week, but already her experience and resolve were making themselves felt once again.

She shot an inquisitive look at Oscar.

"What are you doing here, anyway? It's not even ten o' clock."

Oscar sighed.

"Forgive me, Madam… it's Charlotte Bellamy."

Melissa froze. She stubbed out her cigarette and rose to her feet.

"She's talked."

CHAPTER XVI

The Tower clock struck four, and Charlotte headed home. Her eyes roved everywhere. She couldn't stop replaying what she had said to Miss Gilbaut. The anxious part of her insisted she had done something terribly wrong, but most of all, a weight lifted from her shoulders. She had carried it since she was eight years old. Now, she felt as though she was walking with a lighter step than she had in a long time.

And then there was Julian.

Charlotte glanced at her hand, where his finger had knocked against hers. She smiled. Yes, everything was going to be alright. Perhaps, soon, she could truly be Charlotte Bellamy again.

She reached the watch shop and burst through the door. The bell jingled so loudly, Malcolm stepped out of the back room.

"Everything alright?" he asked.

"Yeah. Fine," replied Charlotte.

"Then what do you want to talk to me about? You don't come in like a madwoman unless you need to say something."

Charlotte pulled a sheet of paper from her satchel.

"Doctor Dickinson's taking us on a field trip to her orb workshop. But I need ten solidi for the omnibus. Tomorrow."

Malcolm stared at the form in astonishment. "She's taking you to *Cropper Lane?* What I wouldn't have given to see that place when I was your age!"

"What you wouldn't give to see it *now*," Charlotte said

with a smile.

She fetched her work apron and tied it over her dress. Malcolm had kept his promise: every night when she had returned from school, he taught her the ways of his craft. When she'd managed to completely disassemble and reassemble the old mantel clock without any direction, he had named her his assistant. He'd even set up a second workbench beside his own.

Charlotte's love for mechanics had never waned. The three Rs were still all she needed, and a steady hand and patience. But alchemy was different. It was a dance of magic and science, which remained as fascinating as it had when she was a child. And soon, she would be qualified. She could take the next step: the one which both she and Malcolm had spoken about for years.

Malcolm placed the form on her bench.

"Mr Downey should be here tomorrow morning to get that phonograph. Take ten solidi out of his payment before you leave."

At once, Charlotte set to work. The phonograph's entire mechanism had needed replacing, and the mainspring was so old, it wouldn't coil properly. She had already fixed most of it. Now all she needed to do was put it back into the casing.

"I think Julian likes me, you know," she blurted, unable to contain her excitement about it any longer.

Malcolm glanced up with a witty smile.

"I dropped my book today and he got it for me," she explained.

"Oh? That was nice of him."

"And he touched my hand."

"Did he?"

Charlotte looked over her shoulder. "You think I'm being silly, don't you?"

Malcolm shrugged, still smiling. "No. I'm just glad you've finally admitted it."

"What? You already had an idea?"

"It's been written across your face since last term."

Charlotte's heart sank. Who else had seen right through her?

"It was that obvious?" she asked sheepishly.

"Only to someone who knows you like I do," Malcolm said gently. "Don't overthink it, kiddo. He's a nice boy. And it's fine for you to like each other. Your father and I used to chase girls when we were your age. But it was your Uncle Leo who always ended up with the admirers. Even when we were kids."

A nostalgic shine came into Malcolm's eyes. His face bore a few more lines, and his hair was streaked with grey, as though someone had shaken salt and pepper all over his scalp. But his hands were as sure as ever, moving so skilfully over a thaumatrope, Charlotte thought he would have been able to work it blindfolded.

She rewound a new mainspring, carefully, so it wouldn't fly open and hit her.

"How old was Uncle Leo when he died?" she wondered aloud. "I mean, Papa always said he was young, but if he ended up with admirers…"

"They were just silly little girls with a first crush. Leo was only twelve," Malcolm said. "About two years older than me and your father at the time. But he was the handsome one, if you know what I mean."

"How did he die?"

"Consumption. Your father never got it, but Leo went to hospital. He hung on for a while, but all of a sudden, it took a really bad turn. Killed him in one night."

Charlotte pressed her lips together. Malcolm had told her about Leo before, as had her father. But for some reason, she'd always pictured him older, perhaps closer to the age she was now.

She supposed it came with the 'uncle' title, to assume he'd always been an adult.

"I'm sorry," she said softly.

"Nothing to be sorry for," Malcolm replied. "It was a long time ago."

"Do you miss him?"

"Yeah. He was the first person I ever knew who died. We both know, you never forget the first."

Charlotte swallowed. A remnant of the panic attack twisted her gut like a rope, but she forced it away. Everything was fine. She was safe. She always would be.

She screwed everything down inside the phonograph. But before she replaced the lid, she looked once again at the mainspring: a tight silver coil spiralling around itself. Then she glanced at the watch on her wrist, and imagined a similar spring inside it, with a tiny shining orb at its centre.

A secret smile stole over her lips.

When she was done, she headed upstairs, changed into a pair of dungarees and fetched her emergency kit bag from her satchel. She opened the leather roll to expose the tools strapped inside: screwdrivers, tweezers, loupes, a scalpel, a length of solder and an iron. Then she listened hard to make sure Malcolm wasn't coming.

Hearing nothing, she retrieved a box from her dresser. Inside lay two orbs. They were tiny — the cheapest possible size — and had been spent long ago. She'd found them tossed into the gutter outside a rich house in the Second West. They would be worthless now their energy was gone. But not to her.

While the soldering iron warmed, Charlotte recalled Dickinson's diagram on the board. She held the orb in the tweezers, and slid the scalpel along it. There was no resistance; the blade sliced through like it was butter. After a few careful strokes, she exposed the core: a dull meaty substance, without a single spark left to give it light. But she had reached it. That was the important thing.

She dismantled the back of the old mantel clock, and eased the orb into the centre of the mainspring. Then she loaded the iron with solder and stroked the tip over it. The hot metal fused the core with the spring, and the mechanism ticked for a few seconds before it fell silent again.

Charlotte beamed. She doubted she would attempt the procedure on a live orb, at least for a while, but this was a promising start. Malcolm had been right all along. The only difference between him and her was that she had been able to apply what Dickinson had taught her. And tomorrow, when she stepped into the Cropper Lane studio, she would be even closer to bringing his idea to life.

Somewhere between alchemy and watch mechanics was the key to the graft. And she was determined to find it.

The Parliamentary Moot Hall stood on the lowest floor of the Pavilion, separated from the private areas by a maze of secured corridors and gates. It was a place of crystal and metal, filled to the brim with the highest opulence. Every column bore accents of green, moulded into fake leaves, to give the impression of trees. Some of the volutes were even decorated with carved birds, their wings spread and beaks open in silent song.

Daniel didn't know how accurate they were to real ones. Hardly any birds flew over the City nowadays. If they were anywhere, it would be around the farms, miles away in the Meadows.

The air was smoggy from pipe smoke. It got up his nose

and tightened a band of pain around his head. The Moot had carried on for far too long. From his gold-laced chair, he surveyed the sea of Lords and Fellows. A handful of them — the most prominent and powerful — wore red rings.

"The last item on the agenda, please," Daniel said.

An older gentleman raised his hand. "That comes from me, Sir."

"Go ahead, Lord Rush."

"It's in regards to the body-thefts."

Daniel nodded. "A terribly unfortunate problem."

"One which, it appears, is getting worse," said Rush. "I saw a headline yesterday, claiming another seven graves had been raided. That's the highest increase in three years."

"Are those numbers correct?" asked another Lord. "Or are the news vendors plucking them out of the air? It wouldn't be the first time they've done that. And aren't they just lunafauna bodies?"

"No," said another. "Humans, too. Don't we still have the Constabulary looking out for the body-snatchers?"

"It's obviously not enough," Rush insisted, jowls shaking as he grew more passionate. "*We're* the lucky ones. We have mausoleums and fences to protect us when we're gone. But what about the poor and the lunafauna? What defence do they have, save for a sprinkling of quicklime?"

A man in the front row rolled his eyes. "They're reinterred in the Cavern of Skulls, anyway. All graves are exhumed eventually."

"Exhumed with *respect*, Lord Goodman," Rush said tightly. "Not stolen away like the Shadow Rats snatch silverware. And it's making the people restless."

Goodman sighed. "They're already restless. At this point, being restless is their hobby."

"That is a degrading and disgusting stance," Rush snapped back. "Imagine, for a moment, *you* had the same lack of post-mortem security. Would you be so quick to dismiss their concerns? I've heard all manner of disturbing theories on the street. Some are saying it's for medical experiments. Others believe the bodies are being manufactured into food for Faunatown, so humans can keep the better produce!"

Several horrified gasps filled the chamber, but they were drowned out by the larger sound of amused snorts.

"I'm certain no corpses are feeding the lunafauna," Daniel said loudly, and turned his attention to the back of the room. "Lady Feline? You can put our concerns to rest here. Do your people consume the flesh of the dead?"

Phoebe was wearing a ridiculously unfashionable dress, with a high collar to hide the strip of leather around her neck. She seemed more tired than normal, though not with alcohol. It was an exhaustion which appeared to be eating her from the inside. She looked *old*.

"No more so than your people might," she said, in an unreadable tone.

Daniel nodded. "Well, there it is."

But Rush wasn't finished.

"Regardless of *why* the bodies are being stolen," he insisted, "it's wrong. I'm older than most of the Fellows in this room, and it's been happening all my life. Potentate Carter, if Lord Bellamy was still among us, you know he would say the same. It *must* stop."

Daniel bit the inside of his cheek.

"Heartfelt words," he said. "Your concern is admirable, Lord Rush. Rest assured, I already have Madam Spectre looking into it. Her plate has been rather full since she's returned from leave, but none of you can deny she's the most diligent Chief

Officer for decades. This won't be a simple issue to stop, but she will do everything in her power to make Forest safe. And so will I."

Lord Rush smiled. "I would appreciate that, Sir. And I know the lower Levels would, too."

At last, he sat down. Daniel suppressed a sigh of relief. There was only one final point to address.

But just as he opened his mouth, an alarming groan sounded from the mechanisms along the walls. The lights failed, and the chamber burst into darkness.

A concerned mutter ran among the crowd. Disguised by the gloom, Daniel glared at the ceiling.

After a few seconds, the sconces regained their glow, albeit softer than before.

"My apologies," Daniel said tightly. "That's the third time that's happened today. I'll have it looked at. Now, before we part for the evening, I wish to say a word in regards to my dear wife. As you're all aware, the High Lady Elisabeth has been absent from the public eye for some time. I'm overjoyed to announce the reason. She is with child, and is expecting to deliver any day."

The Lords rapped on their armrests in subdued applause. They had believed him.

Daniel lifted a small bell from a nearby table and rang it.

"The Moot is closed, gentlemen. Go safely and well."

He strode down the steps at the foot of his chair. The others remained seated as he passed, giving him the respect of exiting the chamber first. The air filled with excited mutterings.

"Congratulations, Sir!"

"I wonder if it will be another son?"

"Such wonderful news. Exactly what everyone needs."

"Give our regards to your wife, Sir," said Lord Goodman. "I hope the delivery goes well."

"As do I," Daniel smiled. "Thank you."

He was almost at the door. But when he drew close to it, and to Phoebe, she met his eyes and didn't look away.

Daniel barely kept his composure. He didn't like Phoebe at the best of times. If she wasn't drunk, she was constantly trying to micromanage Faunatown, right under his nose. He glared at her, knowing that to stare at a lunafauna for too long was the way to assert dominance.

Phoebe didn't back down. Her slit pupils seemed to cut through him like razors. Something in her expression chilled him. Could she know it wasn't true?

No, that was impossible. Nobody knew except for him, Elisabeth, Melissa and the medics, who had all been sworn to secrecy.

Phoebe finally lowered her gaze. Daniel smiled. Never mind that she was a Lady; it never took much to remind lunafauna who were the humans and who were the animals. They didn't see because they had sight, only had sight so that they might see.

CHAPTER XVII

After Charlotte climbed into bed at ten o'clock, Oscar left Renshaw Street. He blended into the shadows with ease — that was why Melissa had insisted he hold his surveillance post for the last decade. He was proud he was still able to move so silently, but over the years, it had grown a bitter edge which grated on his conscience. With every passing day, every moment he lurked and listened, the secrets over his head pressed harder and harder. How long would it be before his neck snapped under their weight?

It took only a few minutes to reach his house. Melissa had secured him one in the Fifth West, so he could easily stay on Charlotte's heels. Heat enveloped him the moment he stepped through the door. Richie had cranked the mechanism up to full power, the way he always did in winter. After the two of them had joined the Circulus, they had opted to share a single house. Melissa hadn't argued — it saved her having to pay twice as much. And for Oscar and Richie, to be separated would have been too strange an idea, even in their new life.

Oscar hung up his coat. His eyes fleeted over the red circle embroidered on it, then down to his index finger, and the ring which sat there.

"I'm in here," Richie called from the parlour. "I saved you some dinner. I didn't know how long you'd be."

"Thanks," Oscar replied. Food. Yes, he would feel better

if he ate something.

He fetched it from the kitchen and sat in the armchair opposite Richie. The pork was cooked nicely, but tasted like ash.

Richie sipped a glass of brandy.

"What's the matter? Not enjoying it?"

"No," Oscar said, and put the plate down. "I'm just not very hungry."

Richie shrugged nonchalantly. "It will keep, if you want it later. You're white as a sheet. Did you catch Bellamy undressing?"

Oscar scowled at him. "I've never watched her undress."

"Yeah, right," Richie chuckled. "Come on, out with it. What's bothering you?"

Despite the warmth, Oscar shivered as if he was still outside.

"Madam Spectre had to go and… take care of some business tonight. You know. *That* kind of business."

Richie lowered his glass in alarm.

"Bellamy talked?"

"Yeah. To her teacher. The feline one."

"Well, shit. You've got to hand it to her, though: she did well to last this long."

Oscar ran his fingers over his chin. He had shaved that morning, as was customary for all officers, but the prickle of stubble was starting to break through.

"Do you think she'll be next?" he asked.

"It sounds like she remembers enough," Richie said ruefully. "Madam Spectre will have to do something. If she's started running around telling people, it's too risky. We can't leave loose threads."

"I don't like it," Oscar admitted. "I mean… I always had my suspicions about Rene. I had a feeling it wasn't what the official report said. I was sure Madam Spectre shot someone, when she went into the manor. And then we find out I was right, find out all about the Aeternum and the Keeper... Richie, there are so many lies."

"*Necessary* lies," Richie insisted. "What do you think would happen if the whole City knew the truth? Everything would fall apart. We cover these things up for the greater good, remember?"

He waited until Oscar was looking at him before he spoke again.

"You did the right thing today. You did your job. You know, you'll probably get a raise for this, sticking it out for as long as you have and now finally getting a result."

"*Result?*" Oscar repeated incredulously. "She's an innocent."

"Surrounded by other people who are much more innocent," said Richie. "Oscar, listen, I know this can be a hard path, but it's the right one. Do you think people like us could have risen through the ranks if it wasn't right?"

Oscar stayed quiet. He wasn't sure what was right. When they had been Rats, he'd known stealing was wrong, but it was the only way to survive in Forest's cutthroat underbelly. Necessity overrode moral ground when it meant the difference between eating and starving. But that knowledge had become the reason why he and Richie had fled to August Bellamy's sanctuary house. They had been desperate to get away, and to bring righteousness to the squalid streets.

Twelve years ago, as gullible trainee officers, that was all that mattered. Then they had reached the ultimate height, and Oscar discovered a world even darker than the one they had left behind. Everywhere he looked, he saw deviousness and death; a City built upon treachery as much as it was upon solid Levels.

And all in the name of *the greater good*.

He had never really escaped the nest in the Ninth North. It had just polished itself up to look like a sturdy house and an elegant ruby ring, and followed him everywhere he stepped.

"Do you ever think of them?" he asked in an undertone.

"Who?"

"The Rats."

Richie sighed. "Sometimes. I wonder if any more managed to get out, like we did."

"If they have, I haven't heard of any joining the trainees," said Oscar. "Actually, what surname would they be up to this year?"

Richie closed his eyes in concentration and counted through the alphabet.

"H," he answered eventually. "Yours."

Orphans in the lowest Levels were each assigned a surname, corresponding to a letter matching the year they were born. Oscar was Hargreaves, and Richie, born ten months later, was Irving. Now twenty-six years had passed, and the names had come round again.

"I'll have lots of little brothers and sisters, then," Oscar muttered. "Poor buggers."

Richie grimaced, finished his drink and swirled the dregs in the bottom of the glass. The faraway tolling of the Tower drifted on the air.

"I'm going to turn in," Richie said. "I've got an early start tomorrow."

"Alright. Thanks for waiting for me," Oscar said morosely.

"Don't mention it." Richie walked over and laid a hand on Oscar's shoulder. "Listen, stop beating yourself up. This was the best thing you could have done. Just cut yourself some slack, get a good sleep, and you'll see that in the morning."

Oscar listened to him climbing the stairs, then threw his head back in frustration. Usually, talking with Richie made him feel better, but not tonight.

What would Melissa do? That lunafauna teacher had always looked out for Charlotte…

His gorge rose. He was no stranger to violence, but not like *this*. The Circulus dealt a calculated, perfect, silent violence, which could only come from a foundation older than anyone who carried it out. He was a part of it now. He had saved Charlotte from it so long ago, gathered her in his arms and rushed her to safety. And today, he had swept that safety from under her feet.

Richie was wrong. He *hadn't* done the right thing. Not at all.

Evelyn hurried through the Fifth South with an urgency she hadn't felt in years. Her fur puffed up against the cold night air, and her tail swept so fast beneath her dress, the skirts lifted. Her heart hadn't stopped pounding all day, ever since she had taken Charlotte aside and learned the truth she'd always suspected.

Poor Roger Cunningham was innocent. And that police officer… There were several women in the Constabulary, but only one was formidable enough to shoot twenty-three people in cold blood.

Evelyn walked straight past Phoebe's manor, into the tavern area. The decay of Faunatown had spread even higher over the last decade, and every street held the scars of protests and marches. Remnants of broken placards littered open gutters, and many of the major thoroughfares were a mess of graffiti. A vicious cycle had been set in motion: the Constabulary would paint over the slogans, but then disenfranchised youths would sneak out and create something else on the new blank canvas.

As Evelyn walked, she eyed the latest protests daubed across the bricks:

LUNAFAUNA RIGHTS! EQUALITY FOR ALL!
WHEN WE BLEED, WE BLEED THE SAME!
FIAT JUSTITIA RUAT CAELUM!

The last one struck deep. Ever since it was first written in the Aspinall Square riot, it had started to show up more than any others. Evelyn still remembered the weight in Phoebe's voice when she'd translated it.

Let justice be done though the sky falls.

She headed first to The Ring O' Bells, but Anthony directed her to an establishment deeper into the Level: The Sundial. Evelyn rolled her eyes in despair. That was one of the seediest places this high up in Faunatown, but the alcohol was cheap. Phoebe must have had a particularly bad day.

As soon as Evelyn reached the tavern, she heard a cacophony from inside. She shouldered the door open and her ears flattened in shock. Phoebe was still dressed in her Parliamentary gown, twirling maniacally on a table. A laughing crowd had gathered around her.

"They were *huge!*" Phoebe cried. "The trees… Some of them, so huge, it would take four of you to circle the trunk! Or eight, maybe… depends what form you're in. Back then, you could shift every single night, you see. Every bloody night. You don't believe me?"

"The transnight's once a month, Phoebe," someone protested, equally drunk.

"It is *now*," Phoebe slurred. "Never used to be, though. Oh, no. *Every* night. Not just full moon. Yes, you'd feel that moonlight, and you'd dance…. *Dance!* Come on, move, like this! I need a partner! You can't do Daniel's stupid waltzes without a partner!"

Evelyn tugged at Phoebe's skirt. "Come down now," she said.

Phoebe peered at her with an unfocused smile. "Hey, Evie! Dance with me!"

"No," Evelyn snapped, in the firm voice she saved for only the unruliest students.

"Spoilsport," Phoebe pouted.

Evelyn glanced at the barkeep.

"How many has she had?"

"Too many."

"*One* is too many for her after Moots."

The barkeep shrugged helplessly. "We just want to see her happy and having fun. We know she doesn't get a lot of that. And we look out for her."

"You call *that* looking out for her?" Evelyn retorted. "It's a wonder the Vixen doesn't *look out for her* as well as you do."

The mention of Melissa Spectre was enough to turn a few heads. Evelyn glared at them all.

"You ought to be ashamed of yourselves," she snapped. "This feline is the reason you're here with roofs over your heads to begin with. You claim to love her and respect her? How dare you let her do this as though she's cheap entertainment?"

"We respect her enough to let her do whatever she needs to be content," insisted a nearby canine. "She deserves that. She deserves whatever pleasure she can get."

In reply, Evelyn hissed. The canine drew away in submission, tail between his legs. Several other lunafauna lowered their heads sheepishly. Then Evelyn pulled Phoebe out of the tavern.

This was a run she repeated often in the evenings following Moots. Usually, when Phoebe still had her wits about her, Evelyn would walk her back to the manor and put her to bed. But now the fresh air had hit her, Phoebe became a dead weight, struggling to stay on her feet.

"Alright, I'm taking you to my place," Evelyn grunted.

Phoebe hiccupped. "Nah. Let's go somewhere else. Tavern crawl!"

"Not tonight."

"Why? It will be fun. You're not being much fun lately, you know."

"Too bad."

As Evelyn unlocked her door, Phoebe started laughing hysterically at a squeaking light mechanism across the road. Evelyn raised an apologetic paw at the lightsman, hauled Phoebe up a rickety flight of stairs to the first-floor quarters, and threw her onto the sofa. Her frilly skirts billowed around her like a cloud.

"You're good, Evie," Phoebe said with a lopsided grin. "A good friend. I just want you to know that, alright? I haven't… had many friends as good as you, and that's good."

Evelyn let out a shaky breath. Phoebe hadn't been this drunk in a while.

"What were you thinking?" she snapped. "You know that place is a fleapit! You're lucky they didn't have the coins out of your purse!"

"They can have them if they want them. I've got enough to go around."

"That's not my point."

"Pointy points, all over the place," Phoebe sang. "Sharp points. Too many of them, if you ask me. Always were too many… down, down in the dark…"

She rubbed her chest, then scratched her neck with a hind leg. The collar was hidden under her dress, but Evelyn knew it was still there. And for as long as Phoebe had worn it, she hadn't changed during a transnight. Not one, for the past twelve years.

But now, after speaking with Charlotte, Evelyn suspected the collar and the shooting were linked. That sent a shiver through her body, so violent, all her fur stood on end.

"Phoebe, please," she said. "I know you insist on destroying your liver at every opportunity, but—"

"No, see, that's where you're wrong," Phoebe interrupted. "My liver's fine. My liver will be fine for another five lives. And you know, I'm due. It's almost time for me to keel over. I need to do what I can to get through that. Death number four, coming right up! Ding dong bell! Kitty's in the—"

She sneezed and lapsed into another fit of giggles.

Evelyn froze. "When? When will it happen? Tell me how I can help you!"

Phoebe's laugh became flat and caustic.

"You can't. You've just got to wait until it's over."

"You need to sober up. I have to talk to you. It's important. It's about the Vixen."

Phoebe extended her claws and swept them through the air. "Oh, she needs to be torn a new asshole, that one."

"Phoebe!" Evelyn cried. "Please, listen to me!"

But she could tell nothing was going to get through to her. Even if Phoebe understood now, she would have forgotten the entire conversation by morning. There was no choice but to wait.

Evelyn's frustration boiled over. She held a bowl under the kitchen tap, turned the crank in the wall until it was full of water, then flung the contents into Phoebe's face.

Phoebe leapt from the sofa with a yowl, ears flat against

her head. Evelyn pointed at the spare room.

"Are you sober now? Or close to it, at least?" she asked. "Go in there and don't come out until you can count all your whiskers."

Phoebe scowled, but managed to reach the door and disappeared inside with a discontented hiss. When she was gone, Evelyn collapsed against the wall.

A whimper of exhaustion and anxiety tangled in her throat. She'd often heard from neighbours that if she had any sense, she would have abandoned Phoebe long ago. The community loved their leader, though few risked the turbulence of being her friend. Her drinking was an amusement to watch from a distance, but nobody wanted to clear up the mess.

Evelyn didn't enjoy it, either. Phoebe was a handful. But she knew too much of loneliness already, to be abandoned by those she shared a few brief decades with.

Deciding she'd had enough, Evelyn walked into her bedroom. She would speak to Phoebe tomorrow, before she left for the Academy. One night wouldn't hurt.

There was no need to turn on the light. Her feline eyes serviced her well enough. She sat on the edge of her mattress, pulled her bodice over her head. She was just about to slip out of her skirt when a lamp burst into life.

Evelyn spun around. A tall woman stood in the corner, as still as a statue. She was dressed in black to blend with the shadows, and a braid, equally dark, trailed over her shoulder.

Evelyn leapt towards the door, but Melissa was quicker. She snatched Evelyn by the scruff, threw her onto the bed. Then she pulled a pistol from her belt and pointed it at Evelyn's face.

"Let's not make a scene, Miss Gilbaut. One of my officers told me that you had an interesting conversation with a student today. And an unnecessary matter was mentioned."

Evelyn shook with terror.

"Please don't hurt me!" she gasped. "I don't know what you're talking about! I've done nothing wrong!"

Melissa didn't move.

"*Please!*" Evelyn cried. "Is this because of what Charlotte told me about Rene? She doesn't know anything, either! She just wanted help!"

"Charlotte Bellamy isn't my concern at the moment," said Melissa. "It's just a shame she decided to make this *your* concern."

She replaced the gun in its holster, and a wave of relief washed over Evelyn. But it was short-lived.

Melissa drew one of her own kitchen knives from a back pocket, and jumped onto her chest, pinning her to the bed. Before Evelyn realised what was happening, Melissa sliced the serrated edge across her wrist.

"*Phoebe!*" Evelyn shrieked, but Melissa held a hand over her mouth and cut her other wrist. Then she dropped the blade and forced her down.

Evelyn tried to fight, but each struggle left her weaker. The wounds were so deep, she could barely move her fingers. She felt her strength sapping away like water through a sieve. Hot blood pooled around her.

The Vixen's face was calm and focused. It occurred to Evelyn, distantly, that she knew what she was doing.

"Ad maius bonum," Melissa whispered.

After thirty long seconds, Evelyn's eyes closed.

When the lunafauna had stopped moving, Melissa checked her pulse. Feeling nothing, she climbed off the bed, made sure there were no handprints or bootmarks. She left the bloodied knife within arm's reach on the mattress, and exited through the window, as quietly as she'd entered.

CHAPTER XVIII

Malcolm had left before Charlotte awoke, to fetch replacement parts from one of the Seventh North factories. She had hardly finished winding up all the clocks on the wall when Mr Downey arrived. He paid forty solidi for the phonograph: more than enough to pay for the field trip. Charlotte counted out a quarter as Malcolm's commission, and wedged the notes under his paperweight. Then she pocketed the rest, grabbed her satchel, and locked the shop behind her.

When she reached the Academy, an omnibus was already parked on the road. Doctor Dickinson stood nearby, talking to the driver in a hushed tone. Then, to Charlotte's alarm, the vehicle pulled away, empty.

"Is something wrong?" she asked.

Dickinson turned around.

"The field trip has been cancelled, Miss Bellamy."

Charlotte ground her teeth in frustration. Cancelled, on the morning they were supposed to be going?

But then an iciness crept through her bones. Dickinson's cheeks were as ashen as her powdered hair. Something was wrong.

"What's happened?" Charlotte asked. She tried to brace herself, terrified of what the answer would be.

Dickinson breathed in slowly.

"One of our teachers passed away last night. Miss Gilbaut. So I've called off lessons for today. We're to have an assembly, and then you can all go home. We'll visit Cropper Lane next week."

The world lurched. Charlotte felt as though she was hanging a hundred feet in the air. Miss Gilbaut was *dead?* It couldn't be. Surely, if she walked into the Academy right now, the lunafauna would be there ,with her broad smile and gentle eyes…

"No…" Charlotte blurted. "No, please…"

"I'm afraid it's true," Dickinson said softly. "I think it's best for you to go inside. The others are already there."

Charlotte's feet walked separate from her, across the yard and up the steps. The corridor was full of students heading to the assembly hall. She spotted Tobias and Eugine Clark, then Julian, and shoved her way towards him. Julian's eyes were so wide with shock, they seemed to completely fill his spectacles.

"Charlotte," he said. "Have you heard?"

She knew it was written across her face. In desperation, she pinched her arm, but the horror remained.

"Do they know what happened?" she asked. Her voice came out in a monotone drawl. She wasn't even sure if she had managed to say the right words.

"She killed herself," said Eugene. "People are sayin' she slit her wrists. Not sure if it's true."

"When did they find her?"

"This morning. One of her friends was at her house and called the coppers."

The image wormed into Charlotte's mind like freezing water through a crack. Miss Gilbaut, alone, white fur stained red. She couldn't imagine the surroundings, so her memory swept in to fill the blanks, and turned the ground into snow-covered cobbles.

She covered her mouth before a whimper could escape.

Miss Gilbaut was always smiling. Had she really hidden such depression behind that kindly face? Or was it because of what Charlotte had said yesterday? Those words, *Cor Aeternum*. Both times she had heard them, only death followed.

Her heart beat so hard, she thought it might leap out of her mouth. This *couldn't* be real...

Julian sat beside her in the hall. The other teachers stood together, their eyes cast down. Dickinson entered, and the whole room fell silent at once. Even breathing seemed uncomfortably loud. Charlotte shivered and tried to focus on her mother's wristwatch. Tick tock.

She didn't listen when Dickinson spoke. She couldn't bear to hear any other details. It was too close, like a match held against her skin. She threw careful glances at the younger children when they began crying. Alarm shot across their faces like a sheared thread.

Charlotte recognised it. She had felt it too, when she was the same age as them. They shouldn't know it. Nobody should ever know it...

When the assembly ended, the more raucous boys ran through the gates, cheering their early freedom, but for most, the exit was quiet and sullen. Charlotte slipped out as swiftly as she could. But she hadn't even reached the end of the street when Julian caught up with her.

"Hey, wait! Are you alright?"

"Yeah," Charlotte lied.

Julian saw straight through it, and stood in front of her to make her stop.

"Look at me."

"I'm fine."

"No, you're not. Come on, talk to me."

"I can't!" Charlotte snapped, so ferociously, she surprised

herself. "Sorry. I didn't mean to shout. It's just… It must have been something I said…"

"Like what? You've done nothing wrong," Julian said firmly. "She was your friend, I know that. But she didn't go the way the others did in Rene. That wasn't your fault, either. I know you've been dragging it with you since you were a kid."

"What does it matter, whether it's my fault or not? They're all still dead. They're dead, and I lived."

"Yes, you lived," Julian insisted. "You're still here. And you're not to blame."

Charlotte ground her teeth to hold back tears. They stung her eyes like acid. She couldn't let him see them.

"I just don't understand," she said. "Why would Miss Gilbaut do that? She was so happy… she was so nice to me. Why would she do it?"

Julian took hold of Charlotte's hand.

"People don't always let on everything that's happening to them. Just because she looked happy doesn't mean she was, you know? How many times did *you* smile growing up, when it was the last thing you wanted to do?"

Charlotte gripped her satchel so hard, her knuckles ached. She remembered the time Malcolm had protected the lunafauna lightsman from a beating; thought of all the attacks as soon as they stepped outside Faunatown. Miss Gilbaut was one of the lucky ones: she had a job above many of her neighbours. But she'd also turned to drink occasionally. She had to walk through squalor every day, and ignore insults thrown at her like stones. Even if she hadn't cast a shadow, a larger one forever touched her, as it did all her people.

What weight lurked within that darkness which Charlotte would never know?

In her heart, she felt something wasn't right. But before

she could dwell on it, Julian pulled her into a hug.

Alarm rooted Charlotte to the spot. She could smell the soap in his hair, feel his breath tickling her neck. His arms pressed against her like the warmth of the sun upon a rock. The two of them had grown up together, played in the schoolyard and studied in the library. But they had never touched. Not properly. Not like this.

After a moment, Julian drew away, took off his glasses and made a fuss of cleaning them.

"Well... I'd better go and see if Aunt Bridget needs me for anything. She mentioned taking some stuff to her house."

Charlotte nodded rigidly.

"Are you alright?" he asked again. "I can tell her I'll come back later. I'll walk you home?"

"No. I'll be fine, really. I think I need some time alone, anyway. To think. Thank you, Julian."

Embarrassment pooled in her belly. She bit the inside of her cheek, so hard, she tasted blood. But Julian just smiled, squeezed her hand, and returned to the Academy.

Charlotte's heart flickered like a candle flame. But then Miss Gilbaut flashed back, sharper than a razor behind her eyes. She shook her head, trying to toss the thought aside. This was no time to fawn over a boy.

She couldn't stay on the streets for long. Soon, she'd hear the cries of news vendors, and the horrid possibility that her teacher's name would be mentioned. She tried to think logically. She and Malcolm needed a fresh loaf of bread. Yes, that was the best thing to do: go to the marketplace, then home. And once she was at the shop, she could distract herself with work. If she'd still had Julian's music box, she would have removed every single screw and then put them back, simply to fill an hour.

Charlotte hunched her shoulders, just enough to avoid

attention, and walked along the main thoroughfare near the Interlevel. A team of labourers passed, en route to the mills and factories in the North Quarter. Their jobs were dangerous: darting around huge loom machines and pulsing pistons. It was all too easy to lose a limb, and many workers showed the scars of their harsh reality, with the metal prosthetics attached to their bodies.

Charlotte stood aside as they bustled past, then she turned the corner, and ran straight into a wall of people. Something was going on in the street ahead. She stood on her tiptoes, straining to see.

A group strode down the road, wearing well-made clothes beneath long white coats. That wardrobe immediately told Charlotte they were alchemists. Several held placards in the air.

AD MELIORA!
PROGRESS — THE KEY TO THE FUTURE!

"Citizens of Forest!" a man called through a voice amplifier. "Stand with us against the family which holds you under its boot! The Potentate bends his own rules and plays us like pawns whenever he must!"

"What the hell have you lot got to complain about?" someone called from the crowd. "You never have any trouble feeding yourselves, do you?"

"It's not just for us!" the man insisted. "Don't turn a blind eye! Give your support to the unfortunates and the free alchemists!"

"Rise up with us, for progress!" a woman cried. "When Forest was founded, we were equal to the Potentate! Not anymore! But we will have equality for *everyone!* We will create power from the sun and moon, return to the ancient magic and bring back the trees! Together, *we* are the future of our beloved City—"

Constables swarmed upon the alchemists from the side streets. One snatched the amplifier and pulled the crank out of it.

"That's enough now!" he shouted. "The show's over! Go about your business!"

Charlotte's belly flipped when she saw the blue uniforms. She hurried down the Interlevel as fast as she could, and didn't stop until she stumbled out into the Fifth West.

The officers hadn't followed her. She clutched her chest, tried to breathe normally. Her heart felt like it had dropped into her gut.

She'd seen several protests through the years, but from lunafauna and poor people, not *alchemists*. Theirs was among the highest positions in Forest. Even if they didn't work with orbs, practically all were trained medics. They would never be out of work, or want for common comforts. And what were *free alchemists?* She hadn't heard that before, nor seen it in any book.

She sighed. There would be time and energy to wonder about it later. For now, the emotion was still too hot and close. It choked her, like the sticky humid air of summer. Even the cool wind which shrieked down the street wasn't enough to clear it.

"Come on," Charlotte muttered to herself. The faster she went to market, the faster she could return to the shop. There, she would be safe.

She approached Godstall Square. The weekly array of stalls crammed every available space, and churned with people, like bees crowding a hive. Charlotte kept her head down and slinked around the side. Even now, it was a force of habit, not to go into the open if she could help it. Near the walls, nothing could grab her from behind.

A news vendor pasted the day's headline on the side of a building. She eyed it nervously. But relief surged through her — there was no mention of Miss Gilbaut. Instead, the words read:

ENTIRE PAUPER GRAVE FOUND EMPTY IN EARLY HOURS
11 BODIES STOLEN
ALSO 3 LUNAFAUNA FROM NEARBY

A couple of men saw the text and shook their heads in disgust.

"Awful," one muttered. "Why can't people just leave the dead alone?"

"Who knows? It makes you wonder who's taking them, though."

"Or what for."

Their voices were lost as Charlotte elbowed her way forward. Why did everything have to revolve around death? She could almost smell it, like smoke clinging to her clothes, no matter how much she tried to scrub it away.

She reached the bakery table. Samuel Tiffin regarded her with a stare as icy as the air. His hair was pale with flour, and looked the same off-white powdered colour as gentlemen of rank. But that was where all likeness to nobility ended. Charlotte didn't want to think about when Tiffin had last washed his apron.

A cigarette hung out of the side of his mouth and he took a long puff of it.

"Bellamy," he grunted. "You'd better have good money here today."

"When do I not?" Charlotte replied, equally sharp. "I've been buying for long enough to know how much a loaf costs."

"Haven't you just, little Lady?"

"Look, I'm not in the mood for this today. So can we just get on with it?"

Tiffin sniffed with displeasure. He turned away to serve a customer at the other end of the stall.

"Aggie," he barked. "See to Bellamy."

"Yes, Father," said a young girl beside him. "Hello, Charlotte."

"Hello, Aggie," Charlotte replied, trying her best to sound polite.

Aggie's eyes twinkled. She was twelve years old, small for her age, and only looked more so thanks to the long pigtails either side of her face. A thick winter cloak hung about her shoulders, but she parted it to showcase the dress underneath: blue wool, decorated with frills like a cake. It was similar to the frocks Charlotte had worn as a child, but she knew it was a cheap alternative. Parts of the lace were frayed and the stitching was broken on the sleeves.

"Do you like it?" Aggie asked. She twirled and held the skirt out for effect.

Charlotte raised her eyebrows. She had long outgrown fondness for fashion.

"You look very pretty," she answered.

Aggie's smile grew even larger. "Thanks. I bet you had loads of nice ones. Which was your favourite? Did you have any blue ones, like this?"

"I didn't really have any favourites—"

"Did you have to wear wigs as well? I think mine would go nice with a wig. One of those big poufy ones with beads and paper flowers in it. What do you think?"

"Aggie, it was a long time ago for me," Charlotte said, as civilly as she could. "Can I buy some bread, please? And one of those sponge cakes?"

Aggie rolled a loaf into a length of cloth. As she moved her arms, her cloak shifted, and Charlotte spotted the yellowed spot of a healing bruise near her elbow.

"I made all the bread today," Aggie said proudly. "What's the cake for?"

"My guardian. It's his birthday the day after tomorrow," replied Charlotte. "Listen, Aggie, what's that on your—?"

"Hey!" Tiffin roared.

Fright sliced down Charlotte's back. She looked around for what had made him shout. Was it the tall woman? No, it couldn't be…

It wasn't. A trio of street urchins had snatched some doughnuts off the side of the stall. Tiffin gave chase, his long limbs flying in all directions as he skidded on the cobbles.

"Not again," muttered Aggie. She glanced over her shoulder, took the largest cake and wrapped it. "Three solidi, please."

Charlotte blinked in alarm.

"*Three?* That's only enough for the bread."

"I know. The cake's free."

"Aggie, I can't—"

"I made it, so I say it's free," Aggie whispered. "Please, you're my friend. Just don't say anything to Father, alright?"

Charlotte leaned closer. "Where did that bruise come from?"

"Just take the cake," Aggie insisted.

Realising she wasn't going to get anywhere, Charlotte hid it inside her satchel and covered it with the bread. Aggie instantly relaxed.

"Three solidi," she repeated.

Charlotte handed it over. "Thank you."

"You're welcome," said Aggie. "Now, you'd better go, before he comes back. I'll see you around, alright?"

She smiled again, thinner than before, and turned to another customer. She yanked her cloak shut as she moved.

Charlotte went to speak, but stopped herself. What would be the point? Aggie was busy enough, and she didn't know how much longer she could stand the market crowds. She had the bread, after all. There was nothing else to do here.

Charlotte wrestled her way towards the exit. A woman came from the other direction, clutching a basket of eggs. Charlotte leapt aside to avoid her, and fell into someone.

"Excuse me!" she cried. Then she saw a blue uniform, and she forgot to breathe.

A constable turned around. She had spotted him several times over the years — the Fifth West was his patrol area — but never this close. He was older than her, in his mid-twenties, with strong features and thick black hair. His jacket swept about his knees, a small red circle embroidered over the left breast. His belt hung heavy with paraphernalia: a truncheon, case of matches, flintlock pistol in a holster.

A pair of striking eyes scanned her. One was ice blue, and the other brown. She wasn't sure which one to look at.

"What was that with the cake?" he asked.

Charlotte's heart jumped. His voice was soft, familiar. She could have sworn she had heard it before.

"It was a gift," she said, hoping she didn't sound as shaken as she felt. "The baker's daughter will say the same if you want to check, sir."

"No, it's fine. I believe you. You'd better run along now."

The man surveyed her for a moment longer, then tugged his gloves down and vanished like a shadow.

When Charlotte returned to the shop, she was surprised to find the door locked and the sign turned to *closed*. There was no sign of Malcolm, and the money she'd left for him was gone, replaced with a note.

Hello, kiddo. 11 o'clock. Smithdown Street water mechanism collapsed. Gone to fix it. Probably home late. Bowl of stew in oven for you. Hope you had a good day at Cropper Lane. P.S. Thank you for the solidi.

A strange relief overcame her at reading the message. She could still distract herself before having to tell him the news.

She checked the clocks on the wall and adjusted any which were slow. In the kitchen, she put the bread in the cupboard, but kept the cake and hid it under her bed. Then she changed into a pair of old dungarees.

She considered taking the mantel clock apart again. That would take several blissful hours. But her attention shifted to the gold watch on her wrist. She remembered her mother wearing it; how the metal glinted as it caught the light, and sent little shining dots over the walls. As a child, Charlotte had tried to catch the trails, only to have them slip through her fingers like dust.

She brushed the little knob on the side. She'd never needed to wind it. The mechanism had kept ticking without fail, year after year.

Her fingers stilled. It never had to be rewound because there was a live orb inside it.

The idea hit Charlotte like lightning; one she was amazed to have never thought of before. She didn't stop to think if it was foolish or not. First, she laid out her solder, screwdrivers and tweezers. Then she wedged a loupe against her eye and removed the back of the watch.

She gasped when she saw the movement inside. She had dealt with small timepieces before, but this level of craftsmanship took her breath away. For a moment, she fancied the wheel train was gold, rather than brass. Some of the teeth were so tiny, she could barely see them.

It would have taken months to construct from scratch. Malcolm could manage making something like this, but not her. This was watch mechanics at their finest, transformed from logical science into pure art.

Charlotte located the mainspring: as fine as a hair. At its centre sat a miniature orb. It didn't simply rest as the spent ones did, but rotated on the spot, with a strange translucent quality that spread to the metal around it.

She swallowed nervously. She would have to be careful. If she applied too much solder, it could stifle the orb and kill its energy.

She picked up a scalpel. She had practised the infinity incision on boiled eggs, and the occasional spent orb, but never on a live one. Luckily, the position of the scalpel in its surface forced the orb to still, and she made a clean cut that exposed the glowing white core.

Her mouth fell open with wonder. It looked like a droplet of sunlight.

She switched the scalpel for her soldering iron, gathered the minimum amount, and tapped the core with it. The entire thing trembled. Charlotte drew back in alarm, but then the orb recovered and began spinning again.

"Alright, don't touch it directly," she whispered, and went in again with the iron. This time, she placed a drop of solder onto the mainspring's centre. It latched itself to the orb and trailed along it in a silver vein. She repeated the process on the opposite side, until the orb was completely coated.

Anxiety stabbed in Charlotte's throat, as if she had inhaled a needle. Had she ruined it?

This was such a stupid idea. That orb was worth more than anything in the shop, and now she had poured molten metal all over it? Had she just destroyed her mother's watch?

She flung down the iron with a snarl. She waited for tears, but just like when she had woken in the hospital, they refused to come.

There was a sudden dull sound, like a heartbeat. Then the mainspring coiled tight, and the gears continued as normal.

Charlotte snatched the watch. Every part of the movement was still ticking. She turned it over to check the face. Sure enough, the second hand was working its way around the numerals, as though it hadn't been disrupted at all.

Her anguish transformed to shock. She had done it.

High above, from inside the Tower, the Timekeeper gazed across the City. He looked into the Fifth West, sensed the pulsing orb in Charlotte's hand.

Perfect.

CHAPTER XIX

The lamps of the Roots burned at full daylight capacity as Melissa traversed the bridges. She smiled at the officers who passed her, doffed her cap to those who greeted her by name. Then, when she was sure nobody was looking, she slipped into the infirmary, and descended a hidden staircase to the foundations of the building.

The room she entered was pleasantly decorated, with baskets of perfumed paper flowers trailing from the ceiling. A nurse sat behind a desk, her nose in a book. As soon as she saw Melissa, she jumped to her feet.

"Madam Spectre," she said. "I wasn't expecting to see you until later."

"I wasn't expecting such a sleepless night," Melissa replied. "I thought I'd come and see her. Do you need any more milk? I brought some, just in case."

"Well, since you're here, there's nothing better than the real thing," the nurse smiled, and led her towards a neighbouring room.

When the door opened, Melissa stopped in mid-step. Daniel stood against the wall, dressed inconspicuously, to make it harder for passers-by to recognise him. Beside him was an incubator, and inside the glass-covered bassinet lay a tiny baby, laced with tubes. A chain of cogs and pumps formed a carefully-controlled heating mechanism over her. On the end, a chart spelled her name in cursive hand:

Euphrasie Carter.

Melissa settled on a chaise lounge and unbuttoned her shirt. The nurse removed the baby and laid her belly down on top of her. Euphrasie gurgled in protest at being awoken, but settled when Melissa guided her towards her nipple.

"Ring the bell if you need me," the nurse said as she let herself out of the room.

Melissa turned her full attention to Euphrasie. Her skin was softer than silk and glowed with a healthy pink flush. But she was smaller than she should be — she had been born four weeks early. It wasn't enough to spell her doom, but she'd spent most of her little life inside the incubator. Those machines were expensive. They had been pioneered only a few years prior, and needed constant monitoring. Melissa knew of only nine babies who had been saved thanks to their warmth. Euphrasie would be the tenth. Daniel had made sure to get the best one in the City. And tomorrow, she would come out of it, permanently.

"I wasn't expecting you to be here," Melissa admitted.

"I could say the same to you. I just wanted to be with her," replied Daniel. He sat beside Melissa. "Any more news on Charlotte Bellamy?"

"Nothing we need to be concerned about at the moment. I'm still going to have her brought in. But I don't want to talk about it now. Let me be with my girl."

Daniel nodded and stroked Euphrasie's head.

"Sweet thing," he said tenderly. "She's got black hair, like you."

Melissa sighed. "That's... not a good thing."

"It's fine. My mother had black hair, too."

His words were warm, but no tone would have lessened Melissa's pain. She felt it, cold and heavy, like a lump of ice inside her heart. She pressed on her breast to encourage more milk to flow. Euphrasie sensed it and sucked harder.

Melissa had discovered she was pregnant just after Midsummer. She'd remained working for as long as she could, but both she and Daniel knew it couldn't continue. He had insisted she have six months away so she could confine herself. They concocted the cover story that she had broken her leg, and she retreated into her house, with only sporadic visits from Daniel, Victor Paley, and trusted nurses.

But the contractions came early. Melissa had tried to recall the moment many times, but it morphed into a haze of pain and delirium. And over it all, fear, unlike any she had ever felt. It tied her stomach into a solid knot, swept her feet above her head and spun her around like a snowflake in a blizzard.

The one thing which had snapped her back to reality was a sound; soft and rhythmic: Euphrasie's first cry. She had only managed a glimpse of her daughter before she was whisked away for specialist care. Melissa had lain in the bed, exhausted, gasping for air as though half-drowned.

Then, in a heartbeat, she grew desperate for the child she never thought she wanted. The child she could never have.

She was the most skilled assassin of the entire force. The youngest Chief Officer in Forest's history, and the longest-standing. She couldn't maintain that position holding a baby on her hip, especially out of wedlock. And if anybody discovered the father was none other than the Potentate himself…

Euphrasie slowed down. Melissa tickled her foot to wake her up, and patted her back until she burped. Even that little sound warmed her heart. Melissa had never thought she could love something so much. How could she have created such a pure and perfect being?

"She's getting stronger every day," Daniel said as he

returned Euphrasie to the incubator. He held her as gently as if she were made of glass.

"I just hope she'll be alright," Melissa said. "Sometimes, when they're early, they become blind or have fits."

"I don't think that will happen. She's got your blood in her."

"That doesn't make me feel better."

"Why?"

"The blood of someone like me? With all I do? And… even if that was of no consequence, she's *my* daughter, Daniel. *Mine*."

Melissa's voice cracked. Daniel closed his eyes with a sigh.

"I know this is going to be difficult for you," he said. "But we can't back out now. I've had Elisabeth out of the public eye; people know she's 'expecting.' This is the best situation for all of us. I can still claim to be Euphrasie's father, you can see her whenever you want, and the alchemists will know the Potentate has two children. Our bond is secure, because of what *we* have created together."

A sob threatened to rise up Melissa's throat. She bit her tongue to keep it in check. When Daniel had concocted the idea eight months ago, she knew in her heart it was the only option, but it still hurt her as nothing had before. The Invisible Law between the alchemists and Potentates called for at least two offspring. One would inherit the leadership of Forest, and the other — in the eyes of the public, at least — always seemed to die. Not even the most powerful family in the City could stave off illnesses and accidents.

That was the official stance. Only a select few knew the truth, and what a single child could mean for the delicate Invisible Law. For years, the alchemists had been waiting for an opportunity to overturn it. One wrong step now, only one heir to the Carter name, and everything would crumble.

Melissa's fingers trembled as she buttoned her shirt. Daniel noticed, and placed a comforting hand on her knee.

"It's only a step further than what my father did to save me," he insisted gently. "I'll have the Tiffin girl fetched soon. Nicolas will be the next Potentate. Now, all *we're* doing is covering our tracks. Nothing more."

The weight of his words pressed into Melissa's chest like dull blades. Daniel hated to speak of his father, and she didn't blame him. She could remember what the previous Potentate had been like, and all he had done. Daniel was a ray of sunshine in comparison, still picking up the pieces; a thousand eyes on him from every angle, waiting for him to fall.

But that didn't lessen the situation *she* now faced. Her fragile little Euphrasie would grow up in another woman's arms. She would call Daniel's wife her mother. She would never know the truth.

Harder than ever, Melissa willed herself not to cry.

"I can't believe you managed to convince Elisabeth this was a good idea," she said.

"Neither can I," Daniel admitted. "But if she wasn't so damn barren, we would never have had to resort to this. It's a good thing she can think as well as look pretty."

"You do her a disservice sometimes, you know. She's a Dickinson. She's smart."

"So long as she's smart enough to keep her mouth shut. That's all that matters."

Melissa kissed her fingers and pressed them to the incubator. Euphrasie was already falling asleep. "I want you to promise me something, Daniel."

"What?"

"Ten years. That's how long it can be before she 'dies' like all the others. Then your tracks will be covered. Yes?"

Daniel frowned. "What are you asking me, exactly?"

Melissa took a deep breath. She turned her eyes on him with a fierceness she had rarely let him see.

"When that time comes, I will tender my resignation. I'll be fifty anyway. There will be others who can step into my shoes by then. And I take her away from all this, to a life where she can be mine."

A muscle twitched in Daniel's cheek.

"It will be difficult," he said.

"I've dealt with *difficult* before," Melissa replied at once. "I'll never forgive you if you don't do this for me. I mean it."

Daniel pursed his lips, then sighed, and gave a small nod.

"Fine. I owe you that much."

A slow smile of relief rose over Melissa's face. It took all her strength to keep her tears in check. They stung like a hundred pins in her head, but she refused to let him see them.

She kissed him.

"Thank you," she breathed. "Thank you."

The sun was high by the time Melissa emerged into the Fifth West. She forced herself to think of other needs — of anything except Euphrasie. There would be paperwork to complete when she returned to headquarters. She also had to wash her black clothes from the night before, and scrub out the lunafauna's blood. Then, that evening, she promised herself she would take a bath and try to forget the entire day.

She stopped at a market and bought two pies from the baker. Then she carried on her way, until she came to the watch shop on Renshaw Street. She glanced through the window, and spotted Charlotte Bellamy heading into the kitchen with a loaf.

Melissa paused for a moment. In some respects, it was difficult to recognise the terrified little girl in the woman before her now. Melissa remembered the moment she had raised her gun and pulled the trigger. The only time she had ever missed.

And here Bellamy was. Alive, as if nothing had happened. But it *had* happened, now, twelve years later: the moment she'd opened her mouth and said those fatal words. Daniel had hoped she would forget them. He had been wrong. And there would be consequences.

Melissa took a shortcut to the neighbouring street and let herself into a dilapidated apartment. She had purchased it several years ago, when she realised it provided a direct view of Bellamy's bedroom. And, just as she knew he would be, Oscar Hargreaves sat at the window.

"Madam Spectre!" he exclaimed. "Is everything alright?"

"Perfectly," Melissa replied. She held one of the pies towards him. "I brought you some lunch."

Hargreaves smiled and the two of them ate at the same time. There were dark circles under his eyes. He hadn't slept the night before, either.

"I saw our Lady friend on the way here," Melissa said. "I assume the Academy let the students out early?"

A shadow passed across Hargreaves's face.

"Yes. She hasn't long come home. She'll go to her room in a moment, to get changed. I imagine she'll stay in there. She's not the type to face people when she's… troubled."

His attention was fixed on the window across the way, but his spare hand clutched the arm of the chair, and Melissa saw faint perspiration on his upper lip.

"Are you alright?" she said.

Hargreaves shook himself in an attempt to loosen up. "Heartburn. That's all."

"There's no need to lie. You want to know the reason I'm here? This morning, Irving paid me a visit. He was concerned. He said you were feeling unsettled when you got home last night."

"Unsettled?"

"About reporting what you heard to me."

Hargreaves's face remained relaxed, but Melissa saw him swallow. That was all the confirmation she required.

"Listen carefully," she said. "You're one of the best officers I have. I knew from the beginning you would be. That's why I chose you. You're skilled, in many ways, and not many have the patience to do what you do. Yesterday was a long time coming, but *you* have done nothing wrong. Do you understand? It's *my* job to do the dirty work."

Hargreaves gnawed his lip. "I'm sorry you had to hear about it, Madam."

Melissa arched an eyebrow. "Hear about your report, or your anxieties?"

He deliberately didn't look at her. "Both."

"Why?" she asked. "Don't you trust me?"

She watched his throat. He didn't swallow again, but a hard sheen came into his eyes.

"What will happen now?" he asked carefully. "Is she a liability?"

"She's always been a liability. That's why you've tailed her."

"I know that, but have the circumstances changed now? What are your intentions?"

"The Potentate wants her brought in," said Melissa. "If she's remembered enough to talk about it, then there's only one place for her."

"But you're not going to kill her?" Hargreaves pressed.

"Not unless I have to," replied Melissa. "You sound concerned."

Hargreaves went to speak again, but then he sat up straight and swept a collapsible telescope off his belt. Melissa peered at Bellamy's window. She was sitting at the dresser under the sill, focused on something in front of her.

Hargreaves frowned. "What the hell…?"

"What is it?" Melissa asked.

"I'm… not entirely sure."

Melissa took the telescope. Through it, she saw watchmaking tools, a soldering iron, the soft white glow of a miniscule orb.

Then her throat tightened in alarm. She dropped her pie and it burst over the dusty floor.

What she had just seen shouldn't be possible. But, all the same, it had been done.

CHAPTER XX

Phoebe staggered into The Three Cogwheels and threw herself down at the bar. The place was empty, aside from a couple of canines eating lunch in the corner. Phoebe paused for just long enough to make sure the collar was hidden under her shawl, and hollered for the barkeep.

He peered out of the back room.

"You're early today."

Phoebe shook her head. "Get me the strongest stuff you have, Timmy. Please."

"Why? What's happened?"

"Haven't you heard? You know what, I'll tell you in a minute. Just, please, the stuff. Anything."

Timmy regarded her cagily, but ducked behind the bar and emerged with a bottle of absinthe.

"This good enough?" he asked.

Phoebe blinked. Just looking at the green liquid made her head spin.

"How did you get your paws on *that?*" she asked. "I've never seen it below the Third Level."

"It doesn't matter. But if anyone asks, you didn't drink it here, alright?"

"Who am I going to tell?"

Timmy fetched a glass and poured the absinthe into it through a sugar cube. He had barely finished when Phoebe snatched it.

"Hey, take it easy!" he cried. "You'll knock yourself out."

"Good," Phoebe growled.

She knew she was still drunk from the night before. Her words slurred, the edges of her vision pulsed, and her skull felt as though it was going to split open. But she didn't care. She wanted nothing more than to enter a state where she couldn't think straight, and stay in it for as long as possible.

"Alright," said Timmy. "Tell me."

Phoebe drank again. The absinthe tasted sweet and herby; it sent clouds drifting through her brain and the smell got up her nose. She sniffed hard to keep herself from sneezing.

"Evelyn's dead."

Timmy's ears turned back in alarm.

"The schoolteacher?"

"Yeah," Phoebe muttered. "She took me back to her place last night. I don't really remember. I just woke up there in the middle of the night. I turned on the lamp and saw blood coming from under her door. Opened it and there she was."

Phoebe held up a paw and mimed cutting the wrist. Timmy's eyes widened with horror.

"Oh, hell," he gasped. "I'm so sorry. It was suicide?"

Phoebe nodded. "I've only just managed to get away from the coppers. They've been quizzing me all damn morning."

She downed the rest of the absinthe and poured more, straight from the bottle, not even bothering with the sugar cube. As she moved, the collar twitched and pulled at her skin like a vicious hook. Twelve years had passed and Daniel still hadn't removed it. Twelve years of being trapped in her taller form, unable to change, not even for a few seconds. In one respect, that time was nothing, but she still bit her tongue to keep herself from crying.

She stared into the emerald depths of the absinthe. The way the light hit it reminded her so much of the trees.

"See, this is what happens if someone gets close to me," Phoebe muttered. "It's hard enough for me, seeing people be born, making friends with them and then having to watch them die. But what's it like for all of *you?* Meeting me, seeing me never change while you do? What does that do to a person?"

"Less than what you probably think it does," Timmy said. "You're one of us. You're not like Carter or the others in Parliament, and we love you for it."

"At what cost?" Phoebe snarled. "I can't remember what she said; I was too far gone. But she was upset about something. She wanted to talk to me. She must have needed help and I wasn't there to give it. I was too busy doing… whatever I was doing. I could have saved her, if only I'd listened!"

Phoebe snatched the absinthe again. The alcohol was starting to muddle her brain. Good. She would finish this glass, then take the rest of the bottle home and swallow it all until she was in a stupor. Hopefully it would incapacitate her for a few days. Maybe it would even kill her.

She scoffed at that idea. She should be so lucky. How wonderful it must be to not exist and lie senseless, like those stony leaves which decorated the buildings. No love, no loss, nothing but the rain to slowly wear her away.

She fished a wad of solidi from her purse and slammed the whole pile on the bar. She didn't know how much was there, but she could tell it was a lot.

"For this," she said, motioning to the absinthe. "And treat yourself. Get yourself a new suit, or something. Take the wife out for a meal."

Timmy stared at the notes. "Phoebe…"

"Take it," she snapped.

She sipped from the glass, slower this time, as flashes of light burst in front of her eyes. Her heart pounded like a hammer against tight cloth. Then it fluttered, skipping beats. The pads under her paws started to tingle.

"Ah, crap. Here it comes," she muttered. "I need to go home."

"I couldn't agree more," Timmy said. "Go to bed. I'll come by later to check on you."

Phoebe shook her head. "No, not like that," she replied. "You don't want to see this…"

The world tipped and she crashed to the floor.

Timmy and the couple in the corner ran to her side. She gasped for breath, saw through tunnel vision. Her feet turned cold. Then she vomited up all of the absinthe.

She knew what was coming. It had been due for a while. She had lived through four lives now, each one roughly eighty years long. And now the next death was on the horizon, advancing by the second, like a speeding train.

"Home," she rasped. "Please…"

She was aware of being lifted and held like a baby in Timmy's arms. The air changed and she stared up at a vacant blue sky. The clouds looked far away, as though they were painted on a fresco. Concerned voices swarmed around her. She moved her ears so she could hear them. Words slurred into a senseless wall of noise. It was too much. She closed her eyes.

After several minutes of hurried walking, Timmy carried her through a door. Phoebe's nose twitched as she smelled herself, her furniture and rugs. Timmy laid her on a couch in the drawing room.

"Get some water," he snapped at someone.

Phoebe shook her head. She wouldn't be able to drink anything now. She never could when the end was near. With every breath, her lungs wheezed more and more. Her body was shutting down.

Please, she begged silently, *let it go all the way this time.*

The rim of a glass was placed to her lips. Only a little of the water entered her mouth, and she immediately coughed it back up.

"Stop," she breathed. "Leave."

"Phoebe…"

"Leave!"

She hated people witnessing this. What must she look like? What emotions did it stir in those still lucid and alive?

Her heart slowed. She couldn't feel her extremities anymore.

With a final feeble gasp, she let herself drift backwards into oblivion, and hung there in the wonderful dark. No light, no warmth, no sound, not even a body. It stretched on forever: a huge expanse where there was no need to breathe or think. She didn't know whether it lasted for years or seconds. It pulled her under, and she didn't fight it. She had been here before.

But she was still conscious. That was the worst thing. That proved it wasn't the *true* end.

The Fabric of Time wrapped around her, and suddenly she was falling, pulled in all directions. White noise drove so deeply into her that if she had a mouth, she would have screamed. Then she sensed her body again, but it was much younger, in an era and place long since gone.

Magic sang in her veins. She transformed for the first time under the full moon and changed from four legs to two. She wasn't a human, but it was close, still a person; a sentient, living thing. She met the others like her: canines and felines alike. The power of nature united them, spun them together in a never-ending dance. Back then, in the beginning, they could change between forms whenever they wanted. They were free. And so, she gathered them, and they walked away from everything they had ever known. They headed west, followed the setting sun towards the rumour of the place where all would be welcome.

They entered a huge forest: so dense and lush, the canopy blotted out the sky. She strode at the head of the lunafauna convoy, encouraging them when they grew tired, tending their wounds when they fell. Eventually, they reached the City in the middle of the woods, which measured time by sundials and made energy from running water. The no-tails who had founded it were building from the ground up, each terrace smaller than the one beneath. There were five of them back then: five hundred feet high. No First Level. There was no need for it in the days before a Potentate.

The lunafauna were welcomed with gentle caution, and given the fledgling South Quarter to themselves. Canines and felines worked with the early alchemists, and spun ancient magic throughout the Levels, so they could be erected stronger and higher. It wove into the bricks like the shine of the sun upon mist. Nature and science, walking hand in hand. Harmony.

She was happy, and so were her brethren. They would be safe here. A new beginning was theirs for the taking.

And then the alchemists started harbouring other ideas. They descended upon her, told her they were looking to unearth truth and progress for the greater good. She fought, tried to escape, but there were too many of them. They took other lunafauna too; ripped men and women from their families in the dead of night.

The sky disappeared. Thick leather straps pinned her limbs down. Her brethren were beside her. Their screams pierced her eardrums until she became one with the sound. Blades cut her flesh and needles dug into her muscles. They drew out her blood with syringes. They swept a scalpel across her forehead to see what lay under the skin. Then they cut deeper, through her ribs, to her heart. And something tore, fused with it… something which should *never* have been altered…

The other prisoners sputtered, coughed up blood, and died. But not her. She proved strong enough to endure what they couldn't.

The alchemists stood in their white coats and scribbled on pieces of paper. They laughed and cheered, and the air filled with the popping of corks. They tried to bind her further, but she was too powerful, in both the right ways and the wrong ways. So instead, another suppression device pierced her neck. They released her from the gurney and took her underground, where a new title was bestowed upon her head. Lady Feline.

Her life drew to an end. She felt the breath leaving her, only to be slammed back into the same body to endure once again. She awoke inside an airless coffin, thrashed until somebody let her out. She was in a hearse, being carted towards the eastern graveyard. Everyone flew back in fright, but none were more terrified than her. She looked at her paws with horrifying realisation and screamed until her vocal cords tore.

The alchemists had done this. They had violated her magic, stretched it as tight and long as it could go without snapping. Nine lives had the cat, was the saying in the land she had come from. And so it would be. Nine lifetimes, each following the last.

They took what they had learned from her and repeated it, but to one of their own this time: an innocent little boy. And with him, they managed what they had originally wanted. An invisible line was drawn through the air between the alchemists and the first Potentate. The Levels grew higher, and through their centre rose a Tower which threatened to touch the sky. A door was closed in its topmost chamber and sealed the child inside.

Darkness descended. Her life ended again and jolted back, no matter how hard she tried to fight it. The last lunafauna, who had made the journey with her when they were mere kittens and puppies, died before her eyes while she endured. Their children looked to her as their leader. They could no longer change under any moonlight, only when it was full, at its strongest. The magic had been warped; the ties to the natural world breaking fibre by fibre. The no-tails sensed the lunafauna weakness, forced them into slavery while alive and stole their bodies when they were dead. Collars were clamped around their necks and she fought to free them.

She turned to the bottle as the City turned to the clock. An industry of gears and cogs spun over the broken remains of sundials and hourglasses. The soil became dead and the beautiful trees tumbled to the ground. Their wood was harvested and carved, while the buildings were moulded to take the image of the very thing the people sought to destroy. Birds fled. Foliage disappeared, leaf by leaf. Greenery turned red, then brown, and then was gone.

Eighty years passed. She died and breathed once more. With every decade, corruption spread. The City she lived in was not the one she had come to. Her old comrades' children were forced ever lower and ever tighter, quashed while she was rendered powerless to stop it. Even the thieves hissed and spat on them. The Potentates looked down from their palace and wallowed in their success. The Timekeepers looked down from higher still, one after another, in perfect timing.

The final tree was felled. No more grew. The alchemists had done their job too well — a job based on knowledge she had handed to them on a plate.

Then she felt August's terrified grip on her shoulders, recognised the desperation in his eyes. He had seen what he should not have seen. She promised to send a private cab to fetch him from Rene Square. She tried to help and he died anyway. Bullets split the air and turned the snow red. Only his daughter survived. It was all for nothing.

Her pulse strengthened and blood moved through her veins. Her lungs swelled to full capacity. She smelled the musky odour of cat hair and undusted surfaces.

Her eyes opened. She was lying on her couch, in exactly the same position as she had left it. The sky was dark outside. She distantly heard the Tower clock chime eleven times.

"No…" she breathed.

She ran her paws over herself, found all her limbs and features. She could even still taste absinthe on her tongue. She was alive.

"Phoebe?"

Timmy scurried over from the shadows. He touched his nose to hers.

"Are you alright?" he asked nervously. "I know you told us to go, but I didn't want to leave you. Can I do anything for you?"

Phoebe stared at him blankly.

"Please go away."

Timmy hesitated. "Are you sure?"

"Go."

To her relief, he did as she said. She lay still until she heard the door close and his footsteps fading into the distance.

"No," she said again, louder now. "No, no! *No!*"

She rolled off the sofa and her legs buckled underneath her. Then she felt the collar around her neck, the sharp needle digging into her scruff.

In desperation, she snatched it, tried to pull it off. The needle pressed deeper, but she carried on scratching at the buckle, tugging at the leather, anything to get the infernal thing away. But nothing worked. The pain only grew, until it consumed her.

Her rage exploded. She raked her claws along the couch and shredded the cushions. Then she collapsed in a wretched heap. She had been so close, yet so far, and so it would continue. Now she was awake, there were still five lifetimes to go.

She saw Evelyn's face in her mind, and screamed.

CHAPTER XXI

"Father?" Nicolas asked, peeking out from under his blanket.

Daniel closed the book he had been reading aloud. "I thought you'd fallen asleep."

"I was just resting my eyes."

Daniel chuckled. He caressed Nicolas's face, smelled the sweet soap from the bath he had taken that evening. It took all his self-control to not whisk him from the bed and hug him.

"You should still try. You don't want to be tired in your lessons tomorrow. Did you enjoy the story?"

"Yes," Nicolas said. "But what are the sundials?"

"They're what people used to tell the time before clocks were invented, back when Forest was founded. If you put them in a certain position, then you could see what time it was from where the sun's shadow fell on the numerals."

"Why don't we use them now?"

"Because clocks are better. Sundials were a lunafauna thing, not good enough for us. And if we hadn't moved on from them, we wouldn't have lighting mechanisms or carriages."

Nicolas frowned as he thought about it.

"So, what comes after clocks?"

Daniel shrugged. "I don't think there'll be anything else. Clocks do everything we need, and we don't have to wrestle with keeping magic under control. There's no need to fix what isn't broken."

"Were the sundials broken?" asked Nicolas. "Is that why we changed to clocks?"

"No, they weren't broken *literally*. But they weren't useful anymore. You find that happens a lot. When something runs its course, then you need to leave it behind."

Daniel tucked the blankets around his son. When he was first born, he thought the child would be awkward; a nuisance which he could leave for Elisabeth and the nursemaids to take care of. But the moment he had looked into those wide eyes, every notion of disinterest had been washed away. He would always adore this boy above all others.

"Will you sing to me?" Nicolas asked groggily.

Daniel let out a soft sigh. He was twelve now, getting too old for this, but he couldn't bring himself to stop.

"Off to dreams you go, little one,
Off to the skies you fly, my dear.
Off to faraway lands, little one,
And I will always be right here.
Here, beside you, forever it will be
Eternally you and eternally me."

Daniel caressed Nicolas's cheek until he was sure he was asleep. Then he kissed him on the forehead and crept towards the door, but stopped, startled. It was open, and Elisabeth stood there, a mellow expression on her face.

"That still works," she said. "You do sing it beautifully."

Daniel pulled the door ajar, just enough for the hallway light to creep into the room. The two of them surveyed Nicolas through the crack.

"I see him every day," Daniel whispered, "and every day

might as well be the first. He's so beautiful."

"I know. I feel the same," said Elisabeth. "He's the best thing we've made."

Daniel cast his eyes down. "How are you feeling?"

"I'm well."

"Good."

Elisabeth didn't look at him. Her face was rounded and childlike, much like Nicolas's, which made her appear much younger than her years. Though a few age lines had creased the sides of her eyes, her skin was as smooth as a doll.

Daniel remembered their wedding day: both of them teenagers, her gazing at him from beneath her veil. She had held a paper bouquet of roses and peonies, which had itself cost a small fortune. Their kiss was chaste and delicate, unsteady with doubt. They had been so frightened.

There wasn't much of a courtship. The whole thing was arranged by their parents: the future Potentate with an heiress of the most powerful alchemical family in history. It was with Elisabeth's ancestors the Invisible Law had been struck, centuries ago. And now a new alliance awaited: one of politics and convenience.

Alastair Carter had risked the very foundations of Forest to protect his only son. Marrying a Dickinson was a small price for Daniel to pay in return. And he and Elisabeth had honestly tried to find love for each other. They copied how the adults behaved, not playing as children would. But when they spoke, there was a hollowness to their words, and days of awkwardness turned to years of coldness.

Daniel hated his father for what he had done. Yes, it was a small price to pay, but for a debt that didn't belong to *him*. So long as he and Elisabeth could produce a child — or two — it didn't matter. They tried, going through the motions, as quickly as could be managed. But for true passion, it was no wonder why Daniel had fallen into the arms of someone who was her complete opposite, as scandalous as it might be.

Elisabeth tucked a stray strand of hair behind her ear.

"Have you prepared everything for the Aeternum meeting?" she asked.

"Not quite," said Daniel. "Just a few final details to write down. I should only be an hour, at most."

"I'll probably be awake. I haven't been sleeping well lately."

Daniel read the meaning to her words at once.

"You're concerned about the baby, aren't you? Don't tell me you're having second thoughts now."

"No, I'm not. I know it's gone too far now… it's the best we can do," Elisabeth replied, so soft and dismal, he hardly heard her. She looked at Nicolas again. "I'm sorry I couldn't give you another, Daniel. But… can you understand how difficult this will be for me? Having to pretend it's my own baby when I know it's hers?"

Daniel paused for a moment. Melissa had said something very similar.

He took hold of Elisabeth's hand.

"I know. But it's also *my* baby. We'll manage. We always do."

Elisabeth bit her lip. The two of them shared a sad smile, then she walked past and disappeared round the corner. As soon as she was out of sight, Daniel heard the sound of muffled sobs.

He rubbed his face wearily. There were moments when he looked into her eyes deeply enough to feel a stab of guilt. And, in its own perverse way, that always brought a hint of something he might call affection. It was faint and near-invisible, but it was there.

He descended to his personal suite. In his study, an antique oak desk stood in the centre of a lush red carpet. He cranked up the lamp on its top, poured a glass of wine, and retrieved his ledger.

"I need to speak with you."

Daniel jumped at the sudden voice. Melissa was standing in the doorway.

"It's something so important, you can't even bother knocking?" he said.

"What are you going to do, arrest me?" Melissa shot back. "And you should know I wouldn't break your precious rules unless there was good cause."

"What is it? Euphrasie? Is she alright?"

"She's fine. I've just left the infirmary; it's nothing to do with her. It's Bellamy."

Daniel set the wine down and groaned into his hands.

"Why? What's happened this time? Who's she talked to now?"

"Nobody."

"Then what's the problem?" he snapped. He was still glad of his decision to let the girl live out the life she'd managed to keep. The last thing he'd wanted from her was any kind of trouble. Her mentioning the Aeternum to her teacher had been bad enough.

"I saw into Bellamy's bedroom today," Melissa said. "And I watched her doing a… procedure. It's like nothing I've ever seen before. She managed to physically attach an orb to a mainspring, by the core."

Daniel frowned. "So, she inlaid an orb. Isn't that what the alchemists do?"

Melissa shook her head. "It's close, but not the same. Whatever she did completely fused the two components. The alchemists have only ever got them to work in conjunction with each other, not become a single mechanism."

"Maybe she just got lucky."

"I don't think so. Before today, I didn't care that she was a watch mechanic. No alchemist has a background like that: clockwork over medicine. But what if *that's* how she figured it out? She's only a year away from being qualified. And her tutor is Bridget Dickinson. Somehow, she knows what she's doing."

Melissa's concern immediately made sense. Daniel's chest curled in on itself like a tightening spring. For generations, the Invisible Law had kept Potentates and alchemists away from each other. If Bellamy had managed to do what Melissa was saying...

"Is it even possible?" he asked. "It sounds..."

"I know, I thought the same thing. But I saw it," said Melissa urgently. "We cannot let this get out, Daniel. She must not be allowed to make... whatever she did... public to anybody. Forget just fetching her. I need to pay her a more serious visit. Do I have your permission?"

Daniel thought quicker than he had all day. He gripped the glass between his hands, so tightly, he worried it might break. Then an idea uncoiled in his mind, with such cool calmness, he couldn't help letting out a sigh of relief.

"No," he said. "You're not to kill her."

Melissa threw up her hands with a snarl.

"This is no time for your sentiment! She's not an innocent little girl anymore! Didn't I tell you at the start, how dangerous this could be?"

"Getting rid of her would be more dangerous, now we know this," Daniel insisted.

"Then I'll just make it look the same as I did for the lunafauna. Problem solved."

Daniel put down the glass harder than he needed to.

"No," he said firmly. "Listen to me. The lunafauna was a nobody. But Bellamy... She's the only survivor of Rene, and people are aware of that. Even if they don't know her personally, she's still familiar enough — her name, her title, what happened to her parents. If it was anyone else, we could get away with it. The whole point is to maintain the status quo. Killing her would just create a bigger risk than it's worth."

Melissa pursed her lips in annoyance. "You said that if anything changed with her, so did our stance. She needs to go."

"You're not to kill her, Melissa, because that's not my main reason for saying no," Daniel continued. "If she did what you say, it might be useful to us. If we treat it properly, present it to the alchemists in the right way—"

"Out of the question," Melissa cut in. "The alchemists can't know about this. If they use their knowledge to refine whatever she's done, or combine it with magic, it could make the Keeper obsolete. I've had enough hard work trying to keep them quiet these past few years."

"I didn't mean the *free alchemists*," Daniel snapped. "Only our little handful in the Aeternum. Victor Paley and his people. They're bound by oaths. What damage could they do?"

Melissa pressed a hand to her eyes. Her shoulders slumped with fatigue.

"This is *not* what I was hoping for when I came back," she said. She snatched Daniel's glass, downing the remainder of the wine in two large gulps. "First Euphrasie, then the lunafauna, now *this*..."

"And you'll manage it," Daniel said, softer now. He approached her. She didn't move, so he slipped his arms around her from behind and pressed himself close. Then she finally yielded and let her head roll onto his shoulder.

"What are my orders?" she asked.

"First of all, I want you to go home and get a full night's sleep. And then, tomorrow, send one of your men to fetch Bellamy and take her to the Roots. It's time she followed in her father's footsteps."

Melissa twisted so she could see him. "What about her guardian?"

Daniel's hands tightened on her stomach. "Malcolm? What about him?"

"Bellamy learnt all her watch mechanic skills from him. You don't think she came up with that technique on her own, do you?"

"Good point. But that's going to be difficult. The two of us didn't part on the best terms."

"It doesn't matter. They're both under *your* terms now," said Melissa. "And if he taught the girl, maybe there's a place for him, too. We'll find a way. Just make them both an offer they can't refuse."

"That reminds me," Daniel said anxiously. "Tomorrow, I need you to send someone to get the Tiffin girl. I saw the Keeper today. He told me the time's come."

Melissa scoffed. "Only now? It's taken him long enough to admit it. He's been falling apart for years. So have half the mechanisms across the City."

"I suppose he's held on for as long as he could. Who knows how his brain works?" said Daniel icily. "But, to be honest, I don't want to know. Every time I see him, it just reminds me of everything I might have been. Everything I did to him…"

Melissa put her arms around Daniel's neck.

"Well, let's forget for a little while. I don't need to go home just yet."

She closed the distance with a kiss and pushed him backwards. Daniel snatched her shoulders, spun her onto the desk.

He hadn't been able to lie with her for months. And so long as they were quiet, it wouldn't matter. The servants and Elisabeth knew not to disturb him when he was in his study.

He ran his hand up Melissa's side, under her shirt, felt the flesh quivering at his touch. She was tired, but he could tell she wanted him, too, and that need was greater.

"You torture me," he panted.

Melissa cocked an eyebrow. "And don't you love it?"

She reached towards his belt. And then nothing existed except for her lips and fingers and skin on his.

CHAPTER XXII

Charlotte's feet sank into the snow as she ran. Each print welled with red. The lighting mechanism shifted and warped. Its gears swung forward like giant claws. A monster in front of her, and an even worse one at her heels. The tall woman was coming, gun at the ready…

Shots, followed by screams. Among them, Charlotte heard Miss Gilbaut.

The bullets hit her, and she jolted awake.

Darkness surrounded her. It was early; the sun hadn't risen yet. She was sitting, slouched forward, with something hard against her cheek. For a moment, she didn't know where she was, then realised she had fallen asleep in front of her dresser.

Charlotte eased herself up and massaged her neck. A blanket fell off her shoulders. Malcolm must have come in and draped it there, but it hadn't done much. The freezing night had pushed under her skin, and every bone ached, as though they had turned to metal.

She wiped condensation off the window pane, and looked at the Tower. Seven o'clock. Two hours until classes would begin.

Charlotte's heart flipped at the thought. How could she bear to walk past Miss Gilbaut's classroom? She pictured the doorway, and it transformed into a black hole in her mind; a deep, dangerous emptiness. Just like the Bellamy manor. Just like Rene. She couldn't go back there…

Then she heard the soft ticking of her mother's wristwatch. It was still lying beside her soldering iron.

She suddenly remembered what she had done to it. She pushed Miss Gilbaut away, hurried downstairs, and bolted through the back door, so fast, she almost ran into Malcolm.

"Hey, slow down!" he barked.

"Sorry."

"Nice to see you up, anyway. You were fast asleep by the time I got home. But, saying that, it was almost midnight. That bloody mechanism took forever to fix. Why didn't you eat the stew I left you?"

Charlotte didn't answer. She dragged him to his workbench and threw the watch at him.

"Open the back of that."

Malcolm frowned. "Why? Is there something wrong with it?"

"Just open it."

He threw her a quizzical look, but nevertheless took his screwdriver and did as she said. Charlotte hovered excitedly as he exposed the movement. The orb's glow shone on his face.

Malcolm's hands, usually so steady, began to tremble.

"You *grafted* this?" he gasped. "Where did you get the orb?"

"There was one in there all along, remember?"

"You..." Malcolm's voice trailed off in astonishment, then his eyes filled with tears. "Oh, kiddo... I can't believe it! How did you do it?"

"The way you said," Charlotte smiled. "Only, you need to make an alchemy incision for it to work, and you can't touch the orb directly with the solder."

"Unbelievable," Malcolm breathed. He grasped her hands. "I'm so proud of you."

Charlotte's heart swelled. He didn't say those words very often, so when he did, they were meant.

Her stomach rumbled loudly. Malcolm heard it and flicked her nose.

"Go get your breakfast."

Charlotte headed into the kitchen. She listened to the clicks as Malcolm wound all the clocks on the wall. Then another sound sliced through them, sharper. The front door bell.

Charlotte paused. It was only fifteen minutes past seven, still dark outside. The shop wouldn't open for another two hours. Nobody came this early.

"Good morning, sir," Malcolm said. His voice was clipped, like a taut cord had been wrapped around his neck. "How can I help? Has another lighting mechanism gone down somewhere?"

"No, Mr Godwin. But I do need to speak with you. And Miss Bellamy."

Ice burst through Charlotte's veins. She recognised that voice. The constable.

She peered around the doorframe. As soon as she saw him, his eyes flicked up and locked onto her. She looked straight back, hoping her nerves weren't showing. His mere presence, standing there in his blue uniform, made her hair stand on end like pins. Had he changed his mind about the cake?

"There you are, miss," he said. "Would you please come out here?"

Malcolm looked over his shoulder. "Charlotte? What's this about?"

Charlotte shrugged. She stepped into the main room and Malcolm subtly angled himself in front of her.

The constable regarded her for a moment which seemed to drag into eternity. He removed his cap and gloves, and she spotted a band of pale skin on his left index finger, where a ring had sat.

"My name is Oscar Hargreaves," he said. "Do you remember, we met yesterday afternoon?"

"He was at the marketplace," Charlotte quickly whispered to Malcolm. "Yes, I remember. If I may ask, why are you here now?"

Hargreaves tucked his gloves into his belt. His eyes didn't leave hers for a moment. They were so intense, Charlotte wanted to fall through the floor, just to get away from them. He was looking at her as though they weren't strangers at all. And his voice rang in her head like the echo of water dripping into a cave. It was so familiar, yet so distant...

"Miss Bellamy, first of all, I want to offer my condolences," Hargreaves said. "I was so sorry to hear about the passing of your teacher."

"What?" Malcolm looked at Charlotte. "What happened?"

Charlotte's heart felt like a knife had been plunged through it.

"Miss Gilbaut. She killed herself."

Malcolm fell into his chair in horror. His hand flew to his pocket, in search of his watch.

"Why didn't you tell me?" he demanded.

"You weren't here. And... I couldn't believe it myself," Charlotte said. Her words trembled, thin and reedy. The black hole yawned behind her, threatening to pull her down. She felt her chest constricting and snatched the workbench to steady herself. She couldn't let it overwhelm her, not now, in front of an officer...

"Hang on," she said to Hargreaves. "How did *you* know about her?"

For the briefest second, his gaze wavered.

"I was part of the team who... well, attended the scene, yesterday evening," he said carefully. "And I'm familiar enough with the area to know you were both acquainted. Forgive me, I know this is hard. I don't want to cause you any further distress. But, you see, Miss Bellamy, I don't believe she took her own life. I think it's more likely someone else did."

Charlotte's insides jerked against themselves. She gripped the bench even harder.

"Why?"

"I saw her," said Hargreaves. "I can't be certain, but in my opinion, there's more to this. And since you yourself are quite a high-profile case—"

"What, you think *Charlotte* killed her?" Malcolm interrupted.

"Of course not! But you've been on my mind for a while."

Hargreaves glanced all over the place, as though he was searching for something among the clocks and contraptions. Then he took a step closer.

"I was in Rene Square, Miss Bellamy. I was one of the first to get there. I took you to Bentham Hospital myself."

Charlotte's head rang like it had been struck with a tuning fork. But uncertainty still chilled her, ran up her spine and then back down again. She wasn't about to take his word that easily.

"Whereabouts on my body was I shot?" she asked.

"In the left shoulder and top of the left arm," Hargreaves said at once. "You were wearing a white nightgown and black coat, with leather boots and a hat, and you had a doll dressed in pink. You were under a collapsed lighting mechanism. That protected you from the worst of it."

Charlotte swallowed. All of that was true, even the detail about her doll. And like a missing puzzle piece slotting into place, the familiarity solidified itself in her memory.

"Are you still awake? Squeeze my hand if you can hear me."

"That was you," she said. Her words trailed up, as though asking a question, but she knew.

Malcolm got to his feet.

"In that case," he said, "I owe you my most sincere thanks, sir. You saved her life."

Hargreaves hesitated, then shook his hand. However, Charlotte noticed a thin veil of wariness running beneath Malcolm's gratitude. They both knew the truth about what had happened in Rene, and Hargreaves was still a police officer. Just like the ones who had pulled the triggers.

"It was one of the longest nights of my life," Hargreaves continued. "After I left you at the hospital, I was summoned to stand guard outside the manor. I'll never forget it. But that's not the only place I know you from, Miss Bellamy — or, *know of you*, I should say. I met your father when I was young. Believe me, I'm a friend. I helped you once, and I'll help you now."

"Help her with what?" Malcolm asked cagily. "She's perfectly safe here. She always has been."

"Not necessarily."

"But why would anyone come after her? She's done nothing wrong."

"I don't know, Mr Godwin. But the ones responsible for Rene may be behind Evelyn Gilbaut's death as well. I'm not willing to take a chance on the lone survivor's life. She is the only one, and I want to make sure she stays that way."

"The *ones* responsible for Rene?" Charlotte cut in. "So you know the truth, don't you?"

Hargreaves's eyes moved back to her. Once again, their different colours unnerved her, like the ground was shaking under her feet. She'd never thought it possible to have eyes like that. If she had still been a child, she might have fancied he'd stared up at the moon for too long, and the ancient magic had bleached one of his irises.

"It wasn't that lunafauna convict who was all over the papers," she said sharply. "What was his name? Roger Cunningham? There were only a couple of lunafauna in the square, and all of them were killed. If you saved me, you must have seen—"

"I arrived *afterwards*. The place was deserted when I found you," Hargreaves insisted. His voice grew more desperate by the second. "Miss Bellamy, listen. I say this as someone who has already saved you, and someone who was saved by your father. You should take shelter elsewhere. At least for the time being — a week at most — until I can figure out a way to help you more. All I'm asking is that you trust me and just lie low for a little while."

"Isn't that a bit suspicious?" Malcolm challenged him. "Us leaving here immediately after Evelyn dies, and you thinking it might not be what it seems?"

"If suspicion could be placed on you at all, then I wouldn't suggest this," Hargreaves said. "*Please*. I want to help you before you need to ask for it."

He stepped closer and rested his hands on the workbench. It took all Charlotte's resolve to not move back.

"I've told you everything I know. It isn't much, but that's why I'm so frustrated myself. I'm not doing this on any command from my superiors. Mr Godwin, if you don't wish to come, I understand. But I would urge Miss Bellamy to take heed."

"I'm not going anywhere without him," Charlotte snapped.

Hargreaves didn't answer, just looked into her eyes. It was beseeching, almost protective. Like the way her father had often watched her when she tried to slide down the banister.

"I... can't leave," Charlotte said. "I have to go to the

Academy. This is my most important year."

"One week," Hargreaves said again. "That's all. And wouldn't you rather be safe?"

"You honestly think Miss Gilbaut was... murdered?"

"Yes."

Anxiety coursed through Charlotte's chest like cold water. Then it flared with the hot red of anger, as her teacher's kindly expression transformed into the face she'd never forgotten.

"Well, if it's the same people who were in Rene, I can give you one clue," Charlotte said. "A tall woman, with a long black braid. She knew my father. He was scared of her. I think he knew what she was going to do."

Hargreaves didn't move. "I'll keep that in mind."

"And she was wearing a uniform just like yours," Charlotte added. "So she shouldn't be too hard for you to find, should she?"

Hargreaves countered with a glance sharper than a knife.

"You'd be surprised," he replied. "It might have been a stolen garment. That's happened before, mainly in the North. There are thief gangs there. Things are more secure now, but back then, they could rob a police store and get hold of our uniforms and firearms."

Charlotte paused. That was a good point. Her father had often visited the North Quarter to help the orphanages, and some were notorious for supplying child pickpockets. The tall woman might have known him because of that. And many people in the North didn't need an excuse for killing anyone they didn't like.

Hargreaves had her in a corner. Defeated, she let out a heavy sigh.

"Alright. I believe you. I'll go."

Malcolm took hold of her arm protectively.

"Where to? I don't know anyone. Would any of your

friends help us?"

"Julian, maybe," Charlotte suggested. "He's the only real friend I've got."

"No," said Hargreaves. "He's the nephew of Evelyn Gilbaut's employer. It's too strong a link."

"Well, who else?" Malcolm asked. Then his eyes lit up. "What about that girl in the market you talk to?"

"What girl?"

"You know... the one with the long hair. Samuel's kid."

"*Aggie?* Oh, no."

"Why? She likes you. She'd help."

"Yeah, but her father can't stand me. You know he's a nutter, Malcolm. You really want to stay with *Samuel Tiffin* for a week?"

"He's not dangerous," Malcolm insisted. "Can you think of anything better?"

Charlotte rolled her eyes.

"Fine," she growled. "What should we take?"

"A spare pair of clothes should be enough," said Hargreaves. "And jackets. The weather looks like it might turn." He threw a glance at Charlotte, still clad in her old dungarees. "And maybe a skirt?"

Charlotte glared at him, but traipsed upstairs to change. She laced a pair of stays and threw on the dress she had worn to the Academy the day before. Then she tore a brush through her hair and pinned it, upended the books out of her satchel and stuffed a nightgown inside.

Her hands shook. She tried to breathe, but every inhale sent a dart of pain through her ribs, like she had been speared from front to back.

It was all too much to take in. She was tempted to storm back down to Hargreaves, tell him to leave and never bother her again. The years since the shooting had been like stumbling through darkness without a light, but she had still managed. She had put her past behind her and laid the foundations of a new future.

But then she thought, once again, of Miss Gilbaut. Her scars twitched. She had changed the way she talked, the way she walked, but had the taint of Rene ever really left her?

Her eyes caught her emergency kit, still on top of the dresser. She tried to stuff it into the satchel, but there was no room, so she fastened it out of sight beneath the first fold of her skirt. Lastly, she clipped her mother's watch back onto her wrist. She couldn't bear to go without having some forms of comfort, even if they were only a timepiece and a roll of tools.

CHAPTER XXIII

Hargreaves was right about the weather. A heavy cloud blocked any signs of dawn and cast the City into a strange lightless purgatory. Everything looked like it had been dragged through a bowl of blue dye. Even the ice seemed more intense than normal. And then, with almost deliberate slowness, snowflakes fluttered in front of Charlotte's face.

She snarled under her breath. This week was only getting worse.

By the time they turned into Smithdown Street, the snow had started to bank against the buildings like mounds of sugar. Charlotte kicked her heels into it to keep from slipping. Ahead stood the bakery, but the curtains were drawn and the sign on the door turned to *closed.* Samuel Tiffin never opened until nine o'clock, but she knew he'd be awake. Bakers were always up early to prepare the day's loaves.

Charlotte glanced at the apartment over the shop, and grimaced at the thought of being stuck inside it for a week. Where would they sleep? On a couch? The floor? Tiffin would surely make it clear that any option was too good for them. And if he flew into one of his rages and turned them out, then what?

There was no time to think about that. Hargreaves was already climbing the flight of stairs to the door.

"Mr Tiffin?" he called.

There was a scurrying sound from within.

"Who is it? Bakery's the other side! And shut!"

"I'm aware of that. Open up, please."

A bolt was drawn away and the door opened a crack. When Tiffin saw Hargreaves, his eyes grew huge.

"No..." he muttered. "I'm not ready to say goodbye to her yet!"

He went to slam the door, but Hargreaves thrust his foot forward. Tiffin whimpered like a child.

"Please... don't take her away," he cried. "Please, sir! I beg you! I know I made a deal, but I was young and stupid!"

"What are you talking about?" asked Hargreaves.

Malcolm and Charlotte exchanged a confused look. Tiffin suddenly noticed them and his jaw clenched.

"Bellamy. What are you doing here?"

"I've brought her and Mr Godwin here for protection," Hargreaves explained. "They won't be on your hands for long."

"They're not staying in my house!" Tiffin barked. "What makes you think I have the room?"

"They don't need much room."

"You haven't got any right to force them on me like this!"

"I have," Hargreaves said. "I invoke the Potentate's Decree of Sanctuary."

"Never heard of it before."

"Shows how much attention you pay to things," Charlotte noted sourly. "You get taught that when you're eleven."

"Bugger off," Tiffin spat at her. "Look at you, still strutting around everywhere as if you own the place. You know it's all a farce as much as I do, Bellamy."

Malcolm eased Charlotte behind him.

"There's no need to talk to her like that," he said, trying a softer approach. "We mean no harm, Samuel. We won't get in your way."

"And I'm afraid I must insist," Hargreaves added. "If

anyone is brought to a residence for protection by the Constabulary, it's an offence to deny entry."

Tiffin glanced over Hargreaves's uniform. He stared at the red circle. Then he looked at the officer's hand, as though searching for something.

"Listen," he whispered. "If I let them in, you won't take Aggie away. Deal?"

Hargreaves frowned. "I'm not going to take your daughter anywhere."

Tiffin snatched his lapel. "Deal?"

"Fine!" Hargreaves snapped, pushing him away. "Deal."

The baker held his eyes for a long moment, then nodded. "Come on, then. Get in."

Charlotte and Malcolm hurried out of the snow. At once, the yeasty smell of fresh bread hit her, like inhaling a warm blanket. But aside from that, there was little to welcome them. The sharper aromas of long-settled dust and unwashed laundry swam forward, exacerbated by a heating mechanism in desperate need of oiling. The small windows were framed with curtains at least two decades old, and equally aged furniture lined the bare walls, all yellowed from tobacco. Everywhere was so dirty and untidy, Charlotte's skin crawled just to look at it.

Hargreaves began speaking with Tiffin in a hushed tone. Curiosity getting the better of her, Charlotte turned her head to hear what they were saying.

"I assure you, I haven't the faintest idea what you're talking about."

"But you've got the red mark! You must know! My girl! When I met with the Potentate after she was born…"

"Father?"

Charlotte jumped. Aggie was peering over the banister, half her hair woven into a single pigtail.

Tiffin sprang to her.

"Sweet dearest, you aren't finished getting ready," he said desperately. "Go back up and tidy yourself."

But Aggie had already glanced past him and seen Charlotte.

"Hello!" she said. "What are you doing here? Father… why's there a constable here?"

"It's nothing, my dear," Tiffin cooed. He put a shaking hand on her cheek to force her to look at him. Aggie flinched at the touch. "Absolutely nothing. Now go back upstairs like a good girl."

Aggie nodded obediently, but her eyes strayed to Charlotte again.

"Can she come with me, Father? Charlotte, would you like to see my room?"

Charlotte tried to think of a polite refusal. She turned to Malcolm for help, but her heart sank when he brushed at her with his hand, urging her to go.

"Wouldn't that be nice?" he said, putting on a cheery façade. "That's alright, isn't it, Samuel?"

Tiffin huffed, then tossed his head to tell Charlotte she could follow Aggie. Charlotte threw a glare at Malcolm.

Eyes alight with excitement, Aggie snatched Charlotte's hand and dragged her up the staircase into the furthest bedroom. It was much better lit and furnished than the parlour, and the walls had been painted pink. A mound of toys sat in the corner, and among the stuffed dolls common for children in the area, Charlotte also spotted things she'd had in the Bellamy manor: a rocking horse, thaumatrope, detailed music boxes. Marionettes hung over the heating mechanism, their strings tangled around the coil.

How could Samuel Tiffin afford all those on a baker's pay?

Aggie spun on the spot with her arms open. "Do you like it?"

Charlotte was too stunned to answer, so Aggie busied herself with plaiting the remainder of her hair into a second pigtail. She looked in a mirror and pointed at the braids.

"Are they even?"

Charlotte nodded.

"Good," said Aggie. "What's the matter?"

"It's nothing. Today's just been a little... strange. That's all."

"It's only eight o'clock."

"I know. Hopefully it won't get any stranger. I don't really want to talk about it."

Charlotte fingered the strings of the nearest marionette. It was beautifully made, likely by someone at the same level of craftsmanship as Malcolm was with his mechanisms. The face and hands were porcelain, and a quaint pastel suit overlaid the body. But, in a rather bizarre detail, the eyes weren't painted on, or even made from glass. Instead, two small gears had been stuck there, and the longer Charlotte looked at them, they seemed to spin in the sockets.

Aggie appeared beside her and beamed at the puppets.

"Is it because your teacher died?" she asked. "I heard about that."

Charlotte gritted her teeth. "I said, I don't want to talk about it."

Aggie took a step back. Realising she had been too sharp, Charlotte sighed and offered a small smile of apology.

"I'm sorry. It's not your fault. I shouldn't take it out on you."

"Don't worry about it," said Aggie, albeit a little meeker. "I know it's horrible."

The way she spoke made Charlotte look at her again. The bruise near Aggie's elbow was covered, but another was forming on her wrist, with the unmistakable shape of fingers. Charlotte took her hand to inspect it, but she pulled away.

"How did that happen?" Charlotte asked.

Aggie kept her gaze on the floor. "Father wasn't happy with me, after he found out I gave you that cake."

"Did he hit you?"

Aggie shrugged.

Anger flooded Charlotte like hot steam. Tiffin was unstable, but to strike his daughter? How long had this been going on?

Then a horrible thought burst into her mind. Had *she* been the cause of those bruises? Another person hurt because of her, and all over a *cake?*

She bit her tongue, hard. Her entire body felt like it had turned to lead.

"I'm sorry," she whispered. "I should have made you take my stupid money."

Aggie opened her mouth to speak. But before she could, a loud bang sounded on the front door. Tiffin yelped like a terrified dog.

Aggie ran towards the noise, but Charlotte grabbed her and flung her back.

"Stay here," she said.

"I need to help him!" Aggie argued.

"Stay here! I mean it!" Charlotte repeated.

She bolted down the staircase, and took stock of what she saw. Tiffin had opened the door. Another constable was on the step. Charlotte hurried to Malcolm, went to ask what was going on, but the officer cut her off.

"Please don't make a scene," he said to Tiffin. "You knew

this day would come. Where is she?"

"No! You can't have her!" cried Tiffin, then brandished a finger at Hargreaves. "He made a deal with me!"

The officer peered into the room, and both he and Hargreaves froze when they saw each other.

"Oscar?"

"Richie? What are you doing here?"

"I'm on orders. What are *you* doing here?" The officer glanced at Malcolm and Charlotte. "Why are *they* with you?"

At that, Tiffin whirled around, panicked tears in his eyes.

"This is your fault! You brought them here to take her away! Get out! All of you! *Get out!*"

"Mr Tiffin, calm yourself, or I'm authorised to use force!" snapped Richie. He walked through the door, kicked it shut.

Hargreaves moved towards him carefully.

"Richie," he hissed, "maybe you and I should go outside for a minute."

"I've got orders," Richie repeated. "I don't know why you're here, with these two, but you can sort that out later with Madam Spectre. Mr Tiffin, where is she?"

Tiffin sank pitifully onto his knees and sobbed.

"Please, please, go away!" he begged. "Leave us alone!"

Richie shook his head with a sigh and shouted up the stairs.

"Agatha! Come here!"

"*No!*" Tiffin shrieked.

Charlotte sucked in a shaky breath. What was going on?

She heard footsteps on the landing, then Aggie appeared. All the light vanished from her eyes until only a frightened shine was left.

"Who are you?" she asked in a tiny voice. "Father! Are you alright?"

Aggie flew down the steps and took hold of her father's shoulders. As soon as she was within distance, Richie grabbed her wrist. She yelped in terror. Tiffin went to pull her back, but Richie drew his pistol and pointed it straight at him.

At once, Hargreaves raised his own.

"Stay your hand!" he barked. "Now! That's an order!"

"Oscar, my orders outrank whatever you're playing at. I'm sorry."

Sparks of panic flared in Charlotte's chest like a firework. She couldn't tear her eyes away from the flintlocks.

Then the door opened again, and a third officer entered. It took all her self-control to stay on her feet.

It was the tall woman.

The edges of Charlotte's vision warped as though she was looking through the bottom of a glass. She heard the faraway cacophony of screams and flying bullets, saw the terror in her father's face…

The woman looked straight at Charlotte. The force of her eyes was so intense, she almost fell over.

"What the hell is this? At what point did I authorise you to bring them here?"

"Madam Spectre, I can explain," Hargreaves replied, but his voice cracked and his cheeks turned pale with fright.

The woman shot him a terrible glare.

"I'm sure it will be an interesting account. And you, Irving, what is this mess? Must I do everything myself?"

She strode up to Samuel Tiffin, took his head in her hands, and twisted it. A sickening crack split the air.

"Ad maius bonum," she said.

Aggie screamed. Four more officers streamed through the door. Three of them ran straight at Charlotte.

She leapt towards the stairs. This couldn't be happening.

They had come back for her, they would kill her, kill all of them…

One of the men caught the hem of her dress and forced her to the floor. The others restrained Malcolm and Aggie. Charlotte thrashed as hard as she could, but the officer straddled her and pinned her arms behind her back.

Hargreaves took a step towards the tall woman.

"You knew her?" Charlotte cried at him. "*You knew?*"

A cloth appeared over her face. The heavy, acrid smell of ether slithered into her lungs like a snake. The room sprang out of its contours, then vanished completely and swept her away with it.

CHAPTER XXIV

Melissa strode to the headquarters with a ferocity which sent dread racing in Oscar's veins. Even the sound of her boots on the stone was terrifying. Richie walked beside him, but neither risked a glance at each other. There would be time for words later.

Oscar tried to swallow, but his mouth was completely dry. What was he going to do?

They reached Melissa's office. Her face was unreadable, and that scared him more than anything else.

"It takes some skill to make me as angry as I am right now," she said. "Or, perhaps that should be *lack* of skill. I'm aware neither of you knew the other's movements, but that's no excuse for what I saw today. So, who wants to explain themselves first?"

An uncomfortable silence fell over the room. Oscar fought to keep his breathing steady.

Melissa's eyes flickered between the two of them. "Well?"

Richie cleared his throat. "Madam, I'm sure I can speak for both of us when I say we're sorry—"

"I didn't ask for an apology," Melissa cut in, "I asked for an explanation. But since you're the first to speak, Irving, let's start with you. Your instructions were to go in, take care of Tiffin, and fetch the girl. That was it. Beyond simple. I was even debating whether it was worth me staying to make sure you managed. It's lucky I did."

Richie shuffled uncomfortably.

"I'm sorry—"

"I'm not finished," Melissa snapped. "I know this was your first sensitive assignment, but I was sent on my first mission when I was eight years younger than you, and the mark never even knew I was in the room. You can start toying with them when you know you can trust your own efficiency. You are a Circulus Officer for a reason, and that means there's no excuse for sloppiness. Do you understand me?"

Richie nodded so fast, Oscar was surprised he didn't pull a muscle in his neck.

"Yes, Madam," he said. "I was going to do exactly that, but when I went inside, I was... well, distracted."

Oscar could tell Richie was aching to look at him. Melissa, however, didn't move a muscle.

"Distracted," she repeated icily. "Do you think *I* was distracted when I had to go into a burning building and shoot four people? Or when I had to give the very impromptu order to seal off a square and kill everyone in it?"

She snapped her fingers. The sound was so sharp, Richie jumped.

"Distractions don't matter. It's how you deal with them that matters," she said. Then she turned her attention to Oscar. "Which brings us to *you*."

She stood directly in front of him — so close, he could see a faint line of moles on her left cheek. A bead of sweat ran down his neck. He was already in trouble, but one wrong move now would spell disaster.

"A simple question, Hargreaves," Melissa said. "Why did you take Bellamy and her guardian to the bakery?"

Oscar ran his tongue across his lips, willed his voice not to wobble, and replied.

"As a ruse, Madam. It was to get them away from the shop for a few days, so I could infiltrate it and inspect the procedure we saw. Then I could bring it back to you to investigate further."

The Tower chimed. Oscar heard the ringing distantly, but didn't bother to note the time. He was too focused on watching Melissa, for the slightest muscle twitch or change in posture; anything which would tell him he had fooled her.

Eventually, she sat in her chair and lit a cigarette. Then she fixed Oscar and Richie with a gaze like venom.

"I appreciate your forward thinking, Hargreaves," she said, "but you know very well you're not to do anything without my order."

Oscar bit his tongue so he wouldn't sigh with relief. She had believed him.

"I was planning to check the shop myself, after Bellamy and Godwin were retrieved," Melissa said. "If you'd continued to show your impeccable patience, you would have known that, because I would have asked you to accompany me. But I'm disappointed in you. You've committed the opposite offence as your friend here: he didn't act quickly enough and you acted too quickly."

"I'm sorry, Madam Spectre," Oscar said.

"I'm sure you are."

Melissa drew a deep lungful of tobacco and breathed out the smoke. It bloomed around her for a moment, then rose towards the ceiling and disappeared.

"Hargreaves, now Bellamy has been taken into custody, your old post is obsolete. Whatever happens to her now is not your concern. I'll find a new assignment for you. But before that, I would say that both of you need time to think on your faults."

She rested the cigarette on the rim of an ashtray.

"I'm a forgiving woman, but if any more accidents

happen, then they are not accidents. They are errors, and the Circulus is only as strong as the weakest link in the chain. Do I make myself clear?"

"Absolutely," said Richie.

"Good," Melissa said. "You're both stripped of duty for three days. I'm being generous with that. Use the time wisely and report back to me here at seven o'clock on Saturday morning. Now, get out."

As soon as Oscar was out of the building, he slipped along the wall until he was safely concealed by the Tower. Two of its flanks reared behind him, stretching a hundred feet to west and south on either side. An encased staircase wound along it like vines on a tree, held in place by huge struts. One of its arteries opened behind Oscar and allowed the sight of only a few steps before disappearing into darkness.

Richie rounded the corner and came straight at him.

"Alright, care to tell me what the hell that was all about?" he snapped.

"I already did," Oscar replied. "What was that about the Tiffin girl?"

Richie pursed his lips and started pacing back and forth.

"It's classified."

"Classified? Damn it, Richie, when has that ever mattered? I told you about the… well, whatever it was I saw Bellamy do."

"That was your decision. This is mine. I think we both know I'm in worse trouble than you. Even though *you* were the one who made me mess up."

Oscar scowled. "Don't be so melodramatic."

"You pointed a gun at me!" Richie snarled.

"And you were pointing one at an innocent man!" argued Oscar. "How was I supposed to know what was going on? Don't blame this on me!"

For a moment, he thought Richie might punch him. But instead, his friend stormed down the path and out of sight.

Oscar stayed still, shaking with adrenaline. He felt as though a hollow had opened straight through his chest. Richie wasn't the priority. He couldn't believe he'd managed to fool Melissa, but now he had, what was he supposed to do?

When the two of them had witnessed Charlotte performing the strange procedure, Oscar had known it would be her last night as a free girl. His mind had flung all the options in front of him like a horrific hand of cards. A quiet assassination, imprisonment in some gaol or asylum... Every single one filled him with such panic, he could hardly think. Approaching her and Malcolm had been stupid; ruled by desperation, not logic.

He looked at the red circle over his pocket, then the ring on his finger. He had taken it off when he went to the shop, but slipped it on again when Melissa's back was turned. He had been so proud and desperate to possess both those symbols, until he learned all the hidden truths they entailed. Those truths, and the gilded lies which shrouded them, beat at his integrity like water against stone, trying to wear him down. Just as the thieves had done when he was a boy.

It was wrong. It was all so terribly, unbearably *wrong*.

Cold reality struck him. He needed to help Charlotte. He couldn't leave her down here to face whatever lay in store.

"A wise decision, Oscar Hargreaves."

Oscar spun around. The voice tore through him, made every hair on his body stand on end. It was completely monotone, neither young nor old; so calm, it completely immobilised him. For a second, he even forgot to breathe.

His eyes locked onto the tunnelled staircase entrance, and he reached for his pistol.

"Who's there?" he said. "Show yourself."

A small figure appeared, as though the shadows themselves had taken solid form. A dark cloak enveloped its entire body, and a hood was pulled low over its face. Oscar noticed a pair of buckled ankle boots under the hem: what a wealthy child might wear. But every step they took down the staircase juddered and clicked like the bones of an ancient man.

Oscar's belly writhed; every part of his brain screamed at him to run as far away as possible. He didn't need to ask who it was. He might never have seen him before, but only one being in Forest could carry such a pressing, sickening weight as this.

"Why... How are you here?" Oscar asked. "You're supposed to be in the Tower..."

"I can come and go as I please. You wish to assist Charlotte Bellamy, and so do I. You also know the streets of the City like no other. Would you like me to tell you how you can help her?"

Oscar trembled. "How do you know about her?"

"Answer me. Will you help her?"

"Yes."

The Keeper nodded. "Very well. Then listen carefully."

Charlotte's eyes snapped open. She was lying on a bed, in a small yet well-furnished room. Her emergency kit bag pressed uncomfortably into her leg, still hidden under her skirt. Her throat stung from the ether she had inhaled, like an entire bottle of cleaning solution had been forced down it. Then she noticed a glass of water on a table and swallowed the contents in a few gulps.

"Kiddo?"

She looked up. Malcolm was sitting in a chair, nervously fingering his pocket watch. He snapped it shut and wrapped his arms around her.

"You alright?" she wheezed.

"I'm fine," he replied, his voice just as hoarse as hers. "I've been awake for about fifteen minutes. Are you hurt?"

"No. What happened? Where are we?"

"I don't know."

They inspected the room. It had no windows and was lit only by a single lighting mechanism overhead. Charlotte quickly checked her wrist, and was relieved to see her mother's watch still there. The hands read five minutes to twelve.

Alarm clenched her stomach. They had arrived at the bakery shortly after eight o'clock. Had four hours passed since then? Or was that twelve o'clock at night? It was impossible to tell.

Then she remembered the tall woman and a panicked cry flew from her lips.

"What's wrong?" Malcolm asked.

"It was *her!*" Charlotte cried. "And those words, what she said…"

"What are you talking about? Slow down. It's alright."

"It's *not* alright! That woman, she was the one who—"

The click of a key cut her off. The door opened to reveal a police officer. Charlotte didn't recognise him, but she noticed a red circle on his jacket. Just like Hargreaves wore.

Malcolm positioned himself in front of her.

"What's going on?" he demanded.

"We were just waiting until you woke up," said the officer. "Would you come with me, please?"

"To where?"

"Don't be upset, Mr Godwin. You're our guests. You were

simply put in here for your own protection while you recovered. Come, your host is waiting."

He spoke civilly, but a dangerous glint shone in his eyes, like the sun striking ice. He wasn't going to leave them in peace.

Malcolm wove his arm around Charlotte's.

"I've got you. We're going to be alright," he whispered, but he couldn't keep the nerves out of his voice.

They followed the officer outside and climbed a steep flight of stairs. At first, Charlotte thought they were inside an Interlevel tunnel, but the windows in the walls showed no hint of the sky. Instead, the views were of a vast underground chamber, lit by lamps turned to maximum brightness. Colossal gears turned in a dizzying array of movement, each component larger than the last. Winding around the various clockworks were more routes, some exposed and some covered. Below, the compound stretched down, into the bowls of the earth, until the lights dimmed against a sickening black abyss. And across everything was a strange pearlescent shimmer, like moonlight woven into threads. Charlotte didn't need to ask to know it was magic.

Her hair stood on end. It was as though she was looking at a whole other City. Were they not in Forest anymore?

"What the hell is this place?" Malcolm blurted.

Then Charlotte noticed the giant stone girth running through the centre. They *were* still in Forest, just *beneath* it. That structure could only be one thing.

"The Tower," she gasped. "How...?"

"It's not my place to answer questions, Miss," said the officer.

They reached a thin bridge. On the other side, an immense building hung suspended between stone pillars, decorated with festoons and oriel windows. Inside, an opulent room swelled around them, with a wooden table in the centre, silver bowls scattered across its top. A beautiful fresco of the sky filled the ceiling — it was so lifelike, it made Charlotte shiver with uncanniness. Two more constables stood in the corners.

Her jaw dropped. She hadn't been anywhere this magnificent since she was a child.

Two more constables stood in the corners, and the one who had accompanied them also took a place, by the door.

"Please have a seat," he said.

Charlotte glared at him, but did as she was told. Malcolm sat beside her and took hold of her hand. A tense silence dragged through the air, grated against her ears like sandpaper.

Seeking distraction, she inspected the bowls. They were filled with sugared nuts and dried fruit pieces. She was tempted to cram handfuls into her mouth, but anxiety tore the edge off her hunger as quickly as it surfaced. Everything about this place felt threatening. The soft colours seemed to hide edges harsh enough to cut her if she looked too closely.

And *that woman* had brought them here.

Charlotte shivered at the thought of her. That face which had haunted her nightmares, terrified her father. There was no doubt it was the same person. Was *she* down here, somewhere? Was *she* their mysterious host?

The door swung wide. Charlotte spun around in her chair.

But there was no blue jacket or black hair. Instead, a man stepped into the chamber. He was about Malcolm's age, and wore a tailored purple suit; so intricately decorated, it would have taken months to sew. A curled wig covered his hair, like the ones her father had worn to Moots. A wedding band and red ring were just visible under the lacy cuff of his shirt.

He turned his eyes on Charlotte, and a shiver rippled through her body. They were a striking shade of leafy green. And there was a certain fierceness to them, carefully controlled —

along with something else. Curiosity? She couldn't tell.

Suspicion gripped her, and it was confirmed when the officers respectfully removed their caps.

It was Potentate Carter.

CHAPTER XXV

The Potentate took a seat at the table — so close, Charlotte could smell his perfume. The simplest movement sang of poise and authority. He held himself with the same rigid grace her mother had drilled into her as a child: shoulders back, spine impeccably straight, as though a pole had been shoved through it.

Charlotte threw a glance at Malcolm. But his expression was not that of a watch mechanic who had suddenly found himself before the most powerful person in the City. It was pure recognition.

"Please forgive the manner in which you were brought here. I didn't intend for it to be so... rough," the Potentate said. Every word was perfectly pronounced, as though he had practised reciting them. When neither Charlotte nor Malcolm responded, he continued.

"I'm sorry for the delay in meeting you, too. There were errands this morning which had to take priority. Now, I'm Daniel Carter. You probably know that already. I'm very glad to receive you, Miss Bellamy. And Malcolm, good to see you again."

Malcolm pressed his lips together. He looked like he had inhaled acid.

"It's been a long time, hasn't it? Since Leo died," he said, in a tone so harsh, he barely sounded like the person Charlotte knew. "Was it too much to keep in touch while August and I were grieving? Or to come to his funeral? You just disappeared without so much as a goodbye."

Carter averted his eyes. "It wasn't my choice. My father kept me from seeing you."

"I didn't spot you at August and Lena's funeral, either," Malcolm added. "I don't think there was anybody stopping you then."

"We can discuss this later," Carter snapped. "I know I owe you an apology, and I'll make it to you. But for now, there's an important matter we need to speak about."

"You've got that right," Malcolm said curtly. "What's the meaning of this?"

Charlotte suddenly realised there was someone missing from the chamber.

"With all due respect, Sir," she said, "where's Aggie?"

"I'm sorry, who?"

"Agatha Tiffin. The baker's daughter. She was… with us."

"I'm afraid I have no knowledge of her."

"Then what about the woman with the black hair? The one who brought us here?"

"Seeing to other duties, I presume," Carter said.

Charlotte swallowed nervously. "What other duties? Who is she?"

Carter ignored her. He plucked a candied plum from the nearest bowl and bit into it with absurd delicateness.

"Please, help yourselves."

"No, thank you," Malcolm said coldly.

Charlotte's tongue felt too large for her mouth. There were so many questions, she scarcely knew where to begin.

"What is this place?" she asked in the end.

Carter dabbed at his lips with a handkerchief.

"It's called the Roots. All these buildings and passageways were built by the founders of Forest as the City grew.

A feat of ancient engineering, to be sure, but forgotten by many nowadays. They're used by the Parliamentary for the most intimate of business."

"Why are *we* here?" Malcolm asked.

Carter took a deep breath. "Well, before I answer that, I must ask a question of my own. Miss Bellamy, how much do you remember?"

Charlotte knew at once what he was referring to.

"Not much."

"There's no need to be afraid," he coaxed. "You're not in any trouble."

"Then why were we knocked out like your officers were subduing a *convict?*" Charlotte snapped before she could stop herself. Under the table, Malcolm kicked her.

The Potentate drew back in surprise. Silence hung between them, so sudden and sharp, Charlotte didn't dare to breathe.

"I apologise," he said. "As I told you, I had no part in what happened in the bakery. I'm talking about—"

"Rene Square," Charlotte finished. Her anxiety transformed into anger, as though a hot poker had been thrust into her chest. "I remember everyone saying that was who had done it: a lunafauna convict. Someone who'd escaped from gaol and gone mad. But that is *not* what happened."

"Do you also believe your father was a stable man?" Carter cut in.

Charlotte's blood boiled. With every second, her respect for the Potentate shrank like an icicle under the sun.

"He wasn't mad. If you knew him for as long as you did, then you would know the same."

Carter sighed. When he spoke, it was with surprising gentleness.

"I'm afraid, my dear, there were parts of him you didn't know at all. Nobody did, not even his wife. Not until he decided to disclose that classified information to her, and then flee with both of you. And we all know what the consequences of that flight were."

He adjusted the position of his hands so the ruby ring became visible.

"Do you see this jewel? Your father wore one as well. Several Parliamentary Fellows do, and certain members of the Constabulary. To most people, it's just a simple piece of jewellery. But for the wearers, it's how we may recognise each other, as the members of a secret sector of the Parliamentary. The Cor Aeternum."

Charlotte froze. Noticing her reaction, Carter nodded to himself.

"I know August shouted those words in Rene. And you remembered them, didn't you? I sincerely hoped you wouldn't."

Malcolm grasped Charlotte's hand, then leaned forward to take over the conversation.

"What does this Cor Aeternum do, exactly?"

"It protects the inner workings of the Tower, and its relationship to life in Forest," said Carter. "You've heard of the Timekeeper?"

"Everyone's heard of the Timekeeper."

"He's one of us, but he can never be seen. The way he is, and how he is responsible for the maintenance of the whole City, would alarm many of our citizens. We stand as his guardians from anyone or anything which could threaten his responsibilities. That's why it's imperative for people to remain unaware of the Aeternum's existence."

Carter twisted the ring. The jewel's facets shone in the light.

Charlotte's heart pounded at the back of her throat. She had woken this morning in such high spirits. Now, she could barely believe it was the same day.

"Sir," she said, "what does all this have to do with my father?"

The final word was no sooner out of her mouth when the answer hit her like lightning.

"You knew there was no convict. He shouted *Cor Aeternum* and everyone in the square heard him."

Carter looked at her directly. His cool expression confirmed her suspicions like a rock dropping into a still pond.

The weight plunged through Charlotte, straight to the pit of her stomach. Carter carried on talking. She heard the words slowly, half a second after his mouth moved. She felt as though she was floating in water; everything beyond her own body was too far away to discern.

"I know this can be difficult to understand," he was saying. "Sometimes, a minority of innocents must be sacrificed, in order for the majority to live in peace."

Malcolm slammed his palm on the tabletop, so hard, the sugared nuts jumped in their bowl.

"Live in ignorance, you mean?" he snapped, choking on furious tears. "They're just words! Your secret group felt threatened over a couple of *words?*"

"It's more complicated than that, Malcolm," said Carter. "Words are simple, but they can be more dangerous than all the guns in the world."

"Well, forgive me, but I think August *did* have something to be afraid of! Maybe he ran because he saw something you didn't want him to see! And then he tried to tell the truth, and you shot him! *You* gave the order, didn't you, Daniel? Don't deny it! You murdered him! You murdered all of them!"

Malcolm leapt out of his chair. Before he could reach the Potentate, the officers ran forward and forced him back down.

"Malcolm, calm yourself. There's no need for violence," Carter insisted. But Charlotte heard a waver of emotion in his words. And, in a strange way, that made the whole situation worse. Behind those piercing green eyes, she could see this man as a child, with her father at his side. How often had they sat at this very table, snacking on sweet fruits?

"Why didn't you kill *me*, while you were at it?" Malcolm continued raging. "I knew the truth from the day I brought her home. I had a feeling it had been covered up for her protection, so I told her to keep quiet."

"Exactly. You were intelligent enough to know better."

"Don't try to throw empty compliments at me!"

Charlotte found her voice again.

"Why are you telling us this?" she demanded.

Carter pulled his chair forward a little, like a comforting parent. Charlotte pressed herself away from him. The cloying scent of his perfume wormed up her nose. It made her think of silk, with a stiletto blade concealed beneath the folds.

Malcolm struggled, but the officers held him fast.

"Don't you dare touch her," he snarled.

"She's in no danger from me," replied Carter gently. "I'm telling you the truth because I'd like to offer you your father's seat, Miss Bellamy. I would make you a Lady, as you were born to be. I would invite you to join us in the Aeternum. You're a smart and resourceful young woman. You would be a valuable asset in helping us protect the heart of the City."

A stone formed in Charlotte's chest. Hidden by the tablecloth, she pressed her fingers together until her knuckles cracked.

"Join the group that murdered my parents?"

"Join a Parliament that has helped to raise Forest into what it is today," replied Carter, not missing a beat. "This isn't how I would normally conduct these matters, but you're a rather unique case."

"Why? Because I've left all that behind?"

"It took her long enough to come to terms with what happened," Malcolm growled. "This is the last thing she needs. This, or anything to do with you."

Carter glanced between them, and the quiet fierceness returned to his features. He waved a hand and the officers let go of Malcolm.

"I understand it's a lot to take in. But I'm afraid, due to the high secrecy of the Aeternum, I can't allow either of you to leave the Roots until I'm sure of an answer."

Panic froze Charlotte's veins. "You're going to keep us here?"

"I have no choice."

Her mind raced. It was clear only one answer would do. And what of Malcolm? He had no connections — what would happen to him? Would Carter protect him? Based on this meeting, she doubted it.

She refused to whimper. She would not let the Potentate see her distress…

The door opened again. Carter's eyes moved up, then grew as wide as saucers. The officers drew back.

Charlotte and Malcolm whirled around. A boy had entered, his head lowered, a long black cloak cascading to the floor. His walk was stiff, as though every joint in his body protested at being moved. He stopped in front of the table and stood absolutely still.

Carter jumped to his feet. Anger and fear chased themselves across his eyes like sparks.

"What are you doing?" he hissed. "You cannot be here! Don't make me have you dragged away!"

"You *will* drag me away. But you're going to be disappointed when you do," the boy said.

His voice scraped through Charlotte like dirty fingernails. It sounded wrong, not quite human...

"Don't let him touch you," warned Carter. "You will leave right now. Turn around and go back to the Tower. That's an order!"

Charlotte's mouth fell open. He had come from the *Tower?* That could only mean one thing.

The boy pulled off his cloak, and she recoiled with fright.

He was about twelve years old, clad in dark knee-breeches with stockings and an untucked shirt. Dishevelled brown hair fell to his shoulders. His hands were stark white, as though they had never seen the sun. But that was where all normality ended. In places, his skin hung from his body like scraps of fabric. There were no bones, only metal rods and pistons, interlocking gears and escapements. A section of brass plate shone through an open hole in his cheek. The mechanism forced his body rigid, back permanently straight, shoulders pressed down. He was a living automaton, coated in flesh.

He looked straight at Charlotte. Two golden cogs spun around his pupils in place of irises.

Malcolm let out a horrified cry.

"*Leo?*"

The boy blinked.

"Timekeeper," he replied.

With alarming speed, he lunged forward and tore Charlotte's bodice open. Before she could react, he pressed his hand over her heart.

"*No!*" Carter roared.

White light exploded out of Charlotte's chest. It was hotter than fire; pain beyond pain.

The room liquefied. Her pulse shot up. Barbs drove into her bones. She was spinning through darkness. Stars flew past as though she were a mote of dust in a sunbeam. She had fallen through a rip; reality fractured like a broken mirror and she saw everything with such clarity, it terrified her. Past, present and future became one: a million threads, turning wheels, suns and moons whirling against the sky…

The boy pulled away and Charlotte's eyes rolled back into her head.

CHAPTER XXVI

As soon as Julian walked through the Academy gates, he sensed something was wrong. Several students were huddling under the porch roof to keep out of the snow, but the bench where Charlotte always sat was empty. He shrugged it off — he knew she hated weather like this and was probably just waiting inside. But then he reached the advanced academics classroom, and she wasn't there either.

The only person in the room was his Aunt Bridget. She stood before the chalkboard, the beginnings of an orb diagram drawn in strong, confident strokes.

"Did you finish the dishes, like I asked you?" she asked.

"Yes," Julian replied.

She pointed to a line of text. "Can you read that?"

Julian peered through his spectacles. The letters seemed to swim around, and some twitched like a trapped nerve. He tried to concentrate on one, but that only made the others flicker even more.

"Uh… orb congopents? No, *components*. Sorry."

The heat of embarrassment rose through his face. He whipped off his spectacles and started polishing them.

Nobody knew why he struggled so much. Children half his age could manage the alphabet better, and his father loathed him for it. Sometimes, to help him, Charlotte had even written out longer words on a piece of paper, the troublesome letters extra-large, and slipped them to him while the teachers weren't looking.

Aunt Bridget sighed softly through her nose, but before she could say anything, the door opened again and the Clark twins strode in. Julian peered into the corridor, waiting for Charlotte to follow them. But there was no sign of her.

Uncertainty trickled into his mind like cold raindrops. She was never late. She was often at the Academy even earlier than him.

In his pocket, he felt the bulk of another handful of caramels from Mr Kane's sweet shop. He hadn't needed any more — he still had some left from Monday. But he'd gone back for Charlotte, hoping they might cheer her.

The lesson dragged by, filled with words which Julian's ears understood, but which he couldn't make his eyes or hands translate. He clutched his pen so tightly, he almost bent the nib. No matter how he tried to apply himself, his mind was full of nothing but Charlotte. She had been so upset...

Finally, the bell rang for the end of the day, and the Clark boys darted outside. While Aunt Bridget turned to a pile of essays, Julian perched on the windowsill. The snow had turned to rain, and turned the yard into a blur under a dull, directionless sun.

"Julian," Aunt Bridget said, "what's wrong?"

"Nothing. I'm fine."

"Don't lie to me. You're not fine."

Julian puffed out his cheeks.

"How am I supposed to be an alchemist when I can't read?"

"Because reading and writing aren't the only indications of a good alchemist."

"Yeah, tell Father that," muttered Julian. "Why else would he throw me onto your doorstep, if not for you to fix me?"

She met his eyes evenly. Julian was next in line to inherit the Cropper Lane Orb Works: the oldest studio in the City. It had been the jewel of the family for centuries. Even Aunt Bridget had served time there, alongside working as a medic. But Julian's father, Basil Dickinson, had made it clear he wouldn't take his son as an apprentice until she was happy.

"You're not the first person I've known who's like this," she said. "It's not an insult to your intelligence, or your ability. It just means you learn in a different way."

"Father doesn't think so."

"I don't care what he thinks. If he respected my opinion as much as he does my skill, you wouldn't be going anywhere near alchemy in the first place. I wouldn't even be here teaching it, if I had the choice. But I'm not the one who controls the Dickinson finances."

"So what would you have me do? Just be a medic?"

"Your conscience would be much lighter if you were," Aunt Bridget said darkly. "There's a reason I left Cropper Lane. One day, you will unfortunately learn it. But, in the meantime, I will say that you and Miss Bellamy have some of the finest dexterity I've seen. Which reminds me, where was she today?"

"I was wondering the same thing," said Julian.

"Was she ill yesterday?"

"No, just shaken, I think. Like we all were."

Julian bit the inside of his cheek. Charlotte had never taken bad news well. He'd lost count of how many panic attacks he'd helped her through. That was probably what had happened, he thought. She must have suffered one and Malcolm insisted she stay home. It wouldn't be the first time.

"Aunt Bridget," Julian said, "why don't you want me to be an alchemist?"

"When you take the Alchemical Oath, you'll know," she replied grimly, and laid down her pen. "Well, I think that's everything. Let's go home, before the rain gets heavier."

They retrieved their outdoor clothes, and walked towards the road under the shelter of a large umbrella. Julian spotted a cab and waved at it.

"Bridget!" a voice called.

They turned around. A feline lunafauna was standing beneath her own umbrella near the lighting mechanism.

Aunt Bridget frowned. "*Phoebe?* What are you doing here?"

"Waiting for you. You took your bloody time."

"Why didn't you come inside?"

Phoebe shook her head. "No. I can't walk past Evie's classroom yet."

Julian hoped his surprise wasn't showing on his face. He'd heard of Lady Feline, but never seen her in person. Though she was a Parliamentary Fellow, she was much shabbier than Miss Gilbaut had ever been. She wore no coat or shoes, only a scarf and a plain dress which might have once been blue. Her ears were torn, one of them pierced with a ruby ring. A scowl, surrounded by scars, was etched so deeply into her features, Julian wondered when she had last smiled.

"Are you alright?" Aunt Bridget asked. "You look… well."

"Like crap. I look like crap. You can be honest," said Phoebe. "It's been a rough night."

"How many did you have?"

"Not rough like that. Just… Actually, I don't want to talk about it. I only came to let you know the funeral's going to be tomorrow. Eight o'clock in the morning. I thought you might want to be there."

Julian blinked in alarm. "*Tomorrow?* But… it's only been a couple of days!"

"That doesn't matter in our parts, sonny. We don't have

much choice," Phoebe said morosely.

A shiver ran along Julian's arms. Her eyes were friendly enough, but filled with a strange sadness and longing, and a sharp edge of impatience. She looked tired. More tired than any creature he'd ever seen.

Aunt Bridget offered her a rare, gentle smile.

"Thank you for coming all the way here for that. I appreciate it," she said. "Evelyn was a wonderful woman. An asset to the Academy. I was proud to know her."

"And *I* appreciate *that*," Phoebe replied sincerely. "I know some of the alchemists claim to look out for us, but you know how I feel about them. No offence."

"None taken. I completely understand."

"There aren't many no-tails who have my personal respect. But you're one of them."

Phoebe drew closer and pressed her forehead against Aunt Bridget's. Julian blinked. He had seen felines do that to each other before, as a mark of companionship, but never to a human.

A tiny purr rolled in Phoebe's throat. Then she walked away, tail flicking from side to side in discomfort as the rain washed over her feet.

"She's not what I was expecting," Julian admitted.

"She rarely is," his aunt conceded. "She might be a Lady, but she's had a rough life. Well, *lives*."

"Lives? What do you mean?"

"She can't die. She lives as long as any person can, then just wakes up again."

Julian couldn't believe his ears.

"How is that possible? The other lunafauna can't do that. Is it some kind of magic?"

"In a way. Let's not talk about it now," said Aunt Bridget. She hailed another cab. "Well, it's a good thing tomorrow has no lessons. Do I need to ask if you want to go to the funeral with me?"

"Of course I do," Julian. "Actually… Charlotte will want to, as well. Do you mind if I go and tell her, and make sure she's alright?"

"Suit yourself," said Aunt Bridget as she climbed into the carriage. "Here, take the umbrella. And some solidi. I don't want you walking all the way back to the house in this weather."

Julian stood aside until the cab rolled off, then hurried toward the Interlevel. The enclosed tunnel provided a welcome reprieve from the rain, but water had been traipsed onto the staircase, and left it treacherously slippery. Julian took his time descending to the Fifth Level, then walked onto Renshaw Street.

He stopped dead at the end of the road. The watch shop's windows were dark, with no sign of movement within. Even though it was still working hours, the door read *closed*. It didn't look as though it had been open all day.

Julian knocked, and bent over to call through the letterbox.

"Charlotte? Are you there?"

The only answer was silence, and the sharp spatter of raindrops hurling themselves upon the umbrella.

The huge pendulum swayed back and forth as Daniel ascended the staircase inside the Tower. Anger lent him new strength and he climbed faster than he ever had before. The shaft was enormous, with not even fifty lighting mechanisms enough to cast a glow into its shadowy corners. Each of the four walls stretched almost seventy feet across, and he shuddered to think of its length vertically.

Eventually, he stepped into the topmost chamber. The pale glow of afternoon light streamed through the clock faces. The entire expanse churned with movements of every conceivable kind. They wove together in an intricate moving jigsaw puzzle; some mechanisms as large as a house and others as small as dinner plates, all shimmering with ancient magic. Some were for lighting, for heating, for water and the artificial river conduits. Others manned alarm systems, communication, and Interlevel control. And of course, there was the single component they all connected to: the timekeeping one at the heart of the Tower itself.

The floor creaked under Daniel's shoes. It was so old, the boards were wooden, smoothed from age and generations of feet walking across them. He hated the sound. It was like the groan of a dying man, stretched out across eternity every single time he stood on it.

He dug a pair of leather gloves from his pocket and slipped them on.

"Come here!" he shouted.

"I would advise you to cover your ears, Daniel."

The four colossal minute hands moved to o'clock. There was a whirring as the hammers lifted in the bell chamber below, then slammed down. The vibrations rattled Daniel's bones. From outside, the chimes were pleasant and tuneful, but here, it felt as though his head might explode.

After several seconds, silence fell. The Keeper emerged from the overhead platform, clutching his chest with one hand. He staggered down a staircase, approached a heating component for the South Quarter, and began winding it with a crank as big as himself.

Daniel took a step closer. The Keeper continued his work until the mainspring was tight. He had no sooner let go of the lever when Daniel slapped him across the face.

"I should do more than that!" Daniel snarled. "You bloody little idiot!"

The Keeper raised his own hand, calloused and stained with grease.

"Be careful."

Daniel scoffed, but still took a small step back.

"You won't touch me, Leo."

"Won't I? You assume to see how I see?"

The golden eyes sent shivers through Daniel: childlike, ancient, as flinty as a corpse but alight with intellect. They were the eyes of a being who saw *everything*, whether it had already happened or not. The Keeper was two full heads shorter than him, but whenever he was near, Daniel felt like a cowering infant. Something small and insignificant before an unfathomable force.

And yet he shook with guilt and fear in equal measure. The two of them had played in the Bellamy manor grounds with August. One day, they called Malcolm over, and the Third West filled with the sounds of their laughter. Now, Daniel couldn't remember the last time he had heard Leo laugh, or seen him smile or cry. Whenever he faced his old friend, heard him talk, it was as though he read his thoughts and twisted them like cat's cradle.

"Your ears will stop ringing momentarily," Leo said. "Then you can interrogate me."

Daniel ground his teeth. "Have all Keepers been as troublesome as you?"

"Troublesome is a meaningless word. What is troublesome for one is treasure to another."

"Then what *treasure* do you hope to glean from this?"

"There's no place for such things here, Daniel. You know that. In the greater scheme of things, I don't matter any more than you do."

"In that case, what were you thinking in bringing Charlotte

Bellamy into this?"

"*You* were the one who brought her here," Leo said. "It's not as though you would have let her just walk away after she performed that procedure."

Daniel struggled to suppress a squirm. "Petty opportunism? The fact she was already here? You're too intelligent for that to be your only reason. Why the hell did you do it?"

"I am aware. Nothing more," replied Leo. "As I speak to you now, it's also thirty-four years ago, and you're swinging from the walls of the Pavilion while your mother orders you to get down. And you're eating strawberries in creamed ice with your son tonight. And as the lowly thieves lie together, so too do you yesterday, on your desk with Melissa—"

"Get out of my head!" Daniel shouted.

"—and all these things are as they should be," Leo finished.

"Stop trying to play mind games with me! You knew your heir was already agreed upon, and you deliberately infected someone else — a member of your own family! Your niece!"

Daniel clasped his hands behind his back, in an attempt to fool himself they weren't shaking.

"I can't allow that," he said, a little quieter. "Leo, you saved me from becoming Keeper. Help me again now."

Leo narrowed his eyes.

"I didn't save you, and you know it," he remarked coldly.

"It wasn't my fault. It was my father."

"You weren't the one who chose to steal me away, confine me up here, and strip any agency I had in the matter. But you also did nothing to help me."

"I wanted to. I tried," Daniel insisted. "You can't blame me for what my father did."

"I place no blame. It's another thing which is meaningless," said Leo.

Daniel's heart pounded like a drum. He decided to try a softer angle.

"Listen to me. I have other plans for Bellamy. She's skilled in alchemy, so I'll have her and Malcolm turned over to Victor Paley. I want to know what that procedure is, and in return, she becomes a Lady. I said that to her face. I just need *you* to stop acting like a fool and help me."

Leo shook his head. "You can say many things to someone's face. They are hollow unless they're true."

"It *was* true! You know that!"

"I also know that either way, the Circulus would ensure Charlotte Bellamy never left the Roots. You wouldn't rebuild her manor or give her a new one. She would never see the light of day again, whether she takes my place or not."

Leo's leg let out a horrid squeak. He eased a hand inside a gash in his calf, and pulled at something until it clicked back into position. Daniel grimaced.

"You see?" he snapped. "This is why you should have let me do what I'd planned, and give you the Tiffin girl! I went out of my way to secure her! You're falling apart! And the street mechanisms! The power's failing almost every day now! How much longer do you think you have?"

"How much longer *I* have is immaterial," said Leo simply. "The *Keeper* will survive, and that's all that matters."

Daniel thought quickly. "Can you take it out of Bellamy?"

"Yes."

"Fine. She's asleep now. Tomorrow, I'm bringing her and Tiffin up here, and you will move it into your true heir."

Leo looked at him with infuriating calmness.

"I will do no such thing," he said.

"I need Bellamy in the Aeternum!" Daniel shouted.

"So you can make me redundant?" Leo countered. "That procedure will mean the end of everything the Keeper does. Do you think I will allow that to happen? If she refines it, then all of this will fall."

He swept his arm around the chamber, at the intricate clockwork puzzle surrounding them.

"You will do as I say," Daniel warned. "I won't let it end your position. We need you — we need every Keeper who will come after you. Do you think I want to give the alchemists an excuse to overthrow *me?*"

His anger boiled again, and he struck Leo a second time. The boy fell to the floor, then placed a single finger on a nearby mechanism. A wave of light fleeted through it; two gears swung forward and locked onto Daniel's hand, trapping it between their teeth.

Leo surveyed him coolly. "I told you to be careful."

The gears ground together. Daniel screamed. Two fingers dropped to the ground, completely severed.

He stared at his mutilated hand in horror, and fled.

CHAPTER XXVII

Pain radiated along Charlotte's bones. She felt as though her skeleton was turning inside out under her skin, shifting in ways it was never meant to. She couldn't even scream; her ribs hurt too much to inhale. Something was ticking in her ear — or, around the place where she knew an ear should be. She was liquid, stretched across eternity. Threads wafted around her, spun together and came apart. She tried to catch one but it floated away, like it was alive.

No, not alive. No living thing moved as perfectly as that…

She became aware of something soft under her back. A distant part of her mind told her it was a bed. She smelled stuffy damp air, heard the creaking of a lighting mechanism, along with the dulled sounds of more gears turning outside.

"Charlotte, can you hear me? Come on, wake up, kiddo…"

She opened her eyes. Shadows swam into their proper places, and out of them came Malcolm, perched beside her on the mattress.

"Are you alright?" he asked frantically.

Charlotte took a careful breath. The air stung as it entered her lungs. She eased herself into a sitting position, felt hairpins digging into her scalp. Her bun had worked loose and splayed behind her in a tousled mess.

"I think so," she said. Her voice crackled like an old lamp. "What the hell happened to me?"

"You… had some kind of fit. It was horrible!"

"I'm fine… I think. What time is it?"

Malcolm snatched his pocket watch and began twisting the knob intently.

"Almost six. You've been asleep for ages," he said. "I was so scared. I didn't know when you were going to wake up."

The dam of emotion he had been containing suddenly burst. He shut the pocket watch, and his eyes flickered back and forth like a terrified mouse.

"It's impossible!" he cried. "Leo died thirty years ago!"

The boy's face leapt back into Charlotte's mind. She had been so stunned by his appearance, she hadn't even thought to check if he looked anything like her father.

"Malcolm," she said carefully, "are you *sure* that was Uncle Leo?"

"As sure as anything," Malcolm breathed. His voice broke on every word.

"But he's a kid!"

"I know! But that was him, I swear! I don't understand… I *saw* him! When the consumption had him, I always went to visit. I was with him just a couple of hours before he died! And I watched his coffin go into the mausoleum! He *died!*"

Charlotte gripped the side of the bed as though the sheets might swallow her.

"Where is he now?" she asked.

"The officers threw the cloak over him and took him away. I don't know where."

"The Tower, maybe?" Charlotte suggested. "He said he was the Keeper."

"That makes no sense," Malcolm said. "The Keeper's been around ever since the Tower mechanism was installed!"

"Maybe there's more than one? We all know he's there,

but we never see him. This must be why. Didn't Potentate Carter say the Cor Aeternum exists to protect the Keeper?"

"It didn't seem Leo needed much protecting," Malcolm muttered.

He buried his face in his hands. He looked so frail, as though all the energy had streamed out of his body. Charlotte had never known him so shaken.

She went to move closer, but pain flared through her chest, tore itself out of her mouth in a cry. It wasn't the constricting pressure of anxiety — it was sharper, both on her skin and *beneath* it, like the edges of a million blades as fine as spider silk.

She looked down. The top two buttons of her dress were missing. Leo must have torn them off. She pushed the material aside to reveal her stays, and directly over her heart was an angry red mark. She prodded it, expecting it to sting, but nothing happened. The pain was all inside her, like the touch had burned straight through her torso.

Malcolm peered at it, respectfully keeping his distance.

"That looks sore," he said.

"It's alright. I've had worse off the oven door."

"Not on your chest, though."

Charlotte trembled. What had Leo done to her?

The Tower clock struck the hour. She gasped so hard, she almost choked. She *felt* those chimes; her own pulse seemed to slow to keep time with them.

"What's wrong?" Malcolm asked. He reached towards her.

"No, don't touch me!" Charlotte cried.

She dropped onto her side. She felt separate from herself; her thoughts were a book, and the wind was whipping the pages back and forth, too fast to focus on one before the next flew forward. She smelled baking bread, heard the snap of bones as

Samuel Tiffin fell to the floor; Aggie's scream: so shrill, it cut like glass. And then the tall woman, with her face of stone and hair darker than night… And Leo, with the gears turning under his flesh… There had been so many, just like him…

The Tower fell silent. As soon as the final chime ended, the pain went with it.

"Are you alright?" Malcolm asked.

"No," Charlotte muttered. "I mean… Yes, I'm fine now. It's gone."

"Can I touch you now?"

"Yeah. Sorry."

"Don't apologise. It's alright."

"No, it's not," Charlotte said. She glanced at her hands. "It's not just Leo. That woman… It was her. *She* was the one I told you about. The one who…"

Hargreaves had called her Madam Spectre. At last, Charlotte had a name for the monster, but she wasn't sure if that helped or made things worse. Could it have been more appropriate? A ghost, haunting nightmares, drifting through the shadows?

Malcolm's cheeks drained of blood.

"Are you sure it was her?" he asked.

"Positive," Charlotte replied. "Even those words she said, *ad maius bonum*… she said them in Rene, too."

"And she said them to Samuel," Malcolm added grimly. "Maybe they're words used by the Cor Aeternum, whenever… someone is killed."

Charlotte screwed her eyes shut.

"What do they want with us?" she cried. "Twelve years of nothing, and now, they bring us here, tell us all this, try to get us to join their group? Why? And if we say no, they'll kill us."

"You don't know that."

"Malcolm, come on. You think they'll let us just go home after this? All Papa did was shout two words, and twenty-three people died for it…"

Charlotte broke off in horror.

"It's my fault," she said in a tiny voice. "This whole thing is completely my fault! I asked Miss Gilbaut what those words meant, the day she died!"

Her throat closed; her lungs squeezed against themselves. The room started to swim, but her own body trapped her. There was nowhere to run or hide.

Malcolm immediately sprang forward and grasped her hands.

"Hey, no, no," he said softly. "Don't panic, it's alright."

"I can't!" Charlotte gasped. "They must have heard me, then gone there to kill her, and came back for us! Hargreaves said he didn't think she'd killed herself, and I couldn't believe it, either! She never would have done that! *Never!* And what about Aggie? She got mixed up with me, too! She could be dead already!"

"You don't know any of that," Malcolm said. He locked his eyes onto Charlotte's like anchors. "Come on, calm down. Breathe."

He inhaled slowly and waited for Charlotte to do the same, then exhaled with her. Every gasp ended in a sob. The panic dragged hard fingers across her skin and caught on the edges of her bones.

"I've got you," Malcolm said gently. "Keep breathing. It will pass, you know it will."

Charlotte forced herself to listen, and sucked in more air than she thought her lungs could hold. But they did, and the oxygen flooded through her in a wonderful cool wave. The tension peaked and she collapsed into Malcolm's arms, panting with exhaustion. She felt like she had inhaled hot sparks.

She opened her mouth to speak, but he beat her to it.

"Don't you dare say you're sorry."

"But—"

"No. You've got nothing to apologise for," Malcolm said. "You're not to blame. Not for this, and not for anything which has happened in your life."

A tear dropped down Charlotte's cheek. Normality had never felt further away. She couldn't bear to ponder what might come next.

The ticking of Malcolm's watch cut through her thoughts. She focused on it. Like anything to come out of his shop, it was a beautiful piece of craftsmanship. But it was battered with age, and in places, some of the engraved filigree had smoothed clean from years of his anxious fingers caressing it.

"When did you make that?" she wondered aloud, desperate for distraction.

A hint of a smile curled Malcolm's lips.

"I didn't. My father did. It's a funny little tradition my family has: whenever a Godwin comes of age, their father gives them a watch. I've still got his, and my grandfather's. They're in my nightstand at home."

He closed the lid, slipped it back into his pocket.

Charlotte sighed. *Home.* All she wanted was to be back there, winding the clocks, washing a mountain of dishes. Doing anything except sitting here.

Voices spoke in the corridor. They were muffled by the door, but Charlotte still tried to listen.

"I've come to relieve you."

"You're early. And I thought Reece was on duty."

"Change of plan. You look exhausted. Go home."

"Alright. Thanks. See you tomorrow."

The key turned in the lock, the door swung open, and Hargreaves slipped inside. Charlotte propelled herself backwards in alarm.

"What are you doing here?" Malcolm barked.

"Ssh!" Hargreaves hissed. "I'm going to get you out!"

"You brought us here in the first place!"

"*I* didn't! Madam Spectre did! I was trying to keep you hidden at that bakery. I didn't know she was going to turn up!"

"And you did nothing to help when she did!" snarled Charlotte. "She's the one who shot my father, and you knew her!"

"Look, we don't have time for this!" Hargreaves said. "I've been planning to fetch you for hours. I'm offering my help. So you can come with me, or stay here and let the Potentate make you both an offer you can't refuse. And he will, now you've come into contact with the Keeper."

Charlotte pulled the top of her dress closed.

"How do you know about that?"

"I'll explain later. Right now, we have to move."

Malcolm shot him a suspicious glare. "How do we know we can trust you?"

Hargreaves sighed. "You don't. But what other option do you have right now?"

None of them moved for several long moments. But Charlotte felt an insistent wave of logic seeping through her mind. Any chance of escape was better than none at all.

"He's our only ticket out of here," she whispered to Malcolm.

"He was our ticket *in* here, too."

"What have we got to lose? I'd rather risk it than see Spectre again. What if she…"

Charlotte's words trailed off as the memory burst in front of her like a bomb. Flying bullets, plumes of blood, the pistol at her father's head…

Malcolm noticed her expression, and his steely eyes softened. Then he turned to Hargreaves and gave a single nod.

"Alright," Hargreaves said. "Follow me, stay close. Don't make a sound."

He checked the coast was clear, then led the way into a twisting labyrinth of passages. Amazingly, he never took a wrong turn. Charlotte supposed he must have spent a lot of time down here.

They broke free of the maze and reached a long thin bridge. Hargreaves sprinted across the chasm with practised ease. Charlotte followed, hands out to help keep her balance. Hargreaves bundled her behind him, out of sight, and waited for Malcolm to join them.

They ducked into a small chamber with a single elevator against the far wall. Beside it was another door, which Hargreaves opened to reveal a cloakroom.

"Hide in here," he said. "I'll go first and relieve the guard. He'll come down. As soon as he's gone, get inside and I'll bring you up."

Malcolm and Charlotte did as they were told. Constabulary coats hung in the darkness around them like ghosts. Charlotte tried to focus — if there was an elevator, that must mean the surface was close.

"You alright?" she whispered.

"Yeah," said Malcolm. "I just hope we can trust him."

"I think we can trust him more than we can trust the Potentate," Charlotte replied.

Malcolm grimaced. "I know I fell out with him, but I suppose a part of me hoped he hadn't turned into such an asshole."

After several minutes, the elevator doors opened. Charlotte held her breath, terrified the guard would look in the cloakroom and spot them. But he didn't. His footsteps moved close, then faded. She wasted no time, pulled Malcolm out and hurried to the elevator. As soon as they were inside, the entire thing jolted upwards.

Amazement ran over Charlotte like hot water. How deep underground were they? She fixed her eyes on the clockwork in the ceiling, and her own clarity stunned her. She could see every single gear tooth, as clearly as though she was looking at them through a magnifying glass. Her eyes hadn't been that keen before, she was sure of it. But then she realised it exceeded simply what she could see. She *felt* the mechanism, like it was an extension of herself; sensed the miniscule movements each cog would make to keep time with its neighbours.

Before she could think too hard about it, the elevator ground to a halt. Hargreaves met them in an antechamber, then unlocked a circular door in the ceiling. Several bolts shot back and he hauled himself through the opening. A waft of evening air pooled down. It was sooty and moist, but fresher than a glass of water on a summer day. Charlotte hadn't realised how much she had missed it.

Hargreaves pulled them up, into a narrow alley lined with sweatshops. To Charlotte's relief, it had stopped snowing. Rain had fallen since they had been in the Roots, and tiny streams ran between the cobbles, en route to the open drain in the main street.

A single lighting mechanism illuminated a sign painted on the bricks:

FENWICK STREET. 8TH N. QTR.

"We're in the North Quarter?" said Malcolm in surprise.

Hargreaves managed a grim smile. "Welcome to my part of town."

Charlotte looked at him. "You're from around here?"

"Well, not for a very long time. And strictly speaking, the Level below was mine. But I spent my fair share of nights here, too."

Trepidation washed through Charlotte's veins. This was the unruliest part of the City, and the lower the Level, the greater the danger. At first glance, it looked similar to the West, but once-intricate mouldings above the doors were smashed and rotten, and the roads were coated with a layer of grime that stank from the rain. Alleyways gashed the formidable buildings, broken only by news pages, recent ones pasted over old, until the words gathered into a mess of tattered papers. It was a part of Forest salvaged from history, there to be squeezed for cheap labour and forgotten about at all other times.

After a hurried trek, they arrived at a decrepit building. It was hardly larger than the watch shop, with a single window on each floor, both boarded up with metal sheets. The door was barred too, but that didn't faze Hargreaves. He waved them down a neighbouring alley, so narrow, they had to edge along sideways. Another tiny window appeared at ground level — he kicked the glass out and slithered through into a dust-clogged basement. Malcolm and Charlotte quickly followed.

"Where are we?" she spluttered.

"Lord Bellamy's sanctuary house," Hargreaves said. "I thought you might have recognised it?"

Charlotte shook her head. "I never came here. I've never even been in this Quarter. My father didn't want me to see it until I was… older."

The words died on her tongue. Hargreaves offered a small smile.

"In that respect, I'm not surprised. But this place will do for now. Come on."

He led the way up a set of rickety stairs, into an entrance hall. On the first floor, they were met with a closed door. Charlotte glanced around for another room, but there were none. Hargreaves, however, pulled a sharp tool from the heel of his boot and picked the lock.

"That seemed easy," Malcolm said disconcertingly.

"An old skill. Once learned, never forgotten," Hargreaves replied.

He fumbled about for a lighting mechanism and turned the crank once. The gears squeaked into life, just enough to see by. A metal desk was jammed against a corner, papers still strewn over its surface beneath a blanket of dust. Two upholstered chairs sat below the boarded window, covered with protective sheets. It looked like years since anyone had sat in them. Maybe even a whole decade, since Rene.

Hargreaves swept some cobwebs away. His eyes shone in the lamplight like jewels.

"You should get some rest while you can," he said. "We won't be able to stay here for long. I'll think of somewhere more stable."

"What about you?" Malcolm asked.

"I'll find some food, and stand watch for any trouble." Hargreaves patted his belt, still laden with a pistol and truncheon. "Stay in here. I'll go and check if the water mechanism's still working."

Charlotte took hold of his arm before he could leave.

"Wait. How did you know to come here? And why are you helping us? You led us straight into a trap."

"I didn't," insisted Hargreaves. "I swear, I had no idea that was going to happen. I never would have taken you there if I did. As for this place, this is where I knew Lord Bellamy from."

He ran his fingers across the desk with a strange fondness.

The touch was so light, he barely disturbed the dust.

"It's a long story, but I was from an orphanage. One of the most notorious ones. The mistress was involved with the Shadow Rats, so most of the kids had no choice but to be pickpockets. I was pretty good at it, I have to admit. But I hated it. I wanted to make something of myself, so I went to your father for help. He got me away from the Rats; gave me the opportunity to join the Constabulary. Before I knew it, I was enforcing the laws which I'd been forced to break. I always wanted to personally thank him for everything he did for me."

His voice was quiet, gentle, like a mellow cloud that rolled in during an autumn evening. And Charlotte heard something else in it, too. Pain. A darkness hung behind each word, woven so tightly together, the two couldn't be separated.

"I thought you knew this area a little too well," she said, but immediately winced at how it sounded. "I mean... I'm sorry for doubting you."

"It was common sense to doubt me," said Hargraves.

Malcolm threw Charlotte a glance, but then his shoulders sagged and he held out his hand. The young officer clasped it warmly.

"Thank you, Constable," Malcolm said.

Hargreaves shook his head with a smile. "No need for that now. Call me Oscar."

CHAPTER XXVIII

The dining room doors opened and Potentate Carter strode inside. High Lady Elisabeth hurriedly put aside the bread roll she had been nibbling on, and Nicolas threw his father an unimpressed scowl.

"She's being boring," he complained, and glared across the table, where Aggie sat with her eyes downcast.

The Potentate placed a hand on Aggie's shoulder. She didn't move. He smelled strange, of sweet expensive perfume, but also of blood and medicinal alcohol. Then she noticed his other hand, encased in crisp white bandages. That dressing hadn't been there when she'd eaten lunch with him.

"Now, now, Nicolas," the Potentate said. "Remember, you need to be nice to her. She's our guest."

Aggie stared intently at the intricate chintz designs on her plate, wishing she could somehow fall into the painted flowers and hide there.

The Potentate gave Nicolas a warm hug. Aggie watched from under her lashes. The sight was painful in a strange way. Her own father had often embraced her like that, usually before presenting her with a new doll he'd somehow managed to get.

But Nicolas still had his father here. Hers was gone.

Aggie shuddered. Only this time yesterday, he'd been alive. He'd cooked doughnuts for an after-dinner treat and wiped the sugar off her nose with his thumb. It was a far cry from the rage of the day before, when he found out she had let a cake go for nothing. The bruise on her wrist still hurt, but she let it pass. He couldn't help it. He had said that to her so many times, it must be true. One day, when she was older, she would understand.

Tears welled in Aggie's eyes, but she blinked them away. The Potentate would *not* see her cry.

"What happened to your hand?" Lady Elisabeth asked.

The Potentate regarded the bandage. "I trapped my fingers."

"Are you alright?"

"I will be. Let's not discuss it now."

The Tower rang six o'clock. The sound exploded inside Aggie's head. She yelped and covered her ears, and didn't move until the tolls had ceased.

"Don't worry!" Nicolas said. "You'll get used to it soon. It's not that loud, is it?"

Aggie stared at him. "Don't you think it is?"

"Well, a little, but the walls deaden it enough."

She moved her eyes towards the ornate ceiling. The bells were only a hundred feet overhead. It wasn't the first time she had heard them in the Pavilion, but she could never prepare herself. How could any of these people sleep with that noise every fifteen minutes, let alone think?

Nerves gnawed at Aggie's belly. She felt tiny in the middle of this huge room, with all its gilt and gold. No matter where she looked, she couldn't get away from it. Everything was beautiful, curving in all directions before twisting back on itself. And the smell of the flowers made her head swim. They were the most intricate bouquets she had ever seen, painstakingly painted with colours as delicate as the vases they sat in. The crispness of the paper told her they weren't old; the Pavilion probably had new ones made every single week.

A butler appeared and lit the candles in the middle of the table. Then the food was brought out: a succulent roasted pork joint trimmed with vegetables and gravy. Aggie's eyes widened. She had never seen so much food for a single meal. It could have fed her for three whole days. Even the cutlery was stunning: all elegant silver curls without a single tine out of shape.

She placed a tiny scoop of mash into her mouth. Butter and milk had been beaten into it until it was as smooth as silk. It was perfect. *Too* perfect.

"Does it taste good?" the Potentate asked kindly.

Aggie almost dropped her fork. "Yes, thank you, Sir."

He smiled at her. "If you finish all of it, you can have some creamed ice. I hear the cooks have flavoured a new batch with strawberries."

Nicolas let out a gasp of delight. "Do you like strawberries?"

Aggie hesitated. "I've never had them."

"Agatha comes from below the Third Level," Lady Elisabeth reminded her son. "It's harder to buy them there."

"Oh." Nicolas poured more gravy over his broccoli. "Well, you can have as many as you want here. I'll share with you."

"Thank you," Aggie muttered. "And... My name's Aggie. I'm only called Agatha when I'm in trouble."

"Well, you're certainly not in trouble now," said the Potentate. "Aggie, it is."

"How can you have strawberries now, anyway?" she asked. "It's January."

The Potentate's smile widened. "We have our own private farm in the Meadows. It has special mechanisms which control temperature, so summer fruits can grow there, even in winter."

Aggie hoped her shock wasn't showing on her face. In one

respect, she wasn't surprised, but how much trouble would it be to run something as complicated as that? And all for a few baskets of berries?

She didn't speak for the rest of the meal. It was so rich, every mouthful felt like two. She carried on swallowing even when she thought she couldn't take anymore. She didn't want to risk insulting the Potentate's hospitality. Especially when she wasn't sure why she had been brought to him.

Across the table, Nicolas ate with such impeccable posture, Aggie forgot she was looking at someone her own age. He held himself like an adult, but his eyes shone as though he was a little child. Had he ever been around anyone except his parents and the staff? Had he ever seen *anything?*

The servants cleared the plates. Nicolas leaned forward to catch his father's attention.

"Can I please be excused?" he asked. "I won't be long."

Lady Elisabeth nodded. Nicolas threw a mischievous smile at Aggie, then followed the butler through the door. It banged shut so sharply, the echo rattled her bones. Now Nicolas was gone, her end of the room seemed even larger, as though the walls might sweep forward and crush her at any moment.

She peered nervously at the Potentate. She'd seen her father's neck snap like a matchstick. The woman who had done it had brought her up here. And now she was being treated like a princess?

Trepidation squeezed Aggie's ribs. She might have enjoyed playing pretend, in her frilly dresses and patterned shoes, but she wasn't stupid. Something was going on.

"Are you full, my dear?" the Potentate asked.

"Yes, thank you, Sir," she said.

"You needn't be afraid of us," he insisted. "You're quite safe."

Lady Elisabeth looked at him out of the corner of her eye, but didn't say anything.

"Sir, where are Charlotte and Malcolm?" asked Aggie. "They were with me when… they were—"

"I'm sorry, I don't know about them," said the Potentate.

Aggie chewed the inside of her cheek and fixed her attention on the tablecloth. It was crocheted from fine white linen. She couldn't imagine how long it must have taken to make.

"Why am I here, Sir?"

The Potentate smiled again. "Won't you look at me, Aggie? It's much nicer to have a conversation when people are looking at each other."

Her belly lurched with nerves. He was talking to her like she was a baby. But she steeled herself and met his eyes; didn't dare break away again. This was *Daniel Carter*: leader of the City. She had to respect him, always.

"Because you're a special girl," he said, in a voice like honey. "You're here because we need to look after you. We have a duty to you, now your poor father has passed away."

Aggie started to tremble. "The policewoman shot him."

The Potentate shook his head. "No, it didn't happen like that. He suffered a stroke. Those are very common, I'm afraid. The alchemists and medics still haven't found a way to prevent them."

"No, she shot him! I saw it happen!" Aggie insisted. "Please, Sir, you have to believe me!"

Lady Elisabeth covered her mouth with one hand. She looked as though she was about to burst into tears.

"I believe you're very upset," The Potentate said smoothly. "But I promise you, he wasn't killed. If something like that had happened, I would have heard about it. Do you believe *me?*"

Aggie hesitated. Maybe he just didn't know the whole story. But there was something about the way he spoke, and Lady Elisabeth's reaction, which made her feel like she had swallowed stones rather than mash. She wanted to fall through the floor, anything to get away and out of the First Level. But chains might as well have been clamped around her ankles. She would have to play along if there was any chance of figuring out the truth.

So she nodded.

"What's so special about me?" she asked instead. "I'm nobody."

"That's not true," said the Potentate. "You have a purpose. You're here to save Nicolas, just as I had to be saved when I was his age."

Aggie frowned. "Save him? How? Is he sick or something?"

"No. There's a job which he's supposed to take up soon. A very important one — even more important than mine. But he can't do it. It was never really meant for him, you see. But from the moment you were born, it was meant for you, because you're so special. And it will mean you'll never have to grow up."

Lady Elisabeth let out a whimper. Aggie looked at her in alarm.

"Are you alright, Ma'am?" she asked.

Lady Elisabeth hurriedly composed herself.

"I'm fine, dear," she said, but it was tight, like fingers were squeezing her throat. "Are you looking forward to your creamed ice?"

Aggie nodded, but a chill of unease crept along her spine. What was this job she was supposed to do?

"Please, Sir," she said steadily. "I want to go home."

The Potentate got to his feet and came behind her. For a fleeting moment, Aggie thought he might bend down and hug her the same way he had Nicolas. But instead, he just laid his hand on her shoulder again.

Her skin crawled when he touched her. There was nothing malicious about it, and that was exactly why she didn't trust it.

"This is your home now."

Aggie's heart shuddered. No, it wasn't. She couldn't stay here. As soon as she was alone, she needed to find a way to escape.

Nicolas returned with a silver bowl. The Potentate let go of Aggie, and returned to his seat.

"Strawberries," Nicolas announced happily. He placed them between himself and Aggie. "I got them from Cook. I thought you might like to try them just on their own. We can have them in creamed ice tomorrow, if you want."

The fruits were brilliant red, cut cleanly in half, arranged in a circle. Nicolas plucked one and popped the whole thing into his mouth. Aggie copied with a quiet nod of thanks. The flavour flooded her tongue: sweet and tart all at once, as though it contained the essence of summer itself.

"They're really good," she admitted.

Nicolas grinned. "I knew you'd like them."

In the evening, a footman escorted Aggie through the private apartments. She did her best to not stare at everything around her. Even the chandeliers took her breath away: stunning gold contraptions threaded with diamonds and silver fronds. She knew she should be grateful — not even the Lords and Ladies stepped foot in this part of the Pavilion. But she still couldn't shift the doubt which had hardened in her belly. The twisted columns seemed like giant bars. Beautiful, but confining nonetheless.

The feeling didn't alleviate when the footman showed her

into a bedroom. It was larger than the entire bakery, lined with mirrored sconces and plaster medallions bearing images of trees and birds. A canopied bed sat in the centre, freshly made. Aggie could smell the soap, soft and delicate, like bubbles had been spun into the fabric. In the corner sat a pile of toys, similar to the ones she had at home, but much better made. She picked up a doll. Its face was porcelain, its curls styled from human hair.

The footman wound the cranks on the sconces, then locked the door behind him. Aggie's heart sank. She had a feeling he would do that.

She put the doll aside, peered through the windows. They opened wide, but there was no balcony, or indeed anything she could have climbed down. And the ground was too far to jump.

She thought quickly. Perhaps she could strip the bed? There were enough sheets to make a rope, if she tied them together with the curtains. But if a servant returned and caught her, it would be too obvious to hide.

She peered into the wardrobe, found rails upon rails of beautiful dresses and jackets, petticoats and cloaks. The sight almost made her swoon. If she was anywhere else, in any other circumstances, she would have spent the entire night trying everything on. But now, she longed for nothing more than the scent of freshly-baked bread.

The dresses might do a good enough job. She would have to tear them up, but it would be easy enough to stuff them back out of sight, should she be interrupted. A part of her protested — it was winter; she could slip and break her neck — but she ignored it. For as nice as Nicolas and Lady Elisabeth had seemed, Aggie knew she couldn't trust the Potentate. The very thought of him made her shudder.

She decided to wait until midnight, when everyone would be asleep, and then put her plan into action. Even if there were guards around the Pavilion grounds, there had to be a way to evade them.

Aggie pulled on a nightgown, in case someone came, and climbed into the bed. It was so soft, she thought she might tumble straight through it. The stony feeling of unease flipped inside her again. Like the food and the forks, this was too perfect.

She stared at the canopy, and tried to forge a trail through the gaps in the flowery pattern. Every quarter, the Tower chimed. It didn't sound quite as loud now. She wondered whether she was getting more used to it, or whether the bedrooms had thicker walls than the other areas.

The sconces started to dim. She would have to rewind one of them shortly, to see what she was doing when she ripped the dresses apart. Then her eyes caught the bruises on her wrist. They looked darker now: four long shadows where her father's fingers had pressed the skin.

Tears came. She didn't bother trying to be quiet. The Potentate's family wouldn't be able to hear. Her father had been a difficult parent, but he was hers; the only one she'd ever known. And now he was dead. His last moments had been of terror, and she hadn't been able to stop it.

A horrid thought settled over Aggie. Had he known about the job she was supposed to do? Was that why he had always been so scared?

She took a deep breath and forced herself to stop crying. She just needed to shimmy down the wall and find a way into the Second Level. Then she'd head home; try to find Charlotte and Malcolm. They were the only ones who she trusted to help her now.

The little clock on her nightstand rang twelve times, then silence fell. Aggie went to climb out of bed, but stopped herself. Only *that* clock had chimed. There wasn't a sound from the

Tower.

She frowned. Lighting and heating mechanisms had shut off sometimes, but always started again after a few seconds. But the Tower *never* ceased. Not for anything.

The door lock clicked. Something must be wrong, if people were working this late in the private areas of the Pavilion.

But it wasn't a servant who stepped through, or even the Potentate. It was a small figure, covered from head to toe in a dark cloak. For a moment, Aggie thought it was Nicolas. But then she noticed a pair of eyes glowing from the shadows of his hood. *Golden* eyes.

She scuttled away with a shriek.

"Who are you?"

"My name is Leo," the boy said. "Get up. We must hurry, before we're discovered."

Aggie gasped. The air grew dense; it felt like someone was pushing pins into her ears and down her throat. Every part of her screamed to run away.

"What the hell are you?" she asked.

"An ally."

"I don't believe you."

"Hurry," Leo said, firmer this time. "Charlotte Bellamy and her guardian are waiting for you, and you'll be safe with them."

Mention of Charlotte made Aggie's heart flip.

"You mean she's alright?"

Leo nodded. "She will be fine."

"How do you know her?" Aggie demanded.

"We're connected, in more ways than one," replied Leo. "I know where she is. I can take you to her and Malcolm Godwin, but we can't linger here. So get up and do as I say."

Aggie swallowed nervously. He had to be around the same

age as her, but he spoke like an adult. Even the Potentate's hollow smile and silky words paled in comparison. But, unlike her host, at least Leo seemed to be telling the truth.

She fetched a jacket and boots from the wardrobe. Then, as she pulled them on, Leo lowered his hood. Aggie bit her tongue to keep from screaming.

"What happened to you?"

"Not now," Leo snapped. "Just follow me."

She went to take his hand, but as though knowing she would do that, he pulled away sharply.

"Do not touch me, Agatha Tiffin," he warned. "Ever."

Flustered, Aggie instead took hold of the cloak hem. When Leo didn't say anything, she presumed that was fine, and allowed him to lead her into the corridor. As he passed the lamps, the bulbs flickered, like they knew he was there.

Eventually, he stopped at a tiny door, two feet off the floor. Aggie supposed it was a dumbwaiter — she had seen the servants using them to bring food from the kitchens. But unlike the others, this one had a lock on it.

Unfazed, Leo placed his hand against the keyhole, and the bolts drew back.

"How did you do that?" Aggie whispered.

Leo didn't reply, just opened the door and jerked his head at it. Aggie shimmied through, and found it wasn't a dumbwaiter at all. Instead, she stood on a spiral staircase which twisted into darkness.

A guard rounded the corner.

Aggie gasped in horror. The guard reached for a whistle around his neck, but before he could blow it, Leo caught his hand. At once, the man's eyes rolled back into his head. When Leo released him, he collapsed in a heap, unconscious.

"How did you do that?" Aggie asked again. "Is that why

you told me not to touch you?"

"Come," Leo said.

He climbed through after her and locked the door from the inside. Then he swept down the steps, Aggie still clinging onto his cloak.

CHAPTER XXIX

The incubator was cleared of its bedding and the heating mechanism turned off. When Euphrasie had sucked as much milk as she could, Melissa laid with her on the chaise lounge. Feeding was tiring for her little body, but Daniel had been right. She was strong.

Melissa just hoped *she* could be as strong as her daughter.

When she could wait no longer, she left the room and turned to the nurse.

"Thank you," she said. "Thank you so much for everything."

"You're more than welcome, Madam Spectre. Have a pleasant evening."

"You, too."

Melissa climbed the staircase and slipped out of the infirmary. Euphrasie babbled at the sudden change in light, so Melissa laid a hand over her head to comfort her. It felt like needles were working their way into her heart. Each step was closer to the moment she had been dreading.

"Hush, hush," she said gently. "Mama's here. I'll always be right here."

She took a private elevator to the Pavilion, and walked down the elaborate corridors towards the east parlour. That was where she had agreed to meet Daniel. The route was the same she had taken with the Tiffin girl, but Melissa knew both she and

Nicolas would both be in bed by now. Good. After this was done, she didn't want to look at any more children.

All too soon, she reached the door. She could hear soft music playing on a phonograph from within. She hesitated. This had been coming for so long, but she wasn't ready.

A part of her snarled at her own weakness. It wasn't goodbye forever. All she was doing was leaving her baby here rather than in the infirmary. But the deeper meaning of the moment burned worse than the hottest flame.

Melissa raised Euphrasie higher and showered her cheeks with kisses.

"I love you," she whispered. "I love you so much. And I'll *never* leave you. No matter what they tell you, you're mine. Ten years will go by so fast…"

She knew Euphrasie wouldn't understand, much less remember; that she was only speaking for her own piece of mind. But she didn't care. She needed to believe her daughter could know this, before it all came to an end.

Then Melissa forced her mask back into place, and knocked on the door.

Daniel opened it. His hair was damp from a bath; the fragrance of essential oils bombarded Melissa's nose. Lavender. She had smelled that on him for years, but now, it swept a wave of nausea through her belly. Too sweet. Too strong. Like an invisible wall, waiting to slam down in front of her.

"You got here without interruption, then?" Daniel said.

"Of course," Melissa replied. With extraordinary control, her voice sounded the same as it always did, and in a strange way, that broke her even more. Half of her hoped her tears were hidden, and the other half wished he might see them.

She stepped past him, and spotted Elisabeth. Her face was pinched and uncomfortable, not much different than how Melissa felt.

"Madam Spectre," she greeted tensely.

"My Lady," Melissa answered.

"So… this is Euphrasie," Elisabeth said, as she laid down an alchemy book. "I know this will be difficult, but I'll care for her well. I promise."

Melissa swallowed hard. "I appreciate that, My Lady."

The moment felt as though the very air had broken into sharp splinters. Melissa pressed Euphrasie tighter to her chest, trying to memorise the milky smell of her, the softness of her skin, the way her small hands curled around her jacket.

Then Melissa summoned all her resolve and passed her daughter to Elisabeth.

She didn't stay to watch. She strode back through the door, along the corridors, until she was out of sight. She reached an atrium, snatched a pillow off a window seat and wept into it, harder than she had since she was a child.

When all her energy was spent, she let herself out of the Pavilion before Daniel could find her. She would be back when the emotion was under control. She'd visit every single day, if opportunity allowed it.

Ten years would fly. And until then, as she did with all things, she would find the strength to endure.

M elissa had no sooner stepped foot into the Roots when she sensed something was wrong. Circulus officers were running everywhere, their voices raised and weapons drawn. She flagged down the nearest one.

"Fletcher! What's going on?"

"Madam Spectre, we were looking all over for you!" the

girl replied. "It's Bellamy and Godwin! They're gone! Reece went to take their dinner and found the door unlocked!"

Melissa frowned. "That's not possible. Show me."

They took an elevator to the building where the prisoners had been held. Melissa kept her eyes straight ahead. She could think about Euphrasie later. The worst anyone could do in a situation like this was panic. Panic only slowed everything down and muddied the path to the solution. And if *she* stayed calm, the others would have no excuse but to do the same.

Reece was still standing outside the room, his face ashen with fear.

"Madam, it wasn't my fault!" he cried.

Melissa glared at him. "The door was unlocked when you got here?"

"Yes, but closed. That was half an hour ago."

"And nobody saw them leave?"

"Not to my knowledge."

Melissa peered inside. There was nothing to suggest a struggle, and the lock hadn't been forced. Somebody had let them out from the corridor. Someone with a key.

Anger shot through her. Only Circulus officers had keys to this area.

"Who was here before you?" she asked Reece.

"Yellen, Madam," he replied.

"Fetch him at once," she snapped. "Wait!"

Melissa squinted at the carpet, plucked a hair from the fibres. It was black and thick: too short to be Bellamy's, but too dark to be Godwin's. Suspicion crept over her shoulders like icy water.

"Fetch Yellen," she repeated, "and Fletcher, go to 3 Lower Bridge Street in the Fifth West and check if Oscar Hargreaves is there. If he isn't, get Richard Irving. Then meet me at the headquarters."

Melissa hurried to her office, and didn't have to wait long before Reece appeared with Yellen in tow. Right behind him came Fletcher and Irving. He had obviously dressed in a hurry: his hair was bedraggled and his buttons fastened in the wrong holes, but Melissa didn't care. The two of them together gave her the answer she had assumed.

She pointed at Yellen and his dog ears immediately drooped.

"You first," she said. "Who came to relieve you and what time was it?"

"Hargreaves, Madam," he said awkwardly. "And it was just after six o'clock. I thought Reece was supposed to be coming, but—"

"And you," Melissa said to Irving. "Do I even need to ask if he went home with you this morning?"

"He didn't," Irving confirmed. "I thought he'd gone to the marketplace, or the tavern, or something. I haven't seen him since our meeting."

Melissa's mind raced with a thousand thoughts.

"Alright," she said. "I need you all to come with me and retrieve them. Put a team of officers together, no more than ten. Irving, you too. Your leave is postponed. You know Hargreaves better than any of us."

Irving swallowed uneasily. "Madam Spectre…"

"I also don't want a repeat of Rene," Melissa added coldly. "The longer your friend is out there, unchecked, the higher the chances that I'll have to take care of him in a way I'd rather not. Now, where do you think they've gone?"

Irving opened his mouth, shut it again. He lowered his eyes, first in submission, but then a flinty edge came into them.

"Oscar said he was sceptical about our work for a while. I

should have known he'd do this. As soon as he starts doubting, he runs. That's how he got us away from the Rats. He's... too moral for his own good. He'll fall back on the skills we learned as kids, the places he knows which he thinks we don't. So my guess is somewhere in the North Quarter; the Eighth, Ninth or Tenth Level... No, wait. I *know* where they'll be. There's only one place Oscar would consider safe down there. August Bellamy's sanctuary building."

"Of course," Melissa smirked. "See, this is why I knew I'd need you. You're intelligent, Irving."

She cracked open her pistol to count the bullets, but then the room burst into darkness. Outside, all the lights in the Roots failed. The only glow came from the faint shine of the ancient magic woven into the walls.

Melissa waited for the systems to reactivate, but nothing happened. She frowned, peered at the clock, and her heart leapt into her mouth. The minute hand was on twelve, yet the Roots remained eerily silent. She looked up, and in her mind's eye, saw through the brick and mortar to the Tower.

"Oh, shit!" she hissed.

"What is it?" Fletcher asked.

Melissa grasped Irving by the shoulder.

"Go to the sanctuary house. I'll meet you there as soon as I can."

Without waiting for acknowledgement, she left the headquarters, hands outstretched to feel her way, and bolted towards the stairs.

Daniel peeked through Nicolas's door to make sure he was asleep, then walked to his own bedroom. Elisabeth sat demurely by the fireplace, Euphrasie in her arms.

As he watched the baby's little chest rise and fall, his heart fluttered. She was defenceless, innocent to the wicked ways of the world. If only all children could stay like that forever.

Daniel thought of Aggie, but pushed her from his mind just as quickly. He couldn't get too attached to her. Leo had taught him that lesson.

He winced as he tried to remove his shirt one-handed. He had spent a few hours in the Roots infirmary while surgeons closed the stumps of his fingers. They still smarted with pain, but the bandage helped a little, if nothing more than disguising the injury.

Elisabeth took Euphrasie into the neighbouring room. When she returned, she sat at her vanity and began braiding her hair.

"Are you alright?" she asked.

Daniel didn't answer. To his knowledge, no Keeper had ever physically attacked a Potentate. But, he supposed with a bitter snarl, he shouldn't have expected any less than this kind of defiance. Leo had proven to be hard work from the very beginning.

"I'm fine," Daniel said eventually.

"Why did he do that to you?"

"Because he still doesn't like being reminded of his place. Sometimes I wonder why I even bother trying."

"I know why," said Elisabeth. "You care for him."

"Not anymore," Daniel muttered. "You wouldn't understand. Did I ever tell you what happened, the very same night he was brought here?"

"No."

"It was thirty years ago. Both of us were twelve. My father ordered him put in the Tower, with the previous Keeper, so he could be made the heir. I never called him Father after that day. I always used his first name whenever I spoke to him. My own puerile way of showing how disgusted I was, I suppose.

"But that was just the beginning. Leo tried to escape. He was frightened, always crying for his parents. So do you know what I did? I sneaked up there. I tried to hold him, give him some kind of comfort, tell him I was sorry. But as soon as he touched me, it knocked me unconscious. I woke up in bed, and my father brought his cane across my backside. He said, 'don't you ever let the Keeper get that close again.' And I didn't. Sometimes, I'd open the door to the shaft and stand there, but I never went any further. I could hear Leo screaming, even from that far away. He was calling for me... *'Daniel, help me, please!'* And I didn't."

Daniel paused to hang up his shirt. His breath shook with guilt.

Elisabeth stared at him. "I don't know what to say."

"There's nothing *to* say, that's why," he muttered. "I know what you think of me. But this is the way of it. It was all my father's fault. He was the one who chose Leo, not me. *I* never wanted this for him. *Never.* But it's done now. There was no other way, and I've had to accept that. Both of us were pawns. All for the greater good."

Elisabeth closed her eyes sadly. She laid down her hairbrush with a trembling hand.

"Let Aggie go. Please. This is wrong, to keep her locked up like chattel."

Daniel paused in the middle of removing his shift to look at her in the mirror.

"Damn well-kept chattel," he snapped.

"Please, listen to me!"

"I am listening. But my day has been hard enough, without having to hear this."

"She's just a little girl! You don't have to be your father!"

Daniel strode over to her. "Elisabeth, do you think the idea doesn't hurt me? Do you think I want to put another innocent through what Leo and I had to endure?"

Elisabeth raised her hands, as though to ward him off.

"I'm not saying you haven't—"

"Then do what I've been forced to, and find some perspective," Daniel said. "I don't agree with the way things must be done. I don't agree with how the Keeper was made. But it exists, and so do we, whether we like it or not. So we control what little we can. That's all. And you haven't had a problem with this plan for the past twelve years. You've always known Tiffin was to be the next one. Would you have preferred Nicolas to be trapped in the Tower for the rest of his days?"

"Of course not!" Elisabeth insisted. "But the sight of her… I feel awful! This is wrong, Daniel! What right have we to do this to her?"

"The right of our son," Daniel replied firmly. "It was *your* family who imposed the Invisible Law, remember?"

"You can't blame me for that. It was centuries ago."

"It doesn't matter. The point is that there doesn't have to be a Potentate, but there must *always* be a Keeper. And I will be damned the day I hand Nicolas over to Leo. Do not ask me to suffer the sight of that."

Elisabeth shook her head wretchedly.

"It's all so wrong!" she cried.

"*Everything's* wrong," Daniel snarled. "I can't change that. We just have to smile, and keep our heads above the water. Do you understand?"

The lights flickered. Then the mantel clock chimed, but nothing came from overhead. At the same time, both Daniel and Elisabeth looked at the ceiling.

"He's out of sync," muttered Daniel. "Two smacks must be his weak spot."

"You hit him?" Elisabeth gasped.

"He doesn't feel a thing."

"You don't know that!"

"I do. He's a machine now. He can't feel."

"But he's your friend!"

That word struck Daniel deeper than a blade. No, not friend, not anymore. Every day, Leo's cries became quieter as the ability to emote seeped out of him like water from a sieve. Soon, there was nothing left of Leopold Bellamy. Only the *Keeper* remained. The inhuman, immortal Keeper, in the shape of the boy Daniel once knew.

There was a sudden knock on the door.

"Sir? Are you awake?"

Daniel opened it by a crack, and found one of the footmen.

"Deepest apologies for disturbing you this late, Sir. It's Madam Spectre. Apparently, it's a pressing matter. She insists on speaking to you."

Daniel frowned. Melissa had barely left. What could be wrong?

"Tell her to wait in my personal suite," he replied, then snatched his shirt back off the hook. "Don't wait up for me, Elisabeth."

He hurried along the corridors and entered the study. No sly playfulness awaited him this time. Melissa's face was stretched with urgency. He had never seen her look so alarmed.

"What's happened now?" he asked. "It's not something to do with Euphrasie, is it?"

"I can't talk about her right now, Daniel," Melissa said tightly. "You can't not have noticed the Tower didn't chime."

"Of course I noticed. But it's only a couple of minutes out. No need to fret."

"Don't act stupid just because you're tired!" she snapped. "All the lighting mechanisms in the Roots have gone down, too. There's only one explanation."

Daniel stared at her. "Are you sure?"

"Do you want to waste time going up to the Tower to check?"

"I hit him when I went to speak to him. He'll right himself soon enough."

Melissa shook her head. "He's escaped. Do you think he'd forsake his duty for fun? It's ingrained in him to ring those bells, to keep the clockwork ticking. The only reason he wouldn't do it was if he was nowhere near the mechanism to begin with."

"But..."

Daniel's words trailed off. She was right. The Keepers had been able to leave the Tower whenever they wanted, but they never went far, because every fifteen minutes, they had to toll the quarter.

"Little bastard!" Daniel snarled. "Do you have officers after him?"

"Yes. But that's not all," said Melissa. "Bellamy and Godwin have escaped, too. One of my own men helped them."

"What?" Daniel cried. "No, no... you need to find her! And the Keeper... if he's out there and Bellamy's loose as well... Did you hear what he did? He's put the malady into *her!* You have to get her, at any cost! Do whatever you need to, use whatever force necessary!"

Melissa snatched his shoulders.

"Calm down," she said. "I've already got a team sniffing out Bellamy. I'll be joining them shortly. And I'll find the Keeper. You know I will. As for my officer, I'll deal with him. Harshly."

A loud thump sounded from the corridor and the door opened. Melissa pushed Daniel behind her and raised her pistol, but he shoved her arm down. It was one of his guards, groaning in pain.

"Sir! There was a boy here... he took the Tiffin girl... Knocked me out, Sir..."

"What boy? Where is she?"

"Gone, Sir... her room's empty... Boy took her..."

"Shit!" Daniel growled. "Melissa, go now! Bring them back! And you have permission to kill anyone who gets in the way!"

CHAPTER XXX

Charlotte sat in the chair with her knees drawn up to her chest. Malcolm was asleep in the other one, and Oscar had disappeared downstairs to stand guard. Her kit bag dug into her leg. She was amazed it hadn't been taken from her in the Roots. Dresses were good for one purpose, after all. They made it incredibly easy to hide things.

A glance at her mother's wristwatch told her it was half past eleven. She knew she should try to sleep, but it was the last thing on her mind. Even her aching lungs and burning chest weren't enough to make her eyes heavy.

Once again, overnight, her life had been turned upside-down. Stupid little worries bombarded her. What if customers came to the shop, only to find it closed? How much money would Malcolm lose? Would Julian be worried about her? She had left him in such an awkward hurry... Would she ever see him again, or even Dickinson, or the Academy?

Normality shattered like a mirror. She couldn't stop thinking about the Potentate, about Aggie; replaying the horrors of Miss Gilbaut and Samuel Tiffin.

And then there was Leo. Dead and yet alive.

Charlotte looked again at the place where he had touched her. It wasn't hurting anymore, so she pressed until she could feel her ribcage. Her bones seemed normal, but oddly colder, like ice was running through the marrow. And though she applied more and more pressure, there was no pain.

What had he done to her?

She walked to the desk, turned the lamp's crank up a few notches, and brushed the dust off the papers strewn over the top. Most were logs of provisions sent to orphanages. Charlotte ignored them, fetched a records file, and leafed through to the *H* section.

Name: Hargreaves, Oscar.

Age: 14. Date of birth unknown.

Status: Orphan, runaway. Surname according to orphan naming customs. No known relatives.

Background: Forced/sold into Shadow Rats aged 8 from 9th N. Orphanage (Mistress Brann). Arrived from 9th N. on May 1st. No injuries but malnourished. Accompanied by friend, also from 9th N. Orphanage and Shadow Rats: see records for Irving, Richard.

Possessions on arrival: 1 shirt, 1 pair of trousers.

Provisions: 2 shirts, 2 trousers, 1 pair of shoes, 2 pairs of stockings, 3 pairs of underwear. Weekly stipend of Sol 10.

Other comments: Wishes to join Constabulary. In meantime, organise room in safe house so Shadow Rats cannot locate him. Update June 19th: accepted into Constabulary as junior officer. Stationed for training in 4th W. Stipend total (arrival-discharge): Sol 70 for 7 weeks.

The sight brought a wash of warmth over Charlotte. Not only did it confirm Oscar was telling the truth, but the account was written in her father's hand. Charlotte had never thought she would see his characteristic scrawl again: legible but rushed, a cursive swoop at the ends which would have made Julian grimace. The fingers which had shaped these letters had also scribed her birthday cards, helped her make garlands for Midwinter and Midsummer. Grasped her wrist as they fled through the streets in fear.

What had August Bellamy known about the Keeper that was so terrible? Had he guessed it was Leo all along? His own brother, who he had presumed dead? Had he *seen* him?

The door creaked. Charlotte spun around, but relaxed when she found Oscar there. She marvelled at how quietly he placed his feet.

"Sorry for scaring you," he whispered. "I just came to get some water, and thought I'd check on you both. I thought you'd be asleep."

"I can't," said Charlotte.

"You should still try."

"No. If I can't sleep, then I should do something useful."

Oscar chuckled softly, then looked at the open file.

"Checking my story holds up?"

A blush rose on Charlotte's face. "Do you blame me?"

"No," he said. "I'm actually glad you did. You're smart to question things after all you've been through."

Charlotte lowered her gaze. He sounded like he had been through a lot, too.

"So much for only being away from the shop for a week," she muttered. "What's going to happen now?"

Oscar sighed. "I'm not sure."

"Where did they take Aggie?"

"Tiffin's daughter? I don't know," said Oscar. "I saw her briefly in the Roots. They took everyone back there. But then I got dragged into a meeting. I didn't see where she went."

"They wanted her for something," Charlotte mused. "But she's just a kid. A baker's kid. I don't understand."

"Neither do I. I tried to find out, but apparently it's

classified," Oscar said, with a hint of scorn.

Charlotte looked at the faint area of paler skin near his knuckle. She had seen it in the shop as well. It was the same finger on which the Potentate's red ring sat. Her father's, too.

"I want to ask you something," she said carefully. "You're in the Cor Aeternum too, aren't you?"

Oscar sighed. When he looked at her again, his pale eye seemed even bluer than before, like a sheet of ice had frozen over the top of it.

"Yes. Quite a lot of the police and Parliamentary Fellows are. The officers who are part of it have this red circle on our uniforms. It's the sign of the secret squadron: the Circulus. But I'm not protecting you and Malcolm under orders. I hope you know that."

Charlotte thought back to the way Oscar had acted when Spectre entered Tiffin's house. He'd looked alarmed, even a little frightened. He hadn't been acting.

"I think I believe you," she said slowly. "But you lied to us. You knew the truth about Rene, about that woman…"

"I did what I could. You didn't know what the Aeternum was, and I had no intention of mentioning it. I only twisted the truth a little, to make sure I could get you somewhere safe. That's all."

"But why?" Charlotte pressed. "If you hadn't come, she never would have found us."

"She would," Oscar said darkly. "It's going to take some careful movements to make sure she doesn't find us *now*. But I'm prepared this time. I won't let her get anywhere near you."

Charlotte frowned. "That's a lot to promise. And to risk."

"Risk is nothing new for me. Neither is conscience," said Oscar. "I was inducted into the Aeternum under false promises. I've been losing my faith in it for a long time."

"Not one for keeping secrets?"

"Not when they hurt people. In some respects, the Circulus and the thieves are just two sides of the same coin. Madam Spectre runs things just as tightly as King Rat. But she does respect people. I'll give her that."

Charlotte stepped back as though stung. "*Respect?* You're *defending* her?"

Oscar paused. He glanced at his hands, inspected his fingernails, as though he might find his response there.

"This was before my time," he said, "but when she first took over the Circulus, it was all men, and half of them wouldn't think twice about raping someone or beating them to a pulp. Once, she caught a group of officers attacking a woman in the East Quarter. She took them down by herself, and then cut off all their fingers. Everyone in the Circulus knows the story. Nobody dares get on the wrong side of her now."

Charlotte swallowed nervously. "Except you."

Oscar smirked to himself. "This has been coming for a while. After your father was killed... Well, I supposed saving you, and keeping an eye on you, was the least I could do to repay him. Madam Spectre has her morals, and I have mine."

"But... she was the one who came after us in Rene," Charlotte insisted. "It doesn't make sense. They killed my father, killed everyone, just because he said *Cor Aeternum* out loud. If they're willing to do that and cover it up, why are you doing *this?* Doesn't it put you in danger if you're going against them? What will she do if she finds out you're helping us?"

A cunning gleam came into Oscar's eyes.

"A long time ago, *she* was the one who needed *me* to navigate this part of the City. I can outsmart her if it comes to that. And anyway, she thinks I'm at home on disciplinary leave for three days."

"And the money doesn't tempt you? I've seen the houses the police officers get. You're honestly doing all this for us because you feel you owe something to my father?"

Charlotte didn't blink. Oscar refused to look away either, and a long moment hung between them like a rope pulled tight. Then he reached into his pocket, and withdrew the ruby ring.

"Why aren't you wearing that?" Charlotte asked.

"I took it off before I went to the shop to find you," Oscar said. "I didn't want it to interfere while I was putting you under protection. And we both know how well that plan ended."

He regarded the ring for a moment, and tossed it onto the desk as though it had burned him.

"Screw them. And screw Melissa Spectre. I'm not part of her club anymore."

Charlotte finally let her guard down, and allowed a smile. She imagined the fourteen-year-old Oscar had once been, in this very room, standing before August Bellamy with nothing but the scrappy clothes on his back. That same fourteen-year-old who, six months later, had saved her life.

"I'm sorry for doubting you," she said.

"I'd have done exactly the same if our roles were reversed."

"Funny old world, ain't it?"

That earned a grin from Oscar. "I wonder what Lord Bellamy would think of the way you say some things now. Nothing like an aristocrat."

Charlotte shrugged. "I'm not an aristocrat."

"Will you take your title? You can, can't you?"

"I've been able to take it ever since I was fifteen. But I decided a while ago that I wouldn't. And I definitely won't now. How can I ever stand beside the Potentate, after all this?"

"He'll probably try to make you, for that very reason,"

Oscar warned.

"I know," said Charlotte. "He told me so. I know too much. Just like my father." She wove her fingers together nervously. "You don't think he'll order Spectre to kill me as well?"

Oscar shook his head. "You're too high-profile."

"You sound very sure."

"I know how the Circulus works. You're a liability, but things would only be made more difficult if you disappeared."

"Is that why nobody came to finish me off after Rene?" Charlotte asked. "And what about my father? He was a *Lord*. Isn't that considered high-profile enough?"

Oscar ran his tongue over his lips. "In many respects, Rene was exactly what it was made out to be. A horrible accident. It was never intended to be a massacre. Your father was marked, whether he'd run or not."

"Do you know why? What made him run, I mean?"

"Not a clue. If I did, I'd tell you. But it's—"

"Classified?" Charlotte finished.

Oscar smiled at her pithiness. "Yeah. It's standard practise. Everything's on a need-to-know basis."

"Why doesn't that surprise me?" Charlotte muttered. Then, suddenly, her blood ran cold. "Wait... do you think he *knew* all those people would die? He stopped on purpose. He stood there and shouted, deliberately..."

"I don't think he intended anything malicious," Oscar said, in such a gentle tone, her heart wrenched. "Bear in mind I wasn't there until after the fact, so I don't know everything. But from how Madam Spectre and the other officers described it, he was trying to create a distraction."

"So my mother and I could get away," Charlotte realised.

Oscar gave a grim nod. "Unfortunately, Madam Spectre is

very good at dealing with distractions."

The woman's face flashed in Charlotte's memory. That nightmarish emotionless expression, as icy as the snow. August Bellamy had gotten the better of her at first, when he hit her with the bag, but she would never have let him escape. Any of them. They were doomed from the very beginning.

"Is there anything else you can tell me?" Charlotte asked. "You knew we'd seen Leo. The Keeper."

At that, Oscar's cheeks turned white. "*Leo?* He has a name?"

"Yeah," Charlotte said begrudgingly. "He's my uncle. Leopold Bellamy. But we all thought he'd died a long time ago."

Oscar raised his arms in apology.

"I don't know anything about that. The Aeternum's purpose is protecting the Keeper, so we all know he's there, but only a handful of people actually *see* him. The Potentate, the Chief Alchemist — I don't even think Madam Spectre's ever been into the Tower. He's not locked in. Apparently, Keepers are naturally inclined to just stay up there, where the mechanisms are."

"Well, he didn't *just stay up there*," said Charlotte.

She shuddered as she thought of Leo, the way his hand had come down on her. It was cold, clear, precise. She had never seen a human move like that.

"I know," said Oscar cagily. "He came and saw me first, before he went to you. He said he wanted to help you. He told me whereabouts in the Roots you were being held; that I could bring you here and it would be safe."

"He told you that? And he calls *this* helping me?" Charlotte motioned at her bodice. "What the hell did he do to me?"

"I wish I could tell you," Oscar said. "Until today, I hadn't met him at all, and I only saw his shoes and hands."

Charlotte turned away. She had hoped talking about

everything would help her feel more in control of the situation. But the uneasy knot hadn't shifted at all. Why would Leo attack her and then employ Oscar to get them to safety? How would he even know about the sanctuary house? If he never left the Tower, there was a nine-hundred-foot distance between the clock faces and the Eighth Level. He couldn't possibly be aware of every single building in the entire City.

But then a shudder passed through her, and with a strange, inexplicable certainty, she knew he *could.*

The idea of him filled Charlotte with even greater trepidation than the Potentate. She'd assumed the Keeper to be similar to a lightsman: a regular person who maintained the mechanisms, rang the bells, then retired to eat and sleep and dream. She wasn't sure Leo could even smile, let alone do any of those things. The very air around him felt like it would drown her if she breathed too much of it. And beyond his haunting appearance, she sensed there was more to him. Something deep, dark and incomprehensible. No wonder the Aeternum tried to keep him a secret.

And what other secrets did they hide?

Charlotte snapped at herself to focus. Leo wasn't with her now. She needed to concentrate on the things she could actually work with.

She picked up Oscar's ring. The sight was both nostalgic and wicked: the thing her father had worn and which had brought about his doom.

"Are you going to put this back on?" she asked.

"No," Oscar said at once. "I told you, I'm done with the lies."

"Then, if you don't mind, I'm going to put it somewhere *I* don't have to look at it."

She tugged at the topmost drawer of the desk, but it didn't

budge.

"I can pick it, if you want," Oscar offered.

Charlotte shook her head. "There's no keyhole."

"Is it stuck?"

"No. I think it might have a secret lock. Hold on."

She ducked into the leg space, grimacing as dusty cobwebs stroked her face. At once, she spotted a faint glow, barely larger than a pea. She snatched the lamp off the desk and stood it on the floor so she could see.

A small smile traced her lips. An inert chain of cogs, dark with dirt, was pressed against the drawer. And the light emanated from the tiniest orb she had ever seen, nestled at the centre of a slack mainspring.

Oscar bent beside her. "What is that?"

"I don't know. But it looks like my father didn't want anyone looking in here."

Charlotte reached under her skirt for her kit bag. Oscar hurriedly cleared his throat and stood up. Once she had the pouch in her hand and rearranged herself, she smacked him on the leg to tell him he could come back down.

"Warn me next time you do that," he snapped. "Have your modesty in mind."

"Is that why nobody frisked me in the Roots and found this?" Charlotte countered. Without waiting for an answer, she upended the bag's contents into her lap, and collected the iron and a length of solder.

"What are you doing?" Oscar asked.

"There's not much power left in that orb, and if I just rewind the mainspring, it could damage it. I'll graft the two together, then I can get the gears turning again and open the drawer. Hopefully."

Charlotte paused for a moment, and glanced at Malcolm.

He was still asleep in the chair.

"Get him, will you? This is his baby, and he hasn't ever seen it done before."

Oscar gently shook him awake. Malcolm jumped, but he calmed when he saw Charlotte waving him over.

"Watch this," she said, motioning at the orb with her iron. "I just hope I can do it again."

Charlotte fetched her scalpel, and incised the orb. She scarcely had to touch it; the blade was so sharp and the orb so small. After a few careful seconds, the glowing core was exposed. She loaded the tip of the iron with solder, let a drop onto the centre of the mainspring. Before long, the entire thing was covered. There was a faint beating sound, then silence.

Malcolm's face lit up. He clasped her shoulder.

"I am so proud of you, kiddo!" he said. "You have no idea how much!"

Charlotte's heart swelled. She twisted the knob, then the gears clicked, and unwound a small secret compartment. She felt inside, and drew out a single piece of paper. Unlike all the other documents, this one wasn't in her father's handwriting.

Oscar took it and held it close to the lamp.

"*Thursday, December 17th. Leaving this here to avoid interception. All is prepared and I've arranged everything for you and family. Carriage will wait at the south side of Rene Square, Fourth West. at midnight tonight. Send word when settled and safe. Good luck, and may magic shine on you.*"

Charlotte's throat felt like she had swallowed sand.

"That was the night of the shooting."

"It looks like Lord Bellamy had some help in his plan to get away." Oscar studied the paper again, and his eyes widened. "I know who it was."

He pointed to the bottom of the letter, and the

unmistakable shape of a cat's paw print.

"A lunafauna?" Charlotte said.

"Not just any," Oscar replied. "There's only one Aeternum lunafauna who's also a member of the Parliamentary. Phoebe Feline."

"Wait," Malcolm said. "Isn't she the crazy one?"

Oscar gave a conceding shrug. "She's... rather unconventional. But she's got a backbone of steel. I've seen her in action. I'm actually not surprised to learn she was on Lord Bellamy's side."

He folded the paper and pocketed it.

"Alright, get ready to leave. We'll have to go to the South Quarter, and it will be best to move while it's still dark. Hopefully we'll catch Phoebe on one of her better nights."

Charlotte threw the ring into the drawer, then turned off the lamp. Oscar led them back out of the basement window and through the streets. She breathed through her mouth to avoid the smells of oil and stale urine, and kept her head down, so passers-by wouldn't see her face. She spotted a sign for a train station, but to her surprise, Oscar waved in the opposite direction.

"Shouldn't we be going that way?" she hissed.

"In a minute," Oscar replied. He retrieved his tool from his boot, and picked the lock on a nearby warehouse. It was dark inside, but Charlotte made out the shadowy shapes of market stalls against the walls.

"The vendors store them in here, to keep them safe," Oscar explained, pulling back a tarp to expose a table laden with drab clothes. "We should change. Madam Spectre will know what we were wearing when we left."

Without another word, he grabbed a bundle, and ducked into a corner to strip. Malcolm did the same, and Charlotte worked free of her dress. She went to take another one, but decided against it. If they needed to move fast, it would be easier without a skirt. She considered doing away with her stays as well, but supposed she'd be better keeping them. If she laced them tighter around the top, they would flatten her breasts enough to fit under a shirt. When that was done, she slipped on a pair of thick woollen trousers and tied her emergency kit to the waistband.

She felt her hair on her neck and hesitated.

"What's the matter?" asked Malcolm.

"It's too long," Charlotte said. "It will be less conspicuous if I can pass as a boy."

Before she could think about it, she seized a pair of scissors from the stall and cut her hair off. Then she blindly hacked at the back of her head until the strands fell to just below her ears.

She glanced at her companions. "How does it look?"

"Bloody awful," Malcolm remarked.

"Perfect, in other words," said Oscar. "Good thinking. Now, come on. We'll catch the midnight mail train."

Charlotte kicked her discarded hair under the stall, grabbed a cap and jacket, and stepped outside. Oscar pulled on a long coat to hide his pistol and truncheon, then locked the door behind them.

Pain suddenly plunged through Charlotte's chest like a knife. She fell to her knees. Her old scars flared. The bullets tore into her flesh, sent a cascade of blood down her back. And something else was tearing, too. Something deeper. A million threads; a magic which should never have been touched...

Those threads wrapped around her, tossed her about like a speck of dust. She was running across the square, then the Godstall market appeared and she was pointing out a pair of dungarees to Malcolm, then she saw the Potentate's Pavilion as a mess of scaffolding as it was built on the new topmost Level.

Birds flew in the air and greenery clogged the Meadows. Leo lay trembling with a handprint on his chest, and let out a scream which turned her blood cold. Her mother sat in front of her in a pale lilac wig, but then she realised it was a mirror, and *herself*...

A force beat at her. Not quite a voice, but a *feeling*, as instinctual as the need to pull away from a hot stove. She shouldn't be *here*. She should be *up*, higher, at the source, in the heart of all things…

Tick tock.

Hands appeared on her arms. In a snap, Charlotte was back in the street, gasping for breath. Malcolm was beside her, eyes bulging with fright.

"Are you alright?" he asked.

"I don't know," Charlotte wheezed. Then she froze. "Wait…"

She looked at her wristwatch. The minute hand had just passed twelve o'clock. At the same time, an alarmed expression came over Oscar's face, and Malcolm checked his own watch.

The Tower wasn't chiming.

"What's going on?" Malcolm breathed. "It *never* stops…"

"I don't know," said Oscar. "But we can find out later. Come on. We need to catch that train."

He helped Charlotte to her feet, and then the three of them ran into the maze of alleys.

Behind them, the old lighting mechanism in the street wound down. A lightsman hurried over and tried to activate it. But no matter how many times he turned the crank, the mainspring refused to tighten.

Windows were flung open. Alarmed people wandered out into the dark. Nervous mutterings filled the silence left by the great bells. And Forest sat still upon itself, like a giant creature holding its breath against an endless night.

RUN LIKE CLOCKWORK

VOL II
THE ETERNAL HEART

The City of Forest is on the brink of collapse. After centuries of steadiness, the clocks have ground to a stop. The Timekeeper is missing, the seeds of discontent are growing, and revolution simmers just below the surface.
It is not a question of if, but when.

On the run, Charlotte Bellamy and her companions race against time to uncover the dark truths binding their world together. But even as the Cor Aeternum pursues them, its leaders are facing battles of their own. There are some secrets which can never be known, and some truces which can never be broken.

Phoebe Feline must rally her people, Oscar Hargreaves must face his past, and Melissa Spectre must choose between duty and love. As danger spreads, the very nature of free will hangs in the balance. And there may be more to the mysterious Timekeeper than anyone could have anticipated...

Printed in Great Britain
by Amazon